SAVING HIS HEART

AVERY MAXWELL

THE BEST OF US LLC

DISCLAIMER

*This romance novel is a work of fiction with a happily ever after. However, the theme of death and grieving is an issue all these characters face.

If this is something you are struggling with, I am genuinely sorry. I hope I was able to tell Preston's story respectfully and if you are ever in need of help, please reach out here:

https://findtreatment.samhsa.gov/

All characters, storylines, events and locations in this novel are a work of fiction.

A NOTE FROM AVERY

Hi Luv,

Saving His Heart is Book #3 in The Westbrooks: Broken Hearts Series. While it can be read as a standalone, I strongly encourage you to read them in order. Each book has a new set of leading characters that build on the previous book. You will get so much more out of these stories if you fall in love with the characters from the beginning!

Happy reading,
Avery

Book 1- Cross My Heart
Book 2- The Beat of My Heart
Book 3- Saving His Heart
Book 4- Romancing His Heart

PROLOGUE

Emory
One year ago

I'm numb. I must be. It would explain why I'm not reacting to the gut-curdling, mind-exploding heartache that is happening right now. I've spent my life doing the right thing. I've followed all the rules, listened to all the authorities, and never once questioned right or wrong … until now.

Sitting in the office of Dr. Terry, my mentor, my hero, and my friend, I know my world is about to come tumbling down. His expression says it all.

"Emory, I'm sorry. I don't know what to say other than we will keep fighting this." Sighing, he removes his glasses from his nose to inspect me. "Do you have any idea how Donny could have compromised records in this manner?"

How? How? How? It's been running through my head all day. Until the hearing last week, I had no idea Donny had forged records. I've been racking my brain ever since, trying to come up with a plausible explanation.

"I … the only thing I can think of is when he used my

1

laptop a few months ago. He wasn't working, and he needed to draft a new resume for an interview he had coming up. But, sir, I would never have given him access to my files, and he isn't smart enough to figure this out on his own." *I've always known that.* "I'm willing to bet he doesn't even know what half of those words mean," I tell him, my voice beginning to waver.

"Oh, my dear, that's what I'm afraid of. It's also why I'll keep pushing the hospital to reopen this investigation. I'm worried that the one doctor Donny went to for the mandated medical examination is the one doctor we have on staff whose ethics are questionable at best."

I chance a peek at my mentor. "I'm so sorry, Dr. Terry. I would have never imagined Donny could do something like this."

"Emory, if I didn't believe in you implicitly, we wouldn't be sitting here having this conversation." Turning his head, he looks out the window. After a long pause, he asks, "How are you faring? With life, I mean. I know you have some rather extenuating responsibilities at home?"

Dr. Terry is one of the few people in my adult life who knows about the shitshow that I come from. One day, during my residency, I had no choice but to tell him about it when my sister Sloane's appendix burst, and my father refused to go to the hospital.

Averting my eyes as shame washes over me, I admit to him where we stand now without my income. "My two oldest sisters had to leave school. Luckily, they could take a leave of absence until I can afford to pay their tuition. *Somehow.* For now, they're working at the supermarket trying to save up again."

Dr. Terry nods in understanding as I continue. "My youngest sister, Sloane, I guess you could say, is a free spirit. She's somewhere in Pennsylvania working on her next book as she makes her way across the country. I sold a lot of my

2

medical journals and textbooks, so they can stay afloat for now. Without my medical license, I'll have to look into teaching or something, I guess." Saying the words out loud hurts. I have only ever wanted to be a surgeon.

"Emory, we are going to sort this out, but I honestly have no idea what kind of timeframe we're looking at. I cannot, in good conscience, believe that your surgical days are over. You're too talented, too good of a surgeon for that to be the case. You have more promise than the last three classes to make it through their residency combined. The fact that your malpractice insurance paid Donny's claim so quickly is another area of concern, so I have a feeling we are fighting an uphill battle, and you need to set yourself up for that. You are going to lose precious time in the OR, but I might have a rather, let's say unorthodox solution," he says cryptically.

"But without a medical license, how am I supposed to do anything in the hospital?" I ask uncomfortably.

"As I said, it will be unorthodox for sure and will not take place in this hospital. I have a patient coming in tomorrow morning who I'd like you to meet. He's a very wealthy man, with limited options due to his specific cardiomyopathy. However, he is interested in trying other forms of treatment. Trials if you will, and he needs someone to travel with him to get these other therapies. Mr. Westbrook is also a close friend, or his father was, I should say. I've known his family for many years, so I am comfortable telling you he will pay you fairly and treat you well. All agreements will be between the two of you after I make the initial introduction, though. As you probably assume, this is skirting a fine line as it is, but I believe this is your best option—for now."

I sit back, stunned. *How has this become my life?*

∼

THERE ARE few people in this world I trust, but Dr. Terry is one of them. Knowing I have no other options, I set out my clothes for the morning, take a long bath, climb into bed, and pray for some good news.

That night I barely sleep as I roll Dr. Terry's comments over in my mind again and again.

≈

WALKING through the doors of Mass Mercy Hospital the next morning is painful. My heart hurts, and my brain is very aware of all the whispered conversations going on around me. The news of my hearing would have filtered down through all hospital channels by now, so I'm not surprised. That doesn't mean it hurts any less, though.

Noticing a door sliding closed, I put my head down and walk straight toward it. I could make this walk in my sleep, having lived here the last four years of my life. Sometimes, when money was tight at home, I literally lived here, too. Often sleeping in the resident lounges, always thankful there were so many of us, no one ever noticed me living out of my locker.

I slip my hand into the door just as it's about to close, and the doors slide open. I'm not paying attention as I burst into the small space and run right into an expensive smelling wall. My entire body reacts in a way it shouldn't. Before I can apologize, a large hand wraps around my elbow to keep me from bouncing off of him.

"I'm so sorry," he says in a silky, almost Southern drawl.

"No, I should have been looking where I was going. It's my fault." Lifting my eyes to meet his, "Holy shit," slips past my mouth unfiltered. My entire body flushes so deeply I feel the need to fan myself.

I watch as a sly grin plays over the handsome stranger's face. "Hi, darlin', going up?"

"Yes," I say in a stunned stupor. I'm staring at him unabashedly, I know, but I've never seen someone so attractive up close before. His dark hair is styled in a way that would look messy on anyone else, but it's his eyes that suck me in and threaten my airways—the lightest shade of blue I've ever seen. Tucking a strand of strawberry blonde hair behind my ear, I look down at the file I'm holding, hoping he will lose interest in me soon, but no such luck. I feel him take a step closer.

"I'm Preston," he says, and I see the humor on his face as my own flushes crimson.

"Nice to meet you, Preston." I can tell by looking at his shoes he is light years out of my league, so I take a step back.

His chuckle is deep and soulful. It makes my toes curl … like, actually curl. I thought that was only something that happened in Sloane's dirty books. Remembering he never asked for my floor, I take a step forward to push the number eight when I realize he has already pressed it. Knowing the eighth floor on the west wing of Mass Mercy Hospital is only for cardiac, I assume he must be a sales rep. *I wonder where his samples are?* The thought has me choking on my own spit.

Suddenly, I feel his presence invading my space. "I would love to know what just went on in that gorgeous head of yours," Preston whispers before wrinkling his nose.

I'm so out of my element, I laugh. Not a pretty laugh, either. I laugh like a crazy hyena. He takes half a step closer, and I'm hit with a pungent smell that makes my eyes water. Glancing up, I can see he has a finger under his nose, attempting to mask the scent.

"D-Did you …"

"Me? Sweetheart, I thought that was you."

I'm used to terrible smells. As a surgeon, you become desensitized to burning flesh the first time you have to cauterize an artery, but this? This is the sewer, rotting flesh, and dead fish all rolled into one, and my gag reflex kicks in.

Doubled over, I can't control the dry heave as Preston rubs my back.

"Why the hell is this elevator so slow?" he grumbles, now covering his full face with his hand.

That's when we hear it. It starts off low, just air, then slowly escalates like someone pinching the sides of a balloon. It ends on a high-pitched squeal. With my hands on my knees, Preston's hand on my back, we both turn our heads to the left.

"I'm sorry," a little old lady smirks, "it's this new medicine they put me on. I can't control the flatulence." She giggles, which turns into an all-out laugh. "Farts are funny, young man. Start laughing every day, and you'll live longer."

The door pings just before it opens, and I rush through it. Heading straight for Dr. Terry's office, I can feel Preston staring at my ass, but I don't dare look.

As I reach for the heavy door, a dark-clothed arm comes around me and pulls it open. "Farts are funny," he says in that voice that has my ovaries doing the tango.

I pause to look at him, trying desperately to contain my laughter. *Good Lord, how can he say fart and still turn me on?*

"Right. Okay, thank you," I manage with a straight face as I head for the front desk. "Hi, Carla," I say to Dr. Terry's receptionist.

"Hi, Emory, so nice to see you, hun. Glad to see you two have met." She glances at one of the elderly men sitting in a chair.

Is that Mr. Westbrook?

Turning in place, I take in all the patients in the waiting room. As I expected, everyone but Preston and I are getting on in years.

"What a mighty fine looking couple you two make," comes a voice I recognize.

"Fred! Oh my gosh, I didn't know you were coming in today," I say, making my way over to one of my favorite patients. Well, ex-patients now. I'm surprised when I feel Preston following me.

"I was so sad when Dr. Terry told me he would take over my care. He isn't nearly as nice to look at as you are, Red," Fred tells me cheekily.

"I know. I'm so sorry about that."

Fred doesn't respond; he just looks over my shoulder at who I assume is Preston.

"You going to put a ring on it soon, or what, young man? Dr. Ems here is one mighty fine woman, you know. You're liable to lose her if you don't get your shit together, no matter how smart you two look side by side," he scolds, and I suddenly feel sick, realizing he thinks Preston is Donny.

"Oh, no, Fred—"

Preston cuts me off, "That's the plan, Fred. That's the plan." He places an arm around my shoulders.

I'm trying to shake him off when the door to Dr. Terry's office opens, and he steps out. Surveying the situation in his waiting room—me standing with Fred, and Preston standing a little too close with his arm around me—he shakes his head. *Shit! I cannot let him get the wrong idea.* I'm trying desperately to shake him off, but he persists, and Dr. Terry chuckles, waving his arm for me to come in.

"I see you've met Mr. Westbrook, Emory. He is his father's son. There is no mistaking that," Dr. Terry laughs.

I'm so shocked, I trip over my own feet, thankfully catching myself before I hit the ground. I take a second to process what he just said, then look back and forth between Preston and Dr. Terry.

"D-Did you say Preston is Mr. Westbrook?" I ask incredulously.

This has both men laughing.

"Come on in, Emory, and I'll make proper introductions. But yes, Preston is Mr. Westbrook, and he can be a real pain

7

in the ass," Dr. Terry whispers as I pass him on my way into his office.

With that cleared up, my mask goes on. Gone is Emory, the enchanted woman getting choked up by a handsome man in the elevator. In her place is the no-nonsense Dr. Camden.

Preston

GRASPING EMORY'S ELBOW, I lead her out of the office. My entire body takes notice. From the tips of my ears down to my toes is a current of awareness. *You cannot sleep with your doctor, asshat. But how fucking amazing would it be?*

We arrive at the elevators, and she has barely said a word since Dr. Terry explained my situation. I get the feeling she is the epitome of a rule follower.

I could break a few rules with her.

"Dr. Camden, I was hoping I'd catch you," comes the voice from earlier.

He has her attention immediately. "Fred," turning to look at the man, her soft smile is genuine, "what are you doing out here?"

"Well, I thought since you're not my doctor anymore, I'd try to take you out to lunch. See if this one's worthy of you," he says, scowling in my direction.

"You're so sweet, but that—"

"Would be great, Fred," I interrupt. "However, it's my treat. I insist." I wink at him. *She is going to be fun to rile up.* "It'll be fun, won't it, sweetheart?"

"I gotta say, Dr. Camden, I thought Donny would be a bigger loser than this. I'm glad to see he has some manners," he tells her while continuing to give me the stink eye.

Clutching my heart, I feign shock. "What? Me? A loser? Sweetheart, what have you been telling people?"

"Mr. Wes—"

"Donny, remember?"

"This isn't funny," she says as her face turns red.

"Oh no, Fred. We'd better get moving. My little love muffin here gets cranky when she's hungry. Plus, we've already had a minor incident in the elevator. I can't let her stomach get all twisted up again."

"I'm not going to lunch with you," she seethes.

"How does The Capital Grille sound to you, Fred?"

He eyes me skeptically, "You're paying?"

"I am," I say, taking Emory's hand in mine. Her little body shivers next to me. *Jesus, I wonder if I could make her do that all over?*

"Maybe I misjudged you, son. I love The Capital Grille."

I swear, I hear Emory hiss, "Traitor." And I chuckle.

She repeatedly tries to remove her hand from mine, but I hold tight. "You'll have to forgive us, Fred. We had a rather hectic morning and haven't settled things yet," I tell him.

"Ah, making up is the best part of fighting now, isn't it?"

The dirty old man has the grace to look embarrassed when Emory scoffs.

"We have nothing to make up for—"

"I do love a good steak, son. Let's get going before Dr. Camden explodes over there."

I sneak a glance at Emory and see he is mistaking her anger for hunger. *Why are you teasing this poor woman? She is going to be in charge of keeping you alive at some point, dickhead. You really should cut her some slack.*

I should, but staring at her gorgeous face, I know I won't. In a couple of months, I know we'll be relegated to a doctor-patient relationship. We might as well have some fun while we can.

"Come on, sweetheart. Can't have you starving over there," I say with a wicked grin.

"You are going to pay for this, Mr. Westbrook. I can eat my weight in meat," she grumbles.

"I would pay good money to see you eat my meat, Dr. Camden." I know I've just moved the conversation to the R-rated variety with my tone, but I'd do it again to witness the reaction it causes in sweet little Emory.

"Oh my God," she gasps.

"I think you are going to make my remaining time on Earth a lot of fun, Dr. Camden. Hard, but a lot of fun." I can't help but slide a little more innuendo into the conversation.

She flushes in such a unique shade; I know it's now my new favorite color.

CHAPTER 1

PRESTON

Present Day

"*M*r. Westbrook, do you have a minute?" I hear Seth ask, and I cringe. Turning, I see him flanked by one of my friends, Trevor, and his fiancé, Julia. *Freaking Spy Guy Seth. I realize he helped bring Julia home and is Loki's right-hand man, but Jesus, he's a real pain in the ass sometimes.*

Laughing, I finally catch Trevor's eye and get a sinking feeling. *Fuck.* "This looks ominous, and considering the shit that just went down, I'm guessing it doesn't bode well for me?"

Julia hasn't been home for an hour, and I can already sense trouble. Trevor's father abducted her. *Now there is a sentence you don't get to say every day.* Turning back to Seth, I wait for him to continue.

"I need you to come with me. We heard from Loki, and he needs us to secure your penthouse." Even Seth, who's a real-life special agent, looks nervous.

"Guys, seriously. What the hell is going on? Let's just do a quick rundown of the last forty-eight hours, shall we?" My patience and stamina are quickly fading. "My best friends, Dexter, Trevor, Loki, and I, were all targeted by the mob. A mob that Loki's father ran and Trevor's father worked for. A goddamn real-life mob that killed Trevor's mother. The reason Loki has been rogue for over ten years with a secret government agency trying to take them down. Loki, who has been playing a merry fucking fairy in all our lives for years and who is now God knows where, wants me to go home and secure my penthouse?"

I see Trevor grimace, but it's Seth who speaks first. "Yeah, that's about it."

"Jesus," I say, giving in. Mostly because I am overdue for my medication, and if I don't get out of here soon, I may have an episode that will spill all my secrets. "Fine, let's go, Spy Guy. Can you at least tell me what the hurry is?" I swear I see Trevor and Julia exchange a look, but I don't speak their language of love.

"Ah, well, it appears you'll be having a houseguest," Seth informs me, tripping over his words.

I shoot Trevor a glare, but he refuses to make eye contact, and Julia is literally pinching her lips closed with her fingers.

Throwing my hands in the air, I give up. "Alright, Spy Guy. Sounds like we will spend a bit of time together. You might as well call me Preston.

"Doll," I say to Julia, knowing it'll get her worked up, "I don't know what you have up that pretty little sleeve of yours, but nothing can be as bad as Lanie's psycho cousin, so I'll survive." I toss her a wink and am shocked as hell when she hugs me but says nothing about the 'doll' comment.

"Losing your touch there, doll? I thought for sure you'd threaten my balls again." I choke on my words when I see her face. "Hey, are you okay?" I ask, bringing her in for another hug.

God, sometimes I can be such a prick. This girl has been

through so much in the last few days. What am I doing teasing her like this?

"Sorry, Jules. I should have been more sensitive. You've had a rough week."

"No, it's fine. I'll threaten your balls the next time I see you if they're still attached." Her eyes go shockingly wide, and Trevor pinballs between the two of us before whisking her away with a promise to call me later.

"That was fucking weird, even for Julia," I tell Seth, but he just ushers me out the door to a waiting car.

Sliding into the back, I'm thankful when he climbs into the passenger seat. I'm not sure how much more small talk I can take. My body is fighting me, and I know I don't have much time.

"Hey, Seth? How long until this houseguest arrives?"

"We don't have a definitive time yet, sir. Loki said to expect at least four hours. That gives us just enough time to do the necessary checks."

"Thanks," I tell him as I pull out my phone to text Emory.

Preston: On my way home, can you be at my place in an hour?

Emory: That's what you pay me the big bucks for, big guy! (Winky face emoji) I'll be there, you doing okay?

Preston: I'm okay. Just need you.

Emory: Got it.

Preston: I'll be having a houseguest, so we will need to work out an arrangement.

Emory: Done.

Slipping my phone back into my pocket, I lay my head against the plush, leather seat. I should wonder who the fuck Loki is sticking me with, but I'm too tired and too weak to do anything but shut my eyes.

I've tried to fool myself, but I know I have deteriorated at an alarming rate over the last year. I visit Dr. Terry once a week; it's a lot easier now that I can access the corporate jet and can explain it as a work trip. The reality is, I know my time is coming to an end. I've had almost ten years to prepare, but I'm still not ready. I'm nowhere near completing my mission of taking care of everyone I love. It helps that both Trevor and Dex are now happily off the market and engaged to two amazing women, but none of my brothers are even close. Then there is fucking Loki.

"Mr. Westbrook? We're here, sir," Seth tells me.

"Jesus, Seth. Stop calling me sir ... just Preston," I bark. *I'm more tired than I thought. I rarely snap at people.* "Sorry," I mumble.

"It's fine, sir. I mean, Preston. It has been a long few days for everyone."

Taking out the keycard to the penthouse, I let us all into the elevator. Somewhere between Dexter's house and mine, we accumulated around six men. Nodding to them all, I ask, "Is the muscle really necessary? I know I've never dealt with the mob before, but I do have money, a lot of money, so I already have to take more precautions than the average person."

A lot of money is an understatement. Westbrook Enterprises is a multi-billion dollar conglomerate. As the eldest son, I had to take over when my father passed away, even though I was still in college and nowhere near ready.

"I believe that is part of the reason Loki chose your place."

"Why wouldn't he take the houseguest, as you keep referring to them, to his place? He only lives a few floors down."

"I can't answer that, sir," Seth responds quickly.

I roll my eyes. It's been a hell of a few days. I need Emory to get here, so I have the energy to deal with whatever bullshit Loki is trying to pull.

"Of course you can't." I shouldn't take this out on Seth, he is just doing his job, but the person I want to scream at isn't here yet. "Sorry, Spy Guy. Do you need me for any of this?" I ask, sweeping my arms around the great room that is already swarming with guys and equipment.

"No, we have it covered. I'll brief you when we're done. You'll need to be aware of any changes or adjustments we make to your security system."

"Great, thanks. I am going to my bedroom to lie down. I have a visitor coming in thirty minutes. Her name is Emory Camden. Please let her in, and don't give her a hard time. She is on my approved list, and until Loki tries to tell me differently, this is still my house."

Seth looks like he wants to argue but smartly bites his tongue. He goes back to work with a nod, and I head to my room. I have a feeling whatever happens next will suck the life right out of me.

CHAPTER 2

PRESTON

"*L*oki? Is that you?" I ask when I hear the front door open.

"Oh no, you cannot be serious?"

As soon as I hear the voice, I cringe. She's right. Loki cannot be fucking serious. This cannot be happening. I round the corner just in time to catch Lexi trying to make her escape. *Good. At least we agree on this.* If her body language didn't give it away, her goddamn screeching would.

"Fuck no," I yell. "You're out of your goddamn tits, Loki!"

"I am not staying with this asshole, Loki," Lexi shrieks at the same time.

"Me? I'm the asshole? You're the one who's had her knickers in a knot since the moment I met you." Immediately, I want to slap myself. *Why do I keep saying this shit around her?* Oh, that's right. Because it bugs the hell out of her. I cross my arms over my chest as a smirk takes over my face.

"Knickers? In a—" she yells, but Loki interrupts us both.

"Hold on," Loki bellows. "There is no other option. You two will have to learn to get along for at least a few months."

"A few months," we both yell.

"Yes, a few months," he repeats.

"Why can't I just stay with you?" Lexi asks with desperation in her voice.

This is the best idea I have heard in years. "Yeah, that's a brilliant idea. He lives a few floors down. You can stay there."

We are both waiting for Loki's reply, and I am boring holes into his eyes with Jedi-like focus. We are definitely in a face-off, just like when we were kids. I feel Lexi's attention on me, and am fascinated when I catch her checking me out.

Don't get me wrong, Lexi is a beautiful woman, but I have grown to think of Lanie as a sister. Since these two cousins could pass as twins, being with Lexi in any manner, even if I could, would feel incestuous. *Yuck*. I shrug off the thought.

Finally, Loki breaks eye contact. Raising his hands to the scruff on his face, he says, "I had to sublet my apartment. As I was telling Lex, this fucked-up situation is not over. I'm only here to drop her off, then I'm back in the field."

Oh no. Is that the apartment I just put Emory in? Jesus. Mental note, call Mona ASAP.

Turning my attention back to Loki, I take a minute to look at him—really look at him—and I can tell he has been through hell and back already.

"Loki, you don't have to do this on your own. Let us help," I beg.

"I love you, Preston, but this is what I've trained for. Until I have taken down Black's organization brick by brick, none of you are safe. I can't live with that, so let me do what I need to do. Alone."

"Jesus, Loki. Why are you so fucking stubborn?" I shout, pulling at my hair that I can feel is a bit too long.

"This is my fight, Pres. I need you to do your part by staying with Lexi. That goes for both of you," Loki says, turning his attention to Lexi. "The best thing either of you can do is get along for the next few months. I don't want to be worrying about you while I'm in the field. That's when mistakes happen. Can you do that for me? Can you try to get along?" he asks.

After a few seconds pass, Lexi finally utters, "Fine."

"Preston? Can you at least try to be happy about this? We're all alive, and there's an end in sight," Loki pleads.

"Oh, I am. I'm as happy as a dead pig in sunshine," I say before turning on my heel. "Come on, your room's this way."

I'm heading toward the opposite end of the apartment when I hear Lexi whisper, "Thank you. For saving me, I mean, not for dumping me here."

The vulnerability in her voice and the knowledge that she has likely just lived through hell has me changing directions. Instead of putting her at the other end of the penthouse, I move toward the master. There is a bedroom across the hall; she can stay there. I'm not a complete asshole. I hear Loki grumble something just before the door opens. Seconds later, Lexi is behind me. My southern manners kicking in, I open the door to the bedroom for her.

"Is Loki sending your things here?" I ask, and notice for the first time that she has blood all over her. "Jesus, are you bleeding?"

I'm reaching for her to check when she swats my hand away. "No, that's … that's Loki's blood."

Turning to glance over my shoulder, I know it is no use; Loki has already gone.

"What do you mean? Is he okay?" Loki has been my friend since we were kids, but when his parents died in our junior year of high school, he moved into the Westbrook compound. I consider all my friend's brothers, but that year Loki became even closer to my siblings and me. My mom hangs a stocking for him every year, even now.

In a whisper so quiet I'm not sure I heard her, Lexi says, "I don't have any 'things'. I'll just wash this and figure everything else later. And I-I packed Loki's knife wound the best I could. He promised he would get it taken care of as soon as he dropped me off."

With that, she closes the door in my face. *Holy Hell.* Unsure of what to do next, I head to my room and grab a few sets of clothes. I know my cleaning staff keeps all the suites well-stocked, so she should have everything she needs in the bathroom.

Standing just outside of her room, I knock three quick times and place the items on the floor. "I'm leaving some clothes out here for you, Lex. I'll make food if you're hungry. Come out whenever you are ready."

Walking through the penthouse toward my office, I realize Trevor and Julia knew all about this. Those assholes knew Loki was dropping Lexi off with me, and that is why Julia's behavior was even more bizarre at Dexter's house than usual. I make a mental note to kick Trevor in the nutsack for this one.

Surprisingly, I'm an excellent cook, so I know I can spare a few minutes and head to my office. First, I call my assistant to find out if I just screwed myself by leasing Loki's apartment for Emory. Then, I leave a message for Ryan from EnVision Securities. He needs to find out why Lexi doesn't have any belongings.

$$\approx$$

PRESTON: **I know you assholes knew about this. Couldn't you have warned a guy? WTF am I supposed to do? We're going to kill each other.**

Julia: **Hide.**

Trevor: **Just try to make the best of it.**

Dexter: **Don't kill her.**

Preston: **Make the best of it? Are you fucking kidding me? Trevor, I'm going to kick you so hard in the balls they'll land in your throat.**

Trevor: Ouch, man. Not cool.

Dexter: I hope little Charlie doesn't mind being an only child.

Preston: Dexter, you're next. I swear you all suck.

Lanie: I don't know why you guys don't get along. I think you would make a cute couple.

Preston: Never. Seriously, Lanes. You're delusional.

Dexter: Yes! Let's _Make _Lexi _Preston's! MLP is a go!

Preston: Over my dead body.

∽

I'm TAKING the steaks out of the skillet when I sense Lexi behind me. Turning, I find her standing on the other side of the large, granite island. I want to make a smart-ass comment, but even I'm not that much of a dick. She looks tired and a little lost.

"You actually cook?" she asks, all the fight leaving her body as she slides onto a stool.

"Yeah, I-ah, my mother made sure we all knew how to cook and clean before we left for college. Cooking dinner with her was always our favorite chore, and we fought over it every night," I tell her.

"That's nice," is all she says. I can see her hands are shaking, and her eyelids are droopy.

"Hey, so this will be ready in about ten minutes. Would you like some wine? It might help you sleep," I suggest.

"Yes, please," Lexi replies, the last bit of fight leaving her body in a whoosh.

I wish I could fix her.

That's how I used to be. I used to be the fixer, the helper. I hated to see people hurting, but when I got the news of my condition, I knew I had to learn to keep people at arm's length. My need to help Lexi is rooted deep, though, and I know I'll be making another call to my assistant soon.

"Preston, you're a billionaire, right?" Lexi asks.

"Ah, yeah," I say, uncomfortably.

"Then why do you use such busted up pans?"

Usually, Lexi would have sounded sarcastic, rude even, but tonight it just comes out flat. Looking down at my pans, I shrug my shoulders.

"I don't know. I've had these since college, and they work fine. I guess I never thought about it."

Lexi doesn't reply. I watch as she runs her finger around the empty wineglass. Turning from her, I grab the bottle and fill it for her.

Dinner is quiet. We eat in near silence, and before Lexi has finished half of her meal, she stands and clears her plate.

"Just leave it, Lex, I've got you."

She looks at me, nods her head, then wobbles back to her room. After a few steps, she turns around. "Dinner was delicious, thank you. You need new pans," she says.

She is far too thin, is my last thought before I realize I'm going to have more than a few problems on my hands. *How the hell am I supposed to get Emory in here every night now?*

One problem at a time, Preston. One fucking problem at a time.

THE NEXT FEW weeks fly by in a blur. Lexi and I have come to an understanding, at least I think we have. We attempt pleasantries. It doesn't always work. She spends a lot of time visiting Lanie during the day, and for the last week, I have been spending a few hours a night in Emory's apartment downstairs. We figured with Lex in the next room, it was best to do our thing in her apartment. Loki's apartment, I should say.

That was a gut punch when I realized I had, in fact, sublet his apartment for Ems. I cook most days, leaving stuff in the fridge for Lex, and I've noticed her doing little tasks to help like emptying the dishwasher and running loads of laundry. But, mostly, we do our best to avoid each other. The tension that's building is going to end in an explosion. I just know it.

At some point, GG sent Lexi a box of old clothes. They look like they must be from high school, and she is too proud to ask anyone for help. The information I got from Ryan this morning had my blood boiling. *How can that damn girl be so stubborn?*

He found out Lex had been the most requested buyer for a large department store in Boston. Then she was terminated, seemingly out of the blue, and no one else would hire her. I don't know what could have changed public opinion so drastically, but knowing that Loki had to rescue her tells me all I need to know. Somehow, she's mixed up with the Black family.

When Ryan investigates, he leaves nothing out, which is how I learn that she only has $1,044.36 in her account. That is all she has to her name and no job. By the looks of it, no prospects either until we can clear up whatever the hell happened with the Blacks.

Deciding enough is enough, I grab my phone to text Lanie and Julia. Staring at it in my hand, I am suddenly overly aware of how much our lives are changing. Now I just need to get Loki and my four brothers settled into stable relationships before my time runs out. *It can't be that hard, can it?* Deciding to put that thought off for tomorrow, I text the girls.

Preston: Lexi arrived with nothing, and I'm done with her bullshit. My assistant will have clothing waiting for her at Nordstrom's tomorrow morning, but we all know she won't take them from me. Can the two of you pick them up and bring them to my apartment?

Julia: Why, Preston Westbrook, is that a friendly gesture toward your sworn enemy?

Lanie: Aww, you're so stinking sweet. Lexi has won

you over, hasn't she? You know we all offered to buy her stuff, but she keeps refusing. So, I'm assuming you two must be getting pretty cozy, huh? (winky kissy face emoji)

Preston: STOP. No one is getting cozy with anyone. She's run down, too thin, and has literally nothing. Can you do this or not?

Julia: Just tell us when. You did good, Preston.

Preston: Thanks, doll. Goodnight.

Switching over to make a call, I press Mona's number.

"Kind of late, isn't it, boss?" Mona answers coolly.

I love this old bat. I inherited her when my father passed away. She was his assistant, and now she is mine. I wouldn't be able to function without her.

"Sorry, Mona. It's sort of an emergency. Lanie's cousin is staying with me, and for whatever reason, she has nothing. Can you have my Nordstrom's shopper pull together everything a woman would need for all seasons? She is the same size as Lanie, so if you call her, she will help you out there."

"Ohhkay," she draws out. "Is this a special someone, boss?"

Jesus Christ, is everyone in my life going to keep saying this shit?

"No," I bark. "She is just Lanie's cousin, and Lanie is a dear friend. Also, tell the shopper that I need it by tomorrow. The girls will be by to pick it up in the morning."

Mona laughs. "It'll be ready, sir." Then she hangs up. Mona doesn't take my shit, but she sure as hell gives it to me by the truckload.

One problem solved, ninety-nine more to go.

CHAPTER 3

PRESTON

*I*t's almost eleven, and Lexi still hasn't come out of her room. If I hadn't just gone to check on her and heard the snoring from the end of the hallway, it would worry me. *Jesus, that girl snores like a chainsaw.* I don't know what the hell she is doing at night, but I hear her pacing or typing away on an old laptop Julia or Lanie must have given her.

From my desk, I hear a commotion at the front door and realize Lanie must be here with the clothes I ordered. Walking toward the great room, I'm shocked by the racks and racks of clothing she and Julia are dragging in. This is going to piss Lexi off to no end, and that makes me happy. *I love messing with that girl.*

"Hey, Pres," I hear Dex call from the kitchen.

"Shh, Lexi is still asleep." As soon as I say it, I feel her come up beside me.

Standing in the great room entrance, she takes in the chaos, and I see the confusion.

I attempt to view everything as she sees it. A wall of floor-to-ceiling windows looking out over the ocean is across from us. The space is enormous. After all, it is the penthouse, but I did what I could to make it less pretentious when I moved in. I wanted a home, a place people could relax in, so there's oversized furniture with pillows and throw blankets placed throughout the space. I had the room painted a warm dove gray with accents of navy strategically placed. But it's the new wardrobe that is causing her face to scrunch.

"L-Lanie, what is all this?" Lexi asks.

Like Vanna White, Lanie tosses her blonde hair over her shoulder and makes a show of introducing the clothing. "This, my dear, is your new wardrobe. Isn't it great?"

Worried about what is about to happen as I see ball-buster Julia stand, I take a giant step away from Lexi.

"Why would you do this?"

"Oh, we didn't do it," Julia begins. I try to tell her to shut the fuck up with my eyes, but she stares right back with a mischievous grin. "*Doll*," she stresses the word, knowing I always use it to get her riled up, "you don't mind if we give credit where credit is due, right?"

"What are you talking about?" Lexi screeches.

"Hold on," my friend Dexter cuts in. "You were both so thoughtful ..."

I look around, confused. Lexi appears guilty. *What the hell is going on?*

"Yes," Trevor takes over, smiling like the Cheshire cat. "Imagine our surprise when we get a text last night from Lexi asking us to pick up new pots and pans, as a thank you, I assume, for Preston."

Jumping up in an excitable way I've only ever seen from Lanie, she says, "Oh, then Jules and I got a text from Preston asking us to pick up these clothes."

Not to be left out, Julia chimes in, "And here we were thinking you guys hated each other. There is some love here, isn't there?" The hope in her voice churns my stomach.

Lexi has also taken a big step away from me, and I let out a sigh of relief. That is when I register what Trevor said.

Turning on Lexi, I feel my face grow hot. "You did what?"

"What did *you* do?" she yells back.

"I did what a friend would do when they have the means to do so. You, Lexi, do not. You have just over a thousand dollars in your account, and from what I can tell, no one in your industry will hire you right now." *Oh, shit. That was a mistake.*

"How the hell do you know how much I have in my checking account, you entitled asshat?"

In my peripheral vision, I notice our friends watching us like a tennis match.

"I had Ryan look into you for your own safety. You show up here with nothing but the clothes on your back. Bloodied clothes, might I add. What did you expect me to do? Turn a blind eye? That is not what friends do. Not when you are so thin that if you turned sideways and stuck out your tongue, you'd look like a zipper! And I know, trust me, I know, we are not friends, but you are family now, and I take care of family even when they are being so stubborn they could make a preacher cuss."

Turning my head, I see all our friends take a seat on the couch just as Trevor says, "Oh Lord, the southern's coming out again."

Is it? Jesus, I can't deal with this girl. *Why does she make my ass itch? Ass itch?* I really am conjuring old grandad. I'm so lost in my head, I don't notice Lexi heading for me until it is too late. The stinking girl flicks me, hard, in the forehead.

"I take care of myself. Do you hear me?" she seethes, poking me in the chest with each word. "I will never rely on a rich asshole again. Never again," she cries and heads in for another flick. Or maybe she was going to punch me. I'm not really sure, but I cut her off by wrapping my arm around her neck and holding her in a headlock.

"You're out of your mind," Lexi screams, hitting and kicking, trying to break free.

I act on instinct. "Stop pitching a hissy fit and just let us do something for you," I bellow, and then shock everyone by giving her a noogie.

"Oh my God. You are the female version of a Westbrook," Trevor reveals in a moment of silence while Lexi and I struggle against each other.

"The two of you. You're the same person. I can't believe I didn't notice it before," Dex continues.

"No wonder you two can't get along, look at you! You're fighting like siblings." Lanie says, turning to face her fiancé. "Sorry, Dex, you can't name the group messages MLP now."

"MLP? You're joking," I say, still holding Lexi in a choke-hold. Having been through this with Dexter, and then Trevor, I know that MLP stands for Make Lexi Preston's.

Finally, catching her wits, Lexi struggles again. "Let me go, you overgrown caveman."

"Not until you agree to take the clothes and return the pans. I can buy my own damn pans, Lex."

"I will not. I can buy my own clothes, too, you jerk. Let me go," Lexi screams.

"Oh my God," Dex sighs. "Will you two stop fighting? It's like you need a buffer, and you're grown-ass adults."

In between our fighting, we hear, "What the hell is going on?"

Our heads whip to the entryway. Standing there with hands on her hips is Emory, and it hits me like a strike of lightning. *I need her to be my buffer.*

Finally, remembering that I have Lexi bent over in a headlock with my fist on her hair, I let her go. I quickly step back with my hands in the air like a child caught raiding the cookie jar. *Please, please, let her know me well enough to agree to this.*

I would say we have become friends over the last year, but this is definitely crossing a line. Praying she has some sort of ESP, I take a step forward and put on my game face.

"Well, this is one way to make introductions, I guess. Here we go, Ems, this is … well, this is everyone. Everyone, this is Emory," I swallow thickly, "my girlfriend."

Everyone in the room speaks at once, and Emory looks faint. I just stare at her as I make my way across the room. Embracing her in a stiff-armed hug, I whisper, "Please, please, just go along with me. I'll double your pay."

"This is going to cost you more than that, Preston," she hisses before pulling away and plastering on a smile. "Hi, everyone?"

Dex speaks first, "Your girlfriend? What do you mean? How long has this been going on, and why didn't any of us know?" He sounds hurt. This poor guy just can't catch a break.

Trying to stick as close to our truth as possible, I tell them, "About a year."

"Why didn't you say anything? Or bring her to meet us?" Trevor asks.

Finally, the craziness of the last year does some good. "Well, things have been a little … intense. I didn't want to throw anything else at y'all with everything going on."

"Emory is who you were talking about every time you said you had a date?" Lanie asks quietly. "So, you're not really a man whore?"

I can't help but laugh. I'm not even sure Lanie realizes she just swore. It's a rarity when she does, and usually, I love it when it happens, but I'm wound tighter than a three-day clock.

Placing an arm around Emory, I feel her tense, and I know I need to move this along. "We had just discussed moving in together when Julia went missing," I tell the room and feel Emory clench my side, painfully. Trying not to wince, I rub my hand up and down her back in an attempt to calm her and pray she doesn't blow my cover.

"I didn't want to say anything before because Lexi looked

so tired, and we are all stressed about Loki, but I was the one who sublet Loki's apartment. I wanted it to be ready for him whenever he returned." Before I continue, I do something I haven't done since I was twelve, I cross my fingers behind Emory's back. "Ems had already given up her place, so she moved into Loki's apartment while everything settled. I think once we talk to Seth, it will be okay for Lexi to move down there now, though."

"Thank God!" Lexi exclaims, attempting to tame the rat's nest I made of her hair. "I mean, listen, I appreciate everything you were doing for me, but I think Lanie might be on to something, and we can never be friends if we're living together."

"Agreed," I blurt. "Okay, now that that's settled, I'm not kicking anyone out, but I promised I would help Emory pack tonight."

"All the goddamn secrets," Dex says, stopping me in my tracks. Emory and I both tense, knowing we are holding onto a big one. "Let me make this clear to everyone in this room, and Loki will get the message loud and clear if I ever get my hands on him, but the secrets in our family are over. I don't know how we got to this point. I don't know if it happened over time, or all the shit hit the fan at the same time, but we are a family. Emory? Lexi? That means you guys, too. No more secrets. Please." He stands but looks defeated, and I feel as guilty as I ever have.

Everyone nods in agreement as Emory and I bite our tongues.

CHAPTER 4

*A*fter a quick round of introductions, Preston takes me by the hand and leads me out of his apartment. I'm so gobsmacked, I can't speak. A year ago, I never would have imagined I'd have any chance of doing anything with medicine again, then in walked Preston.

I don't know how he convinced Dr. Terry, who is the most by the book doctor I know, to do this. If I had to guess, though, I'd say the Westbrook Wings that keep popping up all over the hospital have something to do with it.

Preston hired me to take care of him. *What the hell is he thinking, introducing me as his girlfriend? His freaking live-in girlfriend?* My feet are tapping in time to my racing heart, but I'm also pissed. This is precisely what got my medical license taken away. If Dr. Terry finds out about Preston's little prank, I'll never have a chance of being reinstated.

As if sensing my inner turmoil, Preston says, "Don't worry. I'll explain everything to Dr. Terry. I'm sure you're worried about this breaking some code of ethics or something, right?"

He hit the nail on the head, but he has no idea how hard he hit, and it kills me. Tears fill my eyes, and I can't even tell him why. He never needs to know what I allowed Donny to do, or how it ruined my sisters and me.

"Hey, hey," Preston coos. "Don't cry, I'll explain everything. Come on."

The elevator doors open on the tenth floor, and he ushers me out. When we reach my front door, I open it with a sick feeling.

"What the hell, Emory? Why isn't your door locked?" Preston scolds.

"Oh, please. You guys have this building locked down like Fort Knox. Leaving it unlocked for an hour while I run up to stick an IV in you, check your vitals, and administer the meds isn't the end of the world."

"Lock your damn door. I swear, what is it with you girls? Julia didn't even have a lock on her door, and Lanie leaves the door wide open half the time. Just please, lock the door," he sighs, stepping into my apartment.

I haven't been living here long, but I've been trying to make it comfortable. It looked like a model home when I first moved in. Even as sparse as it is, it's a million times better than my last place. I'd been staying in a rundown building by the highway until Preston had to pick me up to go to the airport unexpectedly. He was pissed.

"What the hell is this place, Emory? I know how much I pay you. Why are you living with drug dealers and bed bugs?"

"I'm just saving money. I have expenses, and my sisters count on me. It's really not that bad."

"Emory, there are rat traps in the foyer."

"At least they're being proactive about them."

"You cannot live here."

"You don't get to make that decision, Mr. Westbrook. This is what I can afford right now."

When we returned from Boston, I found out my building had mysteriously been condemned. They moved all my stuff into Preston's apartment building, and he still won't admit it was his doing.

"You know, Loki only ever had a single picture on the mantel. It was of the four of us. Everything else was sterile," he tells me, looking around like he has done every night for the last few weeks. "You've done a great job of making this place your own."

Remembering why we are down here in the first place, I pull myself together. "First, I'm sorry I barged in there like that, but you were late, and I was afraid you weren't feeling well. Now that I've said that, sit. Explain. Now," I command.

I watch as Preston sinks into the couch and runs his fingers through his thick, dark hair, tugging at the root. I'm not a saint. Objectively, I recognize he is a handsome man. Ridiculously so. But he is also off limits. No matter how much those crystalline blue eyes pull at something deep in my soul, I've learned my lesson. After what seems like an eternity, he talks.

"Listen, I'm sorry I dragged you into this. I don't even know what happened up there. Lexi has disliked me since the day I met her, we're like oil and water. Trevor said we're basically the same person, and he might be right. After Loki dropped Lex off, I thought we might be able to cohabitate, but witnessing that display upstairs? It's more likely we are going to end up killing each other. I had her in a goddamn headlock and gave a grown woman a noogie," he sighs and leans farther back into the couch.

"I don't know, Ems. Dexter said we needed a buffer. Then you walked in, and it was a lightbulb moment. But honestly, the more I think about it, the better it sounds. We couldn't figure out how to get you to Vermont for Dexter's wedding without bringing up all kinds of questions, right? This might be the perfect solution. No one will question you being there if you're my girlfriend."

"Preston. I don't know about this—" I begin, but he cuts me off.

"I'll double your pay, and you can have your own room. The room Lexi is in right now is across the hall from me. That way, if anyone stops by, it looks like we are coming out of the same room," he says, making it sound less crazy by the minute.

Double the pay, Ems! Think of how much that extra money could help the girls. I've already screwed up their lives so much. Preston is basically handing me their education on a silver platter. Turning it down to save my own career would be like ruining their lives all over again.

Preston pulls me from my thoughts when he speaks again.

"We have an appointment with Dr. Terry coming up, right? I'll explain everything to him then. If we can't get his approval … well, I'll figure something out if it comes to that," he tells me. His beautiful blue eyes are pleading. "Plus, if I have a date for these weddings, my friends will stop pushing the MLP plan, too."

"The what?" I've definitely missed something here.

"When Dexter decided he couldn't live without Lanie, he started texting Julia, Trevor, Loki, and I nonstop. He changed the name of the group text to MLM or Make Lanie Mine. We got updates every single freaking day for a year. We all had front row seats to their love story. I hate to admit it, but that first Christmas, when he took every single one of those text messages and made them into a book for her, we all got a little choked up. That asshole is a real-life Prince Charming. So, when they found out Lexi was staying with me, I'm sure he immediately made an MLP plan. Make Lexi Preston's." He is trying to sound put out, but I can hear the love he has for his friends in his voice.

"That's really sweet, Preston."

"It is, but I can't have them thinking there is a happily

ever after for me. We both know that. I just need you with me so I can get through the holidays one more time."

I rarely hear Preston speak like this. He is usually upbeat. *The last visit to Dr. Terry must have hit him harder than I thought.* Seeing him like this, knowing his inevitable outcome, and my desperate financial state, how can I say no?

Crossing the room, I flop onto the couch beside him, ready to sign away my future, this time, maybe for good. "Okay."

"Okay?" he asks hopefully.

"Okay, but there have to be ground rules. And if we have been dating for a year, we will have to go through some intense speed dating rounds. I'm not about to get caught unawares."

"Speed dating, huh? Like, where's your dream vacation?" he asks with the silky grin I have grown accustomed to. This is the playboy Preston, an act. This is who he transformed himself into, thinking it would protect those he loved, and perhaps, to some extent, his own heart.

"Yup, mine is Italy. I've always wanted to go. I've probably romanticized it so much that I'll be disappointed if I ever get there, but it's my dream trip. What else have you got? Throw it at me?" I say, bending my leg beneath me so I can face him on the couch. To my surprise, he sits crisscross as well to meet me. His stare is intense. Bright, blue eyes search mine, his tanned skin making them pop even more, and my belly does a little flip. *That can't be a good sign.*

He looks me up and down, and I feel my body flush. *Damn Irish genes.* As if he senses my discomfort, Preston leans in to make it worse, "Nice legs." He pulls back just enough to watch my reaction. "What time do they open?"

I stare at him—mouth hanging open, brow furrowed as I process what he just said. Glaring into his smiling eyes, I realize this is part of the game. The pretend relationship, the 'get to know you'. Until now, our relationship has been superficial at best. It's how I wanted it, so he has no idea what he just walked into. My sisters and I have laughed at the worst pick-up lines since they were old enough to date.

Rubbing my hands together, I search the recesses of my mind and come up with, "Do you have any Irish in you?" His lip twitches as he thinks of a reply. When he says nothing, I continue, "No? Do you want some?"

His burst of laughter has all the earlier tension leaving my body.

"Please don't tell me someone said that to you?" he says while sucking in air.

"I grew up in Camden Crossing, the only town in this state with a mostly Irish community. I've heard that one since the eighth grade."

His face hardens, and he deliberately pauses before answering, "Eighth grade? That's young, isn't it?"

"Have you ever been to Camden Crossing?"

"Not that I'm aware of," he replies.

"Most girls are pregnant by the time they graduate high school." It's a statistic I've never been proud of and one I could never escape. *That's why I'm agreeing to this*, I tell myself. The sooner I can get my sisters out of the Crossing, the less likely they will become a statistic.

"Wait. Camden Crossing? Is the town named after your family?" he asks. I was wondering how long it would take him to make the connection.

"It is, but I have a feeling the great-great whatever they named it after were better people than my parents."

"Do you have a big family?" he asks tentatively.

Sighing, I know it's best to be upfront with him about this. He deserves the truth. As one of the Westbrook brothers, he is a high-profile man. The last thing I want is for my background to tarnish his family name. *Maybe if I tell him everything, he'll think twice about this crazy scheme?*

Choosing not to look at him, I tell the short version of my

story. "My mom took off when I was three. My dad is an alcoholic and not a nice one. Stepmom number one lasted a little over a year before she left. I was almost seven years old when I first started raising my sister. Stepmom number two lasted a little longer. She was around for almost two years before she committed suicide, and I started raising two sisters. The final stepmom lasted for almost three years, Moira, and she was lovely. I came home from school one day, and she was gone. I don't know what happened to her, but I know she wouldn't have left us if she didn't absolutely have to. She was the only example of a mom I ever had. With her gone, it was just me raising my three little sisters. I don't remember a time when my dad ever actually parented." I finally take a breath to glance up at Preston, expecting to see pity, which I hate. Instead, I find compassion, understanding. Maybe even a little admiration, and it's enough to cause my lip to tremble. I bite down on it to keep the tears at bay.

Expecting him to linger on the seedier part of my story, I'm flustered when he asks, "Where are your sisters now? How old are they?"

CHAPTER 5

S *hit.* Maybe I shouldn't have asked Emory about her sisters. Perhaps she needs to ease into her life? It doesn't sound like it's been easy, and she did just drop a lot of truths. The longer she gives me a blank stare, the more worried I become that I've ruined this before we've even started.

"Emory?" I ask softly, moving my face in front of her, hoping her glassy-eyed stare will focus on me.

"Ah, right. Sorry. I mean, that's just not what I thought you were going to ask," she mumbles.

"What did you expect me to ask?"

"Well, most people want to know about all the stepmoms. The one who went missing. My alcoholic father. I've never had a boyfriend ask me about my sisters." I watch with mirth as she jumps from the couch. "I-I-I didn't mean you. Not you as a boyfriend, I mean. This is just pretending—we're just pretending."

"Right," I say as she moves around me, gathering supplies for the new treatment we are starting tonight. She is a ball of nervous energy, and I feel bad for putting her in this position. Reaching out, I place my hand on her forearm, and pull back as if it scalded me.

"Jesus, did you feel that?" I ask, looking under her arm and around the couch. "That was the strongest static sting I've ever felt in my life. I can't believe we didn't see the spark."

Emory follows me with her eyes, and I catch her biting her bottom lip.

"Yes, static cling. That's what it was. That was crazy, right?" she asks nervously.

Tucking her blonde hair behind one ear, I see the moment she composes herself, and it reminds me of our first meeting. This is the look I usually get, where I am the patient, Preston, and she is Dr. Camden. Even though she won't tell me why she can't practice, I refused to listen when she told me to drop the doctor and call her Emory with tears in her eyes. This woman loves being a surgeon, and from what Dr. Terry has said, she has the potential to be one of the best. Vowing then to right whatever is wrong, I add Emory to my list of 'must-fixes' before I die.

"Okay, Preston. Any shortness of breath today? Any nausea? Sweating for no apparent reason? Shakiness? Weakness or fatigue? Blurred vision?" she runs through the list just like every night before.

"Your hair. It used to be redder," I say instead of answering.

Emory stares at me like I have six heads. "Preston, I've been here for almost a year, and you're just now realizing my hair is different?"

I stare at her, wondering why I never noticed. Gone is the strawberry shades of red. Now she's blonde with golden highlights framing her heart-shaped face.

"When you put it like that, I sound like an asshole," I acknowledge. "Why? I mean, it looks great, but the red was stunning."

"I just needed a change." She sighs, then as an afterthought, adds, "I guess I wanted to hide."

"Why would you need to hide, Ems?"

"What?" She finally looks up from the machine. I have a feeling she just dropped a truth she hadn't planned to share.

"Your hair, Ems. Why did you change it?" I ask again.

"Women's prerogative, I suppose," she evades. "So, any symptoms?" She is back in Dr. Camden mode.

I don't take my eyes off of her even though it causes her to fidget uncontrollably. She is a mystery I'm now determined to solve. "Nothing, Doc," I finally say with a wink. "Maybe Dr. Terry is wrong. How can I be this healthy and only have a handful of months left?" I'm aiming for light-hearted, carefree fun, and fail miserably.

"Preston..."

"I know, Emory. I know. No transplant is a death sentence. I'm just trying to, Christ, I don't know. I just have to aim for the positive sometimes," I tell her.

Placing both hands on my shoulders, she forces me to look at her. I know she is checking my pupils, but I notice something different in her eyes when I meet her gaze tonight. A pit the size of Texas forms in my gut.

"Alright then, shirt off and lay back so I can get you hooked up. This will be easier when Dr. Terry implants the portable catheter. Once that's available, we won't have to continue damaging your veins and it will help with all this bruising, too," she murmurs while inspecting my arms. "Get comfy, I'll get the pillows for your feet."

Doing as she asks, I reach for her one more time to see if she recoils. As I do, I get the same shock, and from her wide-eyed stare, I know she felt it, too. *What the hell is that?*

"Ems, listen. I know we have known each other for almost a year, but is this the first time I have touched you? That can't be right, can it? I don't know if you know this about me, but I am a really affectionate guy. My entire family will know something is off if we aren't demonstrative. You're going to have to get used to me, touching you," I breathe. *Yeah, if you get that electric shock every time you touch her, you will have to get used to it, too!*

Wait. *What the hell is going on?* I know Dex and Trevor both said they started having very loud consciences when they fell in love, but that's not what this is. This, between Emory and me, is pretend—it's fake. I don't get the happily ever after. My conscience would do well to remember that.

Emory is waiting for me expectantly, and I know I missed her response.

"Preston, I said, we've had a strictly professional relationship. Okay, well, a pseudo-professional one, at least given the circumstances. You've had no reason to touch me. I can promise you, though, if I could pretend to be happy with my ex for so long, I can definitely pretend to be your girlfriend."

I have so many questions for her, but I'm afraid to push too much too fast.

"We will need to have ground rules, though—real ground rules, and maybe a contract," she says distractedly. "I definitely need my own room. That isn't a question. We can show affection when absolutely required and in moderation." Emory moves around me, setting up the IV and drip bag infusion, and I take the chance to stare without being caught.

Her hair falls a few inches below her shoulders in waves while her delicate features fight to be seen. I notice she works hard at blending in and want to kick myself for missing what's been under my nose for so long. Emory is beautiful, with a light smattering of freckles covering her nose and fanning out across her cheeks. Her eyes are deep pools of emotion, and I know I could get lost in them for days. *If only I were a different man.*

Scared to touch her again, I say, "Emory, we have plenty of time for the details, okay? This is a lot all at once for us both. Let's just let it be for tonight so we can both wrap our heads around our expectations, okay?"

Emory nods her head and mumbles something I don't catch. Knowing I'll be in this position for at least an hour, I try to relax.

"So, Ems, tell me about your sisters."

Her shoulders lower with a genuine smile I realize I have never seen before, and it brightens the entire room.

"Where to begin? Honestly, Preston, they're amazing. Even after I ruined their lives with my stupidity, they have never held it against me. Eli is twenty-three, Tilly is twenty-two, and Sloane, the baby, is twenty-one, but never call her the baby to her face." She laughs.

I want to ask why she thinks she ruined their lives, but it feels like prying. How have I spent every single day for a year with this girl and know nothing about her?

"Are they still in Camden Crossing?" I ask.

Emory's eyes cloud over and dart away. "Two of them are. Eli and Tilly are in community college, part time, and living with our dad. That wasn't the plan, but without my income, everything kind of went to Hell. Anyway," she says, moving on quickly so I can't ask a question. "Sloane? She is the wild card. She refused to go to college and moved out of Dad's place the second she turned eighteen. Apparently, unbeknownst to any of us, she had been writing romance novels and self-publishing since she was sixteen. She said she always knew she wanted to be an author and wasn't hanging around to make us care for her. She squirreled away a nice little nest egg from her books and is now traveling the country writing. I worry about her, though, because we are pretty sure she lives out the romances before she writes them. I have a feeling it will bite her in the ass eventually, but she's an adult. I just do my best to keep an eye on her."

I laugh as she explains why she could come up with a bad pick-up line so quickly, and sit with her as she tells me the

41

dreams of her sisters. When her tone turns melancholy, I do the only thing I can think of. I try to pick her up. Badly.

Pinning her with my gaze, I lean in and whisper, "Excuse me, the FBI called demanding my penis. Help me find it?"

I'm rewarded with the sweetest sounding laughter I've ever heard. It has me questioning if this is a good idea, but since when have I ever listened to good ideas? I just have to make sure 'pretend' doesn't break her heart because she just might have the potential to bust mine wide open.

"Oh, gawd, that was terrible, and not terrible in a good way. Is that the best you have, Preston? Tsk, tsk. I expected more from you," she laughs.

Leaning in closer, so my mouth is almost touching her ear, I lower my voice and try again. "Are you a haunted house, Emory? Because I am going to scream when I'm inside of you." Pulling away slowly, I love the shiver that covers her body.

Jesus, Preston. What the fuck are you doing? This will go down as your worst idea ever. How the hell do you get that voice to shut up?

Emory's face and neck flush a deep crimson before she pulls at the collar of her shirt. "Ah, okay. That one was better," she acknowledges, but jumps up quickly and puts her doctor hat back on.

"Trust me, sweetheart, I only get better the longer we go," I tell her, watching the flush she is trying desperately to hide.

"I bet you do, Preston," Emory says under her breath.

I sit up, knowing she is about to pull the IV, and watch as she bends over to grab her supplies. *How have you never noticed her ass before?* Okay, this is ridiculous. How am I supposed to tell my own conscience to shut the fuck up?

After placing a Band-Aid on my forearm, Emory stands. "You're all set," she tells me, inspecting her handiwork. Typically, this is when I bolt, and I definitely need to tonight. This day went from one extreme to the next in less than two hours. I have to get out of here and think, but first, I need to thank her properly.

"Ems, listen, I really appreciate that you're going along with this."

"You didn't really give me much choice now, did you?" she replies through a smile. It's a smile I love way more than any of the other ones I've seen in our interactions together.

My neck tingles with guilt, and I clutch it. Now it's my turn to blush. "Yeah, I guess I didn't. I'm sorry, Ems. I just want to make the next few months the best I've ever had for my family. Having you with me is the only way to do that." As I say it, I wash away our intimate moment from before with the stifling promise of death.

"I know, Preston. And I'm happy to help, as long as Dr. Terry approves. If he doesn't, I—"

"If he doesn't, I'll either come clean with my family or find another solution," I interrupt. "Just really, thank you."

"You're welcome," she whispers.

Suddenly feeling like I can't breathe, I stand. "We'll talk tomorrow and go over the details, okay?

"Mmhm," is her only response.

Not wanting to leave her like I'm feeling, I step toward her. "Ems?" I question. When she finally raises her eyes to mine, I continue. "I'm going to hug you now … just a hug. We will work up to a kiss because that is going to have to happen. But for tonight, a hug. Okay?"

I'm relieved when she opens her arms to welcome me. Not to brag, but I am a pretty damn good hugger. Wrapping my long arms around her, I squeeze and breathe her in. I hear her breath catch in her throat, and I smile. Holding her, I can't help but notice she is my perfect size. She fits with me in every way. She is small, but not short like Julia and not an Amazonian like Lexi and Lanie. Ems is my own Goldie Locks, just right.

Emory clears her throat, and I'm aware I've just made this

hug awkward. I pull back, even though I want nothing more than to hold her.

"Right. So, do you want to come up to the office tomorrow around ten a.m.?"

"Okay. I'll see you tomorrow," Emory replies, walking past me to open the door.

I have one foot in the hallway when she calls my name. "Hey, Preston?"

"Yeah?"

"Was your mother a beaver?" she asks, resting her head against the door, looking very earnest.

"A beaver?" I ask, trying to think of what colleges have a beaver as a mascot. I'm about the tell her my mother went to Brown when she hits me with the punchline.

"'Cause daaamn," Emory drawls, a little more southern than is her norm, then breaks out in laughter.

"I can't believe I fell for that," I tell her.

"I'm the queen of bad pick-up lines, Preston."

"And that, sweetheart, makes me the king." I give her a kiss on the cheek, then rush down the hall toward the elevator before I do something else stupid. I don't look back until I am pressing the up button, and when I do, she gives a small wave. "Goodnight, Ems."

"Goodnight, Preston."

I wait until she closes her door and strain to hear if she locked it. I'm tempted to go check but control myself. Instead, I step into the elevator and head to my apartment. *What a freaking shitshow.*

CHAPTER 6

EMORY

Holy shit. I plop down on the couch and fan myself. What the hell was that? When he leaned in and said he would scream when he was inside of me? I swear to all that is holy, I almost orgasmed. From words! I allow myself a moment to live in the dreamland of what-ifs, then text my sisters.

Emory: Eli and Till, I have more income coming in for a few months. Both of you sign up for two more classes next semester. I'll still be able to cover the costs at home.

Living in Preston's building has opened up money, so I'm trying my hardest to get them both through school. I want them out of Camden Crossing as soon as possible.

Eli: Ems, what did you do?

Emory: Don't you worry about it. I've picked up some extra hours, that's all.

Emory: Sloane, I have a ticket waiting for you any time you want to come home.

Sloane: I'm good. Seeing a guy here in Seattle and working on the whole grumpy boss trope. (winky face emoji)

Tilly: (Barfing emoji) Sloane, I swear to god if you end up with an STD, I am disowning you.

Emory: Please, just be safe. I've got to run. Love you, girls.

Eli: Love you, too, Mis.

Tilly: Love you, Mis.

Sloane: Love you to the moon and back, Mis.

Seeing my sisters all call me Mis in succession like that makes me weepy. Eli started mixing up Mom and Sis when I was nine. The rest followed suit. I've been Mis ever since. Knowing it does no good to wallow, I go about hiding all the medical equipment back in the front closet when a loud banging on my door startles me. *Shit, maybe I should be more careful about locking the door.*

"Ems. It's me, open up," I hear Preston call through the door. *Hm, guess I did lock it.*

Panicking that something is wrong, I rush to the door, yank it open, and check him over.

"No, no, Ems, stop. I'm fine, but I had to run down the stairs to beat the girls. I'm sorry, I tried to warn them off, but once Lanie gets something in her head, she's like a dog with a bone. They're on their way down here to have 'girl time'. They raided my wine fridge; I'm sorry! All I told them was that we met when you worked for me briefly. I didn't know what else to say. I wasn't expecting them all to still be in my apartment. I guess, just do your best to make up our relationship," he whisper-yells.

"What? Preston! I know nothing about you except what is in your medical records. I cannot do this," I whine until I hear the elevator. Taking a step toward each other instinctively, we turn our heads and watch as two six-foot blondes, and a teeny, tiny brunette comes laughing down the hallway arm in arm.

"Preston, what the hell did you do? Run down the stairs

to get here first? What's wrong with you?" Lexi asks. It seems like a question she asks a lot.

"Seriously, Preston. We won't scare her off. We just want to get to know her," Lanie interjects.

"I know," Preston says, using the opportunity to wrap an arm around my waist before he continues. "But it's been a long day. Ems wasn't expecting to meet you all today; it's a little overwhelming."

"Geez, don't I know it. Don't you remember the first time I met all of you guys? And I was alone! That is a story Emory definitely needs to hear," Lanie grins.

"Jesus, fine. How about if we promise no inquisition? Tonight, anyway. Tonight we will just eat, drink, and be merry. What do you say, Emory?" Julia asks in the no-nonsense way that she has.

Placing my hand on Preston's chest, I gently push him back. "Preston, it's fine. It might be nice to have some girl time." *Since when? You have never had girl time in your life!* I turn to the three ladies determined to be my new best friends. "But you have to promise, no firing squad tonight. I need a full twenty-four hours' notice before my relationship gets picked apart."

"I like this one, Preston," Julia says, pushing past us into the apartment.

Preston silently mouths, 'I'm sorry!'

"Who would have guessed," Lexi says. "You found a gorgeous girl with brains. I'm impressed, dickwad."

Preston rolls his eyes but bites his tongue.

"We really are not that bad. I promise you'll have fun. Come on, girl rules start now. That means it's time for Mr. Westbrook to head to his own firing squad." Lanie smiles while looping her arm with mine and dragging toward the apartment.

Something tells me Lanie will keep her word, and I am in for the fun night the girls promised, but somehow, I don't expect Preston will get off so easily. Giving him a tight wave, I allow Lanie to lead me back into my own apartment.

As soon as the door closes, my heart rate picks up. I don't know these women from Adam, but walking into the small family room, I burst out laughing. Julia and Lexi are both removing their bras through the armholes of their shirts. When Julia notices me, she slingshots it. Her baby blue bra goes whizzing past my head.

"What kind of girls' night is this exactly?" I ask.

"The best kind. No bras, no glasses, and junk food for days. The only rule is to be yourself," Julia informs me.

"Jesus, girls, you cannot just throw Ems into our wicked ways. Warn a girl," Lexi says, handing me a bottle of wine. "Cheers, Emory."

I watch in amusement as all three of them raise their own bottles and drink. *If you can't beat them, you might as well join them.*

"You see, Emory," Lexi continues, "the three of us have known each other since birth, but we are not the mean girl crew."

"No way," Lanie interjects. "Mean girls can kiss my tush. We are the 'more awkward, the better, just don't be a jerk' kind of crew."

"Honestly, we think the devil invented bras, so we lose them every chance we get," Julia informs me.

This is all a little weird, but since I'm a modest B-cup, I don't really need to wear a bra most days, anyway. Handing my bottle of wine to Lexi, I reach around my back to unhook my bra. I pull it out of the armhole just as the others had. Looking around, I shrug my shoulders and toss it over my head.

All three of my guests break out in applause, and I feel like I just scored the winning basket. I've never really had girlfriends, but these girls seem determined to fill me in on all I've missed.

"First things first, there are a few requirements of our girls' nights," Julia enlightens me, and my palms get sweaty waiting for her to finish. With a glint in her eye, she smiles. "Thanks to Preston, we have the alcohol. Thanks to us, we have the company, and thanks to Door Dash, we will soon have the food. Do you have any allergies, Ems?" she asks while typing away on her phone.

"Ah, no. I'll eat just about anything," I tell her.

"You'd have to if you're sleeping with Preston," Lexi quirks.

"Lex," Lanie admonishes, and I feel my face flush beat red. "We promised no inquisition tonight, and we are going to stick to that."

"Food will be here in twenty minutes," Julia informs us. "And Lanie is right, no inquisition. We invited ourselves down here, so we have to cut her some slack. But," she says, and I sit up straighter on the couch, "we should play a game."

"Yes," Lexi jumps in. "A get to know you game."

I look around nervously. Lexi and Julia look like trouble, while Lanie at least seems as nervous as I am.

"What kind of game?" Lanie asks.

"Never Have I Ever," Julia and Lexi say in unison.

"I've never played," I tell them, and watch three heads whip in my direction.

"What do you mean? Even Lanie has played, and she is usually the goody-two-shoes. No offense, Lanes," Lexi says.

"You've really never played?" Lanie asks kindly.

"No. Um ..." Do I really want to tell these girls how tough my life has been? By the looks of them, I can all but guarantee they won't be able to relate. Deciding to just get it over with, I tell them a little about me. "I didn't do most things. I didn't exactly have a normal childhood. I started raising my sisters when I was seven years old, so I never really had the time for, well, fun, I guess." For the first time in a long time, I feel embarrassed about my past. I lower my eyes to my knees.

I wouldn't change it because I know my sisters needed me, but it has its own sense of shame in times like these.

"Oh, honey. I'm so sorry." Moving in close, Lanie wraps me in a hug. It's an odd sensation. I've only ever received hugs from my sisters, and tonight I've been attacked twice. Donny was against hugging, the asshole.

"Listen, if it makes you feel any better, Julia is the only one who had a normal childhood. Lexi grew up with our grandmother, and my mother was an alcoholic, abusive mess. I only recently came to terms with what that meant and how it has affected me into adulthood," Lanie confesses.

I'm shocked by her open confession and angry with myself for making assumptions I had no business making.

"My father is an alcoholic, too," I tell her, for once not feeling the shame that generally accompanies that statement.

Nodding her head in understanding, Lanie takes my hand in hers. "Well, then, I guess you have some catching up to do. Tonight will be all about filling in the experiences you missed," she says excitedly.

"Lanie," Julia warns.

"What?" I ask, glancing around.

Julia and Lexi have concerned expressions on their faces while Lanie is positively exploding with happiness.

"Nothing," Lexi replies. "Lanie just has a tendency to go overboard, and she looks like she has a plan formulating in her head."

Clapping her hands and bouncing in her seat, she admits, "I do, I do! We can do girls' night once a week. It'll give us a break from all the wedding stuff that is all-consuming, and we can use that time to help Emory have the experiences she missed out on."

She looks so excited I hate to burst her bubble, but this sounds like trouble in the making.

"How about if we see how tonight goes first?" I offer.

"That sounds good," Julia agrees. "So, Never Have I Ever. The rules are easy. We each take turns saying something we have never done. Everyone else will drink if they haven't done it either. If no one drinks, then the person asking has to. Got it?"

"I think so." Feeling nervous, I take a drink from the bottle. Each of them also takes a sip straight from theirs. *These girls just might be my kind of people.*

"Good, I'll start," Lexi tells us. "Never have I ever been on a dating website."

I look around the room. "So, if I have never been on a dating website, do I drink?"

"Yes," all three girls say, so I lift the bottle to my mouth, as does Lanie.

"Julia! When did you go on a dating website?" Lanie screeches.

"Ah, I don't know. I guess before your attack. Remember? I was horny as hell. I was ready to try anything at that point," she tells us honestly, and I can't help but giggle.

"Okay, my turn," Lanie says. "Never have I ever tried a keg stand."

Everyone but Lexi takes a drink.

"What? I played basketball in college, remember? House parties are like Beer-Olympic training grounds."

These girls each have fascinating stories. *I hope I get to know them one day.*

Julia goes next. "Never have I ever given a lap dance."

Lanie and I both drink.

"Who the hell were you giving lap dances to, Lexi?" Julia asks, and I notice we all lean in for the answer.

"Oh, one of my boyfriends in college. I was awesome at lap dances, by the way, right up until he puked all down my back," Lexi says, cringing.

"Ugh," I say, but we're all laughing. I'm surprised to find that I'm having a lot of fun.

"Your turn, Emory," Lanie says while adjusting herself on the floor, so she is sitting crisscross.

"Okay, um. Never have I ever …" Shit, I really have done nothing, so this shouldn't be so hard. "Okay, never have I ever had sex outside."

I glance around the room, and no one takes a drink.

"Isn't that interesting," Lexi says. "Ems, looks like you have to drink."

"Wait," Julia interjects. "Lanie, when the hell did you have sex outside?"

Lanie blushes from head to toe. "When Dex took me out on the boat," she tells the room on a hiccup.

"The first time you slept with Dex was outside?" Julia asks in amazement. "You lil' hussy," she laughs.

"Well, we didn't have sex, have sex, but I came. That counts, doesn't it?" Lanie asks seriously.

"We'll give it to you," Lexi says as the intercom rings.

"Oh good, food's here," Julia announces.

I silently thank God for his perfect timing. I don't know how much I have drunk so far, but I'm a little tipsy.

Julia hands the doorman some cash, and he brings in three paper bags' worth of food. She must notice my bulging eyes because she laughs and wraps her arm around me. "Girl's nights, we order a little of everything, and with the amount of wine we drink, it is a good thing."

I follow the others into the little galley kitchen and watch as everyone makes a plate. Once I have mine, I find they have rearranged the family room so we can sit around the over-sized coffee table.

Lexi grabs her bottle of wine, "Cheers, ladies." I have barely taken a sip when she looks right at Julia and says, "Never have I ever had a bedroom injury while doing something naughty." Her evil grin tells me there is a story here, and damn if I don't want to hear it.

"That was once. Okay, twice. Fuck it. Yes, I have a

tendency to get a little excitable and head-butt Trevor. Sometimes. He has gotten excellent at bobbing and weaving during sexy-time now, though," Julia says with a wink.

I laugh so hard I choke on my food. I honestly cannot remember the last time I had this much fun.

"Never have I ever had sex after prom."

"Ah, I didn't go to prom," I say, beginning to slur.

"What do you mean? Everyone goes to prom. Even I went," Lanie says as if that's the magical scale of who does what.

I shrug my shoulders. "My sister, Eli, needed an orthodontist. We couldn't afford it, so I used the little money I had saved for a dress on a down payment for her braces."

"We need to fix that," Lanie says seriously.

"Ah, I'm a little old for prom, but thanks."

"Hmm—"

"No," Julia and Lexi say together. "Whatever you're thinking, Lanie, just let it go for tonight. We can take Ems to the prom another time."

When I look at Lanie, I see she may have really been contemplating arranging a prom tonight. *These girls are amazing human beings.*

The questions keep coming, we keep drinking, and I keep laughing.

"Never have I ever done it more than three times in a day."

"Never have I ever gone commando."

"Never have I ever watched another couple get it on."

"Never have I ever screwed around in an elevator."

Minutes or hours later, I'm not sure, I turn to Lanie. "I fink next time she asked if I never had ever blacked out, I won't have to drink," I laugh.

Lanie cracks up, too, and is squeezing her legs together. "Don't make me laugh. I'm gonna pee my pants," she cries.

"You sounded funny," I tell her.

"Okay, you two. I think girls' night is over," Lexi says. "Julia, you help Goody over here, and I'll get Lanes."

"Is I Goody?" I laugh.

"Yes, you are Goody," she says through a smile. "We are going to have to speak to Preston about getting a little more adventurous with you in the bedroom, though."

Somewhere I recognize that those words should sober me up, but with my judgment impaired, I get lost in the warm feeling that spreads throughout my body.

"Yes, pleeeease," I hear someone say. *Was that me?*

CHAPTER 7

I linger outside of Emory's apartment for a few beats. When I hear them all laugh, I finally pull away and walk to the elevator. Rubbing a hand over my face, I press the button for the penthouse. I'm not ready for this, but I know by the excessive amount of text messages on my phone, there is no getting out of it now.

Trevor: Preston has a girlfriend.

Dexter: A live-in girlfriend.

Trevor: Who knew about this?

Easton: You've got to be kidding me?

Loki: Bull shit.

Halton: Since when?

Ashton: Is she of the blow-up variety?

Colton: Ah, man! Why am I always the last to know?

Colton: The blow-up variety? (Crying laughing emoji)

Trevor: No, a real one. We just met her.

Halton: Is he paying her?

Dexter: I don't think so.

Ashton: There is no way he has hidden this from us. He's the most ostentatious of us all.

Easton: He is also physically incapable of keeping a secret.

Oh, if he only knew the truth.

Preston: Jesus. You're all worse than GG.

I open the door to my home quietly and hear Dexter and Trevor speaking softly. Taking a deep breath and plastering on my devil-don't-care façade, I enter the great room. They stop talking immediately, and the fight I was building up to leaves in a whoosh of air.

"She seems nice," Dexter starts.

With the memory of her smile, I sit down across from them. "She is," I admit. "She's great, actually."

"Preston, listen," Trevor says. "We want to apologize. We're sorry that we have been so wrapped up in our own lives and all the drama that you didn't feel you could share something this big with us."

And just like that, I know I'm going straight to Hell.

"No. That's—"

"We know how messed up everything has been, and we're sorry you felt like you had to hide this from us," Dexter agrees.

"Guys," I try to sound upbeat, but I'm speaking through razor blades right now.

"Are you happy?" Trevor asks, and for the second time tonight, I cross my fingers.

"I am," I force out.

"Then we can't wait to get to know her," Dexter says, handing me a glass of scotch.

I'm not supposed to drink, but fucking hell, I need a sip tonight.

"Tell us about her?" Trevor asks.

Sinking back into my chair, I let the memories of the past year wash before my eyes. Except, seeing them now, replaying these scenes as Emory and not Dr. Camden, does something funny to my soul.

"Holy shit," Trevor exclaims, and I sit up, looking around to find what I've missed only to see Dex and Trevor staring straight at me.

"What?" I question, looking behind me.

"You're falling in love with her," Dexter smiles.

"Falling or has fallen," Trevor chimes in.

"What? Guys, come on—"

"You look like our Preston. Preston from before your dad died," Dexter tells me. "It's nice to have you back, buddy."

I don't know what to say to that, so I take a sip instead. Eventually, the subject turns to their upcoming weddings, and I can partially tune them out. They have no idea what they are talking about. I have known Emory for a year, yes, but I know nothing about her. Seeing her through fresh eyes will not cause insta-love. That only happens to ... Well, fuck. That happened to both of these dickheads. *What about the spark?*

"What the fuck?" I grumble.

I get a strange look from the guys before they laugh.

"Yup, it's happening alright." Trevor leans back into the couch like he knows all the secrets.

"What's happening?" I finally ask.

"The conversations," Dex says, as if it explains it all.

I stare blankly at him until Trevor fills in the missing pieces.

"You're fighting your feelings for her, so you're having conversations in your head. It happens to the best of us, my friend. That's how you know it's right, though. You're covering all your bases because, above all else, you want what's best for her. You're trying to figure out if that's you. We both went through it, too," he admits, pointing his thumb in Dexter's direction. They both grin wildly back.

My neck feels hot, and I stand suddenly. Patting Trevor on the shoulder as I pass him, I say, "That's where you're wrong. I already know I'm not what's best for her. I have to take a piss. I'll be back."

In my room, I take a pill to help calm my racing heart. Those guys have no fucking idea what they're talking about. I splash some water on my face and stare into the mirror. "You don't get to have this life, asshole. Don't drag anyone down with you. Especially not Ems."

Pouring half of the whiskey down the drain, I grab my phone from my back pocket to text her. I just want to make sure the girls are treating her okay. Then I laugh. *Of course they are.* Lanie, Julia, and even Lexi are some of the most loyal, honest women I've ever met. Rolling my shoulders a few times to relieve some tension, I make my way back to the guys.

To my relief, they have turned on a Panther's game. Turning his head in my direction but not looking at me, Trevor asks, "You okay?"

"Yeah, I'm good. Thanks. What's the score?"

We fall into our regular conversation for the rest of the night. Lifting my glass, I'm reminded of how easy our lives were once upon a time. "To Loki," I say while sending up a little prayer that our brother is safe.

"To Loki," they say in unison.

"HOW MANY TIMES are you going to check your phone?" Trevor teases.

I hadn't realized they noticed. "I ... this is a lot to throw at her, you know? I just wanted to make sure she's having fun," I say defensively.

"Dude. I know you have Lexi issues, but none of those women would ever do anything to make her uncomfortable. You know that," Dex says seriously.

"Yeah, I—"

"Hooney, weee are hooome," someone slurs from the front door.

"Son of a bitch. Lanie, use your legs," we hear Lexi scold.

Sharing a glance with the guys, we all burst out laughing.

What the fuck is going on?

We're to our feet when the girls come staggering around the corner. Lanie is being held up by Lexi, who has two bras in her hands, but it is Emory I can't take my eyes off of. She is staring straight at me, and I feel the entire room sway.

Trevor laughs. "Jesus, they're wasted."

Hearing him, Julia takes her hands off Emory for a minute to make guns with her fingers. "Pew, pew, pew," she says with her guns before having to grab hold of a stumbling Emory.

The three of us are jumping over each other to get to our girls. *Our girls?*

Lexi seems to be the only one capable of holding herself upright. "Someone had to stay sober enough to watch this shitshow," she tells us.

"Thank you," I say honestly.

"No problem."

"Preston," Lanie begins, suddenly serious, "how is it that Emory has done nothing?"

"Ah, what do you mean?" I ask tentatively.

"I means, she hasn't had sex outside. She's never ever been to a sex toy store. She never had sex after prom 'cause she didn't go to prom. She has never ever never been to a strip club," Lanie shrieks.

"Wait, you've been to a strip club?" Dex asks her.

"Duh. I grew up on the Canadian border. It's eighteen to drink there, ya know? So that's where we all had our birthdays." She says it like Dex should know all that.

"Freaking hell, Preston, she's never even been in a hot tub!" Julia scolds.

How the hell did they learn all this about her in just a few hours?

"Oh, yay!" Lanie yells. "We can fixer that one right now. Preston has a hot tub," she squeals with excitement as she reaches for Emory and drags her toward the wall of windows.

"Oh, man," Emory whines. "I don't own a bathing suit."

How the fuck doesn't she own a bathing suit?

Lanie drags the door open. "That's okay, Ems. We can go in our underpants."

"Oh shit," Lexi says, holding up their bras as Dex goes darting after them.

I stand there like a moron, wondering what on earth is happening.

"Come on, playboy, unless you want Dex seeing your lady's bits, you had better grab some towels and meet us out there," Lexi says as she follows the path of drunken bad ideas.

No way am I letting Dex see her tits before me, especially not when she is blasted out of her mind. Rushing to the guest bathroom, I grab a stack of towels. I'm entering the great room as Dex guides a crying Lanie inside.

"What the hell happened now?" I ask.

"M-My mommy bags are leaking. I have to pump and dump, and I don't even get to go in the hot tub because liquid gold will spray everywhere," Lanie sobs.

I'm not going to lie. I have no fucking clue what Lanie just said. I'm also getting anxious about Emory.

"Ah," Dex says, looking sheepish. "Trevor left with Julia, and what my lovely lady here is trying to say is, she hasn't pumped in a few hours, and the hot water is making her leak breast milk."

I look from him, then to Lanie, who points to her chest, and sure enough, there are two large wet spots. I don't mean to, but I gag, loudly. The idea of breast milk spraying all over my hot tub is enough to make me want to get rid of the damn thing.

"See, Dex. Preston thinks it's gross too." Lanie's sobs are getting louder.

"Nice going, dickwad," Dexter scolds, stifling a laugh. "I'm just going to get her home. Emory and Lexi are out on the balcony. Good luck."

"Great." I give him a pat on the shoulder as we pass. "You too."

We both laugh at the absurdity of it all until I step outside and see Emory standing in the hot tub in nothing but a tiny red thong.

"It makes its own bubbles, Pres," she says happily. Hearing her use my nickname does something funny to my insides.

"Well, Romeo. I'm not sure how you landed her, but she is as sweet and possibly even more innocent than Lanie. I would never have thought that possible," Lexi says, chuckling.

"She is far too good for me, that's for sure," I acknowledge, and lean against the hot tub.

Emory has finally taken a seat and is staring up at the stars.

"I'm not sure what's going on between you two," Lexi starts, and I feel the dread set in, "but she's a good girl. A good girl who appears to have had an even harder upbringing than Lanie. Those two have more in common than I would have guessed," she says just above a whisper.

I swallow and nod in understanding but can't bring myself to speak.

"Listen, Preston. I don't truly think you're a bad guy, and maybe with a little space, we could eventually be friends, but when I look at Emory, I worry. Just don't break her, okay? She seems strong and smart and put together, but I recognize the pain she's hiding. Just make sure you're doing right by her."

I wonder for a moment if Lexi has anyone to talk to, and I make a mental note to check in with Lanie tomorrow. I can't bring myself to make eye contact with her, but I nod and say, "I will."

"Alright then, I'm going to head down to Emory's place for the night. I have a feeling she needs about a gallon of water and possibly some bread."

"Lexi, you don't have to do that. I can bring Ems home," I tell her.

"No need, Romeo. I'm looking forward to a little alone time in a space all my own. I'll see you in the morning," she says, heading for the door.

Great. What the hell am I supposed to do now?

Emory answers that when the water sloshes, and she slides farther down into the seat.

"Okay, Goldie. It's time to get you out and into some dry clothes," I tell her.

"Okay, Goldie," she mimics with a few hiccups thrown in.

I hold open the towel and observe as she attempts to stand.

"Excuuuuse me?" Emory says, and I wonder how long I've been staring at her tits. "Did you just fart?" She has her hands on her knees, and I think she is going to be sick until I hear her laughing uncontrollably. "Because you just blew me away," she says just before she slips in the water, and I have to dive to catch her.

I can't even be fucking mad. The girl just told me my non-existent fart blew her away. I'm laying in the hot tub fully clothed with her on top of me, yet we both laugh so hard my stomach cramps. I don't remember the last time I laughed like this.

"Alright, sweetheart, you win. Again. Now, let's get you out of here."

"Why? Are we going to practice that kiss now?" she asks, concentrating on my lips as I lift her out of the hot tub.

I stare down into her eyes, and as much as I want to, I won't kiss her tonight. Not when she is drunk, and not when this day has been the most confusing of my goddamn life. I feel like I had a better handle on things ten years ago when Dr. Terry essentially handed me a death sentence.

"Not tonight, I need you sober for that," I tell her with a wink. The pout that takes over her face has me second-guessing all my morals, but only for a moment. *Never hook up with a drunk girl. Consent is sexy*, I repeat in my head. "Let's get you into some dry clothes and something to eat."

"Eesh, do ya know how much food tiny little Julia ordered? That would feed my sisters and me for a week." I'm happy that the dip in the hot tub seems to have sobered her up a little. At least she isn't slurring as much.

Patting her dry so she doesn't slip on the hardwood floors, I finally wrap her up. Listen, I'm a guy. I'd be lying if I said I didn't enjoy the show. Peering down at her, Goldie Locks runs through my head again. *My perfect size*. Jesus Christ, I need to get a grip. This day has been too much, maybe for both of us. Tomorrow we will set some ground rules just like she wanted.

Knowing I need to get her some clothes, I guide her to my room, where she plops down on the bed with a heavy sigh.

"Holy cow. This is the comfiest bed I've ever sat on," Emory says, running her hands all around my duvet cover. "It's like a tilt-a-whirl."

"Oh, no. Are you going to be sick, Ems?"

"Mhm. Maybe. You know, my father is an alcoholic. It runs in the family, so I don't normally drink," she mumbles.

"I know, sweets." I run to my closet for a T-shirt and shorts. When I return, she is on the verge of passing out. Grabbing her arms, I lift her to sitting and slump her against my body while I undo the towel. Perfection and pervert are vying for the top spot in my head right now.

After slipping the T-shirt over her head, I guide her arms

through the armhole, careful not to touch her anywhere else. It's a fucking chore, let me tell you. Once it's on, I lay her back onto the bed. Staring at her, I wonder what the hell I'm supposed to do now. Finally, I decide there is only one person I can ask at this point.

Preston: Ah, Emory is passing out. I put a dry T-shirt on her, but her panties are wet from the hot tub. Can I just put her to bed like this?

Lexi: Would you want to go to sleep in soaked boxers, you dip shit? Plus, she will get a UTI if she sleeps in wet underwear. She is your girlfriend, yes? Why are you even questioning this?

Girlfriend. Right.

Preston: I take consent very seriously, that's all.

Liar.

Lexi: Your GIRLFRIEND will be pissed if she wakes up with a UTI. Goodnight, Preston.

Shit. I can't have Lexi questioning our relationship.

Preston: Right. Thanks. Goodnight.

Lexi: (middle finger emoji)

"Nice, Lexi. Real mature," I say out loud.

Okay. I can do this. Staring down at Ems with my hands on my hips, I decide I just need to get it over with. I pull my t-shirt down on her legs as far as it will go, reach up to her hips, and with my eyes pointed at the ceiling, pull down her thong. *Fuck me.* Grabbing my shorts, I place each of her feet into the leg holes and pull them up while staring straight at a wall. Once they are to her waist, I look down. *How the hell are those going to stay up?*

I probably should have just borrowed something from Lexi, but there is not a chance I'm going to change Emory again. Instead, I run into Lexi's ensuite in search of an elastic. Finding one, I run back to my bed, bunch the side up as tight as possible, then wrap the elastic around and around. *Good enough.*

Standing back to inspect my handiwork, I'm pretty happy with it. I've never had to take care of anyone before, so this is unfamiliar territory for me. Then I remember what Lexi said. Bread and water. After I surround her with pillows, I run to the kitchen and grab a bottle of water and a bagel.

When I return, I'm relieved to see she hasn't moved. Lifting her once again, I sit her upright and lean her against my chest. "Ems, drink this water, and have a couple bites of bagel, sweetheart."

She doesn't open her eyes but nods her head and opens her mouth. I can't help but chuckle. Breaking off a piece of bagel, I stick it in her mouth and am pleased when I see her chew, even if it is slowly. When her jaw stops moving, I bring the water bottle to her lips and watch as she swallows. I follow the process for as long as she will allow, but now I'm afraid she'll choke.

Placing the water and bagel on the end table, I say, "Ems, open your mouth, sweetheart." I'm happy when she does as I ask without hesitation. Inserting my finger, I swipe at her cheeks like I have seen Dex do with his girls to make sure she doesn't have any bagel stored somewhere in her mouth. She shocks the hell out of me when she sucks ... hard. I've been walking around with a semi since I found her in the hot tub, and now it's standing at full attention.

No. No. No.

Pulling gently, she releases my finger with a pop, and I swear to God, it is the sexiest sound I've ever heard.

"Okay, Ems. Let's get you under the covers," I say sliding her up farther on the bed.

Once I'm convinced she's comfortable and not in danger of choking on her own vomit, I grab a blanket and move to the chaise in the corner of my room. *What?* I'm responsible for her tonight. If she needs me, I want to be close by. That's what I tell myself anyway as I tuck in for the most uncomfortable yet satisfying night of sleep I've had in years.

CHAPTER 8

EMORY

*O*pening one eye, I peer around. *Where the hell am I?* Slowly and painfully, I open the other eye and attempt to survey my surroundings. That's when I land on Preston, slumped over in a chair. What am I doing here? But before I can remember the answer, I fall back to sleep.

When I open them a second time, I can't help the low moan that escapes. The tiny marching band in my head is making my stomach queasy.

"Oh good, you're up," Preston whispers, smelling like bacon.

Good grief, this guy knows a way to a woman's heart, and still, I can't help but tell him to shush.

"Not feeling great?" he asks. His voice laced with humor.

I can't even answer. I just shake my head with as little movement as possible.

I feel the bed dip and know he sat down beside me. "Sweetheart, I'm guessing you've never had a hangover?" he asks in a buttery soft voice that I shouldn't like as much as I do.

"No," I croak out, "not like this."

Sure, when my sisters turned twenty-one, I took them

out, but I was the responsible one. I made sure everyone got home, so I have definitely never felt like this before.

I hear a clinking noise, then my senses are assaulted by the aroma of all the diner food I could want. Peeking over the covers, I see that Preston has a tray full of every greasy food imaginable.

"I wasn't sure what you would want, but these are all my favorite hangover cures."

"Oh my God, did you order from every diner in the city?" I ask, glancing at the food before falling on his face. He looks embarrassed, and I feel like a jerk.

"Ah, no, actually. You've been sleeping for a while, so I cooked." He gives a little shrug of his shoulders, then averts his eyes.

"You what?" *I can't possibly have heard him correctly.*

"I cooked. Here, bacon cheeseburger, blueberry pancakes, eggs Benedict, and biscuits and gravy. The biscuits and gravy are my go-to, but the others help, too," he says sheepishly.

"But why?" I blurt.

"Why what, sweetheart?"

I watch as he positions the tray near me. "Why did you cook all this? For me, I mean."

"Well, it's my fault, or at least my friends' fault, you ended up in this position." He laughs while sweeping his hands up and down my body.

That's when I notice I'm not wearing my clothes. *Oh no, what did I do?*

"W-Why am I wearing your clothes?" I ask timidly, not at all sure I want to know the answer.

"Well, how much of last night do you remember?"

Placing my fingertips to my temples, I close my eyes and think. *What do I remember?*

"Um, I remember playing Never Have I Ever. There might have been a dance party? Someone definitely knocked on the door and asked us to turn down the music. Everything else is a little blurry," I admit.

Preston's laughter fills the room and makes my head pound. Noticing my discomfort, he chokes on his amusement.

"Sorry. Okay, well, I can't speak to what happened downstairs, but Lexi is the only one who wasn't drunk, so she can probably fill you in there. When the four of you came busting in here, though, that was a sight." He laughs again, and I vaguely remember a hot tub.

"Do you have a hot tub?" I ask, cringing as I see his reaction.

"I do have a hot tub. Lanie made it her mission to knock a few things off your Never Have I Ever list. The hot tub being number one."

"But, I don't have a bathing suit," I say stupidly, somehow praying this isn't going where I think it is.

"We'll talk about that later, but Lanie didn't end up in the hot tub … something about her breast milk leaking. I went to get towels while Lexi stayed on the balcony with you. When I came back, Lexi went down to your apartment for the night," he fills in my ever-growing blackout list.

"So, did I wear my clothes in the hot tub?" I ask as my cheeks flame with heat.

The roguish grin that takes over his face tells me no.

"No, Ems, you most definitely did not. But it was just Lexi and I who saw you, and before you freak out, I only saw you for a minute."

The change in his eye color has me blushing more than I thought possible.

"Then … what happened?" I ask hesitantly.

"Well, after that, you asked me if I farted—"

"I did what?" I screech.

"Oh yes, farts are funny, remember? You were full of it last night. You cracked yourself up, telling me I blew you away with my fart." Even Preston can't say it with a straight face. "It was fine until you slipped, and I had to dive into the hot tub so you didn't hit your head. Long story short, after that, I brought you in here, dried you off, slipped my T-shirt over your head, and then texted Lexi. I felt like a creeper, but she promised me you would be pissed if you woke up with a UTI, so I pulled the shirt down as far as it would go and slipped your panties off. I swear I didn't look until I got my shorts on you."

His confession has me kicking off the blankets in a hurry, and noticing a protruding bump. Looking at him questioningly, I lift the T-shirt and burst out laughing at his creativity. He just shrugs with an uncomfortable grin.

"They wouldn't have stayed on your little body otherwise," he tells me. "Now, eat before this gets cold."

"Preston, I do not need to eat in your bed. I can get up," I tell him, and begin to move.

He places a hand on my leg. "Just, just stay and eat, okay? I've never made anyone breakfast in bed before. Don't ruin it for me," he says with a wink.

"No one has cooked for me since my last stepmom left," I say more to myself than to him.

"According to Lanie, I need to take care of a lot of firsts for you." A crooked grin graces Preston's handsome face. A grin I like a bit too much. "You eat, then we can talk about what this whole situation is going to entail. I never imagined it would get messy so quickly. I guess I should have expected it, though. My friends and family really have no boundaries, even when they mean well. We should probably start the speed dating today," he tells me while walking toward the door. "There is a Diet Coke and Tylenol on the side table. Trust me on this, you want to drink the soda."

Then he leaves, and I'm left wearing his clothes, in his bed, staring at the food he made just for me.

"What the hell am I doing here?" I ask the empty room,

hating myself immensely. *You are better than this, Emory. What if something happened to Preston in the middle of the night? He could have died because of your incompetence.* Sometimes I can't tell the difference between my father's voice and my own, but this time it doesn't matter. This voice is right.

Not wanting to offend Preston, I shovel a few bites of food into my mouth and almost fall back into the bed. The freaking man can cook. I would give my left foot right now to finish this, but I have to get out of here.

Taking a giant swig of the Diet Coke he left, my eyes roll to the back of my head. Holy shit, he's right. I needed that. Glancing around the room, the scent of grease keeps me from sneaking out empty-handed. I run back to the bed, dump all the food onto one plate, grab the soda, and, as quietly as possible, leave Preston's apartment.

With the food in one hand and drink in the other, I use my elbow to call the elevator. Stepping forward, I peek back one more time. This is probably the most immature thing I have ever done, but knowing I need a few minutes to get my shit together, I hit the tenth-floor and make my way to my apartment. Opening the door with one hand, I completely forgot Lexi was down here, and it almost crashes into her.

"Oh my gosh, I'm so sorry," I yelp as Lexi places a hand under my plate, keeping it from crashing to the ground. Then I notice she was just closing the closet door—the closet with all of Preston's medical supplies. I'm wracking my brain for an explanation when Lexi holds up her hand.

"That," she says, pointing to the door, "seems like a story that is none of my business. I was just looking for a broom. I love Julia, but she is a fucking slob when she drinks."

"I—" I'm still searching for some sort of explanation when she interrupts me.

"No need, Ems. What did you bring for breakfast? Did Preston cook all this? He didn't know what you would want or what?"

"Well, I've never really been hungover before, so he had no idea what to make."

Lexi raises an eyebrow at me while picking up half the burger. "Why didn't he just ask you then?"

"Ah, I was sleeping, I guess."

"And he didn't want to eat with you?" she asks suspiciously.

"Ah—" *Shit*. What if he wanted to eat with me? Is this what you call chewing and screwing? Or screwing and chewing? We didn't screw, did we? Lexi must read this all play out on my face because she puts me out of my misery.

"Listen, I don't know what type of relationship you guys have, but I get the feeling you haven't had many chances to let go and have fun. When is the last time you even did something just for yourself?" she asks kindly.

I feel my forehead furrow into a frown. I do stuff for myself. I just … well, I—don't I?

"I'm not asking to be a bitch, Emory. I'm asking because it seems like you might be having a hard time letting someone else take care of you for a change. From what you said last night, it sounds like you have always been the caregiver. There's nothing wrong with that, either. Lanie and Julia are the same way. I just get the impression that you might need to let go a little because as much as I hate to admit it, Preston also takes care of those around him. He wants to fix everyone and everything. And I think you should let him." Finishing her burger, she grabs her purse.

"Trevor and Dexter are coming over in a couple of hours to help us switch places. I think they realize the sooner Pres and I are under different roofs, the better it will be for everyone," she says, laughing. "Just think about what I said. It's not always a bad thing to have someone you can lean on, okay?"

"Yeah, okay. But, Lexi?"

"Yes, chica?"

"Who do you lean on?" I ask.

Fumbling with her purse, she turns away so she doesn't have to make eye contact. "I chose the wrong man to lean on, Emory. It almost cost me my life. I can't do that again, but you and I? We're different. I think we have probably both made mistakes ... I just have a feeling you've always had to choose between bad and worse. Let Preston be there for you. I'm not his biggest cheerleader, and even I know something is up with him. I think you could both help each other," she says before turning and heading out of my apartment. Just before the door closes, I hear, "Two hours, Ems. Get packing."

CHAPTER 9

*H*ow bad would it be if I just turned around and climbed into bed beside Emory? *Bad, very bad. Just get the kitchen cleaned up, you idiot.* This is completely fucking ridiculous. I have been with this woman every single day for almost a year. Your feelings don't just change in a blink of an eye. My emotions and my libido are getting the better of me, that's all. "It is time to check yourself, Preston."

"Before you wreck yourself?" Lexi laughs.

"Jesus, I think I've been hanging out with Julia too long," I tell her.

"Mhm, so what are you 'checking yourself' about?"

"Nothing, I just have a lot going on at work," I lie.

"Liar. I'm not buying it. And I'm guessing you're in here talking to yourself for the same reason your girl was just downstairs on the verge of a panic attack."

Lexi's words have me whipping around in her direction. "What? No, Emory's eating breakfast."

"Yeah, downstairs," Lexi says, obviously enjoying me being the last to know.

I'm dumbfounded, and I end up just staring between Lexi and the hallway to my bedroom.

Laughing, she goes on, "You can go check if you want, but I just left her. Whatever kind of relationship you guys have —" She must notice my mood shift because she changes direction. "I'm not judging, Preston. I'm just saying, whatever kind of relationship you have, it's not something she has experienced before, so you need to be gentle with her."

I can't help the snark that escapes me, "And you know her so well after a few hours?"

Pushing off from the island, I hate the hurt I see in her eyes. "Yeah, Preston. I know this after a few hours. Misery loves company and all, you know. It's easy to see it in someone else when you've lived it yourself."

I'm an asshole.

"Lex, listen. I'm sorry—"

"No need, Preston. Just take care of her. She is more fragile than you think," she tells me as she walks out of the kitchen.

Fuck. "Lexi, wait. Just wait a minute." I jog around the island, attempting to catch her in the hall. "I really am sorry," I say, but she tries to wave me off. "Listen, I don't want to fight with you about this or the clothes, okay? What if I told you we all pitched in, and we want you to have them? I also spoke to my brother, Easton. Give him a call first thing on Monday. He needs some help, so he'll be expecting your call. I'd offer you a job myself, but we both know how that would end up."

"I don't need a handout," she stubbornly argues.

"Can you just let down your wall for two goddamn seconds? I was telling you, Easton's assistant up and left. He needs the help. Dexter and I put in a call to Ryan about your career. You were great at what you did, Lex. And before you go all crazy, we aren't doing this because you can't do it yourself. We're doing it because you don't have to do it your-self. There's a difference. Family helps family, okay?"

Without making eye contact, she nods in understanding, and I'm pretty sure I heard a whispered thank you.

"Okay. Then, maybe you can help me figure out what to do about Emory?" I ask.

Finally, looking at me, she says, "That's easy. Go help her pack. Everyone will be here in two hours to help us switch apartments."

"Pack, right. Okay. Do you need anything before I go down there?"

"I'm good. Apparently, everything I own is already on rolling racks," she spits out sarcastically, but also with a smile. She raises her hand for a high five, and I laugh.

"Baby steps?"

"Baby steps," she agrees.

Shaking my head, I leave her in the hallway. Lexi makes me want to swear at the top of my lungs, but I don't. How the hell is this lie getting fast-tracked and out of control so fucking quickly?

I'M STANDING OUTSIDE of Emory's apartment for way too long. *Grow a set and just knock on the damn door.* As I'm raising my hand, it swings open with Emory on the other side.

"Jesus. I thought that was just a Loki thing," I tell a startled Emory. "Sorry, I didn't mean to scare you. I was just about to knock. We always assumed Loki had cameras set up everywhere because he would open the door every freaking time someone was out here." Sticking my head inside of her door above her head, I ask, "He doesn't have cameras, right?"

"I-I'm not sure. I don't think so," she stutters. Looking down, I notice she has a trash bag in her hands.

"I'll take this to the chute, then we need to talk," I tell her as I grab the bag and head to the end of the hallway. When I return, she is in the same position, hand still half raised. "Emory? You okay?"

"Huh? Oh, yeah. Just a lot of firsts, I guess," she says absentmindedly, while sweeping the door open to let me in.

I stare at her quizzically as I pass, hoping she will elaborate. When she doesn't, I enter the apartment, happy when I feel her close behind.

Glancing around the room, I'm beginning to understand just how much fun the girls had last night, and it makes me laugh. "You guys definitely threw yourselves a party."

This seems to break the ice and pull Emory from her stupor. Taking in the room, she also laughs, then plops down on the couch. I sit beside her.

"Lexi told me everyone is coming to help us switch apartments?"

Running my hands through my hair, I lean forward, resting my forearms on my thighs. "Yeah, uh ... Ems, I'm sorry. I really didn't think this through. I should have known we would get steamrolled like this. They mean well, but Christ, they're on a mission. I will call them and tell them we have to go to Boston tomorrow for a meeting, so it's better to wait until the weekend. That will give us a little more time—"

I'm cut off by my cell phone and hate that it's an annoying ring I can't ignore.

"Sorry, just give me a minute."

Pressing the green accept button, I answer, "Hi Seth."

"I just spoke to Lexi, and while I think the switch will be fine, we can't make any moves until we hear from Loki. I've put a call in, but I have no idea the time frame for a response. For now, just keep the living arrangements as they are."

"Fuck, come on, Seth? What's the difference?"

"Probably nothing," he admits, "but I don't have the authority to make those decisions. You all just have to hold tight."

"Two weeks, that's all you have," I command before ending the call.

"Everything okay?" Emory asks.

"Looks like you were just saved by the bell. Seth says we can't switch you and Lexi until he hears from Loki." I hate the look of relief that washes over her delicate features.

"Okay, well, I guess we should get ready for the infusion center then, right?"

With everything going on, I had forgotten today was an infusion day. We usually go together, but while I get my treatment, Emory volunteers. I've often found her sitting with patients that had to go alone. I would never tell her, but I had to pull many strings so they would allow her to volunteer while on probation. I'd do it again, though, in a heartbeat. Every single person in that medical office loves her, and you can tell how much it means to her.

"Sure, let me run up and tell Lexi to slow her roll on the packing, and then we can go. You sure you're up for it today?"

"Are you saying I look bad, Preston?"

"I would never, but you do look a little green around the gills," I joke.

"Good thing no one there cares what I look like. Just give me fifteen minutes to shower, and I'll be ready. I hope Mr. T is there today. I've been worried about him."

Mr. T, as she calls him, is one of her favorite patients. She started sitting with him months ago when we first starting going to the center. He had on a paper gown with no arms and tubes hung all around his neck. She called him Mr. T, and the friendship grew from there.

"How's he doing?"

I hate the expression on her face when she answers, "I don't think he's doing well. He's all skin and bones. His particular type of colon cancer is about as aggressive as cancer can get. He says he is lucky to have made it this long, but I don't know. It's just sad that he's all alone."

Staring into her eyes, I tell her honestly, "He's very lucky to have you, Emory. So am I. In case I forget to tell you that. I will forever be grateful for all you have done for me."

"You're welcome," she whispers.

"I'll let you get ready. Just text me when you're done."

"Sounds good." Emory walks behind me as I make my way to the door.

Once again, I find myself lost in her eyes. *You have to stop this shit, dickhead.* I really need to talk to Dex. Eventually, I force myself to open her door and walk toward the elevator.

As I'm pressing the button, I hear her yell down the hall, "Hey, Preston? Want to have breakfast tomorrow?"

Cocking my head, I stare at her, completely confused. "Ah, sure. That sounds good." I guess that's what couples would do, right? She must be getting into character.

"Great, should I text you or nudge you?" she says with a wink and a full, throaty laugh.

Fucking hell. She got me again.

Pointing at her as the elevator arrives, I say, "You're trouble, you know that? You should not know this many bad pick-up lines." I'm rewarded by her laughter again. Instead of entering, I let the doors slide closed and stalk back toward Emory's apartment.

Standing right in front of her, I lean down to whisper in her ear. We have to get this over with anyway, right? "Did you know my lips taste like Skittles?" She toggles back and forth from my lips to my eyes before taking the smallest step back. "Emory, you're about to taste the rainbow." I lean in, painfully slowly, so she has plenty of time to back away. When she doesn't, I take her lips with mine.

I only meant to give her a chaste kiss, but the second my lips meet hers, I'm lost. With my hands on either side of her face, I angle it to meet mine. I'm itching to touch her, but I don't let my hands roam. Instead, I nip at her bottom lip, causing her to inhale in surprise. With her lips open to me, I taste her for the first time. The zing I feel when touching her arm has nothing on the full body lightning strike happening right now.

Emory tastes like peaches and bubbles, my own little bellini. Our tongues dance, slowly, methodically, and the slight whimper that emerges from her sweet lips has me remembering this is all pretend, so I pull away sooner than I'd like. She tumbles forward as I release her, and fuck me if that doesn't boost my ego from over-inflated to Jolly Green Giant territory.

"Did you have Lucky Charms for breakfast, Goldie?"

"What? I ... you made breakfast, I—"

"Because you, sweetheart, are magically delicious." I wink with the broadest smile I've probably ever had as I back away. "One point for Preston. Text me when you're ready."

Upstairs, I'm relieved I made it through the apartment without running into Lexi. A raging hard-on in gym shorts is impossible to hide. Magically delicious is the understatement of the century. Christ, if we hadn't been in the hallway or if she had made the slightest move, I would have mauled her and given two fucks about who saw.

In the privacy of my own room, I strip out of my clothes on the way to the shower. I stare down at the one-eyed monster that's already leaking, begging for attention. Turning the faucet to scalding, I wait for the water to heat and grab my phone. Opening the Google app, I type: Is it normal for terminal patients to get the hots for their doctors? I scroll through pages and pages of searches and find nothing.

Just me? Great.

After tossing my phone on the counter, I step into the water and do the only thing a man in my position can do. I turn into the fucking creeper, rubbing one out to the vision of Emory's lips wrapped tightly around my swollen cock.

Closing my eyes, I can picture her so vividly. Ems has her natural red hair in this fantasy, and remembering how sexy she looks, I almost come right then.

"Fuuck." It comes out on a long, low groan.

Emory is on her knees before me, her hair slicked back from the shower. I can see the droplets of water running down her neck and falling from the hardened tip of her breast. When I envision her hand sliding down her belly, I lose control and come harder than I have in a very long time. I actually see fucking stars and have to take a seat on the bench.

When is the last time I got dizzy from an orgasm? Jesus, if that's my reaction to the thought of Emory, I wouldn't survive the real thing. Never one to back down from a challenge, not even one made to myself, I take a few minutes recovering and imagine all the naughty things I would love to do to my little Goldie Locks.

$\mathcal{T}$he mood has definitely shifted between Preston and me. The stress of having things move so quickly has been put on hold. It's replaced with a tension I've never felt before. *It's not sexual tension, Emory. It's not.* But holy balls, that kiss? I'd be a lying sack of shit if I said it hasn't been on constant replay in my head.

We arrived at the infusion center in uptown thirty minutes ago, hand in hand.

"For show," Preston had assured me, but nothing about it felt showy to me.

Mr. T is late again, and I want to ask the nurses about him, but I'm so nervous about being here as it is. I don't want to cause any issues that would have them rethinking my volunteer status. I'm lucky they accepted me as it is.

I'm wiping down a chair that a patient just vacated when I hear my name.

"There's Miss Emory. I was hoping I would see you today," Mr. T says hoarsely as he slowly ambles my way. I've been saving his chair in the back corner in the hopes I would catch him. Since I met him, he only wants to sit in that one chair. I don't know if it's because it keeps him mostly hidden or because he just likes routine, but I always save it for him when I can.

"Mr. T!" I'm so happy to see him. I wrap him in a giant hug and am saddened when I feel how frail his bones have become. "How are you?" I ask as I help him to the back to get settled into the oversized recliner.

"Times a ticking, if you know what I mean. I want to hear about you, Emory, not talk about my failing health. Tell me about that man of yours."

"Mr. T, I've told you so many times, he's just my boss, that's it."

No matter how many times we have this discussion, my old friend refuses to believe it.

"I don't believe you. Does he treat you well?"

"Of course he does. Because I am his em-ploy-ee." I stretch out 'employee' into as many syllables as possible.

"Right, you said that, didn't you?" he says playfully. "How's your new apartment? It's in his building, isn't it?"

"You're cheeky today, aren't you?"

"I'm just making sure when I'm gone, you're in good hands, that's all."

"I don't know if you're aware, Mr. T, but I am very capable of taking care of myself," I say with a kind smile. I know he means well, but he has been barking up this Preston tree for as long as I've known him.

"Are you ever going to tell me what's wrong with him? He comes in here every week, and yet you still won't tell me."

Sighing, I say, "I've told you, it isn't my story to tell. You could ask him yourself if you'd like."

"Nah, I *told you*, I don't like talking to people."

"You talk to me just fine," I point out.

"You're pretty to look at." His eyes crinkle at the corners as I laugh.

"Okay, well, the same rules apply. It isn't my story to tell, so let's talk about something else. Have you had any visitors lately? Have you been able to get in touch with your family?"

He told me once that he messed up when he was younger, and he lost his family because of it. He hasn't gone into more detail other than to say he lost them a long time ago and that they are beyond repair at this point. It makes me sad for him.

We sit and do crosswords, just like every other time. Sometimes talking, sometimes he makes me get the dictionary for a word he is sure I made up. I'm just happy that for this hour every week, I can give him companionship.

I see Preston at the door just as Mr. T is finishing up. He isn't allowed in the chemo room, so he usually just stands in the foyer and waits. I don't know how long he stands and watches, but he has never rushed me. Sometimes, I'll come out in search of him only to find Preston has confiscated two end tables and is working on his laptop.

"Why won't you just text me when you're done? You don't have to wait for me like this, you know?"

"You love being here, Emory. I'm not going to take that away from you."

I can't help but stare at him. What billionaire CEO waits on his employee in the middle of the day every week just because it's something they enjoy? "I have a hard time figuring you out sometimes."

"I'm a mystery for sure," he smirks. Peering over my head, he asks, "Was Mr. T here today?"

"He was," I say sadly. "He isn't doing well, though."

Preston stops, takes my hand, and gives it a squeeze. "I'm so sorry, Ems. Are you okay?"

Pulling my hand away, I shoo him off. "I'm fine, Preston. I'm a doctor, remember? Or at least I was. I wouldn't be a very good one if I couldn't handle death."

"You're an excellent doctor, and you will practice again, I promise."

I hate when he promises that. He has said it so many

times since I met him, but the longer this goes on, the less confident I feel. Even the all-powerful Preston Westbrook can't do anything about this mess.

～

"EMORY, Preston! It's so good to see you both," Dr. Terry exclaims, entering the exam room.

Seeing him in his lab coat with a stethoscope hanging from his neck gives me a pitifully sad longing. I worked so hard for the right to wear those with Dr. Camden stitched into the side pocket, and it was all taken away in the blink of an eye. I try to inconspicuously blow air to my eyelashes to keep the tears at bay, but Preston notices. *Of course he freaking notices. He has been overly observant lately.*

Placing his left hand on my knee, he gives me a gentle squeeze while simultaneously removing a handkerchief from his pocket and discreetly handing it to me.

What the fuck? Who even carries these things anymore?

"I'm happy to see you two are getting along so well," Dr. Terry says gently, nodding at Preston's hand on my knee.

He quickly removes it and clears his throat. "Actually, Dr. Terry, I have something I'd like to explain," Preston says, sounding more like a prepubescent boy than the alpha CEO.

"Preston, I've said this before, and I'll repeat it. You are your father's son. I knew him for over half my life, and I've known you since you were born. I'm just surprised it has taken you this long. I don't need details, but I will put poor Emory out of her misery."

At the mention of my name, I finally lift my eyes that had been planted firmly in my lap for the last ten minutes.

"I can only imagine what is running through your head right now, but I assure you, we can put it to rest. I'd like to remind you that at this time, you are not," he says with a wink, "Preston's doctor. Any relationship you form is completely acceptable."

"No, but it's not real. W-We're just pretending, Dr. T-Terry," I stammer.

"We're only in a fake relationship, Dr. Terry. I just needed my family to back off for a bit. I'm disappointed you would think so little of me. I know I'm dying, sir, and I would never play with her emotions or ask anyone to stand by me in an actual relationship just to watch the inevitable happen."

I hate the emotion I hear in Preston's voice. It's a sadness most people will never truly experience.

"Preston, everyone deserves happiness for however long they are on this earth. I'm going to encourage you to find it while you can with whoever that is." He turns his attention to me. "Emory, you know I have always held you in high regard. Marie and I are sick to death over what is happening with your medical career, but don't you let that stop you from living either. Understand me? Now, Marie? She is sweet as pie, but if she thinks for a second you're closing yourself off from life again, she will have us on a plane to North Carolina faster than you can say hush puppies."

I'm so confused. "Yes, sir."

"Now, I need you to go to HR and speak with Candace. The legal team should also be there shortly. Your appeal is finally being presented to the medical board on January 9th. That only gives us a few months to prepare our case—"

"Wait a minute," Preston interrupts. "I told you my legal and investigative team would handle this."

I spin in my seat at Preston's words. "You what?"

"Son, the first rule of a relationship, real or fake as you call it, is to never leave out the details. Emory, I suggest you take Preston's help. Preston, your team will have to work with hospital representatives. Emory is welcome to her own council, but it is hospital policy to have our own. Now, Emory, you go down and meet with them while Preston and

I start the tests. No results will come in before you return, I'm sure."

Standing, I give Preston's shoulder an unconscious squeeze and a nod of my head to a smiling Dr. Terry. *Why does everything in my life come with a giant side of 'what the fuck' these days?*

CHAPTER 11

I'm sprawled out on the exam table in my paper gown, playing a rather intense Game Of Words on my phone with Dexter's son, Tate. The kid might be a genius because he is kicking my ass, and he hasn't hit double digits yet.

Emory and Dr. Terry are hovered over his desk, discussing my latest round of tests. Normally, I get lost in her voice as she works through each problem, throwing out every possible solution known to man. A few of her suggestions have even taken Dr. Terry by surprise. It's those moments that I love the fatherly look of admiration he has for her. It's well deserved.

Today, though? I'm trying to figure out if Tate has found the cheater app for this game or if he really is this goddamn smart. But when Emory's voice changes, so does my focus.

"But he has already been on the transplant list for two years. Surely he must have moved up by now?"

"He has, Emory, but you know as well as I do that people with group O blood types wait longer."

"Yes, because while I can donate blood for all other types,

I can only receive organs from other group O's. The longer I have to wait, the more damage is done. The more damage, the more likely heart failure becomes. You both know I've done my research, so give it to me straight. What are we looking at now?"

Staring at Emory, I wish I hadn't repeated all my research like a robot. She may be the doctor, but even our doctor-patient relationship has never been normal. She said she wouldn't be a good doctor if she couldn't handle death, but I'd counter she wouldn't be a good person if she could spend every day with someone and not be overcome with emotion when their days get a literal number. It's the emotion in her eyes that gut me.

"Emory?" Dr. Terry says, silently asking if she would like him to deliver the news.

Sadly, she shakes her head. "Your transthyretin has become unstable, creating amyloid fibrils that are building in your heart. That means the heart muscles are stiffening at an accelerated rate, which will eventually cause your heart to fail."

Swallowing, I nod along to her explanation. I know it's coming, and I'm not sure I can make eye contact when she says it. Dr. Terry sits next to me and takes over Emory's diagnosis. Glancing up, I realize she is trying to compose herself.

"I am guessing, based on all evidence, that you have about three months, son," he exhales loudly. "I'm suggesting Emory hook you up to the ECG twice a day. She and I will speak nightly to go over results, and your care will be day to day. I think you should prepare for the placement of the Ventricular Assist Device as a last resort."

The VAD. I haven't decided it's worth it, to be honest. It appears it will only delay my destiny.

"I understand you've turned down a do not resuscitate order? Is that correct?"

I think back to the day my father died. Had he not signed a DNR, there is a possibility we could have all gotten to him in time to say good-bye. I won't do that to my family.

"No, sir. I want everyone to have a chance to say their good-byes. I don't want to live on life support, though, for any longer than necessary. I've thought about it a lot."

"Then I suggest you appoint your medical power of attorney as soon as possible, Preston. Preferably, a family member who will follow your instructions to the letter."

"Th-That means whoever I choose will be forced to decide when to let me die?" There's gravel in my voice, making it hurt to speak.

"Technically, yes."

How can I put that pressure on someone?

"I say this as your friend, not your doctor, but whoever you choose, you must be sure they can go head to head with your mother because she will fight it. She hated me for years for following your father's DNR, and I get it, but it's something to think about. Appoint someone who can help her see reason and understand your wishes.

"And, Preston? I've listened to your reasons for not telling your family for years, but I do believe we're at the point now where it is imperative to let them know."

God, Dr. Nathan Terry really knows how to turn the knife when he wants to.

"Not yet. Help me get through Dexter and Trevor's weddings, then I'll tell everyone."

"Preston," Emory finally finds her voice, "Dexter's wedding isn't for two-and-a-half months. You cannot seriously still be considering holding off on the VAD until that is over? I understand you wouldn't be able to hide open heart surgery, but Jesus, Pres. That will ensure you make it to both weddings."

"Obviously, I agree with Emory," Dr. Terry says pointedly.

"I'll let you get dressed, and I'll collect the equipment you'll need to take home with you. I am going to encourage you to reconsider your plan, though."

Emory and I sit in silence as we watch Dr. Terry leave the room.

"Honestly, Preston, we—"

"Ems, I know that you're the doctor here, but I have done research on this disease for ten years now. We have flown everywhere from Japan to a remote village in Australia, trying different treatments. When the muscles of the heart become stiff, the only treatment left is a transplant. I have also done the research on wait times, and it doesn't seem as though I'm going to make it to the top of the list in time. Please," my voice cracks, "please just help me live the best life I can for as long as I can."

A single tear stains her face before it's hidden from my view. Emory steps behind me to help guide my arms into my button-up. It's entirely out of character for her, and I know it's a defense mechanism because I do the same thing.

Dressed, I turn to her, lowering my face into her personal space. "If you're feeling down, I can feel you up?"

She chokes on a sob mixed with laugher, causing a snot bubble to form under her nose. I want to cry, too; not for myself, but for her. For the first time since I've known her, I realize how well she hides her pain. Her pain right now is caused by me.

"Here you go." I hand her a tissue, and she punches me in the chest.

Now it's my turn to choke on a laugh as her face goes ashen when she realizes what she just did.

"Holy shit, I'm so sorry." Her hands are flying all over my chest, inspecting for injury.

"I'm not that broken, sweetheart. I'm fine. Come on, let's find Dr. Terry so we can go home."

Home? If you were another man, Preston, home might be wherever she is. Thinking about the lucky son of a bitch that gets to make her his causes a pain in my chest worse than anything cardiomyopathy can throw at me.

CHAPTER 12

I've ridden in this plane hundreds of times, and I'm still not used to the opulent luxury it exudes. I've lost track of time replaying everything that happened today. I've repeated every word over and over again. From Dr. Terry all but giving his blessing for a pseudo-patient relationship to Preston's worst-case scenario. *Preston.*

The kiss we shared has been burned into my heart for eternity. It's fucking with my ability to look at his case objectively. *This is why doctors don't treat their loved ones.* I jump from my seat like someone just dropped a can of spiders in my lap. *Preston is not a loved one. He is a patient, Emory. A patient!*

"Miss Camden? Is everything okay?"

Spinning in place, I find Lucy, Preston's flight attendant, staring at me with concern.

"Huh? Oh, yes. No. I mean, yes, I'm all set, thank you. I just realized Preston has been gone for a while. I'm going to go check on him."

"Alright, would you like some water?" She still seems convinced I'm having some sort of episode.

"No, but thank you," I say over my shoulder as I sprint down the aisle toward the bedroom.

Once inside of the small cabin, I instantly know that Preston isn't here, so I knock softly on the bathroom door. When he doesn't answer, I'm immediately put on edge and open the door. The sight before me is soul-crushing.

Preston is gripping the edge of the sink, the water is running at full blast, but it's his reflection in the mirror that is my undoing. His shirt is tear-stained from shoulders to chest. When his eyes meet mine, our tears join in a weepy mess.

"I've tried to prepare. I've spent years getting things in order, Ems, but I'm not ready yet," he chokes back a sob, and my hand hovers over my own heart where I suffer his pain. "I've still got so many things I have to do. There are so many people who need me. I'm not prepared for this all to end. I don't know how to say good-bye." He lowers his head again as if his confession is shameful.

Dr. Camden has left the building, and I'm not sure she will ever return where Preston is concerned. Reaching around his middle, I hold him in an awkward hug. Eventually, he turns in my arms, but I don't let go.

"This isn't the life I thought I'd have. Help me forget, Ems. I can't waste any more time not having what I want."

I'm not sure what he is asking, but he looks exhausted. Taking his hand, I'm pulling him toward the bed when he tugs me to a stop. When I turn my face to his, he's wearing the most devilish smirk, and his eyes are glossy for an entirely new reason. I just don't know it yet.

"Sex isn't off the table for me yet, right?" His haunted eyes are taking in every feature, every blink, every breath.

I ping pong between him and the bed. For the first time in my life, my lady bits fire on all cylinders, begging for attention. I've had sex before, but the thought of sex has never elicited such a visceral reaction. *Do I want to have sex with*

Preston? Yes, God fucking yes, the loud bitches in my head scream.

"Emory?" His voice is raspy as he steps toe to toe with me. "You're not my doctor."

"I'm not your doctor," I repeat.

"Dr. Terry approves of us."

His mouth is next to my ear as his arms embrace me. He's nuzzling himself into the crook between my earlobe and neck, causing me to shiver.

"Do you want me?" he asks as he gently bites the sensitive skin of my neck.

I do, I do want him.

"I don't want to jack off in the shower, only imagining what you look like anymore. So tell me, Emory. Do you want me?"

"You've thought about me in the shower?" It comes out in a squeak.

He takes one step, then two, my body moving in tandem with his until my legs hit the back of the bed. The abrupt stop causes me to lose my balance, and I fall onto the cloud-like navy comforter.

Leaning over me, his lips so close to mine they almost touch, he growls, "Do you want to know what I think about in the shower, Emory?"

"Yes." It comes out stronger and harsher than I intend, but my nerve endings are fried. I'm surprised I can form a coherent thought right now.

Preston slowly encroaches my space with a wicked grin, forcing me to lean back onto my forearms. His arms slowly make their way to the bed just below my bra line, and I'm caged in by this man. The moment is intense. *Oh gawd, I'm panting.* He's going to be the death of me. Internally, I cringe at my choice of words. *He is going to die, Ems. You know this. What does that make me? A distraction? Am I okay with being a distraction?*

"Whatever fears or doubts are running through your head, sweetheart, let me put them to bed for you. But first, you have to answer me. Do. You. Want. Me?" Each word is punctuated by a kiss or a nip. He travels up one side of my neck and down the other.

"I-I-I do, Preston, but—"

"But you're worried about what it means? If you're crossing an ethical line? If it's okay to let go? Do any of your questions have anything to do with wanting me? With wanting this?" he asks as his fingertip trails over my collarbone.

How the hell does he read me so well?

"No, none of my questions have anything to do with wanting you." The voice that speaks is hardly recognizable as my own. I sound … wanton.

"Then, can I tell you what I want?" I find some satisfaction in hearing Preston's voice strain as well.

Swallowing thickly, I nod my consent.

"I want to spend the next few months doing anything and everything I can to forget." His nose runs along the column of my neck. When he speaks near my ear, his voice is hoarse. "I want to spend my time learning every inch of you." I jump when I feel a quick nip at my earlobe that quickly turns into a soft moan of pleasure. "I want to play Never Have I Ever until I know everything there is to know about you. What do you say, Ems? Do you want to play with me?"

"Yes," I croak.

Pulling back so he can look into my eyes, I see the lopsided boyish grin plastered all over his face. "That is an excellent answer, Ems." Before I realize I'm moving, he has me hooked under my arms and has slid me up the bed. Using his knee, he urges my legs apart just enough so he can wedge himself between my thighs.

He says nothing for a long time, and the scrutiny of his stare has me fidgeting. My mouth feels like I've been chewing on cotton, so I break eye contact when I can't stand the silence any longer. That's when he pounces. Aligning his body with mine, the weight of him calms my racing nerves.

"Never have I ever had a man undress me."

My heart rate spikes, and my entire body tingles. He really wants to play this game, but I'm also confused as hell because we aren't drinking. *Isn't this a drinking game?* Turning my attention back to Preston, I see the wickedness in his eyes, fighting to be set free.

"Do you want to know the rules of our new game, sweetheart?"

"Yes," I beg.

Preston lowers his mouth to mine, and I swear my entire body vibrates. "When you haven't done the other person's action, instead of taking a drink, you'll have to kiss. Each kiss has to be placed somewhere new."

"Holy shit." It comes out in a breathy whisper as Preston skims his fingers just under the hem of my shirt.

"Every time there is something you haven't done, we are going to remedy it. Right now, I'm going to undress you."

I gulp audibly, and he grins. Preston's fingers run a line from hip bone to hip bone, and my skin pebbles. I watch in a trance-like state as he raises his hands to the bottom button on my shirt. Methodically, he undoes the first button, then moves up the line.

Oh shit, what underwear am I wearing today? All thought leaves my brain as his fingers caress the underwire of my bra.

"Jesus Christ. You're so fucking sexy, Emory." The desperation in his voice turns my breaths shallow. Painfully slowly, he releases the clasp of my bra. As my breasts fall free from their confines, Preston's eyes go from icy blue to hazy and hooded. They're demanding, and I know I will never be the same after this.

His lust-filled gaze lowers to my nipples that harden under his intense inspection. My chest rises and falls rapidly as he lowers his mouth and licks a line around each peak before lapping at them in earnest. Taking one into his mouth, he uses his hand to manipulate the other. The caress starts butterfly-soft and teasing but quickly turns feverish. Rolling, pinching, pulling at my sensitive flesh, I wonder if it is indeed possible to come like this. The look in Preston's eyes tells me he is wondering the same thing.

I'm just adjusting to the sensations when his right hand wanders south. His left hand, still insistent in its assault, doesn't let up, and I feel his palm glide down my torso and pause at the button of my capris. I gasp as he starts a trail of open-mouthed kisses in the wake of his hand. Peering up at me from the juncture of my thighs, I notice the naughty gleam in his eyes and want to hide.

"Never have I ever had oral until I came."

"I, I thought you were supposed to say things you've never done?" I rasp.

"Our game has different rules, Emory. I've been told I have a lot of boxes to check off, and I can't fucking wait."

CHAPTER 13

I pull away to look at Ems. I'm waiting for her answer, and by the flush taking over her entire body, I think I have it.

"Do you need to pay up, sweetheart?" I know I'm smiling at her like the Joker, but the anticipation is killing me. For a moment, I panic. *Is this something she has done before?* My blood turns to ice, realizing this may be a first I don't get.

I'm taking slow, calming breaths, trying to contain the irrational rage I'm experiencing. *She's mine.* Shocked by the possessiveness I'm feeling for the first time in my life, my vision blurs. *Do not pass out now, fuckface.* Caught up in my own crazy, I don't notice when Emory pulls her body back enough to sit up. Her movement catches my attention, and I try really hard to focus and not scare her off.

As if in slow motion, Emory leans forward so we are nose to nose before her lip twitches and her full, sweet lips kiss the corner of my mouth. "New spot every time, right?"

I exhale loudly, a breath I hadn't realized I was holding.

"New spot every time," I force out. I have an awareness around her that's intoxicating and wreaking havoc on all my senses. The caveman tendencies finally breakthrough, and before she can speak again, I have lifted her off the bed and turned us, so she's now straddling me.

"Fighting for control is not something I'm used to," I confess.

"What are you trying to control?"

"My every reaction to you." I don't allow for more conversation. I cover her mouth with mine. Gone is every plan I had for her. Twisting my hands in her hair, I control the kiss as I'm flooded with sensation. "You're going to break me," I whisper, drunk off her already.

Flipping her over, I lay her back once again. This time I go straight for her pants. Wanting her to feel the same rush I do, I don't waste any time pulling her pants down her long legs and toss them over my shoulder. My body thrums with an eagerness I haven't felt in years as I kneel in front of her. Finding her eyes as I hook my fingers into her panties, I raise my eyebrows in silent question.

"Please." It's one word. A silent plea, and I'm lost.

Ripping the yellow lace panties from her body, I revel in the gasp of surprise she emits, but I give her no time to adjust. I descend on her like a feast being served to a starving man. One lick and I'm a goner.

"Preston."

"I've got you, Ems." And I do. I vow to take care of this beautiful creature for as long as I can. I blow a line of cool air on her exposed sex and delight in her reaction. Taking her clit into my mouth, I suck and flick and tug with abandon.

"Oh-oh," Emory pants. I love how needy she sounds because, as I insert one finger, my thoughts escape in a strangled groan.

Holy fuck, she's tight. Almost too tight. She can't be a virgin, can she? Dr. Terry mentioned she had lived with a boyfriend at one point, didn't he?

I stretch her to add another finger, never giving up my attack on her clit. My dick is throbbing so painfully I have to grab the asshole and give him a hard squeeze so he doesn't embarrass me. I continue to work her, hoping and praying that she will tell me if she is a virgin. I know I'll end up asking, but I don't want to embarrass her if I can avoid it.

"I can't. Oh, God, Preston. I-I—"

"Yes, you can," I growl. "Come for me, Ems. Come now and let me taste you."

In a rush, her body shakes and contorts under me as a string of incoherent babble leaves her mouth. I don't stop my pursuit as I wring every last drop from her orgasm. Her body quivers with the final aftershocks, and I stand quickly stripping out of my own clothes. The painful erection I've been sporting springs free.

I climb over her as she opens her eyes, and an easy grin takes over her face. She's relaxed in a way I've never seen her before, and I add it to my list of things to accomplish before I die. As she comes back to earth, I watch as she takes in my naked form. It might be the single most erotic moment of my life as she stares at my length while licking her lips. Lowering to my elbows above her, I know I have to ask.

"Ems? Are … are you a virgin?"

"What?" she screeches. "Preston, I'm almost thirty years old!"

"I know, and I'm not trying to be a dick. You're just so goddamn tight. I'm afraid it's going to hurt. If you're a virgin, it will definitely fucking hurt."

She smiles at me with a red face partly from her orgasm and now probably because I asked a stupid, but necessary question.

"I'm not a virgin, Preston." The gentleness in her voice sends a chill throughout my body.

When her hand snakes between us to stroke my cock, I have to grind my teeth and count to ten.

"Fuck me." It slips from my mouth as she places my dick at her warm entrance. I didn't have time to prepare, and my body vibrates with excitement. "Shit, hold on." I jump off the bed and run in circles, hoping someone has left some freaking condoms on this plane. As I open and shut door after door, my body tenses.

"What are you doing?"

"I'm looking for a condom, I—" Pulling at the back of my neck, a nervous habit I thought I had broken years ago, I roll my shoulders and then continue. "I wasn't expecting this. I'm not prepared, Ems. I don't have any fucking condoms."

I'm feeling defeated as I stare at her, so I'm shocked when she crooks her index finger in a come-hither kind of way.

"You beckoned?" I can't control my smart ass mouth sometimes.

"I've seen your medical chart, Pres. I know you're clean. Do you trust me?"

"Jesus," it comes out in a whoosh. "So fucking much, and I had a vasectomy when I was twenty-two. I wasn't willing to pass my heart issue onto another generation."

Something like sadness clouds her vision before she hides it. For the first time in my life, I can almost envision a life with kids. It's a stark reminder that my time is limited. Trying to brush reality to the wayside, I climb onto the bed next to her.

"Are you sure?"

"I'm sure, Preston."

I don't wait for another invitation. With my lips on hers, I gently press her into the bed. Holding my weight above her, I lower my gaze to watch as I slide into her with just my tip because holy shit, she's tight. Raising my head, I observe her, waiting for any signs of pain, and feel immense relief when all I see is her beautiful face with hooded eyes.

I push another inch, gliding back and forth to open her when she raises her legs. Hooking them at the knees with my arms, I lift her just enough to slide in fully.

"Oh, oooh—"

"Deep breaths, baby." I don't move. I barely breathe myself as she adjusts to my size. Licking my thumb, I then make slow circles around her clit to help her body adjust. Within seconds, she is rocking against me. *Thank God.*

"Are you ready for me to move?"

"Yes. Yes, Preston, I'm ready."

"Greedy little thing, aren't you?" I grin and pull back. A light sheen has covered her body, and I want to lick her everywhere. Slamming back in, I lower my mouth and do just that. Lapping at her little pink nipple, I stay rooted as far as I can go and start to grind. The moans that slip from her lips tell me how much she likes it.

I raise my face to hers. "Do you like that, Emory? Do you like me buried so deep inside of you? Filling you to the hilt?"

"I've never felt anything like this, Preston. I think I'm going to come again," she says in a rush.

Straightening, I raise her legs higher, resting one on each of my shoulders as I begin to really move. Her body is already a vice on my dick, but I see stars myself when she starts to spasm. Nothing has ever felt this good, squeezed my cock this tight, or felt this right before. Sweat is sliding down my back as I pick up the pace, and she combusts.

"Emory, Jesus." I can't form sentences. I'm pounding into her, but I attempt to hold back just enough that I don't hurt her. Then she wraps her legs around my back and pulls me in farther, and the last of my control slips. Her body is convulsing around me, and I'm a prisoner to sensation.

"God, Ems, you're perfect. So fucking perfect," I say in between thrusts.

"I think I'm going to pass out," she admits when I feel her body tensing again.

"Come with me, Emory. On my cock. Right now, come now."

She's shaking her head back and forth.

"I know you can, Emory, now." I lower my hand to work

her little bundle of nerves again. No sooner do I connect with her heated flesh when her body goes rigid, and I give one last thrust, coming so hard my eyes roll to the back of my head.

When I come to my senses, I glance down at Emory and am assaulted by feelings I've worked ten years to hide. *Why would God give her to me now?* The thought is too real, too harsh, so I do the only thing I can … I run. Getting out of bed, I grab a wet cloth to clean her up.

I need busy work before my mind runs in directions it shouldn't. Tasks keep me focused, but Emory is out cold when I return to the bed, and she takes my breath away for the hundredth time today. I don't take my eyes off of her as I clean her up and chuckle as she moans about not being able to walk. When I've done all I can, I slide in next to her, pulling her so close I can't tell where her body ends and where mine begins.

Emory doesn't wake until we touch down in North Carolina, but I lie awake, barely blinking, and memorize every inch of the woman in my arms.

CHAPTER 14

EMORY

J'm quiet but antsy on the car ride back to our apartments. Thank God we have our own space for a little while longer. I need some time alone to process the best freaking sex I've ever had in my life. *That is not how sex is. Is it?* It was definitely never like that with Donny. Even thinking that man's name makes me shiver.

"Are you cold?" Preston asks. He has not left my side since we exited the airplane. In fact, he hasn't let me out of his reach. He held my hand on the tarmac walking to the car and now has a heavy hand resting on my knee while he scrolls his phone with the other.

"Hmm? Oh, no. Just thinking," I say absentmindedly.

With a devilish gleam, he grins at me, and I feel my body respond. *How can his expressions alone cause such a reaction?* Mercifully, the car ride is short, and we arrive at our building just a few minutes later.

"Why don't I come up with you and get you set up in bed with your IV? It's been a long day, and you're going to need your rest."

"Trying to get me into bed again so soon? You know, if

you want round two, all you have to do is ask." With a wink, he retakes my hand and leads me into the elevator.

"What?" It comes out a few octaves too high. "No, I'm serious. We should have done it on the plane—"

He laughs. "We did *do it* on the plane, sweetheart."

Why does his use of sweetheart make my insides tremble?

"You're ridiculous. I'm being serious here, Preston. We should have administered your meds on the plane."

"So am I, Emory. I can't wait to get you undressed again, and since I have these ..." He pulls my thong out of his pocket.

"What? You jerk? I looked for those for almost fifteen minutes."

"Oh, I know! I had the perfect view, and it's had my shaft hard ever since."

The elevator door pings open, and he makes a run for it, but I'm close behind.

"Don't you dare, Preston! Give me back my underwear right now," I yell, but run into his back when he stops short. That's when I get the sensation of being watched. I'm about to move when his hand slides behind him to reach for mine. Once he has my hand in his, he steps to the side. If someone could die of embarrassment, I would do it right this second.

"Ah, hey, everyone. What are you all doing here?" Preston asks, holding my hand in a death grip. I try to shake free, but it only causes him to clamp down harder. Peering around him, I see all his friends and what I can only describe as a pack of Preston's. I assume they are his brothers because the family resemblance is astonishing.

"Preston Michael Westbrook," comes a voice from behind us.

Preston goes stock still, so I give his hand a gentle squeeze in silent support. Preston's eyes are flying around the room, searching for someone to blame, when he glances down and gives me an apologetic smile. I open my mouth as a regal-looking woman comes around the corner, wiping her hands on the apron she is wearing, and I immediately clamp it shut.

By the use of three names, I'd guess this is his mother. She is beautiful and graceful. She could easily have just stepped out of a magazine.

"You have a live-in girlfriend, and you don't think to introduce us or even mention anything to any of us?" Walking over to greet us, she ignores Preston and instead lets her gaze land on me.

If I could shrink into the furniture right now, I would. I'm fully expecting a tongue lashing, but she's smiling at me when I finally make eye contact.

"Oh, my dear boy," she says while never taking her eyes off of me, "she is gorgeous! Hi, Emory, I'm Preston's mom, Sylvie. It is so lovely to finally meet you."

I'm bouncing between her and Preston, not sure what to say, when she reaches in and envelopes me in the biggest motherly hug I can ever remember receiving.

"It's nice to meet you, too, Mrs. Westbrook." I've just gotten the words out when there is a collective hiss from the crowd.

"Oh, there's no Mrs. anything around here, Ems. I learned that the hard way," Lanie informs me. I hadn't even noticed her in the corner.

"She's right, my dear. Just Sylvie will do."

Preston takes a step toward the front door. "Okay, can you guys just give us a few minutes? It's been a long day, and we were not expecting any of you," he says pointedly. "I'm going to run Ems down to her apartment so she can change and have a breather before the inquisition starts."

"Oh, there's no need for that, Broken-heart. We've got everything takin' care of, ya know?"

My head is on a swivel, trying to find where the older voice came from. Preston apparently already knows.

"GG? What do you mean?"

"Oh Broken-heart, don't go lookin' so worried. I got here this mornin' to see all my great-grandbabies, and that demon spawn, Seth, told me I gotta stay with you. So I got Grumpy-growler over there to show me around so I could choose my room. He has his panties twisted up real good, that one."

"GG, there is nothing wrong with my underwear," a Preston clone grumbles.

"Ha! Yeah, right, Easton. You're the grumpiest asshole I've ever met, and that's saying something," Lexi yells from across the room.

"Lexi, Jesus. I am still your freaking boss," Easton bellows.

"Hold on. Everyone, just shut up for a minute. Someone, please tell me what the hell is going on?" Thankfully, Preston is as confused as I am.

"Well, I was a tryin' to tell ya, Broken-heart, before Lex and Grumpy-growler interrupted. Anyway, once I picked my room, everyone came over, packed Emory up, moved her into your room, moved Lexi downstairs, and unpacked my stuff in Lexi's old room. All set, ya see? Now, you go washin' up. Dinner is almost ready."

With a gentle tug on Preston's arm, I whisper, "What the hell is going on?"

He must see the fear written on my face because he tucks me into his arm and tells the room, "Just give us a few minutes, and then we can make all the introductions, okay?" He looks as wild as I've ever seen him.

"Sure, sure. Go wash off that sexin' smell ya got all over ya's. Dinner will be ready soon, so no more fornicating," the old woman called GG says.

"GG!" Lanie, Julia, and Lexi all scold at once.

"What? Y'all know I'm right. Can tell just by lookin' at 'em. And the way that girl there is a blushing? Yup, they went at it real good."

"Okay, GG. Jesus, that's enough," Julia scolds again,

guiding the old woman toward the kitchen, and thankfully Preston is dragging me toward his bedroom.

Preston shuts his door, then goes back to lock it. I stand in the middle of the room as he paces. We both stare at all my belongings in boxes scattered throughout the space.

"What is going on, Preston?" I whisper yell. "Who the hell are all those people, and why is my stuff in your room? We agreed I would have my own space. I can't sleep with you every night. We agreed." My heart is racing, and I'm twisting my hair around my finger like a nervous teenager. My voice falters as the reality of our situation sinks in. *I need time to think.*

Preston is at my side a second later, taking my hand and guiding me to the chaise in the room's corner. "Sweetheart, this is what we call a shitshow. I'm sorry, I had no idea they would all converge like this."

"How did that old lady know we had sex? How does she know about your broken heart? God, Preston, I have so many questions."

Resting his forehead against mine, I feel my breathing fall in step with his. Holding the back of my neck while we breathe in each other's air, he makes no move to separate for long minutes.

"Listen," he finally says, kneeling in front of me. "That was GG, Lanie and Lexi's grandmother. She doesn't know about my heart, per se, she's been reading some sort of tarot cards, and that's what she came out with. She hasn't called me Preston since. I have no words for her because she is the craziest, most well-meaning buttinsky I've ever met in my life. I honestly don't know what the hell is going on, but can we please get ready for dinner and just do our best to get through the next couple of hours? Then I promise you, I'll figure it all out. Okay?"

What did I walk into here? This is not my life.

"How long has Lexi known your brother?" I ask, trying to buy some time.

"Holy shit." He laughs. "Not long, but I haven't seen anyone get to East like that in years. I'm not surprised. I mean, I put the damn woman in a headlock, but Easton's reaction is something to watch for sure."

"I'm not good in crowds, Preston. There is a bonafide crowd out there. I'm not sure I can do this."

Placing his hands on my thighs and lifting himself so we are face to face, he says, "It is a crowd, but I promise everyone out there already loves you. I won't leave your side, though." Taking my hands, he pulls me to standing and walks me to his bathroom. "You shower first. Unless you want some help?"

I can't believe I'm even contemplating this. Preston has some sort of dark magic he has worked on me. My lady parts are screaming no and yes please at the same time. Sex with Preston cannot become a regular occurrence. Not trusting myself to speak, I shake my head and run into the bathroom, quickly shutting the door in his face. Hearing him laugh through the door relieves a tiny fraction of my anxiety.

Twenty minutes later, Preston and I walk hand in hand back into the lion's den.

"Oh good, you're ready," GG says, animatedly rising from her chair. "So nice to meet ya, Miss Fixem', I'm GG." I offer her my hand, and she legitimately swats me away with a loud slap. "No handshakin' here, lady. We're all family. Call me GG." She embraces me in a hug, then pulls me away from Preston toward a dining room full of expectant, happy faces.

So much for Preston not leaving my side.

∾

MY PHONE PINGS WITH A TEXT, so I grab it from the counter. I'm confused when I see a text from Lexi because she is sitting right beside me.

Lexi: Sorry about GG. She's a freaking nutbag.

Julia: That is an understatement.

Peering around the room, I see all the ladies are typing on their phones.

Lanie: But she means well ... she just has an odd way of showing it.

Julia: Odd? Lanie, she is certifiable.

Lexi: It's true. She will also be all up in your business while she's here. I laugh because it will drive Preston nuts, but feel bad for you because you aren't used to her.

Lanie: It's best to just nod and smile with GG.

Julia: And set boundaries early on. That woman still calls me a lil' hussy and throws condoms at me every chance she gets.

Emory: Good Lord. I feel like I should be scared.

Julia: A little fear is always a good thing around GG.

Lexi: (Eye roll emoji)

Lexi: She isn't the devil.

Lanie: She's just a little eccentric.

Lexi: Eccentric is a good word.

Julia: So is bat shit crazy!

Holy hell. For the third time tonight, I ask, *What in God's name did I just walk into?*

CHAPTER 15

PRESTON

$\mathcal{I}$'m beyond pissed, and the only person I can take it out on is my brother, East. So when I get him alone on the balcony, I dig in. "Why the fuck did you have to put GG right across the hall from my bedroom?"

"What are you talking about? You have met that woman, right? There is no putting her anywhere. She does whatever the hell she wants, whenever she wants," Easton tells me flatly.

East and I are the closest in age, and like all brothers, we know how to push each other's buttons. Needing to pick a fight to put all my conflicting emotions at bay, I pull out all the stops.

"What the hell is going on between you and Lexi? She has been through hell recently. The last thing she needs is some grumpy asshole all over her. I knew I should have sent her to Colton instead."

"Fuck off, Pres. Nothing is going on. She is a pain in the ass, that's all."

"Why is that muscle in your jaw ticking then? You know that's always been your tell."

I am such an asshole.

"Oh yeah, what about you? That vein in your neck about exploded when mom called your ass out earlier."

He's not wrong.

"Whatever. Seriously, East, don't be a pecker with Lexi. She's been through enough shit already."

"Why are you all over my jock tonight, Pres. What's really going on with you?" he asks, getting in my face.

Just like we're ten years old again, I shove him off of me, and before I know it, we are a tangle of limbs.

"Seriously, Preston? Get off each other, you morons," I recognize the voice as a very pissed off Emory.

"Ooh, you're in trouble with the missus now," East chides.

With one last shove, I take a step back. "At least I have a missus, asshole."

"Good, keep them away from me. That's an anchor I'll never be looking for."

"Are you two about done? Seriously, how old are you guys? Preston, what the *hell* are you thinking?" she scolds through gritted teeth.

I know she's worried about my heart, but this day has been an epic disaster. First, my feelings for Emory are rattling around my brain, and then we get bombarded by everyone in my life. It's been a fucking day, okay? Sometimes you just have to take it out on your brother.

"I came out here to tell you everyone is heading home. Well, everyone except Lexi. She is waiting for Seth to walk her downstairs. New rules, I guess?"

Easton stands so quickly he knocks over the chair he had just sat in, and I swear I hear him growl, "No fucking way. I'm leaving anyway. I'll walk her down."

He is out of my sight before I can even formulate a response. Freaking East, I'm going to have to keep an eye on those two. I can't think of a worse pairing for either of them.

"What was that about?" Emory asks.

"No idea. Come on," I say, taking her hand. "Let's go say good-bye and get everyone out of here."

"Thank God," she whispers, making me chuckle. For someone who doesn't like crowds, she handled the gaggle of onlookers tonight like a pro.

~

IT TAKES over an hour to get everyone out, and by the time my mom finally leaves and I get GG situated in her new room, I realize Ems has been MIA for a while now. Stepping into our room—*Fuck. Our room*—I find her in sleep shorts and a tank top, hands on her hips as she inspects her handiwork on the bed.

"What's all this?" I ask, amused, then laugh outright when she jumps. Emory was so lost in her thoughts, she didn't hear me come in.

"It ... well, it's a barrier. We really have to set some boundaries, Preston. I know this sounds silly after what happened on the plane." She pauses, running a finger over her collarbone as she composes herself.

"What happened on the plane, Emory?" I ask through a smile as I stand behind her, close enough I can smell the rose and chamomile scented shampoo she used earlier.

"Wh-What? You know what happened."

"I want to hear you say it, Goldie."

"We had sex, okay? Is that what you wanted me to say?"

Taking a step forward, I wrap my arms around her middle and rest my chin on top of her head. "Not just sex, Ems. Fucking amazing, mind-blowing, can't feel my limbs sex."

"I'm not saying that," she chokes out, and I'm hit with a full belly laugh.

Pulling her in closer, I whisper, "You don't have to say it, just agree with it."

"Mhm. Okay, y-yes, I agree."

I don't hide my smile. "Good, now tell me what you did to the bed?" I gesture to the line of pillows she placed down the middle.

"Well, we need boundaries. We don't have any boundaries right now, so this literal one will have to suffice until we have everything in writing."

"You still want everything in writing?" I ask, genuinely a little hurt.

"Yeah, don't you? We come from different worlds, Preston. I don't want anything coming back to bite me in the ass."

I hate how she says that, and I'm more determined than ever to find out what the hell is going on with her medical license. If neither she nor Dr. Terry will tell me, I'll call in the big guns. My brother, Ashton, can find out anything with a few clicks of his computer. I make a mental note to call him tomorrow.

"Okay, so you want us to stay on our own sides then. Is that it?"

"Yes, can you do that? I mean, while we sort through everything?"

Turning her in my arms, I stare into her eyes. "I promise to stay on my own side. But how do I know you'll stick to your own terms?" I'm joking, but I love the spark of sass I spot when I threw down the gauntlet.

"Once I'm asleep, I never move, Preston. Ever. I always wake up in the same exact position. Even when I slept with— Never mind. Just trust me. Staying on my own side of the bed has never been an issue."

I want to know who the fucker is she was just thinking about, so I add it to the list of shit I want Ash to find out for me.

114

"Okay, sweetheart. I'm going to get ready for bed, but I promise to stay on my side." I kiss the side of her head and begrudgingly let her go.

After brushing my teeth and stripping down to boxer briefs, I step out into the darkened bedroom. Squinting until my eyes adjust, I find Ems hanging off the edge of the bed with her back to me.

"Ems?"

"Yeah?" Her voice is small.

"I'm not going to bite, you know? Not unless you want me to," I can't help but add. "You don't have to cling to the edge like that."

"Nope, I'm good. This is how I always sleep," she lies.

"Suit yourself. Goodnight. Oh, and, Ems?"

"Yeah?"

"Thank you for tonight, and for the best fucking sex of my life."

"Ah, you're welcome?"

"Hey, Ems?"

"Yes, Preston?"

"How do you like your eggs in the morning? Scrambled or fertilized?"

The beautiful sound of her laughter fills the room and makes all the other shit from today totally worth it. I will die a happy man if I can hear that every night. *Too bad, you'll be a happy man before you know it.* Where the hell is this voice in my head coming from? I really need to talk to fucking Dexter, and soon.

I lie in bed, unable to sleep most of the night, trying to make sense of the last twenty-four hours. However, I keep coming up empty. The final thoughts that run through my mind before sleep finally overtakes me are, *Make sure Emory is taken care of, and why couldn't I be the man to care for her for a lifetime instead of the man for just right now?*

~

I WAKE myself up trying to swat hair from my mouth, except my hair isn't long enough to reach my mouth. Either GG snuck a goddamn cat into my home, or …

Peeling one eye open, I come face to face with a head full of blonde hair. Trying not to move a muscle, I take in the situation.

Emory is fast asleep on top of me. Her head rests on my chest, just below my chin, and her entire body is plastered to mine. That would also explain the raging morning wood I'm sporting. Ever so gently, I turn my head to the right to see what could have happened to her pillow barricade and almost laugh out loud when I see it parted in the middle. It's like she tunneled through it to get to me, and my heart does a funny little skip it's never done before.

Instead of moving, I lay here, holding her, breathing her in, and enjoying the moment I know she will freak out about. At some point, I started caressing her arm, and feel the instant she wakes up, and her body goes stiff.

"Good morning, Emory." I don't attempt to hide the humor lacing my early morning voice.

Her head springs up like it was shot out of a cannon.

"What are you doing?" she whisper yells.

"Me? I'm not doing anything, Miss I Never Ever Move In My Sleep."

"I … you … how did you get me over here?" She pushes herself up to sit and lands directly on top of my hard-on. "Eeep," she squeals and moves, but is unsure of where to go.

Placing my hands on her hips, I still her. "Goldie, if you keep moving like that, my cock is liable to spring free and impale you."

I love the shocked intake of air my words cause.

"Why do you call me Goldie sometimes?"

With my hands holding her in place, I gently grind up and into her involuntarily. "Because you fit me just right," I grin.

"Huh?"

"The first time I hugged you in your apartment, I couldn't stop thinking you were the perfect size for me. I don't know, Ems. It's corny to say you were just my size, but that's how it felt."

I don't embarrass easily, but admitting that to her has me wishing I had just jumped out of bed and left her to sleep.

"That's ... that's actually really sweet, Preston."

"Sweet enough to make like fabric softener?"

She throws her head back and laughs. Fuck me if my cock doesn't twitch angrily below her as I watch her tits bounce.

"Make like fabric softener, and what? Snuggle?"

"Exactly." In one quick movement, I roll, taking her with me. Grinding my dick into her belly, I say, "I know one part of me is more than eager to 'snuggle' with you again."

"Oh my God. You're ridiculous." She's laughing, but I sense she is also torn, so I back off and push myself to stand.

Leaning over, I give her a quick kiss on the cheek. "I'll never force you to do anything you don't want to, Ems. If you want ground rules, we'll make ground rules. Whatever you want, okay?"

Her eyes get glassy, and I feel like I was sucker-punched. "Okay. Thank you, Preston."

Unable to control myself, I lean in for a proper kiss, but I don't allow myself to linger. "Anytime, Goldie. Anytime. I've got to get into the shower. Make yourself at home, but beware, GG is floating around here somewhere. I don't think that woman ever sleeps, and you never know what the fuck is going to come out of her mouth."

"Okay. Oh, do you know why she keeps calling me Miss. Fixem?"

Laughing, I tell her the truth, "None of us has any flipping clue about three-quarters of the shit that comes out of her mouth. But give her enough time, and I'm sure she'll fill you in." And, because she didn't pull away last time, I lean in for one more chaste kiss. Listen, I'm still a guy. I'll take whatever the hell I can get.

CHAPTER 16

EMORY

I crack open Preston's bedroom door and am relieved to see that GG's door is closed. Hopefully, that means she's still sleeping, and I can have a few minutes alone to clear my thoughts with coffee. I need lots and lots of coffee.

"It's about damn time, child. I've been waitin' on yer asses for an hour."

GG scares the shit out of me, and I almost trip over my own feet. Glancing around, I see her sitting at a little stool in the kitchen corner, looking out over the ocean.

"Don't just stand there, Fixem. Grab yer coffee and come sit."

Looking over both shoulders, I'm hoping someone else will appear. I'm not sure how to handle this kind of crazy.

"I'm talkin' to you, now stop yer fits and come sit down."

Okay, she is talking to me. Walking on autopilot, I go over, pour myself some coffee, then pull up a seat next to the old lady.

She reaches over and pats my knee gently. "It's nice to see ya, Fixem. Now tell me, what's your plan for old Broken-heart?"

Trying not to choke on my coffee, I decide it is best to set it down on the table. "Um, what do you mean, GG?"

"Don't ya go GG'ing me, too. I know that boy's heart is broken. I also know you're the one who's gonna bring his knight and shining armor. So, tell me, what's your plan?"

"I think you have too much confidence in me," I tell her honestly.

"And you don't have enough, child. I saw your cards today, ya know. It will be a rough road, but you'll come out exactly where ya should be. Those sisters need some of yer trust, too. You've raised 'em right. Now it's time to let them fly. And you, my dear? You need to learn how to live for yourself. My Broken-heart's goin' to show you the way, just you wait and see."

I don't know how to answer any of that. How in the world does she even know about my sisters?

"Ladies? How's it going in here?" Thank God Preston rounds the corner just in time.

"Oh, nothin', Broken-heart. I'm just tellin' Fixem here that you're going to be just fine. It's grumpy-growler and that dipshit, Loki, I have to worry 'bout now."

"Loki? What do you mean?" I hear the concern in Preston's voice, and I ache for him.

"That dipshit's goin' to learn the meaning of family sooner than you think. Just you wait and see. Red is comin', and she's goin' to write him a new song."

"GG? You know I love you, but you're as confusing as a fart in a fan factory."

Both GG and I turn to face him, and she busts out a cackle straight from a Halloween movie.

Standing from her stool, she crosses the short distance to rest a hand on his cheek. "You'll see, Broken-heart. You'll see. You better be hungry after all that sexin' yesterday. I cooked enough to get that energy up for the next round."

I stare at Preston, who just stares back, then finally shrugs his shoulders. "If you can't beat her, join her."

He holds out his hand, and I reluctantly take it. For the next hour, we have breakfast with GG while she regales us with stories of the North East Kingdom. Neither of us sure where the truth ends, and the story begins.

~

"Is she okay?" I ask Preston when we're finally alone. Thankfully, he told GG we had some work to do for his company and could sneak away while she started cooking again for lunch.

"It was funny when she was pulling her crazy shit on Trevor, but now that I'm in her sights, I'm regretting making fun of him. GG isn't crazy. Eccentric, maybe. I don't know how she gets her information, but she was spot on with Julia and Trevor. She doesn't pull any punches, that's for sure. She loves fiercely but has even less of a filter than Julia."

"She thinks I'm going to fix you, Preston."

His smile is genuine. "You did, sweetheart. Even Dex said it was nice to have the old me back. You've done that, you know? You bring out a part of me I've fought for ten years to hide. Knowing that it means so much to my family to see me like this? For them to see me behaving like the pre-heart condition me? It means more than you'll ever know. So you have fixed me, Goldie. Just maybe not the way we wish you could."

My throat tightens, and I let my gaze fall to my lap.

"Emory?"

Unsure I'll be able to control my emotions, I raise my eyes just enough to meet his.

"You want to set some ground rules now before we are interrupted again?"

That is not what I was expecting him to say, but I'm

thankful he doesn't harp on my feelings. I'm not even sure I could explain what's going on in my head right now.

"Ground rules? Oh, yeah. I think we need some."

"Okay then," he says, booting up his laptop to take notes. "What's first?"

"My pay needs to be in writing. Exactly as we discussed, with the raise for … whatever you want to call this, but no gifts. No bonuses. No extras, and it ends just as our previous one did. I'm entitled to my full pay and nothing else."

"Emory, as my girlfriend, you'll get gifts."

"Pretend, Preston. Pretend girlfriend." I swear I see his jaw tick, but I'm not backing down on this one.

"We will come back to this one."

"What? No, that is not negotiable—"

I'm interrupted by a ring tone belonging to my sister, Tilly.

"Sorry, that's my sister," I explain as I fumble to pull my phone from my purse.

"Ems, Dad's at it again. He broke all the dishes, and he is going after Eli's room now," Tilly says in one breath.

"Tilly. Till, slow down. What is going on?" My voice cracks, and I see Preston rising from his chair.

"Daddy, Emory. I can't get him to calm down. He's yelling for Susie again, and he doesn't recognize me. He's trashing the place—"

Susie, my mother. Fan-freaking-tastic. Tilly is cut off by a loud crash.

"What the hell was that, Till? Tilly?"

"He threw a vase at me. There's glass everywhere."

"Okay, just get out of the house. Where is Eli? Can you get to Ginny's house without him seeing?"

"But, Ems, he just smashed Eli's computer to pieces. We can't afford to replace all this stuff. We need it for school, and you're already working yourself to death."

I haven't told them about my job with Preston. I was too

ashamed of the arrangement initially, so I told them I picked up an office temp position.

"Tilly, I don't give a shit about the stuff. Leave everything. *Now.* I will find a way to replace the laptop again. Just go now. I'm on my way. Text me as soon as you get into Ginny's house. Do not try to grab anything. Just get your ass out of that house now."

The warm, cozy, relaxed feeling I had started to associate with Preston is gone. Once again, I pull down the mask and become Dr. Camden. Dr. Camden has her shit together. She is calm in an emergency. It's a persona I curated at nine when I realized my sisters could only ever count on me. I'm spinning in circles, formulating a plan, when strong hands land on my shoulders, holding me in place.

"Slow down, sweetheart. What's going on? What's wrong with Tilly?" Preston asks, calmly at first. When I finally make eye contact, he absorbs my pain, my fear, and I see he is trying to control his anger.

"Huh? No, Preston. I can't, I have to get to Camden Crossing. If I leave now, I should be able to get there before dark," I tell him, begrudgingly shrugging from his grasp.

He looks at his watch, then back to me. The next thing I know, Preston has hold of my hand, my phone, and the little bag it came out of, and he is towing me toward the door.

"Preston, I just said I have to go." I try to break free, but he won't let go.

He turns so quickly I don't have time to react. He has caged me into the wall, his voice low and steady when he asks, "Are you going to tell me what's going on?"

"Just family stuff. I have to get to my sister. Please, Preston, leave it at that."

"I can't do that, Goldie. What I can do is get you to Camden Crossing within the hour. GG?" he bellows.

"There's no need to be yellin' young— Oh, dear. What's going on?" GG asks after one look at me.

"Can you call Lexi and ask her to come up here, please? I want her to help Emory pack. We have a family emergency and will leave in twenty minutes. I just have to make some arrangements first."

"Preston, it's not possible to get to Camden Crossing in an hour. The fastest I've ever made it was three hours, and that was going 100mph on the highway," I tell him, my irritation taking over.

"We'll be going faster than that."

"Lexi is on her way up," GG says, holding up her phone. "That touchin' with the ladies has really helped my speed with these messages. Now, come with me, Fixem. We'll get started while Broken over there gets you all set up."

Lexi walks through the door, and her face hardens immediately.

"What the fuck happened? Are you okay, Ems?" She runs to me, scowling at Preston.

As soon as Lexi reaches me, the dam breaks. My face is tear-stained in seconds, the stress of it all finally catching up to me.

Preston

I watch, helplessly, as Lexi comforts Ems and hate it isn't me doing the comforting.

"Lexi? Can you help her pack an overnight bag? I need to make a call. We have to leave in twenty minutes," I tell her.

"We?" Emory sobs. "Y-You can't come with me," she chokes out.

In three long strides, I am standing in front of her, trying to control a temper I rarely have. "Are you going to tell me what the hell is going on and what is wrong with Tilly?" I command.

"N-No," she stammers.

"Then I'm going with you—end of discussion. We will leave for Boston from there if we have to."

Lexi looks back and forth between the two of us, and seemingly takes my side. "Come on, chica. Let's get you packed."

I watch as Lexi and GG guide Emory back down the hallway, soothing her the entire way. At the end of the hall, Emory looks for me over her shoulder. The pain, confusion, and sadness I see in her eyes call to a part of my soul I never knew existed.

"I love you," slips from my lips in a whisper, and I clutch my broken heart as if I can feel it tearing in two. Emory Camden now owns half of me, and she has no idea.

When I hear the bedroom door click shut, I call my pilot, George.

"Boss?"

"I need the chopper. It's an emergency. How fast can you have it ready?" I don't have time for pleasantries, and luckily, he knows better than to care.

"We went through the monthly maintenance this morning, sir. It can be ready in ten minutes."

"Great. Stand by. We'll be up as soon as we can."

My next call is to Mona.

"Hello, boss," she rasps. Mona sounds like an eighty-year-old smoker. She is only in her sixties, and I remind her every day she cannot retire until I give her permission. I also pay her obscene amounts of money. That always helps.

"Hey, Mona. We have an emergency. Emory has a family thing. Can you book two rooms at a hotel in or near Camden Crossing for tonight, please? I don't care how much it costs, just make sure the rooms are next to each other."

"Is she okay, Preston?" Mona asks in a motherly tone I've heard from her since I was a kid.

"She is, but I'm not sure about her sister," I admit. Mona

has signed every NDA known to man, but I know she would never spill my secrets even without one.

"Have you called George? Do you need me to arrange a car?" she asks, returning to work mode.

"Shit, a car, yes. That would be great. Touch base with George because I have no idea where he will land once we get there," I tell her.

"Done. Take care of Emory, Preston. I'll handle all the other details. They will be in your inbox within the hour." Mona may not know Emory personally, but she has seen her enough over the last year to have a soft spot for her.

Why did it take you a full year to find that same soft spot, asshole?

"Thanks, Mona," I say sincerely to an empty line. She hung up on me again.

CHAPTER 17

EMORY

*L*exi walks me to Preston's bedroom, where my stuff is still strewn around in boxes, but I'm in a daze. I'm envisioning every worst-case scenario in my head, so I don't hear her ask me a question.

"Emory?" she tries again. "Let's get you packed up, okay? Do you want to talk about what is going on or why Preston has gone all alpha protective mode?" Lexi asks while rummaging through my boxes in search of something. Coming up with an empty duffle bag, she places it on the bed.

"He, Preston, I mean, he can't come home with me," I plead, hoping she'll understand.

"Ems, are you in danger?" she asks, sitting on the bed to really look at me.

"No, not really. It-It's just my dad," I tell her.

"Sometimes parents can hurt us the most," Lexi says wisely. "Why can't Preston go with you? I won't sugarcoat this, sweetie, because I know how Lanie's mother got when she was drinking. Lanie was an only child." She stops, and I see a pain cross her face even I don't recognize. "Lanie suffered most of her life at the hands of her mother. She had outlets in our grandmother and Julia's family, but it was never easy for her until she met Dex. What I'm saying is, if you have someone willing to stand beside you while you fight your battles, why not let him?"

"I'm, I mean, we're not, it's not like that," I try to explain without exposing Preston's secrets.

"Honey, I'm never going to be first in line for the Preston parade, but what I see when he looks at you is 'that' exactly. He wants to be there for you. I think you should let him."

Is it possible that Preston wants to be by my side? Or does he just feel obligated after everything that has happened lately? The last twenty-four hours have thrown me so far out of my comfort zone. I don't even recognize myself right now.

"Sometimes, when you've known someone for a while, they act out of responsibility more than genuine concern," I say lamely.

"I think even you know that's bullshit, Ems. I admit I don't know this group of billionaires like the rest of my family, but I do know they are the most genuine, kind people I have ever come across. The worry, the fear I saw written all over Preston's face was out of love. Pure and simple. What-ever is going on between the two of you, I think you should trust that the man out there will always have your back," she says solemnly.

"He made me breakfast," I let slip stupidly.

"Oh-kay. Is that a bad thing?" Lexi asks through a grin.

"It's just that no one has ever cooked for me before. I'm not used to people doing things for me. I don't know what to do with stuff like that," I tell her honestly.

"Emory, the thing I am learning about this particular type of fucked up family we have found ourselves in is that they do anything and everything they can for you. Whether you want it or not," she adds a little cryptically.

"I don't fit in with this family," I mumble.

"None of us do, girly. I think talking with Lanie would do

you a world of good, though. For now, let's get you packed up before Preston rips my head off for not having you ready to go."

Standing on auto-pilot, I grab things left and right, handing them to Lexi to put in the bag. When I realize she is no longer reaching for the items I'm giving her, I turn and feel my stomach plummet. In her hand is my badge from the hospital. It must have been in the bag from our last trip.

"Someday, you are going to have one hell of a story to tell me," is all she says as she tucks the badge back into the bag and returns to folding the clothes I have piled up.

"Lexi—"

"I said someday, Emory. I get the feeling your story doesn't have the right ending yet. When it does, you'll tell me."

Choking back the emotion, I simply nod.

〜

TRUE TO HIS WORD, twenty minutes later, we are on the rooftop of his building with the air spinning all around us. The helicopter blades are swirling the air so roughly, I have a hard time walking against the wind. Before I have any time to ask a question, Preston has my hand in his, and he is dragging me towards a navy blue helicopter with the gold Westbrook Enterprises crest on the side.

Reaching the door, he turns to lift me and places me on my feet inside of the helicopter. Seconds later, he has boarded as well, and I'm not sure what the hell I'm supposed to do. The noise is picking up, and I'm getting dizzy.

Placing a hand on the small of my back, Preston leads me to a bucket seat. With light pressure on my shoulders, he guides me to sit, and in the blink of an eye, he has lowered himself to harness me in. I feel like an idiot, but I am at a loss for words. Once he's happy I'm strapped in, he raises his face,

129

and it sucks all the air from my lungs. His sparkling blue eyes bore into mine. A slight nod of his head, followed by a squeeze to my knee, and I feel my anxiety loosen its hold.

There is something about this man. He can wash away fears and instill confidence in the most broken of souls. For that reason alone, I vow to lock down my heart. Unless I can save his, mine cannot feel his warmth without the threat of being buried right alongside him. Donning my doctor's façade once again, I stare out the window and wonder what kind of nightmare I'm about to walk in on.

PRESTON LAYS his hand on my thigh, so I turn to look at him and wish I hadn't. The concern I witness in his handsome features is too much.

"Emory? We'll be arriving in three minutes."

Nodding, I try to formulate a reason he can't come with me before I speak.

"Whatever you're thinking in that beautiful head of yours, you can forget about it. I'm not letting you go anywhere without me." His chest puffs out a little as he speaks.

"Preston," I sigh. "This isn't your battle. Honestly, I don't even know what I'll be walking into."

"It is my battle now, sweetheart, so get used to it. Do you want to tell me why you don't want me to go with you?"

Do I? It's not like I'm embarrassed by where I grew up. Not exactly, anyway. But how do you bring someone like Preston into a world they very clearly have never experienced? Insecurities I haven't felt since my freshman year of college surface again, and I hate it. *You are more than what you come from,* I repeat in my head. Dr. Terry drilled that into me during my first year of medical school. *You are more than what you come from.*

The helicopter drops, and my hands fly to each side like

they're looking for something to hang onto. I hear Preston laugh through the headset, and I turn my gaze to his. Following his line of sight, I'm horrified to find my hand gripping his belt, right above a rather large package twitching for attention.

It takes a second to register, and when my brain works again, I rip my hands back into my own space and hold my head in them. "Geez, what are you doing? What are you doing, Emory? You're not a little girl. You don't get to have childish fantasies anymore. Too many people are counting on you," I scold myself quietly.

"Emory?" I hear through my headset.

Shit.

Raising my head just enough to see a smirking Preston, I say, "Yes?"

"So, the headsets pick up conversations," he tells me, amused. "Even scolding, whispered ones. I would, however, be very interested in what kinds of fantasies you just had."

I feel the creep happening. If you're an Irish girl like me, you know what I'm talking about. That horrid flush that starts at the tips of your ears and screams across your body like an inferno.

A slight shift in gravity lets me know we have landed, and hopefully will spare me from answering. Instead, I feel like a lead weight has landed on my chest. We just touched down in Camden Crossing. I might be sick.

CHAPTER 18

PRESTON

*L*uckily, George carries Gatorade in the cockpit. By the time I have Emory unbuckled, she is positively green. I'm not sure if it's from the chopper ride or the fact that I am forcing her to take me along, but she couldn't get out of there fast enough. As soon as her feet hit the ground, she doubled over. The contents of her breakfast emptied onto the asphalt below our feet.

For the first time in my life, I don't have the urge to sympathy vomit with her. I stand by her side, rubbing small circles on her back until she's done.

When she finally stands upright, I meet Emory for the first time. The real Emory. Not Dr. Camden, not the Emory she shows to the world. Today, I'm a witness to the Emory that has insecurities, fears, hopes, and dreams that have nothing to do with her obligations, and it brings me to my knees.

Placing my hand on the side of her face to wipe away the small streak of mascara with my thumb, I ask, "How have I never seen you before?"

As if she realizes it's more of a rhetorical question, she just stares at me, leaning into my touch ever so slightly.

"Sweetheart—"

"Mr. Westbrook, your car is here, sir. The driver will take you to Rural Route 1, as you requested," George interrupts. "Also, Seth has been all over the airwaves. He appears to be unhappy you left without security."

Biting my tongue so I don't snap at him, I take a deep breath before answering, "Thank you, George. I'll be in touch soon with our plans for tomorrow, and Seth can fuck off."

"Yes, sir," he says before turning and heading back to the chopper. Beyond him, I spot the SUV waiting with its doors open.

Taking Emory's hand in mine, I watch as her nimble little fingers collapse around mine. It surprises me that such an innocent gesture can heat my blood and have me wanting to beat my chest like a caveman.

After helping her into the SUV, I wait until she settles before I root around the vehicle. Mona knows to always request mints and water, and she doesn't disappoint this trip either. I find bottles of water and two tins of my favorite mints in the front seat's pocket. Taking them out, I open them both, handing them in turn to Emory.

Smiling weakly, she says, "Thank you," before chugging the water, then popping a mint.

I make no attempt to hide the fact that I'm openly staring at her as she angles herself toward the door, leaning her head on the window. I'm out of my element here and don't know how to proceed. Arrogant playboy Preston would insist she talk, but I've known for some time, that's not who I want to be to her. *But what can I be to her?*

Mona dutifully sent all the details as I requested, so I know it will be a twenty-minute drive to her dad's house. I decide it's best to let her sit in silence for the first half of the ride. Keeping an eye on my watch, I debate how far to push. When ten minutes have passed, I can't stay silent any longer.

"Emory?" I ask gently, and wait until she looks at me

before continuing, "We are going to arrive at your dad's house soon. Is there anything I should know before we get there? Anything I can do to help?"

I've heard sappy assholes say eyes are the windows to people's souls—it was probably even Dex—but that statement has never held any truth for me until this very moment. Her eyes are distressingly large. They have a ring in the darkest shade of blue surrounding a pool of green and gray speckles, and they are staring at me, begging me. I'm just the asshole that doesn't know what they're asking.

"Ems, what do you need, sweetheart? Anything, I'll do anything, just tell me how to help," I plead.

"Preston," she sighs, "this isn't your fight. I need to go into the house and dump his alcohol. It won't be pretty, and I don't want you to see it, okay? I … I just don't want you anywhere near it. My sister should be across the street. If you really want to help when we get there, you will go over and check on her, but not let her enter my dad's house. Throwing him in the tank is something I have to do alone. Can you do that?"

"Why, Emory? Why do you have to do it alone?"

"You grew up with loving parents, right? Siblings who always had your back?" she queries.

Feeling my neck prickle again, I pinch it before answering, "I did."

"And that is great, really it is. Every child should grow up that way, but it's not how it works for all of us. I started raising my sisters at a very young age, but I took that on, and I will keep taking it on. They were able to have some semblance of normalcy growing up because I did all this. I did the hard stuff. I do the hard stuff. They are all young enough still to be whatever they want, whoever they want. This is my burden to bear. This is my responsibility because the only thing I have ever wanted in my entire life was for my sisters to have better. To have what they deserve, can you understand that?" she asks, and for the first time since my father died, I feel tears pooling at the back of my eyes that have nothing to do with me or my broken heart.

"I'll do my best, Ems," I finally manage. "I'll do my best under the condition that you know from here on out, for as long as I can, I am going to be your person. I want you to experience life without all the weight on your shoulders."

She rears back as if I struck her, sucking in an audible breath. "Preston, please, please don't. I don't need a white knight, and please don't confuse our pretend with our realities. We come from different worlds, and while I can pretend to fit in, I could never run in your circles."

I'm shocked by her response. It is the last thing I ever expected her to say. I'm so taken aback, I don't even realize we've stopped in front of an old duplex. Emory takes my silence as her chance to run, and she does. Jumping from the car, she leans back just long enough to tell me that her sister is across the street, and then I watch as she runs up the walkway and disappears into the aging white building.

Glancing between the two homes, I finally step out of the car and cross the sleepy street. I take the steps two at a time to the ranch-style home that has a fresh coat of paint and pansies hanging from planters on the porch. I knock twice, and the door swings open to reveal a younger version of Emory, but with darker features and black hair.

"Tilly?" I ask.

"Yes. Who are you?" she demands, closing the door a little farther.

"I'm Emory's boy— I'm Emory's friend. I brought her here; she's across the street. She asked me to come check on you," I tell her.

"What? That isn't possible. I just spoke to her, and it's at least a three-hour drive, so I'll ask you again, who are you?" she insists.

"It would take three hours if we drove, but we didn't. We

135

flew here." I watch her eyes grow three sizes. "My name is Preston," I continue. "Are you okay?"

Sizing me up, Tilly finally decides I'm safe and takes a step out onto the porch. "I'm fine," she says. "Why did you let Emory go into hell by herself?"

"Well, she didn't give me a choice," I admit, repeating her words from the other night. *Jesus, that already feels like a lifetime ago.*

"That sounds about right," Tilly replies, watching the house.

"I said she didn't give me a choice, but should I be worried? I'm fully prepared to stick my nose where it doesn't belong if she is in trouble."

Tilly gives me the side-eye. "How do you know Emory?"

"Ah, we're, she is, I-I mean, we're friends," I say, feeling like a teenager being asked about a girlfriend.

"Okay, 'friend', I think she's alright, she usually is anyway, but I think we should cross over to the porch so we can hear if anything goes wrong," she tells me, already moving.

"What would go wrong?" I ask through gritted teeth before noticing she is rubbing her forearm, covered with a bandage. "Tilly, what the hell happened to your arm?" I'm suddenly livid that Ems might be in danger, and I'm sitting here pissing away time.

"I'm sure she's fine," Tilly repeats.

She reaches the porch and sits on the top step that I notice is slanting heavily to the right. Unsure of how to proceed, I pace the yard in front of her. Five minutes turns to twenty before I hear a crash. I run toward the door just as it flies open, and Emory walks out.

"Jesus, Tilly. I almost took you out with the door. Why are you sitting there like that?" Emory asks her sister, then hones in on the bandaged arm. "What the hell is this?"

"Calm down, Ems. Ouch, you don't need to rip the bandage off like that."

Taking a step closer, I grimace, seeing the cut. Staring at the two sisters deep in conversation, I remove the baseball cap Emory has placed on her head and watch the color drain from her face. The gash, similar to Tilly's, has me taking the front steps two at a time.

"Preston! Stop. He's passed out now. There's nothing you can do," Emory yells from her spot on the walkway.

I'm boiling over with a rage I haven't experienced since I witnessed Lexi being manhandled by her prick of a boyfriend. "Take your sister and get the fuck into the car and wait for me. Do not even think about arguing with me, Ems. Get in the goddamn car, now."

Not the least bit affected by my threatening tone, Emory marches straight for me, dragging Tilly behind her.

"Don't you dare, for one second, think you can speak to me like that. I don't care what kind of nightmarish scenes are playing through that protective, neanderthal brain of yours, but for the last time, this is not your fight."

I step forward, menacingly close when we hear another crash from inside.

"Oh shit," Tilly whispers.

"Get in the fucking car, Emory, and take care of your sister." The rage in my voice finally overflows. They must hear it as well because Tilly is walking backward, taking Ems with her.

Without another thought, I enter the home, my feet crunching on glass with every step. I follow the sounds of grumbled, slurred ranting.

"Who the hell are you?" Emory's father slurs.

"I'm the one who is going to clean up your mess and get you dried out. If you don't like that option, I'll have you sitting in jail for assault faster than you can suck down your last drink. Sit down, Mr. Camden."

Whether it is the authority in my voice or the utter and complete acknowledgment of defeat that has him following orders, I can't say. Pleased that he is listening, at least for now, I pull out my phone and call the driver.

"Start driving. When you're out of the neighborhood, ask Emory if they need the hospital. I will cover all expenses if they do. If they refuse the hospital, take them straight to the hotel, and stand by for my call. Oh, and prepare yourself for a fight. Make sure you activate the child locks."

I hang up the phone before he can question the legality of what I just requested. My next call is to Mona.

"Hi, Mona. I need the Camden Crossing sheriff at Emory's father's house. No one else, no other officers, just the sheriff. Then please make arrangements to get Liam Camden into a six-month in-patient rehab facility. He needs to be on a plane tonight."

"Preston, where is Emory?"

"I made the driver take her to the hotel," I admit.

"It sounds like you're being very high-handed, and that girl will not take well to this."

"I know. Listen, I'm not done. I hope you have a pen ready."

As I dictate my list, I walk around the home, never allowing Liam out of my site. School pictures of all the girls hang on the walls, all of them except Emory. Through all the destruction, I can see the attempts at making this hell a home. I have no doubt that would be Emory's doing as well.

"Thanks, Mona," I say, finishing the call. "Let me know when all arrangements are ready."

"You got it, boss."

Liam is snoring away on the couch, so I leave him be and head to the kitchen to make him some coffee. Less than fifteen minutes later, there is a knock at the door. I open it, then place the cup of coffee in front of Emory's dad.

"You must be Mr. Westbrook?" the older gentleman asks. "I'm Sheriff Anderson."

"Yes. Please, call me Preston. It's nice to meet you." I

motion for him to follow me, and we step over the glass on the way to the family room.

"Jesus Christ, Liam. What did you do now?" the sheriff asks. It's easy to see these two have a history that is not all bad.

"This is my house," he slurs.

The sheriff takes a seat opposite him. "Mr. Westbrook, you requested my presence. Has a crime been committed here?"

"Well, Sheriff, that depends on how Mr. Camden proceeds from here on out. In the next two hours, a car is going to arrive. He will then be escorted to the closest airport and brought to one of the country's top rehabilitation facilities. If he chooses not to go, then yes, I will be pressing charges for assault I witnessed against two of his daughters. Should he take the smart option, I will pay all expenses. I will also manage and maintain his home for his return in six-months to one-year, dependent on the facility's recommendation."

"Just who the hell do you think you are?" Liam bellows, attempting to stand.

"Sit down, Liam."

I notice the sheriff has a way of handling him.

"Mr. Westbrook, can I ask what your horse is in this race?"

"I have no stock here, sir. I don't give a shit if he goes to rehab or to jail. I just want him out of his daughter's lives so they can attempt to have some normalcy."

"What one of those whores spread their legs for you?" he spits.

I'm across the room in an instant. I have Liam off the couch and jacked up against the wall of his home. My voice is murderous. "If I ever hear you speak about any of your daughters that way again, and I will ruin your sorry excuse for a life, do you hear me?"

"Okay, let's settle down. Am I right in assuming you are a friend of my nieces?" the sheriff asks.

"Your nieces?" I question, letting go of Liam and allowing him to fall to the ground.

"Yes, sir. Liam here is my ex-brother-in-law. It's a long story, but my ex-wife was Tilly and Eli's aunt. I may have divorced that nightmare, but I've done my best to keep tabs on the girls." As he crouches down in front of the fallen man, I hear, "It sounds like you have a choice to make, Liam. You're out of options, and what Mr. Westbrook is offering sounds more than generous to me."

"Sheriff? I need to check on the girls. They both had nasty cuts," I say, focusing all my hatred in Liam's direction. "Can you handle this while I do that?"

"I've got it, son. If you need anything, call the station, and we'll send over some supplies. I imagine Emory has already taken care of the others, but her stubborn ass may need some help."

I can't help but chuckle. "Thanks, sir. And, Liam? I swear to God if I find out you are not on that plane or that you attempt to leave treatment early, I will end you."

He doesn't look up, but I know a defeated man when I see one.

CHAPTER 19

PRESTON

When I get outside, I'm thankful to find the driver is waiting. Walking to the car, I wave him off when he jumps out to open my door. I slid into the back seat, let my head fall back, and take a deep breath. *I am so exhausted.* Daily activities are becoming more difficult. It makes me worry that Dr. Terry's estimation was too generous.

Instead of worrying about what I cannot control, I pull out my phone and make a list.

-Call the University of North Carolina.

-Get a contractor to Liam's house ASAP.

-Have Mona find an apartment near campus.

-Call Mr. Whipple to set up accounts.

I'm interrupted by an incoming text message.

Dexter: Heard something's up with Emory's family? Let us know what we can do.

Ashton: Why am I just hearing about this now?

Trevor: Lexi told Julia that Emory was pretty upset.

Easton: What is going on?

Dexter: Let us help Preston. No more secrets, remember?

My family has already accepted her.

Preston: Thanks, guys. Everything's under control.

I startle when someone opens my door. *Jesus, I'm losing my mind.*

"Sorry to disturb you, sir. I've already taken your bags to your room when I dropped off Miss Emory and her sister. Here is your room key," the driver whose name is escaping me says.

I can't help but cringe. "How angry were the ladies? Ah, I'm sorry, I've forgotten your name."

"The name is Sam, Mr. Westbrook, and on a scale of one to ten, I'd say Miss Emory was volcanic. Her sister, however, thoroughly enjoyed Miss Emory's displeasure. If I may say so, sir, I believe you have an ally in that one."

"Thank you for the heads-up, Sam." I chuckle. "We should be good for the rest of the night. I'll see you in the morning."

"Yes, sir."

Turning to face the building, I'm not sure how to describe it. It's like a double-decker motel, but I learned my lesson from GG on my last visit to Vermont. *Don't be such an ass about judging places like this.*

Noticing my room number printed at the top of the old-fashioned gold key, I look at my options and see two stair-cases on either side of the building. *Room number 226 has to be on the second floor, right?* I'm out of breath by the time I get to the top—another reason to dread my remaining days.

There are rooms on my left, and the right is open to the road. I watch the parking lot as I drag my sorry ass down the corridor. Exhaustion like this is becoming a real bitch, so I'm not paying attention to my surroundings as much as I probably should. That's why I am not prepared for the door that flies open or the four arms dragging me into one of the rooms.

"Where have you been?" a voice I recognize quietly scolds.

When my eyes finally adjust to the lighting change, I notice Emory's sister, Tilly, is the one talking. Next to her is obviously another of their sisters.

"Why are you whispering, and why the sneak attack in the hallway?" I ask.

"Will you keep your voice down?" the other sister scolds.

"You must be Eli?"

"Yes," she replies with a grin, "and you're Preston."

"Nice to meet you." Glancing around the room, I notice they are a sister short.

"Where's Emory?" I ask, hating the uncertainty that settles in my gut.

"If you will hush up, we'll tell you," Tilly says mischievously. She is reminding me of Julia, and that is scary as hell.

"Fine," I whisper. "Where is she?"

"Next door, probably wearing a hole in the carpet with her pacing. I haven't seen her this pissed off since Tilly didn't come home right after school in sixth grade."

Rubbing a hand over my face, I know I'm in a lot of trouble. "Listen, I know what I did was high-handed, but things had gone too far. How's your arm?"

"Oh, it's fine. Ems cleaned it all out."

"Okay, did you ladies need something? Or should I go face the music now?"

"Why do you think we have been sitting on that door for the last hour? We're here to help you," Eli says with the same devilish grin as her sister.

"Help me with what?"

"Emory," they say in unison, handing me a bag of Twizzlers and a container of chocolate milk.

"What are these for?"

"A peace offering. You're going to need it, and we want you to win her over. I've never seen anyone take care of Emory like that or handle her that way. I think you could be

143

good for her, so whatever happens tonight, just know, it's for her own good." The way Tilly says it tells me they have something up their sleeve, but I am too worn out to dig.

Checking out the room for the first time, I look around in confusion. "Why are there two twin beds in here?"

"Oh, that's how most of the rooms are here at the Crossing. Emory made sure you had a queen bed, though, since you obviously won't fit in a twin," Eli informs me.

I'm irritated now and tired. It isn't a good combo. "How the hell are the three of you going to fit in two twin beds? No one can go back into that house until I've had it cleaned, inspected, and whatever the hell else it needs."

The girls exchange an unreadable look before Tilly finally speaks. "The house is fine. I would be careful how much you push Emory tonight, though."

"We have slept through worse, don't worry. We have it all figured out," Eli adds while ushering me toward the door.

*H*earing the click of the lock, I whirl around to the door. I'm so mad I could spit. *How dare that jerk-off pull that shit with me?* Pretend relationship aside, it was wrong on every level. That is my father, my sisters, my mess. I have handled and taken care of them since I was in diapers. How dare he come in and take over like I'm not capable?

I clench my hands at my sides, and my nails dig into my palms. I'm so angry the pain of the nails breaking skin doesn't even register. The old door creaks open, and instead of Preston, I see two hands, one holding a bag of Twizzlers, the other a container of chocolate milk.

"Those traitors," I bite out, but all fight leaves my body when I finally get a look at Preston. "Shit." I scramble to get to him as he staggers into the room, and I swallow a lump in my throat. This isn't a good sign for his health. "Come on, you need to lie down." Corralling him in the small room makes his vast size that much more noticeable.

Satisfied he is safely on the bed, I get his meds while he unbuttons his shirt. It's a comfortable routine we have fallen into over the last year. Leaning into him, I attempt to start the IV, but he holds me off.

"Let me see your head, Ems."

Annoyed, I raise my eyes to look at him. "Preston, I'm fine. We need to get this IV in you."

"After you show me your head," he says stubbornly. "I have to know if your uncle needs to send someone over to look at you."

I huff out indignity but am overcome with a warm sensation filling my chest.

"Ems, you are not sticking that needle in me until I am sure you're okay."

I stare at him. He isn't going to back down, so I mutter under my breath about stubborn ass patients and take out my ponytail. Preston's eyes are lidded, but with exhaustion, not lust. At least, that's what I think until he speaks.

"You're so beautiful. Promise me someday you won't be scared anymore, and you'll let the right people into your life to help ease your burdens? Come here, please. Let me look at the cut."

"You do realize that I'm the doctor here?"

"Yes, but I think I am perfectly capable of assessing the need for stitches," he deadpans.

Giving in, I lower my head, so it is almost resting on his chest. It's the only way he can examine me since he is lying down.

I'm not prepared for the sensations he causes when his large hands so delicately separate my hair to look at the one-inch cut just behind my ear. Preston's hands caress my head, and I have to force myself not to moan. I'm not used to being touched like this, or maybe even at all. The realization has me choking up a little, and the only armor I have left is to become Dr. Camden again.

Pulling away suddenly, I actively avoid eye contact. "I used the liquid glue to close it up. I don't need any stitches. Can I get your meds started now before you pass out?" I know I sound snippy, but I fear the alternative will be tears.

"Go ahead, Dr. Camden."

He calls me Dr. Camden to acknowledge that I've put my mask back on, but I can't let his words affect me.

On a sigh, he says, "Emory?" It's a command, and I think we are both shocked when I comply by looking at him. "I am sorry for taking away your choice to handle things today, but I am not sorry I did what I did. Just because you are used to doing everything yourself doesn't mean you have to."

I don't respond, I can't. I'm also afraid of what might slip out if I speak, so instead, I go about checking his vitals and tracking them on the iPad Dr. Terry sent us, probably illegally from the hospital.

After thirty minutes or so, Preston's color is back, and he is pushing himself to sit up a little straighter.

"Ems, please explain how the three of you are going to sleep on those tiny little beds in there?"

I'm taken aback by the question, still not used to someone showing concern for me. "Oh, that's nothing. Tilly and I shared a bed growing up. We can do it again, no worries."

"Don't be silly. You three can have this room, and I'll stay on the twin bed. Between the queen bed and the couch, you will be more comfortable in here."

"No," I say harshly as I remove the IV. I take a steadying breath and try again. "No, thank you, Preston. My sisters and I will be fine. Plus, I have to go check on my father and assess the damage."

"He won't be there," Preston says, so matter-of-factly, it feels like I've had the wind knocked out of me.

"Where is he? Please tell me you didn't make my uncle arrest him? That will only make things worse." I'm packing up all the medical supplies because I feel the panic rising, and I need to get out of here.

"No, Ems. I didn't have him arrested."

I see Preston check his watch before he continues.

"Right about now, he should be on an airplane to Arizona

147

to dry out. He'll be at an inpatient rehab facility for at least six months."

"You … what?" I screech. "Preston, I can't afford that no matter how much he needs it. I can't even guarantee he'll stay. How could you do this? I have to pay for my sister's school and probably new laptops for them now if he destroyed them like last time. You can't just come into people's lives and do this shit."

I'm so angry. My brain is working overtime to figure out how to get my father home when Preston speaks again, stopping me in my tracks.

"Ems, there is no cost. It's all covered." Preston stands and crosses the room. "I'm going to hug you now, Ems. I'm going to hug you for taking care of me, and I'm going to hug you because I think you need one."

I get no other warning before he engulfs me with his massive body. I'm a doctor, so I understand the emotion tied to human touch. I took an entire class on it and its benefits, but I'm experiencing its raw power for the first time in my life.

With my head pressed to his chest, I hear the deceivingly steady beat of his heart, and I know I won't be able to hold the tears off for long. I'm much safer in the other room where I can tear into my traitorous siblings. After allowing myself a few minutes of comfort in this remarkable man's hands, I eventually pull away.

"I need to go check on my sisters." It's a lie, and we both know it, but mercifully, Preston lets it slide.

"Okay, sweetheart. I'll order us all some dinner. Any allergies over there?"

"Pres, you don't have to do that. I can order them pizza or something."

"Emory." He says it so sternly, I freeze in place. "I told you to get used to me doing things for you, so I will order dinner.

Just let me know if there are any allergies I need to be aware of."

Giving in because I know he is too weak to continue and too stubborn to give up, I say, "No allergies. Thank you."

I fall in love a little more with the carefree, happy smile that he gives me. It makes me feel like I could actually perform miracles.

"You're welcome, Goldie. I'll knock on the door when it arrives."

Afraid of the lump in my throat, I nod, then make my escape. In the hallway, I take longer than I should to compose myself. When I know I can yell at my sisters without crying, I knock on the door. "Tilly? Eli? It's me, let me in."

The door opens a crack, and I can hear them both behind it. What I wasn't expecting was to have a bag thrown at me and the door shut in my face again.

"What the hell? Let me in. I'm not kidding, girls. I'm freaking tired. Let me in."

"Sorry, Mis. No can do! We tested out the beds and decided they're too small. You'll have to stay with hunka hunka bubblicious next door."

If I wasn't about to lose my temper completely, I might burst out laughing. Hunka hunka bubblicious was our sister, Sloane's, name for her Ken doll. I often pray that her male romance characters have better monikers now that she's older.

"What. The. Fuck. Let me in. I swear to all that's holy, I will strangle you both if you don't open this door right now."

"Everything okay out here?" Preston asks with his head poking out the door and a giant ass smile on his face.

"Go back to bed, Preston. My immature sisters think this is a game. This is not a game, Tilly. Open the damn door," I scream.

I'm thankful when I hear the handle turn, but flush bright red when I realize the chain lock is still in place. I stick my foot in the door anyway and am ready to grab the girls by their hair if necessary when Preston comes up behind me.

"What's happening here, ladies?" The laughter in his voice is bubbling over.

"Hey, Preston."

"Hi, Preston. Nothing, we're good. We were just telling Mis here that she has to sleep with you because after testing out the beds, we realized we won't all fit, just like you said," Eli tells him with a wink.

"Yup, so you two kids have fun. Don't count on us for dinner. We ordered a pizza. Love you, Mis."

I'm about to argue, but Tilly is on the floor and physically removes my foot so Eli can slam the door again. I swear I hear them laugh, and I stomp my foot because I'm so mad.

I could totally break down this door. I just need to find its weakest point —

Sensing danger, Preston wraps his hands around my middle just as my fists and foot land on the door.

"Come on, Tyson. It looks like you've been evicted. Luckily, there is a nice, big bed in my room. I'll even let you make the pillow fort you love so much."

"I. You. Jesus," I seethe. I'm angry, confused, and so freaking tired I don't know which emotion will win out.

Sensing my distress again, Preston guides me by the shoulders back to his room. To his credit, he doesn't laugh. Doctor or not, I probably would have kicked him in the balls if he had.

"Hey, Ems?" Preston asks as we enter his room.

"Yeah?"

"It's a good thing I have my library card."

"What? Why would you have a library card for Camden Crossing?" *God, maybe I'm more tired than I realized.*

After he closes and locks the door, he stalks me, and my pulse quickens. Nose to nose, he leans down to kiss my cheek.

"Because I am totally checking you out." He turns and guides me toward the bathroom. "Get in the tub, and I'll bring you a glass of wine. Mona made sure there are all kinds of girl things in both bathrooms, and the fridges are fully stocked. Your sisters will be just fine. Let's take care of you tonight."

"Preston. You need to be in bed. Your blood pressure was a little high, and your oxygen levels were lower than I am comfortable with. You don't need to take care of me. I am the one who went to medical school, remember?"

Preston walks past me with practiced control and turns on the water, then adds some gel to the tub. As the bubbles form, he turns back to me.

"Emory Anne Camden. What did I tell you on the plane?"

Shit. He expects me to remember anything after sex like that?

Noticing where my thoughts have gone, Preston smirks.

"Not that, Emory. I told you, I want you to help me forget. Help me live for however long I can. Not just medically, help me live a life worth remembering. I also told you I want to take care of you for as long as I can. It makes me happy. It makes me feel useful, like I'm not missing out on so much. Please, baby," he says softly, "let me take care of you."

It's a plea for a full life, and the last of my walls come crumbling down. A single tear falls down my face as Preston lifts my shirt over my head, followed by my bra. He slides my jeans and thong down next. *Oh my God! I'm standing naked in front of Preston, completely uninhibited. What the hell is he doing to me?* The look of gratitude on his face has me reaching for him. Placing my arms around his neck, I allow him to hold me.

"Come on, sweetheart. Let's get you in the tub before the food gets here."

I step into the pleasantly scalding water and slide down into the bubbles. What kind of fractured fairy tale did I just find myself in? *The kind where Prince Charming dies at the end.*

The thought causes such a distressing reaction that I dunk my head to hide my tears. *Prince Charming isn't supposed to die.*

When I come up for air, Preston is sitting on the edge of the tub with a sad smile on his face. He hands me a glass of wine and uses a hand towel to wipe the bubbles from my face.

"One of these days, you'll learn not to hide your feelings, Goldie." He leans in and kisses me on the forehead. "I'm going to give you some privacy while I wait for the food and make a few calls. If you need anything, just yell."

Before I can respond, he's gone, and for some reason, I feel more alone than I've ever felt in my life. Grabbing my phone, I'm shocked by the messages I find there.

Lexi: Thinking of you, chica.

Julia: Let us know if you need anything.

Lanie: Luvs.

CHAPTER 21

LOKI

I've been lying in this cold, wet ditch for three sunrises now waiting for a signal, and all I can think about is Preston. I know something is wrong, but I can't remember much. The mud has lowered my body temperature for sure, but I have a feeling it's more than the threat of hypothermia. I also know my leg is badly injured. Before I took cover, I tied a tourniquet around the gash the best I could, so I don't think my issue is blood loss either.

The agency trained me for every Prisoner Of War scenario, so I quickly learned how to take an inventory of my body in situations like these. There is a small chunk of my memory gone. The clothes I'm wearing are singed, indicating a fire of some sort, and I woke up fifty yards from an explosion site. It doesn't take a genius to figure out I must have been in it. *But why?*

Think, Loki. Think. What happened in that building? Hearing a car approach, I lower my face back into the mud, back into darkness. My brain is running in circles. Like a goddamn hamster on a wheel, and once again, I come up with nothing.

Training. Break it down. *What is the last thing I remember?*

Ashton. I was speaking with Ashton. *Where was I? What did he say?*

"Preston. Boston. Dr. Terry. Hearing. Treatments. Sisters."

I can only remember things in fragments. *Where do I know that name from? Dr. Terry?* What does Preston need a doctor for? Whose sisters? Nothing is making sense.

"If Kane was here, he's long gone now. How the fuck are we going to track him? The guy's a goddamn ghost when he wants to be."

Every other thought gets buried in the recesses of my mind when I hear my name. Here, I'm a soldier. Here, it's kill or be killed. *Who's hunting me?* I ended Black's organization. *Didn't I?* My brain is too fuzzy to piece anything together. For the time being, I'm a lone wolf. That means I need to put my contingency plan into action.

I lie perfectly still while the men walk and talk around the remains of whatever building it was. I need to get to my first destination, Clinton, Pennsylvania. Pressing the small receiver lodged into the ring I wear on my right hand, I send up my Hail Mary. Until I can figure out what the hell is going on, I can only count on my boys back home. I just hope they know where to look.

CHAPTER 22

PRESTON

*I*t's been weeks since the fiasco with Emory's father. I've had the house inspected and cleaned, and there is a crew working around the clock, bringing it up to code. Tilly and Eli can move back in tomorrow, but little do any of them know they won't be there long. I'm not looking forward to this battle, but I know it's one I'll win.

Grabbing the baby blue journal that matches Emory's eyes from the shelf where I store them all, I turn to the first page and am reminded of the day I decided to start these journals. It was not long after my diagnosis when my world had fallen apart. My very first letter was to Loki. Perhaps it should have been to my mother or my brothers, but I remember thinking he would take care of everyone. In hindsight, I had no idea just how involved he would become in all our lives. Taking the red journal with Loki's initials engraved on the front, I open to the first page.

Dear Loki,

Do I write dear when I'm writing to a dude? I can't remember what the etiquette books say, and I doubt you give a shit either way. My dad's been gone a year, it's hard to believe, and yet, at the same time, it feels like a lifetime has passed.

I know when your parents died, and you moved in with us, you became close with him, too. I hate that none of us got the chance to say good-bye, so in a way, I guess that is what these journals will be for me. A final good-bye spread out over as many years as I have. I'm starting with you because you are a Westbrook in all but name, and I'm worried about you. I'm not sure what happened to you the last couple of years, but I'm going to keep an eye on you, brother. Even when I'm gone, you'll always be a part of my family. I want you to know that.

Good old Sylvie Westbrook has eight sons as far as she is concerned, so don't let her down when I pass. She and my brothers will need you to step in for a while, and I know you will. If you're reading this, I've already passed. I'm sorry for not telling everyone the truth, but I had my reasons.

Dad had a heart condition, something called cardiomyopathy, and it had the possibility of being genetic. You might remember my brothers and I all flying to Boston after the funeral for testing. Easton, Halt, Colton, and Ash's tests were all negative. Mine was not.

I have a slightly more aggressive form of cardiomyopathy, and there is no cure. Without a heart transplant, my life expectancy is eight to ten years. I also lucked out in that I have a rare blood type that requires a very specific donor. The chances of me receiving one is less than half percent. It's taken time and a hell of a lot of whiskeys, but I've come to terms with my diagnosis.

I decided early on not to tell anyone, and I'll stand by it for all of my days. Had you known, I wouldn't have been able to live my life with all of you authentically. You would have (rightly so) treated me differently, and that's not how I'm choosing to spend my time. Is this selfish of me? Maybe, but I'm the one dying here, not you. (That was supposed to be a joke, by the way.)

I know you will all be sad. My mom may not recover, but I need you to be there for everyone. Dexter and Trevor will help, I'm getting to their journals next, but I'm asking you, as my friend, take care of everyone when I'm gone. Be the glue for our group and *don't let the guys fall away from each other. We have been friends for this long, don't let anything tear you apart.*

I'm sure you are looking at this book and wondering what the fuck I was thinking. So I'll tell you. I want to live an honest life for as long as possible, but there will always be restrictions, things I will miss out on, and it haunts me. You are each getting one of these books so I can write to you, and you'll have a piece of me with you forever. I won't write every day, but when I do, it will be because something memorable happened that day or because I saw something you didn't.

Some pages will be fucking tear-jerkers, some you may get pissed, and others will always give you a sense of home. What I promise you is that every page will be from my heart, so don't shit on my parade and know that I love you.

Preston

Jesus, it's been a long time since I read that, and it brings me right back to that day. My tears dot the page, blurring the ink where they fell. Each book has them. I never thought about the reaction they might have for the readers until now, though. I wish I had. It makes this whole thing that much fucking harder.

Turning back to Emory's, I grab my pen.

Dear Emory,

I make one of these for everyone in my life. I have been doing it for years now. I'm just sorry yours won't have as many entries because I'm pretty sure if I had the time, I could fill a hundred books for you.

"What are you doing?" Emory's sweet voice asks.

I quickly flip her journal over and put Loki's back on top. "I'm just writing."

The rise of her eyebrow and crossed arms that push her tits up in a fantastic way tell me she is looking for more of an answer. Sighing, I point to the window shelf where they are all lined up.

"A year after my diagnosis, I started writing to everyone I

love. When I decided to keep it from them, I wanted to be able to explain why. Then it turned into my final good-bye of sorts."

Emory walks to the window, sinking to the floor as she runs her hands over the smooth leather of each one.

She runs a delicate finger over the engravings. "Do you ever think that you should allow them their chance to say good-bye?"

Getting off the bed, I walk to her and slide the two other journals onto the shelf with the spine of hers going in backward. Offering my hand, I help her stand.

"All the time," I admit, but quickly change the subject. "How was Mr. T today?" She is continuing to volunteer at the infusion center, even though I ended my treatments. The benefits no longer outweigh the side effects for me.

"I'm afraid he won't make it to Christmas." Emory's voice is soft and shaky. She has grown to care so much for this man. I hate that she will probably lose us both at the same time.

It makes me even more pissed that Ashton is dragging his feet in getting me this information about her license. She will need the distraction of practicing medicine after the holidays. I have a sinking feeling I'm not going to make it to Christmas either.

"Is that why you're spending so much time in my library? Are you researching treatments for him?"

She stiffens, and I know whatever she is about to say won't be a complete truth.

"Partly. I just feel like I'm missing something with the both of you. GG keeps telling me I'm going to 'fixem.' I just can't figure out which one of you she's talking about. I know it sounds crazy, but the longer I talk to her, the more she scares me. Those damn cards of hers keep telling her stuff she shouldn't know."

What the hell did GG figure out now?

"She is a little scary," I agree. GG is still staying with us, though thankfully, she spends most of the day with Lanie and Dex. "But you can't keep coming to bed every night, exhausted." I know she is looking for a needle in the haystack that will save me, but I've come to terms with what my life is. I hate that she is running herself ragged searching for cures that don't exist, though.

"I'm just doing my job, Preston."

Ouch, that one hurt.

"You're not my doctor, remember? Not really." My words make her uncomfortable, and she goes about arranging the bed and pillows. "You know, you could probably just forgo the pillow fort now, Goldie. You're like a heat-seeking missile, and no amount of pillows or weird bed-making is going to keep you from snuggling up next to me."

"I don't just snuggle up, Preston. I wake up sprawled out on top of you every morning. That is not normal. I did a double twist with the sheets tonight. If this and the couch cushions don't keep me on my own side, I don't know what will."

Every night before bed, she builds her pillow fort, and every morning, we wake up with her sprawled out on top of me, right where she was always meant to be. I wait for the moment she wakes every single morning. She's at the point now where she is getting pissed, and it's so fucking cute.

"What if I like waking up with you on top of me every morning?"

"You cannot possibly be able to sleep like that. I don't know what my sleeping self is thinking, but I am determined to let you have as much sleep as you can get."

"Come on, sweetheart. Is it really that bad to wake up in my arms every morning?"

Lifting her head to meet my eyes, I see something like love reflected in hers.

"No, Preston. It's not—"

"I know something that might tire us both out?" I say suggestively.

"Oh yeah? What's that?" She asks it so innocently, I almost feel like a douchebag for even continuing, but who the hell am I kidding. I'm bursting at the seams to be inside of her again.

"Never have I ever tried the cowgirl position."

I laugh when she drops her pillows on the floor.

"Shit."

"I know you wanted boundaries, Goldie, but I'm over them. I just want it to be us, no rules, no worries. We leave for Vegas in two days for the bachelor and bachelorette parties. I want us to go and just have fun, for real. Ems, have fun with me?"

Standing behind her, I run a finger down her spine. When I reach her sleep shorts, I hook a finger and pull her back into my front.

"On a scale of one to ten, you're a nine, and I'm the one you're missing," I whisper, relieved when I get the reaction I was hoping for. Sweet, musical laughter fills the room.

Gently, I turn her to face me. "I know what I'm asking isn't fair. I realize what I'm asking of you goes against everything you've trained your brain to reject. But I'm a selfish bastard, and I'm asking anyway. Be with me, Emory. Really be with me."

I read the conflicts crossing her beautiful face as I wait for an answer. When she reaches up on her tiptoes and kisses where my jaw meets my neck, I tense, waiting for what comes next.

"A new spot for every kiss, right?"

"Fuck," it comes out in a possessive growl, and I don't give a shit. Taking control by holding the base of her neck, I continue to growl as I speak. "You're mine, Emory. From here on out, you're mine."

CHAPTER 23

EMORY

$\mathcal{M}$y stomach tingles, and I lick my suddenly dry lips before answering. One word, one syllable, and it sets my mind free on a breathy whisper, "Yes."

Preston's hands tighten around my scalp, almost to the point of pain, and my nipples harden when I realize I like it.

"Say it, Goldie. Say you're mine." His voice is gruff, and I feel his arousal growing between us.

I've been thinking about this a lot over the last couple of weeks, and no matter how much I try to fight it, I can't lie to myself anymore. I want this man to set me free in a way only he has ever done. I want him to take control. For the first time in my life, I want to be taken care of. I've decided I don't even care if that goes against every feminist bone in my body. I'm not delusional, I know this isn't forever, and perhaps that is what makes it okay in my mind. But as I stand here, looking into his eyes, I know I'm done fighting.

"Say you're mine," he repeats, more desperate than before.

"Yes, Pres. I'm yours—"

He pounces at the word yes, and the rest of my thoughts are swallowed by his mouth. His hands are everywhere at once.

"Preston ... Pres, wait. One thing, you have to promise me something."

"What, sweetheart? Anything. What is it?" he asks while lifting my tank top over my head.

"Promise me that you'll hold back if you start feeling any symptoms that exceed the normal realm."

"I won't collapse in your arms, Goldie. I promise. Okay?" He pulls back to see the concern in my eyes. "We'll be together in every way for as long as we can. I want you to remember me always. I won't let your last memory of me be dying in your arms. I promise."

As a doctor, I know he can't promise such things, but I also know Preston. He will move heaven and hell to try.

"You're here," I say, patting my chest above my heart. "I'll always remember you."

Preston's eyes mist, and he looks to the ceiling in an attempt to ward off the tears I know are trying to fall. Leaning forward, I place my ear to his chest. I've heard thousands of heartbeats, but none have sung to me as his does.

"I think you're going to get arrested, sweetheart."

I smile because he is bringing us back to neutral with our game. I hit the highest of highs and the lowest of lows with this man. He makes me smile even as my body screams out in pain at the unfairness of it all.

"Oh yeah? For what?"

"For stealing my heart."

Raising my eyes to his, the dam breaks. In slow motion, he brings his lips to mine. The kiss is salty as our tears mix, and our pain becomes one. Suddenly, I'm frantic for him, clawing at the hem of his shirt. He helps me remove it, and I pepper his chest with kisses. He hisses as each one covers his heart. I wish more than anything I could just kiss it and make it better. Instead, I do what I can to show him how entrenched he has become in mine.

"You're mine."

"Yes," I reply as he removes my sleep shorts. When I am naked before him, he takes in every inch of my body. As I stand here, his fiery gaze heats my flesh. He starts at my toes and slowly, methodically, allows his gaze to wander higher.

I've never thought kneecaps could be sexy, but when I see his body tense with desire as he reaches that particular body part, I feel the wetness of my arousal begin to pool at my center. When I try to clamp my thighs together in embarrassment, Preston holds a single finger up to stop me.

Without raising his eyes from my thigh, he asks, "Are you getting turned on, Goldie?"

"Oh, gawd." I want to hide, but my response elicits a grin from Preston, and he raises his eyes a few more inches.

"Do you think you could come standing there, Emory? From my words alone?"

"What? Why?" *He cannot seriously be considering not touching me, can he?*

"Turn around." It's a command and sexy as hell. I'm shocked that I respond immediately and do as he asks. I hear the rustling of clothing and think he is undressing. Sensing him moving toward me, I let out a sigh of relief, then whimper as he passes me to sit on the bed.

He sits, with his legs spread wide, three feet in front of me, his cock standing at attention. I take half a step forward, but when he says, "Stop," I freeze.

Gawking at Preston's naked body, I'm not sure what to expect. I've never waited for instructions. I've always been the one giving them. I've never willingly allowed another person so much control, and I'm shocked to find it so freeing. Shifting my weight from leg to leg, I wait for him to say something, anything.

"You're so sexy." His garbled voice draws my attention away from his length. I find he is focused solely on my pussy, and I nearly moan. "Never have I ever masturbated in front of someone."

My body goes up in flames, and I'm unable to speak.

"Is this a first I'm going to get or not, Emory?" His voice isn't harsh, but it's commanding and leaves no room for debate.

I nod, feeling ashamed, which even I know is stupid. When I dare a peek, I find Preston smiling like the king of the castle. My eyes double in size as his hand wraps around the bulging head of his erection. I'm mesmerized as he strokes, up and down, over and over again.

"Do we need a refresher on the rules?" His words snap me back to awareness.

"No," I say more confidently than I feel.

Preston leans back on his forearm as he watches me. "I'm waiting for my kiss."

He says it so cheekily I'm tempted to throw him off his game. As soon as the thought enters my head, I know I will follow through. Taking a step, then another, I stop when I'm standing between his thighs.

I watch as his hand clamps down on the base of his cock, and I smirk. Bending over, I know he is expecting me to kiss his chest, maybe his abdomen, but I shock the hell out of him as I place an open-mouthed kiss on the head of his penis.

"Holy fuck."

With my mouth pressed to his tip, I let my tongue lick a line around the slit, then step back and flash him with the broadest grin I can muster.

Preston's chest is rising and falling with each shallow breath. "Suck on your finger."

Without hesitation, I place my index finger in my mouth, never taking my eyes off of his. His hand begins to move up and down much faster this time as he continues to stare at me.

"Play with your nipple with your free hand."

Automatically, I roll my nipple between my thumb and forefinger.

"Christ." His voice is raspy and turns me on even more. I can feel my wetness coating the inside of my thighs—Preston notices, too. "Show me how you want me to touch you. Show me what you like."

Removing my finger with a pop, I look directly into his eyes. "I just like you, Preston. No one else has ever made me feel like you do." I don't admit that my one and only other sexual partner never bothered to learn my body. Or that I had never had an orgasm I didn't cause myself before Preston, but somehow, I can tell he knows.

"Oh, baby. I fucking love that answer." He leans forward quickly and pulls me to him. My head falls back as he squeezes my ass and begins kissing a line from my navel to the top of my pubic bone.

Reaching up, he offers me his thumb, and I take it greedily, rolling it around in my mouth like a lollipop. Groaning, Preston rips it from my mouth and places it on my bundle of nerves, ripe for attention.

One, two, three circles of my clit, and my legs begin to tremble.

"I love how you respond to me. Jesus, it turns me on." I'm taken by surprise when he wraps both arms around my legs and drags my pussy to his face. "I've never tasted anything so sweet in all my life."

"Gah," is all I can manage as he uses his teeth to separate my lips and clamp down on my clit. I swear someone gave this man a map to my body I never knew existed. Every inch of my body is vibrating, and I feel my release coming for me like a freight train.

"You're so close, baby, but not yet. Don't come yet."

I'm out of breath. I can barely speak. "I can't, Preston, I can't control it," I finally force out, and he pulls away so suddenly I think I might fall over. I should know better than that, though. Preston will never let me fall. He uses his muscular arms to guide me onto him.

Straddling his waist, I watch in awe as his large hands ghost up and down my body, causing goosebumps in their wake. One long arm grabs the back of my neck and guides me to his lips. I've never experienced kisses like this. Kisses that can send you flying with just the slow torture of a tongue.

Unable to stand another moment, I reach between us and guide his hardened shaft to my entrance. I feel awkward and uncomfortable. Donny only ever wanted missionary sex, and it was always in the dark, and never once was it enjoyable. I get more satisfaction from a single Preston Westbrook kiss than I ever got in all my years with Donny.

Preston starts rubbing his hands up and down my back in a soothing motion. "Just go slow, Ems. This position is going to fill you in ways you've never experienced, and I'm not just saying that because my cock is so big."

I laugh and feel my muscles relax. I didn't realize I had tensed up.

"That's it. Just relax and take me in when you're ready."

His voice is so strong, so calm, so loving I can't bear to look at him for fear the tears that are always threatening will spill. Instead, I look down between us and watch as, inch by inch, he enters me. "Holy shit," I whisper.

"It's the hottest thing I've ever seen in my life." Forcing my eyes to his, I see the truth in his words. Preston has had plenty of opportunities to be with other women, yet he thinks this is the hottest thing he's ever seen. That knowledge gives me newfound confidence, and I begin to move the way my body instinctively tells me to.

"Christ! Why did it take so long for us to get here? Hang onto my shoulders, baby. I need to fuck you now."

My mouth goes lax as he does just that. On my knees, hovering above him, he wraps his arms around my back for leverage. Then he pounds into me from below. One orgasm turns into two, maybe three, before I lose all consciousness.

I wake the next morning with my head buried in his chest, my body perfectly in line with his, and I feel no guilt for the first time in weeks. No remorse. Only happiness and contentment I'm beginning to understand I deserve. All thanks to this man softly snoring below me.

CHAPTER 24

"This is, without a doubt, the most unconventional bachelor/bachelorette party I've ever seen in my life," I whisper to Colton.

Glancing around the plane, I see the men and women of honor, Julia, Trevor, Lanie, and Dexter, all of my brothers, our mother, Julia's parents, Lexi, GG, Emory, and all the kids. Of course, Seth and his team of spy guys are also in attendance. They're all sitting at the front of the plane pissed off about this little excursion, but seriously, they can all suck it.

"Dexter, I thought this was a Jack and Jill party, not a Jack and Jill went up the hill party. What's with all the kids?" my brother, Halton, asks as a teetering Harper screams down the aisle.

"Lanie is weaning, but she still has to nurse sometimes, so it was easier to bring everyone along and have the grandparents watch them all together in a suite," Dexter explains.

"Fucking hell," Easton grumbles next to me.

"Swear jar. Swear jar, Uncle East." Dexter's oldest son, Tate, comes flying out of nowhere with a large plastic tub that has money overflowing from this plane ride alone.

"You've got to be kidding me, Tate. You're like a goddamn ninja."

Tate's giggles are infections as he informs Easton that he now has to pay double.

I catch Ashton's eye as he passes my seat on his way to the restroom. This is my chance to corner him. Standing just inside of the cabin, I wait for him to exit. When he does, I drag him into the bedroom and quietly shut the door.

"What the hell is taking so long to get that info, Ash?"

"Nice to see you, too, asshole," he says, sarcastically pushing me off of him. "I'm working on it. There is a lot of shit that doesn't make sense. I'm heading to Boston next week after Trevor's wedding to weed through some shit, so just keep your pants on."

"Sorry, Ash. I-I just can't fuck this up. I need you to pull through for me."

Placing a hand on my shoulder, youngest brother to oldest, I realize how much of his life I'm going to miss out on. "I won't let you down, Pres. Is there anything else you want to tell me?"

I knew asking him for help was a risk. He doesn't leave any stone unturned, so he may discover my secret, but I decided it was a risk worth taking. Emory is worth the risk.

"No, I've told you everything I can."

He glares at me for a moment. *Does he already know?*

Giving me a curt nod, he turns to go. As I follow him down the narrow aisle of our private plane, I'm not ready for the chaos we walk into.

"I swear to God, Colton, I'm going to kill you." East is standing at the front of the plane while Colton is standing up in a seat four rows back, ready to run for it.

"That is enough." My mother's voice cuts through the crowd just like when we were kids. "There will be no killing anyone because your poor mother cannot handle another round of life support, so I suggest you all calm down and take a seat like the adults I raised you to be."

I didn't hear much after the life support comment because it sucked all the air from my lungs. I think I might have a panic attack, but that's when Emory's voice cuts through the cabin.

"Dexter, I can fix her. There won't even be a scar."

"No offense, Emory, but we need to land this fucking plane so I can have a doctor look at her. The cut is on her face. I don't want to take a chance with a scar. I appreciate you trying to help, but this is for the professionals," Dex says, coolly holding a crying Harper.

Emory jolts back as if he struck her, and I know his words hit harder than a punch. I'm running toward them, anger boiling over when I finally reach them.

"Watch it, Dex," I warn.

He looks up at me in surprise.

Emory notices my clenched fists and places a hand on my thigh. She is crouching in front of the toddler and peers at me with watery eyes. She tells me she will handle this without saying a word, just as Lanie pushes through with a first aid kit. Noticing the tension, she sits back.

"Everything okay here?"

"No. Emory offered to help, and I said I would prefer a doctor take care of it," Dex confesses. If I wasn't so fired up, I would be rational enough to understand, but I'm not, so I don't.

"Dex," Emory's voice comes out just above a whisper. "I am, I mean, I was a doctor. I'm not practicing right now, but I can take care of that cut. I'm, I was a surgeon, stitching people up was my specialty."

Dexter and Lanie glance back and forth between us, then Lanie lays a hand on Dexter's arm. "We would really appreciate that, Emory. We trust you completely. Thank you."

We all watch on as Emory expertly cleans and closes the

gash on Harper's tiny chin. Dr. Camden is in full force as she talks sweetly to the little girl, explaining why it is so important to stay still for her, and to all our surprise, Harper listens.

Everyone on the plane is hovering around as Emory does what she does best. When she's finished, she looks around to the astonished expressions of everyone on board.

"Ah, okay. So, she's all set," she tells Lanie. "Her chin is numb from the Novocaine, but it'll wear off in about an hour. Children's Tylenol should be enough to take the edge off if she is in pain. I'll check on her tomorrow, too, though, if that's okay?"

"Of course," Lanie says, wrapping Emory in an enormous hug. "We have a lot to talk about, I guess," I hear Lanie whisper.

"Right. I'm-I'm just going to go get cleaned up."

Before Emory can make her escape, Harper launches herself at her legs. "Tank yoos, Em-wee."

"You're welcome, sweety. I'll be back in a few minutes, okay?" She doesn't wait for anyone to respond as she makes a mad dash for the back of the plane.

I'm turning to follow her when the questions start.

"She's a doctor?"

"Why isn't she practicing?"

"What kind of surgeon?"

Everyone has a question. Everyone but Ash, and now I know he's onto me.

"It's not my story to tell, okay? Please don't make her uncomfortable. Someday, when she's ready, she will tell you. If she's never ready, that's her choice, too. Excuse me."

As I make my way toward Emory, I hear the hushed conversations in the background but do my best to ignore them. As I pass GG, she grabs my arm.

"Miss Fixem, Broken-heart. She's the one you've been waiting for. You wait and see."

171

"Okay? GG. Thanks? I'm just going to check on her."

"Mhm, that girl could give Lanie's childhood a run for her money, but she's a good one, Broken-heart. Trust in her."

"I do, GG. More than I thought possible."

With a grin and a nod, GG speaks in riddles again. "Then you, my broken heart, will be just fine. You just wait n'see."

When I finally reach the cabin, I knock softly then let myself in to find Emory sitting on the bed with her head hanging low.

When she hears the door shut, she speaks without looking up. "I'm so sorry, Preston. I hope I didn't just ruin everything for you. I-I just, when we hit that little pocket of turbulence, and she came up with that cut, I couldn't focus on anything else. I knew I could fix it easily and everything else went out the window. I just—"

"Dr. Camden?" I catch her off guard, and she finally looks at me. "You did good. I'm proud of you. You just took care of my family out there knowing you'd have to tell something deeply painful about yourself."

"You're not mad?"

"Goldie, I don't think I could ever be mad at you," I tell her honestly. "They do have a lot of questions, but hopefully, I bought you plenty of time. You tell them when and if you're ready, and I'll always support you. This," I say, waving my hand between the two of us, "isn't just about me anymore. Those people out there love you and will always be there for you, even when I can no longer be."

"Why would they do that?"

"Because that's what family, chosen or by blood, do for one another, and you have just become part of our messed up family."

I'm suddenly flooded with my mother's comments about life support and Dr. Terry's warnings about choosing a medical power of attorney, and my brain forms a plan right before my eyes. I'm going to marry Emory.

"Preston? Are you okay?"

"Huh? Yeah, I'm good. What were my moronic brothers fighting about out there?" I ask, trying to distract her. I know getting Emory to marry me will take some finesse, so I need to buy myself a little more time.

"Well, we hit a little bit of turbulence, but it was enough to knock Harper off balance. She was closest to Easton when she fell. Colton … Wait, can we just talk about the ton names?"

I laugh as she gets sidetracked. "Yeah, there are a 'ton' of Westbrooks. So, why were they fighting?"

"Oh, right. Colton was teasing Easton, telling him if he hadn't been drooling all over Lexi, he would have caught the baby. Easton charged him, but he bolted over the seats. I'm not sure what happened next because I was grabbing my medical bag."

I pull Emory to stand, and wrap her in a hug. Resting my head on hers, I'm acutely aware that the pain in my chest has nothing to do with cardiomyopathy and everything to do with the heartbreak of knowing I can't keep this woman.

CHAPTER 25

EMORY

"*P*reston, I brought a dress for tonight. I'll be fine."

"I know you're fine, Goldie. And I don't give a shit what you wear, but this is a girl thing. Once Sylvie Westbrook gets a thought in her head, it's best not to fight her."

He places a hand on mine, and I hadn't even realized I was wringing them. Actually, I wasn't aware people really wrung their hands anymore, but here I am.

"Emory, this will be fun, I promise you. Sylvie Westbrook will go out of her way to make sure all you ladies are well taken care of."

"Everyone is going? Lexi too?" I feel close to Lexi even though I haven't known her long.

"Trust me, no one is getting out of this shopping trip. Sylvie never had any girls, and I have a feeling she is going to make up for it today."

"But I'm sure she just meant family. She won't even notice if I'm not there." I don't want to sound ungrateful, but this is my worst nightmare come true. I never had a mother, so I don't know what the hell to do with one now.

Preston stops in his tracks and is in front of me in only a

174

handful of steps. Looping his finger under my chin, he raises my face, so I'm in line with his.

"Don't make me repeat this, Goldie. You are my family—end of story. If you think Sylvie won't notice her oldest son's girl is missing, you're in for a shock."

"It's not that I don't want to hang out with your mom and the girls, Preston. It's just, I've never done this before. I never had anyone take me shopping; I've always been the mom."

"Then, you know what I say to that?"

"What?"

"You couldn't have landed with a better group of moms. GG? Well, she is crazy. We've already established that. But Jules' mom, Mimi, and my mother are two of the best you'll ever meet. They have also never subscribed to the blood is thicker than water mantra. Their families have both always encompassed those who needed them most. You'll see. And you won't be the only one. Lanie and Lexi never had a mother around either. Lexi's died when she was two, and Lanie's mother is an asshole."

There's a knock on the door, followed by, "Git yer'selves ready, I'm comin' in. I'm too old to be waitin' in the hall."

"Fucking GG."

I look to Preston and let out a laugh. GG is followed by Preston's familial entourage.

"Does your family always travel like this?" My belly is starting to hurt from laughing so much.

He lowers his mouth to my ear, "Our family, Goldie. Our family." I physically shiver at his words and hold my elbows close to my sides. "Relax, sweetheart. This is a good thing, or I wouldn't let you go." Preston moves behind me and places strong hands on my shoulders, gently working out the tightness in my neck and shoulders. My head rolls back to rest against his chest involuntarily, and he leans down to kiss my forehead.

My face smiles on its own when he looks at me like that.

Hearing the commotion that comes when twenty people invade your suite, I straighten to find all eyes are on us. Preston has either gotten really good at reading my cues, or he is uncomfortable as well because he gives my neck one more squeeze before taking my hand in his.

"Hi, everyone. You ladies ready to go?"

"If you can part with your better half, the rest of us are ready to go," my mother smiles.

"Oh, I'm ready, Mrs. Westbrook. I just have to grab my purse."

Preston squeezes my hand with extra vigor as our entire group "oooh's" again.

Shit. I look to Sylvie apologetically.

Sylvie tsks the others away. "No apologies, my dear. And no purse needed. It's not every day I get to take my girls shopping, and trust me; you've never done shopping like this, so just grab your phone, and let's go."

I'm scanning the group, looking for an ally, when all the girls hold up their phones.

"We all got the same talk," Lexi informs me.

I turn to Preston for help, and the asshole just hands me my phone with a kiss on the lips. In front of everyone.

Lexi and Easton make puking noises like they are twelve years old, then scowl at each other when they realize they did the same thing. The room erupts in good-natured laughter at their expense.

I've never experienced love on this level, and I have a hard time keeping my shit together.

"You're family, too," Preston whispers.

"How do you do that?" I demand.

"Do what?"

"Read me like that."

"I pay attention, Goldie. Get used to it. You're mine, which means you're also theirs," he tells me, gesturing at the sizable crowd gathered in his suite.

"Mom, dinner will be ready at six-thirty p.m., so make sure the ladies of honor are back here and ready by then."

Checking my phone, I notice that is seven hours from now.

"Preston, that's seven hours away—"

"Oh, good grief. Seven hours is not nearly enough time." Sylvie interrupts. "Chop, chop, ladies. Time to go. We have a big day ahead of us."

Like a deer in headlights, I turn to Preston. "I'm supposed to shop for seven hours?"

He only grins at my discomfort. "Have a good day, dear."

The next thing I know, Lexi is looping her arm through mine and dragging me after the others. "Come on, chica, it looks like we've been adopted by Mommy Warbucks for the day."

"This is going to sound really childish, but please don't leave me today. I don't fit in here, Lex."

Out of nowhere, Lanie hooks my left arm with hers. "None of us do, Ems. But here we are, and you know what I attribute that to?"

"What?" I choke out.

"Karma. Good things happen to good people. You're good people, Ems. It sounds like it's about time some things go your way."

MAN, *my feet hurt*. I'm also nearing an epic meltdown. Sylvie has spent more money on clothes for me in the last three hours than I have spent on all three of my sisters in the previous four years. I'm hiding on a bench in a store that I cannot afford a single sock in, hoping this will all be over soon when Sylvie materializes like a fairy godmother.

"There you are, Emory. I've been searching for you."

I try so hard, but I know I cringe when she speaks. Her tinkling of laughter that follows is a dead giveaway.

"Ah, I just needed a break."

"I hear you. Mind if I sit?"

"Sure. And in case I forget, thank you for everything today, Sylvie. This was way too much, and I don't know how I can ever repay you."

She bumps shoulders with me before she speaks. "Well, that's where you have things wrong, Emory. I should be thanking you. Ten years ago, I thought I lost my Preston for good. He was always larger than life. He was the glue, the one who looked out for everyone, but when his father died suddenly, we lost that carefree, loving boy. You've brought him back to me."

Guilt. It sinks into my gut like a lead weight.

"But Preston isn't why I wanted to take you shopping today."

Oh no, is this where she tells me to take the goods and run? Stay as far away from her son as I can? I'm not good enough. I'm—

"Has Preston told you about my upbringing?"

That has my head spinning.

"No, I don't think so."

She smiles kindly. "I think these boys forget where their momma comes from sometimes. It isn't the white picket fences of Waverley-Cay, that's for sure. I have a feeling you and I have more in common than you think. But I'm not going to push you, yet." She grins, and it's so much like Preston, I can't help but smile back. "I wanted to take you out today because I have a feeling you deserve it, and I'm in a position where I can do that for people. No matter what happens with Preston, you have lots of friends and family here, myself included. But between you and me? I think I'll get the privilege of walking you down the aisle before you know it."

I choke on my own spit at her words. I don't know what

to say to her. I don't want to lie after all the kindness she has shown me today, so instead, I say nothing.

"Don't look so surprised, dear. That GG has been reading those cards again." Even Sylvie can't finish that sentence. We're both laughing hysterically. Finally, she composes herself. "I've never met anyone like GG, but let me tell you, she hasn't been wrong yet. If she says you're not going anywhere, my money's on her. And you."

It must be a Westbrook trait to make you laugh one minute and be on the verge of tears the next.

"What do you say we go check on those brides? Preston will have my head if I don't have you home on time."

I stand with her when my phone rings with Eli's unique tone.

"Actually, Sylvie, this is my sister. Can I meet up with you in a few minutes?"

"Of course, dear." She wraps me up in a hug that has my eyes prickling.

Jesus. The Westbrooks are also good huggers.

"Emory, are you sure you're okay?" Lexi asks again as we walk into the hotel.

We've had our hair and makeup done to within an inch of our lives, and I have to admit, we all look freaking good, but I am so pissed off at Preston that I can't even think straight.

"Yup. I'm fine. Just need to speak to Preston," I say through clenched teeth.

Julia comes up on my other side. "Oh, this is going to be good."

I stop abruptly and look around. Lanie, Lexi, Julia, even Mimi and Sylvie are all surrounding me, showing support, and they have no idea what Preston has even done.

"Oh, don't look at me like that," Sylvie says. "I love my

boys to death, but I'm the first to admit they need a good ass-kicking sometimes."

Something about hearing this prim and proper woman swear sets everyone off, and we all erupt into fits of laughter.

"So, do we get to know what he did before we get up there?" Lexi asks, way too excited.

Everyone must give her a look, because she defends herself. "What? I'm just glad someone else is laying into him."

"I—"

I peer around at this group of women trying so hard to take me into their circle. *Do I tell them?* Luckily, I'm saved by the bell, and I stalk toward the end of the hall, trying not to laugh as my female army marches behind me, ready for a fight they don't even question.

When I reach the door, Lanie places a hand on my shoulder. "Deep breaths, chica. Whatever he did, I'm sure he thought he was doing the right thing. Dexter does the same thing."

"Trevor, too," Julia chimes in.

"Ladies. Men are idiots sometimes, but they are idiots for love, so keep that in mind," Sylvie says with a wink, then pushes the door open and ushers me inside.

If I wasn't so pissed, I'd laugh. Preston's own mother is encouraging me to set him straight. So that is what I set out to do.

CHAPTER 26

EMORY

*W*ith newfound confidence, I lead the she pack into the lion's den. Following sounds of muted laughter, we find them crowded together in the family room. The babies are playing happily in the center of their circle.

This is not your standard suite. There are rooms—so many rooms within the suite. I swear it's bigger than my father's entire house. Someone has transformed the dining room across the hall from where they sit into a magical oasis. It looks as though someone recreated an entire scene from a fairytale, and I lose my momentum for a minute. Leave it to Julia to fuel the fire.

"Remember, you're on a mission."

Turning, I see all the women, my new friends, all standing behind me with their arms crossed, scowling at the offender.

"Jesus, I thought the Westbrook boys traveling in a pack was scary. You guys have nothing on the she-wolves over there," Trevor tells the room.

My eyes don't leave Preston as he scans the room and does a double-take when he lands on me.

"Oh shit," he whispers.

"Dude, what did you do? Even Mom looks pissed," Colton says from behind him.

"Ah—"

"Well, don't keep them waiting, Preston. I don't want the she-wolves to turn on the rest of us," Dexter says, giving Preston a little nudge.

"Ladies?" Preston says, taking tentative steps toward me. His smile falters only momentarily. "Everything alright?"

"No. Everything is not 'alright'."

"Do you want to go somewhere and talk about it?"

"You already know what I'm pissed about, don't you?"

"Well, I may have an idea," he says while grabbing the back of his neck.

"You're pinching your neck! That's your tell. You know what you did was wrong."

"She's got you there, Preston," East chimes in.

"Listen, how about we go into the bedroom and talk in private?" he asks, but he is already guiding me down the hall, so I shrug out of his hold.

God, this jerk. I want to kick him right in the shins. As soon as we hit the bedroom, I spin on him.

"How could you do this, Preston? I'm already a sinking ship trying to figure out how to pay you back for my father. How the hell am I ever going to come up with Tilly and Eli's tuition to UNC-Chapel fucking Hill? You can't just go around playing in people's lives. I'm barely holding it together as it is. This is my family you're screwing with, and I won't let you. How dare you just take over without speaking to anyone? Do you have any idea how much this is going to crush them when I have to tell them we can't accept?"

"Are you done?"

His condescending tone makes me violent in ways I've never even imagined before.

"Done?" I say, stepping into his personal space as he sits on the edge of the bed. "No, Preston. I am not 'done' by a long shot. Just because you have more money than you know what to do with does not mean you get to buy me. I'm not for sale. My sisters are not for sale. What is it exactly that you expect to gain by doing this? I've already slept with you, what else do you want from me?"

Slowly, he stands. I thought he looked pissed off in my father's home, but that Preston has nothing on the one standing before me now.

"What do I want from you, Emory? I don't want anything," he says in a tone so cold my body wants to curl in on itself. "All I've ever wanted, Emory, is you. You are mine, are you not? That means your family is mine. Now and forever. So when your family is struggling, I am, too. Letting you struggle through life is not how my family works. If we can fix something, we do. Get used to that. As far as you being for sale? Don't you dare, ever, speak about yourself that way again. I swear to God, Emory. The rage I'm feeling right now at those comments is not even human, so don't ever say that shit to me again."

"Preston, you can't just throw money at people. Life doesn't work that way," I scream.

"I'm not throwing money at you. I'm throwing money at a fucking miserable situation to make it better. That's what I do, and you're not the only one so you can get off your warped sense of integrity and accept the help I'm offering."

I feel sick to my stomach. "Oh, oh my God. Are you sleeping with other people? Fixing them, too? Is that what you mean? You find broken girls and try to fix them because you can't fix yourself?"

"Sit. Down. Emory."

"Don't tell me what to do."

"Sit the fuck down, Emory. I know I've upset you, but that was fucking low, and I need a minute, so I don't say something I'll regret."

His voice leaves no room for argument, and while I'm not

scared of him, I am scared for him. His heart is not in any condition for the level of anger I see radiating off him, so I sit.

He takes a handful of breaths before he speaks again. "Considering how smart you are, Goldie, you can be a real shit head sometimes, you know that? You are the only person I have slept with in years. Let me say that again, years. And you will be the last person I ever sleep with. Do I need to repeat that as well?"

I shake my head, not trusting myself to speak.

"When I said it's what I do, I mean, it's what I do for my family." Opening his briefcase, he pulls out an arrangement of colorful folders. Holding them up one at a time, I worry that the contents of our ridiculously lavish lunch are going to make an exit.

"Dexter-House of Hope.

"Trevor- Knights and Days.

"Loki-Lost Directions, home for boys.

"Lanie-Hearts and Hands Network.

"Julia-Righting Wrongs.

"Lexi-Women Warriors.

"I started each of these charities in their names, based on their specific shitty experience. This is how I help the ones I love, Goldie. I don't buy people. I take a fucking nightmare of a situation and do what I can to make it better. For you, that means helping your sisters because they deserve it, and you deserve a break. You don't have to be responsible for everyone all the time."

I notice he has two more files that he tucks under the others before shoving them all back into his bag. My head is spinning, and I know if I speak, I'll vomit all over the floor.

How could you be such a bitch?

"You see, Goldie, I do throw my money around because I can do some good in this fucked up world with it. I take care of those I love, even if they don't know it yet. Should I have spoken to you about this? Probably. But I didn't because I knew you'd give me a hard time. You and your sisters deserve a little help. So what if I'm the one to give it to you?" He is trying to catch my eye, but they are so full of tears, I couldn't focus on him even if I wanted to.

"I've invested time and money into each charity for all those people out there. I do it because I care for them, and they have all had some shitty things happen in their lives. I wasn't always able to help them when they needed it, but if I can help others in that same situation in their name, why the hell wouldn't I? What the fuck does it matter if I put money into a charity or into the people that matter the most in this world to you?"

"Pres," I say weakly. "I ... we just can't accept this. It's Chapel Hill. We barely get by with them living at home rent-free. I-I just can't afford for them to go there." My body is trying to give way to the sobs I've been holding back. "It's not that I don't appreciate the thought, I do, but I have no way to make this work. Don't you see? Not everyone is meant for the happily ever afters."

"Bull shit. Did you even listen to your sisters, or did you shut down after they said full ride?"

"What?"

"I tried UNC-Charlotte first because it was closer to you and because I knew you would lose your shit over the money. But because the semester has already started, Mona couldn't find an apartment close enough to campus in a safe neighborhood. I figured you would really freak the fuck out if I bought them a car, too, so we went with Chapel Hill. Their apartment is a two-minute walk to campus, comes fully furnished, and is ready for them to move in whenever they want."

My head is spinning, and I'm drowning in emotions. My body crumbles to the floor, and I allow painful sobs to wreck me. "This isn't real life. I can't do this," I say on repeat, even after Preston sits down and pulls me into his lap. I've spent so long being the only person to care for my sisters. No one has ever taken care of me, and certainly not to this extent. How is it possible this man can come into my world like a freight train and relieve so much stress in the blink of an eye?

I wake with a start. *What the hell happened?* I feel hungover, and I'm forcing my brain to focus so I can figure out what I did last night. A gentle knock on the door has me bolting upright. That's when I notice I'm still in my clothes from yesterday, and memories flood my brain like a bad movie.

Preston laid with me last night while I cried. He left once, I think, to tell everyone to eat without us. When he returned, he tucked us both into the bed and held me.

Knock. Knock

"Come in," I yell with a hoarse voice.

Lexi peeks her head through the door, then she enters with Lanie and Julia close behind. It takes a minute for me to notice, and when I do, I laugh right along with them. They all have hot pink T-shirts on that say The She-Pack. Julia hands me one as all three climb into bed with me.

My sisters and I do this all the time when one of them needs comfort, but this is the first time it's happened to me. It's also, I realize, the first time in my life I have had girl-friends who cared enough to check on me.

"Jesus, I ruined your bachelorette parties," I shriek.

Lanie kicks her shoes off and pushes up next to me in the bed. "Girl, please. I'm still nursing, and after all the champagne Sylvie fed us yesterday, I was passing out in the middle of dinner."

"Yeah, these two dipshits flew us all the way to Las Vegas to be in bed by ten p.m.," Lexi says, rolling her eyes.

"Well, excuse me, miss I rolled in at five a.m.!" Julia snaps back.

"Wait, what? Where the heck were you until five in the morning?" Lanie demands.

I sit in the middle of these ladies and watch the back and forth like I've always been a part of their pack.

"You guys left me high and dry, so I had to go out with the Westbrook boys of bad decisions," Lexi says without making eye contact.

"That's not what Colton said this morning," Julia informs us, thoroughly enjoying calling Lexi out. "He told us he was home by one a.m. Only you and Easton rolled in at five."

My head whips to Lexi, but she is working hard to keep her facial expressions neutral.

"What? If you guys think I'll waste a free trip to Vegas sleeping in my room, you're all insane. We went out, gambled, drank, walked the strip. All the stuff you're supposed to do in Vegas."

Trying to help a girl out, I change the subject. "Do you guys know where Preston is? I think he might be upset with me."

"That man is far from upset," Julia states. "That man is in love."

I snap back so fast I bonk heads with Lexi.

"Jesus, Emory. What the hell has gotten into you?"

"Ah, sorry. Nothing. Sorry. So, where is he?"

Love? No way. We have an inevitable expiration date, and no matter how much either of us wishes it were different, it's out of our hands.

"He had to run an errand. He said he'll be back in a couple of hours. So we are here to snuggle with you and raid your mini-fridge until it's time to head home since none of us want to gamble and the grandmas have the babies," Lanie says while adjusting the pillows behind her and getting comfy.

"None of you are upset that I ruined your night?" I ask in disbelief.

"Chica, we have all been there. You should have seen my reaction when Dexter went behind my back to talk with Mimi. These guys grew up in a world none of us understand, so they may have some autocratic ways of dealing, but they do it out of love. Plus, we have a lifetime to make these memories. We can have a Vegas redo anytime."

"A lifetime," I repeat.

I wish with every fiber of my being that a lifetime was actually possible.

CHAPTER 27

PRESTON

*T*hings have been different since we returned from Vegas last week. Emory has fallen into an easy routine with the girls and my mom, which I'm happy about, but I would be lying if I said I was missing having her all to myself.

Today she is at the infusion center since the rest of the week will be chaotic because of the wedding. Julia had a dress sent over this morning, having invited Ems to be part of the wedding party. Emory is uncomfortable by the offer, but I appreciate Jules for including her.

Using the few minutes GG isn't talking nonsense, I take out Emory's journal. I haven't been able to write in it nearly as much as I would have liked now that we are sharing a room, so I sneak moments whenever I can.

Dear Goldie,

Your ring arrived today. It's beautiful, just like you. I've never once thought about marriage, but I knew the first time I hugged you, something was different. This might elicit our biggest fight to date, but I know we'll get there in the end.

You're probably wondering what was going through my mind when I bought it in Vegas. It's a fair question, so I'll tell you.

Watching my family and friends claim you as their own changed me. I know my time is short, and I decided on that trip I wanted to have all the firsts with you I can. I want to die a married man, Goldie. I want to go, knowing you were by my side because you wanted to be there. That's why I bought the ring. If I had more time on this Earth, I know I would spend every day doing everything in my power to make you mine. Unfortunately, time is not on my side, so I'm having to speed things up to have it all.

These last few months with you have been the best and worst of my life. Why God gave me perfection when I'm destined to join him so soon is something that plagues my dreams. I wish I could have met you years ago. I wish my heart wasn't so broken. I wish life had a different outcome for me, but it doesn't, so I'm not wasting any more time.

I've never feared death until I met you, sweetheart. Now I wake every morning praying for ways to make sure you are always cared for, especially when I'm no longer here. I'm not saying that because I don't think you can care for yourself. I'm saying it because I think you've done it on your own long enough. I know I'll never find peace until I've done all I can for you.

My family will always be there for you, too. That's both a blessing and a curse depending on how you look at it. But I'm a selfish asshole that wants to be the one who cared for you all of your days. That's why we are going to get married. Here's the thing —my family is loaded. My friends are loaded. Their children's children's children will never want for anything. They don't need me to take care of them—

"What are you doing?"

Emory scares the shit out of me, and the journal goes flying. She's closer to it than I am, and in slow motion, I watch as she picks it up, then turns it over. Her face pales instantly.

"Emory Anne Westbrook."

"Okay, just hear me out."

"Hear you out, Preston? This book says Emory Anne

Westbrook. West. Brook!" She paces, waving the book in the air.

I stand quickly and wish I hadn't. The dizzy spells are getting worse, and she notices.

"Sit down, Preston. How long have you been getting dizzy like this?"

"Today?" I ask evasively.

"What do you mean today? How long have you had these spells?" Laying the notebook on the nightstand, she runs to the closet for her medical bag. "How long, Preston?"

I know by her tone not to argue with her. "Probably since Vegas," I admit.

She spins to face me—a mixture of hurt and anger clouding her otherwise perfect face.

"Vegas? That's an entire week, Preston. Seven days. You didn't think to tell me this?"

Placing my hand over hers as she puts the stethoscope to my chest, I get her to stop and look at me. "It doesn't matter now, sweetheart. I spoke to Dr. Terry this morning. I'm too far down on the donor list, and my symptoms are progressing much too fast."

"I read about a new procedure last night. They are testing it in Mexico now, but I'm sure we can get you in. Let me make some calls. We'll—"

"Emory," her name is like a prayer on my lips. "I'm done," two words that hold so much heartache. "Dr. Terry agrees. I want to just live the next few weeks, checking off as many boxes as I can. Having as many of your firsts as I can."

"No, Preston," she wails. "You don't just give up. I told you there's new research. There are other options. We can buy us some time." The first trickles of tears fall down her face.

"We can buy us some time." Does she realize what she said?

"Sweetheart? Our time is now. Right now is what we have."

"What is that journal?"

191

"I told you. I write letters to everyone I love."

A strangled sob gets caught in her throat. "No."

"Yes." I chuckle. "Never have I ever asked someone to marry me."

She stares at me with wide eyes, shaking her head. *Well, that's not the answer I'm hoping for.*

"We barely know each other. You can't be serious, Preston."

"Oh, baby. I'm so serious. There is so much I want to do. So much I know I won't have time for. Some of it for my family, but this? You and me? This is for me, for us. I wasn't lying when I said I want all your firsts, and I realize this is beyond selfish. It's definitely the most selfish thing I have ever done. I want to marry you, Emory. When I die—" The words get caught in my throat, and I have to swallow multiple times before I can finish.

Emory sobs quietly on the edge of the bed.

"When I die, I want to have been a loving husband, even if only for a short time. I want to be your loving husband, so when your life moves on, you know how you deserve to be loved. I want you to remember how life should be. I want you to remember the life I gave you and never settle for anything less. When you get your life back, I want it to be the best version it can be. And selfishly, I want that chance to show you how perfect you are. I want to show you how it feels to be loved. I want to be the first to love you with all of my heart."

"Y-You can't love me, Preston."

Shaking my head, I kneel in front of her. "I'm pretty sure it's too late for you to make that demand." Reaching behind her, I pull out the ring box I had hidden under the pillow when she walked in.

"You're asking me to become your widow," she cries—deep, painful, earth-shattering cries.

My body shudders with emotion. "I'm selfish, I know. I

understand what I'm asking of you, sweetheart. But I'm asking anyway."

Opening the box, I pull out the perfectly round diamond ring. The large center stone is encircled by smaller, intricately placed diamonds. I'd drawn it to symbolize the circle of life set on a platinum band, and the jeweler delivered something better than I had ever imagined.

"Please, Emory, say you'll marry me," I beg.

"I-I … Preston, your family will hate me. And your friends? Oh my God. Preston. This … I'm not what you want."

Her pain-filled eyes never leave mine. She doesn't even look at the ring. All she cares about is my family and me. That tells me more about her than any game of Never Have I Ever could.

"Goldie? This isn't for them. This is for you and for me. When I have to leave you, I never want you to doubt how real my feelings for you are. Not only am I asking you to be my wife, but I'm also asking you to elope. I can't even give you the wedding you deserve because it will raise too many questions, and I don't have that kind of time."

"Y-You want me to be your secret wife?"

"Yes, no. Damnit, Ems. This is not going the way I thought it would. I want to marry you because I love you. I want to marry you for me, not for my family, not for my friends. I want to marry you because it is something that will give me peace. When I die, I want to do it knowing you were truly and fully mine."

"But you don't want to tell anyone?"

I hang my head in shame. "No. But it has nothing to do with you, please believe that."

"Your mother will never forgive us."

"Me. She'll never forgive me, no. But I'll be leaving her with the most perfect stand-in. She will love you for all your life."

"Broken-heart? Miss Fixem? It's time for dinner. Come on out, ya hear? You best be dressed. I don't need to see ya knocking nookies," she says, opening the door uninvited.

"GG, it's not a—"

"Oh, dear. I was wonderin' when this was goin' to happen Broken-heart."

"What the fuck are you talking about, GG? This isn't a good time. We're in the middle of something here."

"I see that, son. Take a seat."

I look from her to Emory and back again. Emory seems as though I just put her heart through a meat grinder, and maybe I did, but I need GG to get the hell out of here so I can fix this. Not seeing any way to get her out of here without man-handling her, I take a seat next to Ems.

"It hurts, don't it?"

I stare at GG in horror as Emory's shoulders shake with tears beside me.

"Some love hurts, but only the truest of loves can shred you to pieces like this."

"GG, I'm losing patience. Honestly, we need a minute." I've never lost my temper with an eighty-year-old woman before, but this one is seconds away from pushing me too far.

"I've been readin' yer cards Broken-heart—"

"Jesus Christ. Enough with these goddamn cards—"

"I'll allow one outburst like that from ya, but the next time I'll tan yer hide, no matter how bad your heart is, you hear me?"

How the fuck do I get rid of this woman? The insanity of it all has Emory in a state of shock.

"I'm going to tell you this, then I'll be on my way, you asshat. Miss Fixem here is going to be your knight in shining armor. I won't lie, it's gonna be a damn close one, but when you see that white light, you run the other goddamn direction and hold on for dear life. Our girl here will be the one to get your heart to beat again. Just you wait and see. Now, you two finish up here and then come eat. Dinner's gettin' cold."

I sit back on the bed and watch her shuffle away. When she closes the door behind her, I don't even know where to begin.

"I almost knocked out a crazy fucking eighty-year-old woman," I say in disbelief.

Emory stands in silence.

"Sweetheart?"

Holding up a hand, she doesn't turn around as she follows in GG's path. "I-I need some time, Preston. Please."

"Okay," comes out in a croak as I choke on my own sadness.

How did you fuck this up so badly?

CHAPTER 28

EMORY

"Then Claira-Rose thought she would be funny and wrapped a condom around Ted Johnson's tailpipe at the senior center. I'll be damned, that thing just got bigger and bigger, I swear it would have fit Monty's—"

"And that's where we call it a night, GG," Preston finally interrupts, standing to gather the dishes.

"Nah, you just leave those dishes be. I'll take care of them. You've got that fancy ass dishwasher in there, so it takes no time at all. I think the two of you should go have that chat now." GG stares at me as she speaks.

Preston was able to make small talk all throughout dinner, but it was strained. I, on the other hand, couldn't get a single bite down, let alone talk.

"Best idea you've had all night, GG." The tenseness of his voice proves his anguish over the past hour, too.

No sooner do I set my fork down does Preston grab my hand and literally drag me through his home.

With two hands on my shoulders, he gently presses me to sit on the bed.

"I know I fucked this all up, and I know I'm an asshole for—"

"Did you ask me to marry you so I can be your medical power of attorney?"

"It crossed my mind, at first, and I guess it's something we'll have to talk about when you become my wife." His confidence, usually so freaking sexy, is annoying as fuck right now. "But the more I thought about it, the more I know, without a doubt, you are what I want. It's not just about a power of attorney—"

"Then why, Preston? Why would you ask me to marry you?"

"Because I love you." He says it so calmly I'm beginning to wonder if I'm the crazy one here.

"You don't love me."

"I do."

"You can't."

"Why not?"

"Because you don't know me," I scream, finally losing my temper and not caring if GG hears us or not.

Grabbing the desk chair, he drags it to sit right in front of me.

"I know that I love you," he says with a grin. "I know that you're the most selfless person I've ever met. I know that you have always put everyone else before yourself. I know your favorite color is baby blue, that you hate cilantro, and that your perfect afternoon is curled up with your medical journals taking notes. You prefer dogs to cats even though you've never had either. You don't drink very often, but you like red wine, not white when you do—hoppy beer, not lagers. You prefer jeans to leggings but would be happiest in scrubs. You have two holes in each ear, even though you never wear earrings. Your right pinky toe slants a little to the right and never keeps polish on it. You check your sisters' checking accounts every week to make sure they have money. You volunteer every week at the infusion center even though you walk in those doors, knowing your heart will bruise a little more each time. Your right eyelashes curl a little higher than the left. You have a chickenpox scar behind your left ear—"

"Stop, Preston. Please, stop."

"I know you, Goldie, and I know I have never wanted anything more than to be your husband. This isn't some weird end-of-life shit. This is me, sitting here, begging you to give me what I never knew I wanted but now desperately need, with you."

My breathing is as erratic as my mind. He wants this. *He's dying.* If he wasn't dying, he wouldn't want me. *Does that matter?* Do I grant his wish? It's not really hurting me. Fuck me. These questions have been rattling through my brain for over an hour, and I can't come up with another argument for why I shouldn't.

Preston must sense my hesitation because he pulls out the ring again, this time forcing me to look at it.

"Emory Anne Camden, will you marry me?"

For the first time in hours, I allow myself a moment to pretend this is real, and I relax as a smile fights to break free. *I can give him this.* When he leaves me, I'll figure out how to pick myself up because I know devastation is in my near future.

"On two conditions."

Preston's head whips back in laughter. "I wouldn't expect anything less from you, Goldie. What are your ground rules this time, love?"

Love?

"There has to be an iron-clad, no exceptions pre-nup—"

"No. What is your other demand?"

I'm so shocked my words come out in a stutter.

"Wh-What do you mean no? This isn't negotiable, Preston. I will leave with everything I came here with, plus my fee for taking care of you until six weeks ago."

"Six weeks ago? What the hell are you talking about?"

"You stopped treatment, Preston. I'm not doing anything

for you now except being your fake girlfriend. You can't pay me for that."

"There is nothing fake about this, Emory." He stands suddenly, but it's his volume as he yells that has me pulling back onto the bed. "This is not fake for me, Emory. I don't know when it stopped, but this is us. This is real to me. Are you saying you don't feel the same way?"

"No, I-I just have to protect myself, Preston. You're dying. My heart is going to shatter when that happens. I can't deal with a legal fight on top of that when your family comes after me for taking advantage of the situation. No matter how much you want it to be different, that is what people are going to say."

"This has nothing to do with anyone but you and me," he says on a sigh, then takes a seat next to me. "My family isn't like that either, Emory. No matter what happens, they will always be there for you. I know you haven't known them long, but that is the one thing I am always sure of. They are going to take care of you."

"But—"

"I'll talk to my lawyer tomorrow and see what we can do. What's your other demand?" I can tell by his body language he is trying to appease me.

"Preston, I'm serious. I will not marry you without the prenup."

"Point made. What else?" he says curtly.

This is going to be an even bigger ask. I try to pull away before I speak, but he clamps his hand down on my thigh, holding me in place. Before I can say anything, he slides me closer and pulls me up, so I'm straddling him.

"Tell me," he demands.

"Y-You have to tell your family, Preston. Give them the chance to say good-bye to you properly. It isn't fair to them. You've had all these years to write them letters, to tell them how much you love them. Don't they deserve that same chance at closure?"

Tears roll down his face as he gives an almost imperceptible nod.

"Okay," he whispers, pulling me into a hug so tight it's hard to breathe. "But not until after Trevor's wedding. I don't want to ruin their day, especially since they are getting married on Thanksgiving. That's always been my mom's favorite holiday. Lanie and Dex aren't getting married until next month, so hopefully, we'll have time to get it all out and not ruin their day either."

"Okay."

Pulling back, he looks into my eyes. "Okay? Is that a yes?"

Nodding like a fool as tears stream down my face, I say, "It's a yes."

This feels more real, more honest, than anything I've ever done in my life.

~

"WAKE UP, Ems. We have a lot to get done today," Preston says with the energy of a little boy on Christmas morning.

Opening my eyes, I find that once again, I'm sprawled out on top of Preston.

"My little heat-seeking missile," he jokes. "Come on, a lawyer will be here in an hour for the prenup you're insisting on. Then we have to run to the town hall to pick up our marriage license, and don't forget our appointments at the bridal shop this afternoon."

He is way too excited.

"We are just going to the courthouse. I'm sure I have something I can wear, and you have rows and rows of suits. Is shopping really necessary?"

With a quickness he hasn't had in days, he rolls me onto

my back, pinning me with his hip and hands holding mine above my head.

"This is my one and only wedding. I want pictures, and I want us dressed up, so deal with it." With a quick kiss to my lips, he jumps out of bed. He has a spring in his step today, that's for sure.

The sense of pride I feel knowing that I am making him this happy messes with my head. GG calls him Broken-heart, but I realize that moniker will switch from him to me sooner than I'd like.

"You told your lawyer to make sure the prenup can never be contested, right? Everything that is yours will go to your family, or however it is you billionaires do stuff like that?"

I hate to ruin his mood, and this conversation always brings a temper, but I want to make sure he did as I asked. It's important to me, and I know it will be best for everyone in the long run.

His jaw ticks twice before he speaks. "Yes, everything will go to my family. I promised you, Ems. You don't have to keep asking. I will leave everything to my family."

"Okay, thank you." I know he hates the relief he hears in my voice, but I needed confirmation one more time.

CHAPTER 29

PRESTON

*O*kay, so I may have crossed my fingers one more time when I lied to Emory. It wasn't really a lie, though. I promised to leave everything to my family, and I will. Once we're married, she will be my family. I just made sure my attorney buried everything in so much legal jargon she'd never figure it out—until she needs to.

"Seth just left to bring GG to Dexter's house. We have to leave in about thirty minutes, okay?" I yell through the bedroom door where Emory is getting ready.

"Okay, I'll be ready soon. Are you sure you don't want to call anyone? Your brothers? The guys? Anyone?"

"I just want you today," I tell Emory. It's true. I just need her today.

I'm getting married today. And I'm dying tomorrow.

That goddamn voice won't give me a break. I will not let my future ruin today. Today is a day I never thought I'd get, and I am going to make every second count.

"Preston?" I hear my youngest brother, Ashton, yell.

Fuck. I'm standing here in a white tuxedo jacket and nowhere to hide. What the hell is he going to think? I don't have time for another thought because he walks straight to me, as pissed off as I've probably ever seen him. He pulls back a leg and nails me hard in the shin.

"What the fuck, you prick? Why would you do that?"

The next thing I know, I'm in a headlock, and Ashton is kicking at my legs again. He gets a few more shots in before he lets me go. When I stand, I see the tears in his eyes and know he found out the truth.

"I couldn't punch you in the goddamn face on your wedding day. Mom would never forgive me if you had a shiner in your wedding pictures. How could you do this, Preston? How could you hide this from us all this time?"

This time, he punches me right in the gut. It's been a long time since I've been sucker-punched, and I'm finding it harder than ever to catch my breath.

"You fucking selfish asshole. Why the hell wouldn't you tell us? This isn't fair, man. You can't die and leave us all here to pick up the pieces."

Taking a seat on the couch, I finally regulate my breathing but wonder if I should call Emory to take a look to be safe.

"Ash, I'm sorry." What the hell else can I say? I don't even know where to begin. "I'm sorry."

"You're sorry? You? Are sorry? Fuck you, Preston. You're just lucky I was smart enough to stay home and mourn this news like an adult before I came here; otherwise, mom would have lost two sons. One when I killed you and two when I ended up in jail for doing it. Why would you let us go through losing you just like we lost dad, without a chance to say good-bye? You, of all people, know how badly that fucked us all up. Why? It's all I've asked myself for days, so you had better have a goddamn good explanation for me."

"How did you find out about the wedding?"

"No way, Preston, you're not changing the subject. You asked me to help Emory. Just where did you think that road was going to lead once I started digging?"

Hanging my head, I sigh. "I knew there was that chance, but I figured her well being outweighed my need for secrets."

"Secrets? This is more than a secret, douche bag. Please explain to me how you go from finding out you're dying to thinking it's a good idea to keep it from your family for ten fucking years? Do you have any idea what kind of devastation this news is going to bring?"

"Ash, of course I know. But put yourself in my position. I was twenty years old. I didn't want to live in a bubble. I made this decision a long time ago because I wanted to live a normal life with all of you for as long as possible. Would you have climbed Mount Washington with me last year if you'd known about my heart?"

"What?"

"Do you think East would have gone scuba diving with me in the Dominican if he knew? What about Colton? Would he have done any of the shit he does to me on a regular basis if he'd known? I wanted to live with you, not watch from the sidelines. Does that make any sense?"

"You mother fucker."

"I'm sorry, Ash."

"You're going to die."

"I am."

He picks up the lamp in between us and sends it flying through the plate-glass window. I try not to react.

"And she knows?" he asks, nodding in the direction of the bedroom.

I look that way on instinct and become dizzy by the sight before me.

Emory stands in the doorway, holding her arms tightly at her sides like she is trying to hide from herself. Her blonde hair falls over her shoulders in waves. No matter how much I pushed, she wanted a simple white dress with ruffled sleeves that hits a few inches above her knees. She was right about the dress. She's so gorgeous, I lose all rational thought.

"Goldie, you ... you're beautiful." I can't form any other words. They all get caught in my throat.

"Hi, Ash." She waves uncertainly.

Regaining some composure, Ashton raises to kiss her hello. "You look beautiful, Emory. Welcome to the family."

Her eyes blink in rapid succession as she looks between the two of us.

"Ah, thank you? Pres, maybe I should give you guys a minute?"

"No," Ash and I say at the same time.

"Thank you for taking care of him as long as you have," Ashton says, softly. "You'll make a great addition to our fucked up family, Ems. Honestly, I couldn't ask for a better sister from this guy."

"Ash, I—"

"Don't we have a wedding to get to?" he says in a falsely cheerful tone.

"We?" Emory asks, as surprised as I am.

"You'll need a witness, right? And no one in this family will ever forgive you if we don't get some pictures. I'll be a witness and the photographer," he says, pulling a camera from his pocket.

Knowing we can't leave without clearing the air, I try again.

"Ash, I'm going to tell everyone ... I am. I just want to wait until after Trevor's wedding. I don't want to ruin their day."

He doesn't say anything but punches me really fucking hard in the arm. I know I deserve it, and I also know it's the best I'm going to get from him right now.

"Okay. Everyone ready?"

I chuckle when Ashton asks, "Can I walk you down the aisle, Ems?"

"Ah, I don't think you actually walk down an aisle in a courthouse wedding, but I appreciate the offer."

"Preston would be the one to get married in a court-house," he mumbles. "Oh, shit. I forgot. Here, consider this a wedding present."

Emory takes the large, manilla envelope he grabbed from the entryway table.

"What's this?" she asks, looking between us.

I have no idea, so I just shrug.

"That, Emory," Ashton makes a show of pointing to the envelope, "is everything you'll need to become Dr. Camden again."

Goldie wobbles on her sexy as hell shoes that have sparkly straps crossing every which way.

"Wh-What?"

Reaching for her, I hold her elbow to steady her. Ashton seems concerned about her as well because he grabs her other arm.

"Sorry, maybe I need to work on my delivery? Anyway, Dr. Terry should receive his copy any time now. You'll have no problem putting Donny the douche-canoe away with everything I pulled on him and that corrupt doctor of his. He really is sleazy, Ems. How the hell did you end up with that Jersey-Shore nut monkey? Never mind, don't answer that. The only thing I wasn't able to do was change your hearing date, so you'll have to wait for the official Dr. Camden name until January. We ready to go?"

I stare at my brother with pride. He was only fifteen when our father died. He had to lean on the rest of us for guidance. With four older brothers, plus Loki, he always had someone around, but I know we were no substitute for a father. Still, I'm so proud of the man he is today.

"Thank you, Ash—"

I don't finish because Emory has flung herself at him, and my body tenses with irrational jealousy.

"Okay, that's enough. We have a wedding to get to," I tell them as I pull Emory away.

"Ashton, h-how did you do this?"

"When you work with Loki as long as I have, you learn a few things," he says cryptically.

I only recently learned that Ash had been hacking for Loki since he was sixteen. Now, he runs the technology branch of Westbrook Enterprises, but I know he and Loki have something in the works on the side. I just haven't figured out what yet.

"Thank you, Ashton. Honestly, thank you so much," Emory sobs.

"Sweetheart, I'm so happy for you, but we really have to get going. Do you want to touch up your makeup, or should I let Ashton punch me so we can both have raccoon eyes in the pictures?"

"I vote for the punch," Ashton grumbles, and I roll my eyes in his direction.

"Oh, Preston. I'm going to get to be a surgeon again. I'm going to be Dr. Camden."

"I know, baby. I'm so happy for you."

"Just give me a second, and I'll grab my bag. I can fix my makeup in the car."

I watch as she practically bounces toward our bedroom. For once, all is right in my world.

All except my broken heart.

CHAPTER 30

I've never pictured my wedding. That's probably weird to admit, but I've never even thought about it. I would spend hours with Eli and Sloane as they planned their weddings down to the smallest of details, but I was always the guest. Sometimes, Sloane would decide I needed to be the mother of the bride. But it never occurred to me to think of a wedding in any other terms. I had goals, responsibilities, plans, and I only had myself to rely on. Even after living with Donny for so long, I never pictured myself in a white dress. Yet, here I am. Standing before the judge in the cheapest white dress I could find that Preston would agree to, preparing to exchange vows.

I may not have imagined a wedding, but Preston, in his white tux jacket and black pants, is every little girl's hero. His dark hair and blue eyes stand out against his tanned skin. He's striking.

"Never have I ever loved anyone more than I love you."

I feel the color drain from my face.

"Are we ready?" the judge asks.

"Yes, sir," Preston blurts. Happiness is radiating from him like the sun shining off a lake in summer.

Swallowing, I follow Preston's lead. "Yes, sir."

"Great. You have all the paperwork for me?" The judge, an older man with glasses perched on the end of his nose, stares down at us.

Preston shifts uneasily next to me. Turning to him, I see him giving me the side-eye as he hands the judge the papers. Unsure of what's happening, I look to Ashton, who just gives me a shit-eating grin. He's trying to mask the sadness of his brother's diagnosis, and he could easily fool most people, but I've seen death and dying too often in my brief career. I recognize the pain he is hiding.

What the hell is Preston doing?

"I understand young Preston here would like to say his own vows, but is just now springing this on his beloved. Is that correct?" the judge asks with a knowing smile. "That's a bold way to begin your life together, son."

Everyone in the courtroom chuckles around us, but I barely hear it. My ears are ringing.

"You wrote something?" I hiss.

"I did." Preston smiles.

"It's kind of tradition," Ashton interjects. "Our dad did the same thing."

My eyes snap to Preston's, and he shrugs sheepishly.

"You asshat. What the heck am I supposed to say?"

"Yes, Emory. You're supposed to say yes."

"Let's get you two hitched before we have a runaway bride. What do you say?"

Even the damn judge is a comedian?

As the judge goes through the formalities, my ears ring with Preston's words. *"Never have I ever loved anyone more than I love you."*

Holy shit. I'm getting married. My sisters aren't here. Why aren't my sisters here? Because it's not real, Emory. If Preston wasn't dying, he wouldn't need to marry you. I feel sick to my stomach. It all runs through my head in the course of three seconds. *But he said he loves me?* I'm scared to acknowledge that I'm falling in love with him, too, because I think my feelings are real.

Preston's deep, melodic, soothing voice brings me to the present.

"Emory, do you believe in love at first sight?"

"Ah—"

"Or should I walk by you again?" He can't say it without cracking a smile. It causes me to laugh away all the anxiety riddling my head. "Some people have that spark, that moment they meet and fall in love instantly. That wasn't us." Glancing around at all the people in the small room, he continues. "It wasn't us because you had a job to do, and I was so sure of a path I had to follow. Some pushy family members, unbeknownst to them, broke that mindset for me in the harshest of ways. It may not have been love at first sight, but it was love at first touch. That moment in your apartment, when I touched you for the first time, I swear God gave me a swift kick in the ass, and I've never been able to look at you the same again. I knew then but didn't want to admit it. You see—"

A single tear falls down his face. Unable to keep my hands to myself, I reach up to wipe it away.

"You see, our story isn't your typical one. I won't get to hold your hand as you give birth to our children. I won't be able to hold your hand on the beach when we're eighty. We may not get the lifelong love story most couples cherish, but we do have now, and I'll do everything in my power to give you a life's worth of love during our time together.

"I will forever be thankful that I am the one who gets to show you what it means to be loved, because from where I stand, you deserve the world. Fifty years from now, when you think of this day, I want you to remember my love for you is real. My heart is beating only for you. No matter your future, I can be at peace, knowing that you have felt my love.

"Never have I ever been happier than I am today. Never have I ever wanted anything more than to be your husband."

Through my tears, I see him reach for Ashton.

"With this ring, I promise to always watch over you." Preston slides a ring on my finger, and even through the cloud of emotion, I can see it sparkle.

"B-But I can't wear this. Everyone will—"

"Shh, sweetheart. It isn't your turn," he smiles. Taking my right hand in his, he slides on another ring, this one much smaller. A single band encrusted with pave diamonds. "Until we tell everyone you are Mrs. Westbrook, you'll wear this one. But, Goldie? As soon as we make an announcement, I want you to wear this ring so I can show everyone you're mine." He gives me a wink, and it feels like a knife to my heart. He's staked his claim. My heart can never belong to anyone else.

"Emory Anne Camden, do you take Preston Michael Westbrook to be your loving husband? To have and to hold until death do you part?"

"I-I doooo," I sob, unable to hold it together any longer. Ashton taps me on the shoulder and hands me a ring.

"And, Preston, do you take Emory to be your loving wife, to have and to hold until death do you part?"

"I do." He says it so confidently, so passionately, I can almost believe he means it.

"Then, by the power vested to me by the state of North Carolina, I pronounce you husband and wife. Congratulations. You may now kiss your bride."

I think I hear Preston growl right before he swoops in for the first kiss. No kiss will ever be the same. Preston may be the one who is dying, but he just ensured my heart will never beat for anyone else. It will go wherever he is.

"Ah-hem. Mr. and Mrs. Westbrook, I do need you to sign these documents to make it official," the judge says, interrupting Preston's assault.

Preston grabs the papers, adjusts them in a neat stack, and then signs as fast as he can move the pen across the paper. It actually makes me laugh. *Where does he think I'm going to go now?* Handing me the pen, I see his jaw is set tight.

"Do you think I'm going to run or something?" At least it gets a chuckle from Ashton.

"Nope, just want to make sure everything is in order," he tells me, grabbing the papers and handing them back to the judge. "Is everything ... everything is all set, right?"

We stare as the judge signs the last of the papers. "You're all set, son. I'll get these to the lawyer as you requested."

"Thank you, sir. Okay, Mrs. Westbrook, let's get out of here!"

"I didn't get to say any vows," I say as Preston pulls me through the courthouse with Ashton close behind.

"He did that on purpose, you know? Dad did the same thing to Mom. He knew if she had time to prepare something, he would be the blubbering mess. They didn't have a big wedding either, but he had convinced her to go with the standard-issue vows. He sprung it on her just like this."

I look to Preston for confirmation, but he won't make eye contact.

"You sneaky little jerk."

Giving my hand a squeeze, he smiles, and his hand might as well have been gripping my heart. "Is that any way to speak to your new husband, wifey?"

"George said he's ready to go whenever you are. Want me to drop you off?" Ashton asks.

"George? Why, where are we going?"

I stop short when Preston tugs on my hand. "I can't take you on a honeymoon today because Julia would have my balls if we missed their wedding, but you didn't think I'd just let this pass, did you?"

"Preston, we can't do this right now," I protest. He needs

all his energy for these two weddings if we have any chance of making it to December.

He silences me with a kiss.

"I know what your concerns are," he whispers, "but this is something I want for me—for us. This is important. Let me have this night with you, please. I packed our clothes. We'll be back tomorrow in plenty of time for the rehearsal dinner. Please, Goldie, for us."

"For us," I agree.

"I won't let you down, Ems. I promise."

"You never do, Pres. And you never cease to amaze me either."

CHAPTER 31

PRESTON

*W*e land in Charleston just before dinner. Emory was quiet on the flight, but I feel a shock of pride every time I catch her staring at my ring on her finger. I hate that she can't wear it for long, but that's what the second ring is for. *Will she wear them when I'm gone?*

I feel insurmountable guilt if I think about Ashton too long. I'm leaving him alone in his grief, asking him to keep it to himself. I know it isn't fair. *It's another selfish dick move I've made lately.* I'm his older brother, I'm supposed to protect him, yet I'm selfish and here with Emory instead.

"Where are we going?"

"Ah-ah, Mrs. Westbrook, it's a surprise."

"I've never really liked surprises."

"Have you ever had a good one?"

"Probably not. Surprises rarely end well for me."

The car slows to a stop, and I flash a satisfied grin. "Then I'm glad I can have another first, Goldie. Come on, we have a reservation."

I offer my hand as she steps out of the car, then snicker at the confusion written all over her flawless face. She glances left, then right, and I know why. We are on an exclusive strip of beach. There are no restaurants or hotels here, only private homes. I'm sure this isn't what she was expecting.

"Who lives here?"

"Tonight? We do," I tell her. "Come on, the chef is waiting." She allows me to drag her behind me. I've noticed it's become a habit when I'm excited or nervous—me in front, holding her close and keeping her protected.

The house is enormous, and you have to climb at least fifteen steps to reach the front door. Though I can't see the ocean, I can smell it. The salty brine of tide fills my nose. The sun is beginning to set, and I can tell from the front steps it falls behind the ocean.

I'm not even to the top step when the front door opens. "Mr. and Mrs. Westbrook, we are so happy to have you here at Hearts Landing. Come in, please, I'll show you to the peak."

"Thank you," I tell our host politely while giving Emory a smile I hope conveys every feeling I can't express right now. *How can this woman's presence elicit so many emotions?*

We follow the woman who introduces herself as Mrs. Archer, the home's caretaker, through the house and up another set of stairs. On the upper floor of the home, she stops at a twisting iron staircase that spirals all the way to the ceiling.

"You go first, sweetheart, but take off your shoes. I don't want your heel to get stuck in the grates of the stairs."

I hold out my hand as Emory removes one, then two high heels. Mrs. Archer happily takes them from me.

"I'll just place these in your room." She turns and leaves us standing in front of floor-to-ceiling windows overlooking the ocean.

The sea is visible from every angle. Ems is fidgety and twirling a lock of her hair around her finger as she takes it all in. *She's overwhelmed.*

"We need to go up, Goldie," I nudge her. "Your surprise is upstairs."

One last glance around, and she takes the steps cautiously. It's a staircase out of a fairy tale, the one that has the princess locked in the castle. This area of the house is why I chose to come here. Every bride deserves a little fairy tale on their wedding day. Even if ours ends with a grim finale. *Stop thinking like that. Live in the moment, asshole.* They have propped the door open at the top of the stairs, so she takes a step through.

"Oh, Preston!" Her hands fly to her mouth as she looks around. "What did you do?"

Wrapping my arms around her waist, I place my chin on her head and sigh.

"I can't take you to Italy for our honeymoon, Ems, so I did the next best thing. I brought Italy to you." My voice is so thick with emotion that she tries to turn in my arms, but I hold her still. "I wish I could take you there and watch you stomp grapes, then taste the wine from your lips. I wish I could feed you pasta in the winery as you take in the orchards. I wish I could take you, Emory, but I'm happy knowing you'll go. Next year—"

I have to pause to compose myself, and she again attempts to face me, but it's hard enough to get this next part out. I can't look in her eyes as I say it.

"Next year, you'll spend today in Italy with your sisters. The crazy family you have inherited will also meet you there, and you'll all celebrate life together. If there is one thing I can give you, Emory, it's a promise that you'll never be alone again. You and your sisters will always be a part of my family."

"Pres—"

"This is my wedding gift to you, Goldie. You'll all need each other, and it makes me happy to know that one year from today, you'll all be together in the one place you always wanted to visit most in this world. Please don't fight me on it. Mona has worked triple time to get it all planned in the last forty-eight hours."

"Poor Mona," she laughs. She doesn't even know half of it. I had to use half my office staff to pull all this off.

"Emory, welcome to your winery."

"My what?"

Letting her go, she spins in place. We are on the roof that overlooks the ocean, but you can only hear it from where we stand. Everywhere she looks is filled with rows and rows of vines.

"What is this?"

"These, sweetheart, are grapevines from Italy. Every year you will receive a barrel of wine that's being bottled in very small batches just for you. This," I say, gesturing around us, "is Golden Ems."

I'm not sure what to expect, and the longer she stays silent, the more I worry that I went overboard. Without warning, she launches herself at me, and I hold her tight.

"This is too much, Preston. Why would you do this?"

"So you'll remember me, Ems. On your worst days in the OR, on your best days, and when you fall in love, I want you to remember this day." My fucking voice is like sandpaper.

"Oh, God, Preston. I could never forget you. How could you even think that?"

"Because life is going to move on, Ems. I know that." I'm beyond trying to hold back the sadness that laces my voice. "I even want that for you, but for now, I just want you to be mine."

"I am yours, Preston. I—"

"Sir? Are you ready for the first course?"

We're interrupted by a man in a white chef's coat. I raise my brows in Emory's direction, silently asking if she wants to continue, but she looks away.

"That would be great," I tell our chef, Miguel.

We eat at a bistro table set for two at the edge of the roof, where the only thing you can see is the sun setting over the bluest of oceans. I force tomorrow out of my mind and focus on the here, the now. I didn't hold back when I planned this, and I want my Goldie to enjoy it all. Course after course is served, and I only wish I could be with her when she experiences the real thing for the first time.

"Dance with me." It isn't a question. I need to hold her. As soon as I stand, I take her hand in mine. Holding her in my arms, Ed Sheeran's "Photograph" plays through the speakers.

"You picked our wedding song, too?" she asks while laughing.

"Yes." I can't elaborate. I just move, and she glides along with me. With her head on my chest, I hope she's listening to the words. As I sing, "You won't ever be alone," her tears soak into my white dress shirt, and I know she hears all I want to convey.

"Preston?"

"Yeah, baby?"

"Can I make my vow now?"

Her request has the hairs on the back of my neck standing at attention. "It's a little late for that, Goldie, but go for it."

"I vow to keep you with me always, like a photograph, in my heart."

I feel my feet shuffle unnaturally, and Emory immediately searches my face.

Fuck.

"Preston?" Her voice tells me Dr. Camden is entering the building.

"I-I'm okay, Goldie. Maybe, just, maybe I should sit down."

"Is there another way off this roof?" She's all business. Turning to the chef who has been standing off to the side, she barks, "Is there an elevator up here?"

"Yes, miss. In the corner," he points, but she is already leading me that way.

"Are you dizzy?"

"No."

"Heart palpitations? Blurred vision?"

"Emory," my voice is more powerful than I feel, "today is not the day. I just need to sit down for a bit, I think."

Today may not be the day, but it's coming soon, and we both know it with heartbreaking certainty.

CHAPTER 32

EMORY

*P*reston has not stopped apologizing or berating himself for last night. Once I could locate the bedroom, I hooked him up to the ECG, but he fell asleep halfway through my exam. I spent my wedding night realizing I am in love with the man I just married, and he will not live to see our first Christmas together.

With a sadness I never knew existed, I forwarded the results to Dr. Terry, who just delivered them to Preston over a video call. I sit, barely breathing on the edge of the bed while he sits in the chair five feet away. He is staring, but not truly seeing me. The phone is still in his hand, but he isn't holding it, and it slips from his fingers.

"Preston?"

"We should call Ash and tell him to get ahold of Loki. If anyone can do that, I'm willing to be it's him," he is speaking on autopilot. "My lawyer's name is Ben Simmons. You'll need to call him when it happens. He knows what to do and will have everything to you within hours. On the way home today, we should call the chef and have them prepare. We can have everyone to the house for brunch after Trevor's wedding. That's probably the soonest I can tell everyone without ruining the next forty-eight hours—"

"Preston!" My voice is terrifying to my own ears, so I'm not surprised when he snaps to attention, standing immediately he is in front of me before I can blink.

"Sweetheart." It's a pained whisper as he sinks to the carpet before me. Cradling my face in his powerful hands, we lock eyes, and I see an eternity pass between us. "I'm so sorry. I've spent my adult life avoiding love. What kind of monster slaps me in the face with it only to rip it away so soon? I never meant to hurt you like this. My life, our life has spiraled in ways I could never have predicted. Everything happened so fast. Part of me wishes I could turn back time—"

"What? No. No, Preston, please don't say that," I cry.

"The other part of me—" His shoulders hunch over. His pain escapes in a sound that will haunt all of my nights. "The other part of me wouldn't change a thing because I got to know this girl, this really fucking amazing girl with so much love and kindness in her soul. I got to know you, Emory, and love you the way you deserve. Please, please, promise me you'll find someone to love you as I do. Never settle for anything less than perfection because that's what you are, Emory. You're perfect, never let anyone tell you differently."

"Why do you do this?"

"Do what, Goldie?"

"Stop trying to take care of me. This isn't about me, Preston. You don't have to manage me. I'm stronger than I look."

He cracks a smile.

As I sit here ugly crying before this man, I look anything but strong. Damnit, I am, though. *Pull your shit together, Emory.*

"You're the strongest woman I know."

"Then, please, tell me what I can do."

Sadly, he shakes his head no. "I'll need your strength to get through this wedding." He swallows loudly. "And I'll need you after—after when I have to say good-bye to everyone I love." My handsome, powerful man breaks.

Resting his head in my lap, I hold him, smoothing back his hair as grief crashes into his body.

"I had plans, Ems. Plans for everyone. I was supposed to take care of everyone. I didn't want to leave a mess. I wanted everything to be easier than when my dad died. I-I failed everyone."

"Oh, Preston. That isn't your responsibility. People are going to be a mess, but not because you didn't take care of everything. Not because you didn't plan or because you didn't organize things. They'll all be a mess because they love you. They will be a mess because they lost someone far too young, someone who had so much good left to do in this world. But—" I have to pause as more tears flow. "The thing about your family, Preston, is they'll take care of each other because that's what you would have wanted. They'll carry each other through on the hard days. They'll remember you together and love you forever."

There is a loud knock at the door, and I know he has used all the energy he can at the moment. "Is that the car?"

"Yes," he sighs.

Kissing him softly, I pull away. "I'll tell them we'll be a few minutes, stay here. I'll be back to help with everything."

He nods, and I see the exhaustion consuming him. *This wedding is going to be the end of him, and he knows it.*

THE REHEARSAL IS as crazy as I would expect after getting to know this group. Lanie's daughters, Harper and Sara, refuse to walk down the aisle. Harper won't even leave Preston's lap, which has been a blessing in disguise. He sits in the back, cradling her, conserving his energy.

"Okay, Preston. We have upgraded you from groomsman to flowerman," Julia, more manic than ever, yells across the room.

"Ah, what does that entail?" I ask hesitantly.

"Don't worry, he just has to walk the girls down the aisle since apparently, they haven't learned the art of not giving a shit from their buddy, Charlie." I look in the direction she is gesturing to find Trevor chasing the naked little boy around the room, trying desperately to get a pull-up on him.

Julia's parents, Mimi and Pete, are in another corner with Lanie's two newest additions. GG is with Dexter's oldest son, Tate, teaching him a card game that is probably highly inappropriate for his age.

Two of Preston's brothers sit at a table arguing over an NFL player while their mother, Sylvie, is attempting to calm Julia down. Ashton is hiding behind a pillar just outside of the room, talking animatedly on the phone. *I hope he can reach Loki.* Turning in place, I notice Lexi is missing.

I'm searching the room for her when I catch myself twirling the ring on my right hand with my thumb absentmindedly. I search for Preston and find him watching the movement as well. A sad smile graces his tired face. *Lexi is probably in the bathroom. I'll find her at dinner.*

Preston's eyes never leave my hand as I cross the room and slide into the seat next to him. Laying my head on his shoulder, I memorize his scent. I'm trying to remember everything, so I take out my phone and take a selfie—my head on his shoulder, his arm around mine. I feel a teardrop land on my cheek. Glancing up, I see it in his eyes.

"Can I borrow a kiss?" The lift of his lip is another splinter in my quickly shattering heart.

"Borrow a kiss? Do you promise to give it back?" I ask with a small smile.

"Always, sweetheart." Repositioning the sleeping Harper, he kisses me tenderly.

He just keeps chip, chip, chipping away.

"Yes!" Dexter yells, startling the crap out of Harper and me.

Sheepishly, he takes the crying little girl. This time in a stage whisper, he tells Lanie, "MEP is in motion!"

Preston stiffens beside me. "Let's get you two knuckleheads through your weddings before you go into full Prince-Charming mode, okay?"

"Oh shit, please tell me you'll include us in the MEP messages this time?" Colton whines.

"Yeah, I wouldn't mind having Emory as a sister," Ashton adds conversationally, but we know better, and my body flushes with guilt.

"What's MEP?" I ask, looking around at the crowd now gathering around us.

"Make Emory Preston's."

Toggling between Preston and the group, I shrug. "Too late, I'm already his."

CHAPTER 33

PRESTON

*T*revor's wedding is small, but I'm thinking the children outnumber the adults. I've been holding Harper for the last hour. She's still a tiny little thing, but it's unseasonably warm. Scratch that, it's fucking hot, and she's getting heavy.

"You good with the title of flowerman?" Trevor asks, kissing Harper on the head.

"Totally. We'll be the best damn flower couple this wedding has ever seen. Isn't that right, Harps?"

"Geez, can you not call her Harps?" Dexter comes up behind me. "It sounds like you're calling my daughter herps."

"That fucking disgusting."

"Preston!" they both scold in unison.

"Sorry, Harper. I don't have the dad filter these two have."

"Yet," Trevor smirks, nodding toward Emory.

I have to swallow down my reaction.

All the girls are wearing deep red, silky, form-fitting gowns. Emory has thin little straps at her shoulders and a deep V-cut in the front that she fought Julia over. I know she feels too exposed, but I lose my breath every time I see her.

"Right."

"I know we haven't had a lot of time to talk, but are you ever going to tell us what's going on with her?" Dexter asks. "You know, we could probably help. We said no more secrets, remember? If something's going on, tell us. I don't want to be forced to knock you out, too."

"Hey, hold up. You did not knock me out. You just got a couple of good shots in," Trevor says defensively. "But I'm with Dex. We'll both take our shot at you if it comes to that."

"Good to know. Has anyone heard from Loki? This isn't like him. He wouldn't miss this." I hate to be the wet blanket, but Ash hasn't been able to reach him, and I'm worried. Judging by the looks exchanged, we're all concerned.

"No, and Seth isn't giving anything away. I agree, though, something big is happening because he wouldn't miss this unless something was stopping him. Or someone—"

"Julia's just about ready," Emory says, thankfully cutting our conversation short. "She wants you two to go to the front, and Pres, you and Harper can come with me."

Dex gives his daughter a quick kiss. "Be good for Uncle Preston."

I watch as they walk toward the altar.

"Are you okay?" Ems asks.

"Yup, let's make this a wedding no one will ever forget."

She nods but doesn't answer. Instead, she blinks rapidly as I take her hand and guide her toward the guesthouse where Julia waits.

I FEEL confident that the chaos that follows our group around is not normal behavior, especially for a wedding. GG is in the front row, shushing everyone, and we're in the back with a gaggle of children who want to be anywhere but here.

"Uncle Preston, we have a problem."

Turning, I find Tate standing with his hands on his hips and a severe expression on his face. He looks just like Dexter. *Would my son have looked like me?*

I try not to laugh, but he looks like he is about to school a boardroom full of toddlers in his little suit. "What's up, buddy?"

He adjusts his hair, then frowns. He really is Dexter's boy. This time I do chuckle.

"Well, have you seen what my charges are doing?"

"Your charges?"

"Yeah, that's what Nannie Sylvie calls them."

"You mean your siblings?" *This kid.*

"Yes," he says, exasperated. "How am I supposed to get them all down the aisle? Charlie won't even keep his pants on. He peed on the roses like a dog. He peed, Uncle Preston, *peed*. In public."

Placing a hand on his shoulder, I get him to look at me. "It's going to be just fine, okay, buddy? I promise. I'm going to rock this flowerman role with the girls, so all you have to do is pull the boys down in the wagon. We've got this." I give him a fist bump like Lanie always does, and I see him relax. *She was the best thing that ever happened to this kid.*

"Yup, okay. We've— Oh, no."

I follow Tate's finger and see that Charlie has become a handful. Glancing back at Tate, I see the poor kid pale.

"I-I have to get him in the wagon?"

"Er, you know what, buddy? Change of plans. Let's go get Emory to carry him. She can hand him off to GG at the end if she needs to."

"Oh, thank goodness. That's a great idea. Let's go tell her. Oh, I almost forgot. Here, this is for you. Keep it in your pocket. Love you, Uncle Pres." He hands me a blue playing card and trots off to find Emory.

Turning it over, I see it's a king of hearts. "Keep it in your pocket," Tate yells again, pointing to my jacket.

Confused and running out of time, I do as he asks, then I follow the crew to line up.

"Tate's taking his job very seriously, huh?" Emory whispers as we watch him walk down the aisle, pulling a little red wagon with his baby brothers strapped in and holding onto the ring pillow.

"Best ring bearer I've ever seen."

"You're up, handsome. Good luck, flowerman." She gives me a quick kiss, and I try to soak up some of her strength. With Sara clinging to my pant leg and Harper in my arms, I take my first step and decide to go all out.

"Hey, Sara?" Little blue eyes look up at me, and I stick out my tongue to blow her a raspberry. "Can you do this?" I ask, taking some of Harper's petals and throwing them in the air. Both girls stare at me with wide eyes, then squeal in delight as they start making noises with their tongues and throwing petals, mostly at me, but they're happy.

I really get into character, and we flamboyantly float down the aisle, merrily sticking out our tongues. The cheers and laugher from family and friends eggs them on with every step. *This is the life I'm going to miss out on.* The thought makes me pause. Rubbing a hand over my heart, I continue moving so Emory doesn't notice.

I should have known better. As soon as we reach the end, I hand off the girls to the grandmothers and take my spot next to Dexter but feel Emory boring a hole into the back of my head.

"It's a good thing Julia couldn't see that display, you know?" Dexter whispers.

I can't help the smile that crosses my face. "She will definitely have my balls for that one. But we made it without any tears, right?"

"No tears until Jules watches that video," Trevor chimes in.

"She won't be able to forget it, that's for sure." My smile catches in my throat at the concern I see in Emory's face across the aisle. My eyes never leave hers, and I miss the entire ceremony daydreaming about what-ifs.

CHAPTER 34

"*Have* you seen Lexi?"

Craning his neck, Preston peers around the room. "No, but now that you mention it, Easton's missing, too."

He doesn't seem happy about that.

"Why are you so adamant they're bad for each other?" I ask out of curiosity.

"Listen, I love my brother, but since my dad died, Easton has been the grumpiest mother fucker I've ever met. He would do anything for you, but he's an asshole. And Lexi? I just think she has been through enough shit. She doesn't need his baggage, too."

"Can I have all my girls on the dance floor, please? Okay, their partners can come, too," a slightly tipsy Jules yells happily into the microphone.

"Speak of the devils," I tell Preston, nodding toward the entrance where a very pissed off Lexi just entered. Easton right behind her, looking murderous.

"Fuck," Preston and Colton say in unison, having both seen the same thing.

"You better go cut in," Preston tells his younger brother.

"Get Lexi on the dance floor and tell East to cool the fuck off for a while."

Preston and I are making our way to the dance floor when I hear, "Not fucking today, Colt. Back off."

Turning my head, I see Easton dragging a pissed off Lexi behind him, trying not to cause a scene.

"Is dragging your woman a Westbrook trait?" I laugh.

"Apparently."

"Yay! Look at how gorgeously amazeballs all my ladies look tonight."

"Oh boy, she's more than tipsy," I whisper.

"He's got her," Preston says, pointing to Trevor, who stands off to the side, admiring his new wife.

I notice Preston is giving East the side-eye. He's holding onto Lexi's hand in a vice grip, and it doesn't seem like she's going anywhere anytime soon. *What the hell is going on with those two?*

"So, now they all have red dresses on, and we can finally dance to 'The Lady in Red' by Chris De Burgh, just like when we were kids," Julia is still babbling. "Maestro, cue it up." She giggles. Julia is living her best life.

Preston wraps his massive arms around my waist and pulls me into him. We are so close I can feel his shaft twitch. He is in no condition for anything, but apparently, no one told his dick that.

"Can you do telekinesis?" he asks. "Because you've been making a part of me move all night without even touching it."

My head falls back in laughter. "Oh my God. Okay, I take it all back. That is the worst pick-up line of all time."

We fall in step with the slow melody the band is playing. I remember this song. It always made me cry as a kid. But listening to it with Preston singing the words into my ear is my undoing. Trying to hide my tears, I bury my face in his chest.

"I'll never forget how you looked tonight," he sings.

We dance in slow circles, the rest of the wedding party fading into the background. Our movements get slower and slower, but I don't notice until Preston's grip loosens on my hips. I glance up just in time to see the moment his eyes glass over. "I love you," he whispers, then goes down, taking me with him.

"No. No. No. No. No," I'm yelling before we even hit the ground. "You promised you wouldn't do this in my arms, Preston. You promised me, goddamn it."

His family is surrounding us, everyone yelling at once.

Dr. Camden

"Lexi, get my bag and the small black bag under the chair." I undress Preston, where he lay. "Dexter, call 911. Easton, get my cell phone and call Dr. Terry. Ashton, c-call Ben Simmons. Tell him to bring everything Preston requested, as well as all the journals and folders under the window seat in the master bedroom, to the hospital immediately." By the time I am done barking orders, Lexi is throwing my bags at me.

"What the hell is going on?"

"Is he going to be okay?"

"What's wrong with him?"

All valid questions I block out and focus on one thing—Preston's broken heart.

"What is she doing?" Sylvie screams as I open the black bag and place the portable CPAP around Preston's nose and mouth.

I listen to his heart; it's weak but beating. With his latest ECG, I know what I'm dealing with. Ripping off my heels, I climb over Preston, dragging the small bag with me.

Sylvie grabs me by the shoulders. "Please, tell me what's going on?" she cries.

I don't have time to stop.

"Ash, get your mother off me, now." My voice is harsh even to my own ears.

After unrolling the sterilized equipment, I roll up his sleeve and pray the months of treatment haven't left me without any options. With practiced movements, I insert the IV and attach the drip just as the paramedics arrive.

"Patient, Preston Westbrook, thirty-year-old male, cardiomyopathy positive. CPAP applied, Nitroglycerin administered intravenously at 10 mcg/min titrated."

We're all moving with the paramedics who have lifted Preston onto the gurney.

"Are you his doctor?" a paramedic asks.

"One immediate family member allowed in the ambulance," another tells Sylvie.

"I'm his mother," she says, but Ash holds her back.

"Emory's a cardiac surgeon—and his wife. She'll go."

At my back, the collective gasp causes my spine to tingle, but one look at Preston's ashen face, and I put my mask firmly back in place.

"Let's go. East, Dr. Terry's ETA?"

"Two hours. The helicopter is landing at MMH now."

Running barefoot beside Preston, I follow the EMT's to the ambulance. It's not a long ride to the hospital, but I do what I can. Once we arrive, I'm held back. No longer Dr. Camden since I have no credentials. The doctors here only see me as Emory Westbrook, the patient's wife.

"Mrs. Westbrook? The rest of your family has arrived. Would you like me to take you to them? Or would you like someone to wait here with you?" the nurse asks kindly.

God, the questions they must have. I know I'm the one who has to give them answers, but I'm the coward that can't face them yet. Instead, for three hours, I sit in a room alone, chanting, "Not now, Preston. Please, not now."

I never told him I loved him.

~

I'M NOT sure how long I sit there, but a coldness that shouldn't exist in a soul washes over me.

"Emory?" My head whips to the door to see the tear-stained face of Sylvie Westbrook, followed by Dr. Terry.

She runs at me, and I prepare for a beating I'd sure want to dole out if I were in her position, but squeak in surprise as she wraps me in the tightest hug I've ever received.

Through her own pain, she does what mothers do, she comforts. With my face in her hands, we stare at each other while tears flow freely.

"Oh, my dear. I bet you were a beautiful bride," she says.

Speaking at the same time, I say, "I'm so sorry."

We sit in the private room for what seems like hours. Dr. Terry leaves to extract some scrubs for me, and then we wait some more. We both know the outcome. Sylvie has lived it, and I've studied it. Yet here we are, waiting on a miracle.

CHAPTER 35

EMORY

*S*ylvie lays with her head on my shoulder, having cried herself to sleep a few hours ago. She'd been the one to tell Preston's family and friends the news with Dr. Terry. I stayed back with Preston, ever the cowardly lion afraid to face the ones I've deceived.

As far as I know, they're all still in the main waiting area even though hospital staff tried to remove them. After making a few calls to crucial hospital benefactors, they decided it was not in the hospital's best financial interest to remove eight of the East Coast's wealthiest people.

A knock on the door has my heart racing, but I'm surprised to see an older, familiar face enter. My change in posture wakes Sylvie, who recognizes the man immediately.

"Ben, thank you for coming."

"Ben? Ben Simmons? Preston's attorney?"

"Your attorney now, too," he replies.

"B-But you're the judge who married us."

"Yes, ma'am, I am. It was a beautiful ceremony."

"Ben here did the same thing to me when he married Preston's dad and I," Sylvie huffs.

"That's true. Still, I'm very sorry we're here again," he tells us.

Sylvie sniffles but says nothing.

"I understand they'll be bringing him to a room soon, is that correct?"

"Yes, they said it would be about an hour," I tell him.

"I suggest we go through the paperwork now then if that's okay? That way, you can spend as much as possible focusing on Preston."

"I'll … I'll just step out so you can have some privacy. I'll be in the hall in case there is any news."

"Wait, Emory. You need to be a part of this conversation," Ben says.

"Oh, no. I'm all set. I knew that we wouldn't have much time together, so we fixed the prenup accordingly. Everything that's Preston's will stay his, or yours, I'm assuming," I explain to Sylvie. "I only agreed to marry him if he promised to leave everything to his family. And really, I'm having a hard time talking about him like he isn't here. He is still here, so I'll let you two handle this."

Sylvie looks at me kindly.

"Emory, he is leaving everything to his family. As soon as you married him, you became his family, and he changed his will."

Sylvie laughs softly beside me.

"No, he didn't. We haven't even been married for three days, and I've been with him every minute since then." My hand flies to my mouth as I remember Preston's nervous ticks at the courthouse.

"He had them with the marriage license. You both signed them. You're now his legal power of attorney, wife, and sole beneficiary.

"No, thank you," I say, standing suddenly. "Sylvie, I'll let you know when Dr. Terry comes back." Opening the door, I step out into the sterile, antiseptic-scented hallway. I take a deep breath, then allow my body to slide down the wall.

The door opens a few moments later. Sylvie exits and joins me on the floor in a dress that may have cost more than my first car.

"I don't think you can just say 'no thank you' to legal papers you've already signed, hun." She bumps her shoulder with mine, and I try to regulate my breathing. "You know, Preston has always been the spitting image of his father. High-handed, charming, caring, and a real asshole when he wants to be."

A shocking sound comes from deep in my throat.

"This will get harder before it gets easier, you know?"

"I know," I say quietly.

"And Preston is nothing if not thorough. If he wanted you to have something, he probably made it nearly impossible for you to walk away from it."

"I really hope not, Sylvie. I never wanted his money, I swear."

"Oh, Emory. Don't be silly. I have eyes and ears. I also have a bullshit radar that goes off the second a gold digger comes within a hundred yards of my boys. I know you were never looking for a handout. Preston wouldn't have fallen as hard as he did, as fast as he did if you were."

"We've had a pretty messed up relationship," I admit.

"I wouldn't expect anything less from Preston."

"I ... he said he loves me."

"Of course he does. I know my son, Emory. If you're sitting here thinking he married you just to make it easier on us when someone has to make that life or death decision, I might have to smack you."

"What?" I gasp.

Sylvie shakes her head. "Emory, if Preston married you just so you could make that decision, he wouldn't have gone to such lengths to ensure you were provided for."

"I don't think I ever told him I loved him. I was, I was—"

"You're scared," Sylvie supplies.

"I think I was."

"But you're not anymore."

"And now it's too late," I cry again.

"It's never too late, honey. It's never too late to tell someone you love them. We'll do this together, okay? Let's get through the next few days, and I'll support whatever you want to do about the rest. But I hope Preston told you that you have inherited a crazy family for life because that is not something any of us will ever budge on."

Somehow, this man, my husband, has done the impossible. He has made sure I'll always have someone to lean on, even if it can't be him. Sylvie and I sit there, waiting for Dr. Terry for an eternity. When he finally rounds the corner, I attempt to pull myself together. I have to remember, Sylvie is losing a son, and everyone else that will come through that door is losing the most amazing man I've ever met in my life.

"Emory? Sylvie? I can take you to him now. As Emory knows, we have done everything we can, Sylvie. I'm so sorry you must go through this again."

She doesn't reply.

Taking her hand in mine, I give it a solid squeeze. "We'll get through this together, Sylvie." Then, just as Preston has always done with me, I take a step forward, dragging her with me, trying to protect her, shield her, comfort her. Behind me, I can hear Ben shuffling papers, trying to keep up.

We enter Preston's room, and try as I might, I cannot keep the Dr. Camden shield in place.

"He's so gray," Sylvie comments.

"The body shuts down in stages, Sylvie. It preserves its strength for what's essential. He has devices helping for now, but Preston was very adamant about not being kept alive on them indefinitely."

"Will he wake again?" she asks just above a whisper.

I don't dare to make eye contact, my own tears forming a river down the sides of my face.

"I never say never, Sylvie. But we have placed him in a medically-induced coma so you all can say good-bye, per his request. Medical evidence suggests, when these are removed, his body will continue to shut down organ by organ," Dr. Terry explains.

"Never have I ever loved anyone more."

Ben sets up in the corner as Sylvie and I each take a seat at Preston's side. After a while, Sylvie stands.

"I need to get his brothers," she tells me. "They need to spend some time with him as well."

"Of course. Would you like me to get them?"

"No, Ems. You stay with your husband. I have a feeling you have a lot to say."

I nod and feel sweat trickle down my spine. Sylvie walks toward the door with hunched shoulders and a hand holding her stomach. As soon as it shuts, I hear her sob. *Oh, Sylvie.* I rise immediately to go after her, but Ben places a hand on my arm.

"I've known Sylvie for a long time. I'll look after her. She's going to need you for this next part," he says, pointing toward all the journals he piled on the side table. "And Preston wanted to make sure the two of you were alone when I gave you this."

Glancing down to his hands, I see an envelope with my name written in Preston's scratchy print. Sadness rolls through my body like an avalanche. It starts in my stomach and spirals until I feel it from my toes to my ears, and my body shakes violently.

Ben gently guides me to the edge of Preston's bed, where I sit beside him. The letter is then pressed into my palm, and I watch Ben retreat in search of Sylvie.

What did you do, Preston?

My eyes search the room for answers but find none. Eventually, my gaze lands on Preston. *My husband.* Lying here in this bed, he seems so small, so weak, it cuts my heart to its core.

"You're supposed to be the strong one. You promised you wouldn't do this in my arms, Preston. You promised me."

No longer giving a shit about hospital rules, I slide my body up against his. Laying my head on his chest, I listen to the beeping of monitors echoing his weakened heart. Beep. Beep. Beep. Three cycles of his labored breathing later, I break down. With my head buried in his chest, I cry harder than I have ever done in my life.

"Never have I ever loved anyone more."

"God, Preston, I'm so sorry. I-I never even told you I loved you. I know it was all pretend. None of this would have happened if you weren't sick, but somewhere along the lines, I fell in love with you for real. I was just too scared to tell you. I'm so sorry," I wail.

Wiping my nose with the back of my sleeve, I notice I'm still clutching his letter.

Can I do this? I have to, right? I promised him.

Rolling a little onto my back, I slide my finger under the seam of the heavy cardstock envelope. Removing the papers, it takes six tries to get through his written words.

My Dearest Mrs. Westbrook, My Goldie, My Ems,

You have made the last year and a half of my life something worth living. No matter what happens in the future, always know that you're my hero. I know reading this, you're pissed off. I've deceived you a few times recently, but it all came from my broken heart, so please don't hold it against me.

Let's start with the tangible. You're pissed off about the money, but here's the thing. When you have as much money as my family does, you can do whatever the hell you want with it, and I'm giving it to you. Knowing you, you're also worried that your new family will think you're a gold digger. That won't ever happen. They love you and will always stand by you because you're my wife. They have their own money. They don't need ours, so you can cross that off your defense list as well. It's yours now. Ben has spent hours ensuring there was no way it can be refuted, just like you asked. So, you see, Goldie, I didn't really lie to you. You made me promise to leave everything to my family, and I did. You are my family.

You'll also know by now that you are my medical power of attorney. I did this because I know you'll do as I ask, no matter how hard it is. I'm sorry to put you in this position. I truly am, but you're not alone. Ben has all my wishes in writing. He will help guide you. It's important to me everyone has a chance to say good-bye, but this is not how I want to exist.

I also have one last request, and I know I'm asking the impossible of you here. I only hope you can forgive me one day for all the pain I have caused you. After my heart beats its final time, I would like you to be the one to give my family their journals. They'll need you to get through them. I know you don't want to hear this, but Ben will make sure you receive yours in Italy next year. I'm doing this for a reason, and when you get it, you'll understand why.

For now, this will be my 'see you later' letter. I can't say good-bye to you, Goldie, because I didn't have enough time with you. I'll only say see you again and pray that's the truth. Thank you for bringing me back to life, even if only for a short time. I spent so long trying to ignore who I was at my core, but that part of me was shocked back to life by your touch. I will die a happy man because of you.

I prepared to die alone for years because I thought it was better for everyone. I didn't realize before I met you that I would leave a hole in my family's lives regardless of how I had lived. By allowing you into my life, they will always have a piece of me through you because my heart belongs to you for as long as you'll have it.

Thank you for your courage, your heart, your kindness, and your love.

Forever yours,
Preston

"Geez, you're the worst, Preston," I sniffle. "I'll do as you ask because I love you, but I'm doing it my way. You promised you would tell your family, and we ran out of time. I asked Ben to bring all the journals here, so they'll read them and have a chance to respond before you go. It's only fair.

"I wish I had told you so many things. I wish I hadn't let my hang-ups ruin the time I could have truly been yours. I'm sorry I never told you I loved you when you could respond. I promise to do everything I can to make your wishes come true. I will carry your heart with me always, Preston. Never will I ever love anyone more than you. I'm yours, remember? I'll always be yours."

A knock at the door has me scrambling, but everything happens in slow motion in my emotional state. I'm still lying with Preston as East and Dexter walk in behind Sylvie. I attempt to move, but Sylvie places a hand on mine.

"Stay there, Emory. That's where he would want you," she tells me, kissing the side of my head, causing tears to start anew.

"This isn't going to work," Easton says, and I shrink further into Preston.

Does he mean I'm not going to work?

I watch in horror as he pulls out his phone.

"No, please don't have me removed. I-I can't leave Preston. I just promised him I'd do as he asked."

Easton raises his head. His standard grumpy exterior softens, making him look more like Preston than I've ever realized.

"Emory, no one will ever make you leave. You're family. I'm sorry if my attitude would ever make you think differently. We may all be different, but family is not something we fuck around with. You're stuck with us forever."

I stare at Easton, slack-jawed. *He's not the asshole he portrays.* The admission has me babbling, "Preston wanted to make it to Christmas for your wedding, Dex. I'm so sorry we hid this from you all. H-He—"

"Emory?" Dex cuts in. "We have known Preston our entire lives. None of us will hold this against you, ever. We just have to make a few adjustments so we can all be here with you."

"Adjustments? I-I don't understand," I admit.

Dexter smiles. "You will, Ems. In this group, family is chosen, and we don't mess around when it comes to family. Preston may have been an asshole for keeping this from us, but I hope he had a damn good reason. He lived with this for too long alone. We won't let him die that way, too." The single tear that falls from his eye tells me we're all experiencing a torturous pain. Some, I recognize, are just better at hiding it.

CHAPTER 36

EMORY

The next twelve hours are like watching a movie. A flurry of activity, threats, phone calls, and more threats happen around me as I lay by Preston's side.

"Emory?" Dex asks softly. I must have dozed off.

"What's the matter?" I ask, feeling Preston's heartbeat under my palm where it has been permanently affixed.

"I'm sorry I startled you. Easton has made progress with hospital administrators," he says with a grin. "They are going to move Preston to the sixth floor where we'll have more room," he continues vaguely.

"More room for what?"

"The family. It's amazing what threatening the loss of funding from Westbrook Enterprises will do for you. We'll all have room to stay with you and Preston down there, together."

"Dex—"

"You okay?" he asks, cutting me off.

"Yeah, I-I just want you to know how hard Preston fought to make it to Christmas. It's all he really wanted. He begged me to help him make it so he could see you and Lanie become a family."

Dexter's strong arms wrap around me, so suddenly, he knocks the wind out of me.

"We're going to do everything we can to make it all happen for him," he promises cryptically. "Lanie and I are already a family. The ceremony can happen anytime, Ems. You've been amazing. Preston is so lucky to have found you."

Within the hour, the hospital is processing the transfer to move Preston downstairs. When the nurse comes to bathe him, I tell her no. Begrudgingly, I climb out of his bed. Ushering everyone out of the room, I strip Preston down and give him a sponge bath while the orderly helps change his sheets.

"This is something I'm supposed to do when we're eighty, Preston. Not yet, but knowing you, you're probably getting a kick out of this."

Oh God, did I just say that out loud?

"It's okay, miss. I've heard doctors tell loved ones it is good to talk to them. I always do." The orderly watches me kindly.

"Thank you," I whisper.

When I've got Preston changed and made him as comfortable as I can, I open the door and tell everyone he's ready. Walking beside the bed as they roll it to the elevator and down to the sixth-floor hall, I realize we're on the labor and delivery floor.

"Why are we down here?"

"The L&D rooms are the only ones big enough to accommodate Mr. Westbrook," the nurse answers from behind me.

I'm about to ask another question when they roll Preston into a room three times the size of his other one. Lining three walls are chairs, all filled with the family I've been thrown into. All four of Preston's brothers sit in a line. Dexter, Lanie, and Julia sit on another. Even GG is sitting quietly next to Lexi.

They all sit in comfortable clothing like they're settling in for a long while. Red eyes give away their sadness.

Keep your shit together, Emory. They are all hurting more than you.

When my gaze lands on Sylvie, my dam breaks even as my brain is yelling at me to bottle it up.

Dexter stands and wraps me in a hug. "We don't do anything alone in this family, Emory. I wish Preston would have realized that sooner, but we are all here for you. We always will be."

"Ah-hem," someone clears their throat, and I peer around Dexter's broad shoulders to see Ben Simmons. "Emory? Knowing Preston's wishes, I believe we should fill everyone in now that you're all together."

"Where's—"

"Incoming," I hear Trevor say from behind me. Dexter immediately moves to help him.

I watch in horror as Trevor drags in one of the most massive Christmas trees I've ever seen, followed by Julia's dad holding about twenty bags overflowing with decorations.

"Trevor, you can't have live trees in a hospital room. There are allergens and—"

"Emory, I know this is going to be the douchiest thing I ever say to you, but money allows for a lot to happen that isn't technically allowed," East says. "Preston wanted to make it to Christmas. I'll pay off as many assholes as needed to bring it to him. This is where it's okay to take off your doctor's hat and just be his wife."

Shocked, I back up until I'm resting on the edge of Preston's bed once again. Someone puts Christmas music on their phone, and the entire room goes about decorating the tree whose scent has already infiltrated the room. Once it's made beautiful, everyone goes back to their seats, allowing the music to fill the silence.

"Emory?" Ben says again.

Glancing around, I know I owe everyone here an explanation. Making eye contact one by one, I stop when I get to Ashton.

"Ash, where's Loki?"

He doesn't answer right away, but when he breaks eye contact to stare at his lap, I feel another pit forming in my throat.

"Ashton?" Sylvie demands.

"I ... he should have arrived yesterday for the wedding. Seth can't reach him. The last contact point they had for him is gone. An explosion of some sort is all the information I can hack from his systems. As of four hours ago, they listed him as missing in action."

"No," Sylvie cries, collapsing to the ground. "Dear God, please don't take two of my boys from me today."

I move to comfort her, but the room is faster than I am. Colton has swooped in and lifted her into the reclining chair set up in the corner as he sits and attempts to soothe her, while Dex and Easton stand by her side.

Don't let Ben push this right now. Sylvie cannot take any more. Waiting a couple more hours so she can digest all of this heartache isn't going to hurt anyone.

"Emory, dear. Please, please, tell us what Preston wanted. Tell us your story," she pleads.

Halton hands her a cup of tea and wraps a blanket around her trembling frame. He looks to me and nods.

Sucking in a deep breath, I start at my beginning, with Donny Growset, and end four days ago with our wedding at the courthouse.

Ashton stands to hand her his phone.

"Oh, Emory. You looked beautiful, and I've never seen Preston look happier," she cries.

I look at him quizzically.

"I told you, I was the witness and the photographer," he says with a shrug.

Crossing the room, I take the journals and coordinating files and make my way around the room.

"Preston started writing in these books a year after his diagnosis. He knew he would miss out on a lot of your lives." I pause to swallow more tears. "He started writing them to say good-bye, and it turned into love letters for everyone he cared about most. He wanted me to give them to you after he was gone, but I don't think that's fair. He's had ten years to say his good-byes. I told him I was going to allow you all to have that same chance."

"What are the folders?" Trevor asks.

I have to swallow multiple times before I can speak.

"H-He started a project called the Broken-Hearts Network. In each of your folders, you'll find a charity he started in your honor. Each one has a Westbrook brother attached to it who will sit on the board and ensure funding is plentiful for as long as you wish for it to continue." My throat is closing up, clogged with emotion. "Ben? Could ... could you take over, please?"

"Of course, dear. Dexter, your charity is House of Hope. It's for children of abandonment, and Preston requested that Colton serves with you. Trevor, yours is Knights and Days for domestic violence. He assigned Ashton to this one." Reading the paper, he continues. "Loki's is Lost Directions Home for Boys with Halton. Lanie—"

"What? Me?" she asks, surprised.

"Yes, he has one for all those he loves. Yours is the Hearts and Hands Network for abused children."

"Fuck me," Ashton says through tears.

"Julia, yours is Righting Wrongs for victims of cyber and identity theft with Ashton."

Julia stands suddenly, quietly excusing herself.

"Lexi's Woman Warriors, it prepares women for the workforce after tragedy with Easton."

"I know this is a lot, but he made me promise not to keep him attached to machines any longer than necessary. We've exhausted all medical treatments. His only hope is a transplant, and he's too far down the donor list. He wanted you to have these as a positive to focus on when you miss him. As hard as it is, we have to start saying our good-byes. I-I promised him."

"Actually, Emory, there is one more charity I need to get through," Ben tells the room.

I look around, trying to figure out who we missed.

"Preston's newest charity under the Broken-Hearts Network is for you. He named it Hearts of Hope and offers free surgical procedures for underprivileged children. It's been assigned to Sylvie."

There is no way I heard that correctly.

"Emory is correct, though. Preston's last request is that you all say your good-byes and let him go in peace," Ben informs the room. "I'll give you all privacy, and ultimately, it is Emory's decision, but I urge you to do as he asked as quickly as you're comfortable."

The room is eerily silent for a long time.

"Fuck you, Preston," Colton screams before punching the wall. "How the fuck could you do this to us? You selfish piece of shit. This had nothing to do with us. It was all about you not having to deal with us when we found out. How dare you leave this responsibility to Emory and the sadness for us to bear alone?"

Not today, Colton.

All reasoning leaves my mind as I charge him, and everyone watches on in horror.

Punching Colton in the chest, I scream. "That's not what he did. That's not it at all. He wanted to live a life worth living. If you'd known, you would have all treated him differently. You wouldn't have played pranks on him. You wouldn't have taken trips or done the stupid shit brothers do together. He would have been forced to live his life in a bubble. He wanted to live authentically. Can't you understand that? Can't you see it was him that had to bear the sadness alone? We all have each other. You all can share your heartache. He suffered alone for years to save you. He wanted to save us all, don't you see?" I sob. "Don't you see how much he loved us?"

Placing his hands on my shoulders, Colton tries to calm me down, but I'm beyond that. I've lost control of myself, and there's no going back right now.

"Emory," I hear Lexi say beside me. "Come here, chica. Come on," she coos, wrapping me in a hug as the room cries collectively for the man we all love—the man we all have to say good-bye to.

Less than a week later, I sign the papers to turn off life support.

CHAPTER 37

EMORY

Day 1

*M*y head rarely leaves Preston's chest as I lay beside him. The hopelessness I feel burns deep in my soul. It's all-consuming knowing I've failed. With my eyes closed and my tears soaking Preston's chest, I listen to Dr. Terry explain to the room what I have just done.

"If she removed all assisted-living devices, why does he still have an IV?" one of the brothers asks. Without seeing them, I can't tell them apart. With my eyes closed, they all sound like Preston, and it twists the knife deeper into my chest.

"Emory left the IV intact so we can continue with pain management. As his body shuts down, breathing will become labored. We want to keep him as comfortable as we can while this process happens," Dr. Terry explains.

"How long will it take?" another brother asks.

I glance up to see Sylvie has laid her head down on Preston's other side. We stare at each other, recognizing and sharing in the other's pain.

"There's no set time, son. It could be a day or as long as a week. There is just no way of knowing with these things."

"And you're sure, Doctor? You're sure that there isn't anything we can do? There are four of us. Can't you take a piece from all of our hearts to fix his?"

Bargaining. There are stages of grieving, but until you experience them, you can never fully understand it.

"No, son. I'm sorry. Without a transplant, the most we can do is keep him comfortable."

Someone kicks a chair, and it screeches across the floor.

Anger.

"Emory?" Sylvie asks quietly. "You need to eat something, sweetie. You haven't left his side in days. We will get through this together, okay? I promise you, but I need you to take care of yourself, too."

Acceptance.

Placing my hand over hers, I give it a meek squeeze. "I'm alright, Sylvie." I close my eyes again and listen to his heart.

When I open them, I notice the light is no longer streaming through the blinds. Lifting my head, I see some tables were brought in, and everyone's scattered throughout the room. They've ordered pizza and beer, which makes me laugh. This is how Preston would have wanted it.

Colton catches my eye and grabs a beer on his way over. Sitting opposite me, he hands me the bottle, but I decline.

"Just take a sip, Emory. Everyone's worried about you. If you're not going to eat, at least drink something that will numb your pain for a bit."

Figuring taking a drink is the easiest way to appease him, I do. The cold, bitter taste of hops coating my unnaturally dry throat feels nice, so I take another sip, and he chuckles.

"Hey, Ems? I'm sorry about the other day. I ... Preston has been more like a father to Ash and me since ours passed away. I, it just felt like—"

"I'm sorry, too, Colt. I know this is hard. We're all doing

the best we can. You're entitled to feel however you feel. I shouldn't have attacked you like that."

His grin is so reminiscent of Preston's it makes me ache. "That's where you're wrong, Ems. That's what Preston would have wanted you to do, put me in my place, and help me see things from a different perspective." Standing, he kisses me on the forehead. "You're the big sister I never knew I needed."

Where the hell did this family come from?

Day 2

"Any change?" Dr. Terry asks as I finish my exam.

"He's shutting down, as expected," I force out. In another of Dr. Terry's miracles, no one has questioned me taking over Preston's care with no license.

"Emory, make sure that you're taking care of yourself. Sylvie said you haven't eaten and have barely drunk anything since you've been here."

"I'm fine," I say bitterly. *I'm not the one dying.* Ignoring his pleading looks, I climb back into my spot beside Preston and close my eyes again.

I hear a phone ring and a whispered hello, followed by the sounds of someone leaving the room.

After a few minutes, I sense someone behind me, so I lift my head and find Lanie. Dexter is rounding the bed to sit on the other side.

"Ems, can I talk to you for a minute?" Lanie asks. Her pained expression has me sitting up.

"Sure, are you okay?"

"We, we need your opinion. Tate is begging Julia's mom to bring him to see Preston. We've told him in a roundabout way what is going on, but we don't know the right answer. How old should a kid be before you allow them to witness something like this? He really wants to talk to Preston. We just don't know if it is the right thing to do."

Shaking my head, I attempt to remove the cobwebs that have settled in my brain. I try to focus and remember what I have told patients in the past, but this isn't a patient. This is family, so I speak from the heart.

"I don't think there is a right or wrong answer, Lanie. You're his mom. You guys know him best and what he can handle. I think you have to go with what your gut is telling you. When my stepmother passed away, we couldn't afford a service, but I knew my sisters needed closure, so I created a service in our back yard. I knew they needed the chance to say good-bye to her. I wish I could give you a more definitive answer, but I think you have to go with your heart. What is it telling you?"

"That we have to let him say his good-byes," Lanie says sadly. The pain of knowing your child will experience heartbreak and also knowing you can do nothing about it is written all over her face. "Do you mind if we bring him in?"

"Of course not, Lanie. Whatever you need to do."

Had I known giving Lanie that advice would also cause the most heart wrenching moment in our lives, I may have tried a different approach.

Day 3

"Hi, Auntie Ems," a chipper, unfamiliar voice wakes me with a start.

Opening my eyes, I see Tate standing in front of Dexter.

"Sorry, we didn't mean to wake you," Dex apologizes.

"Auntie Ems, can I climb up?"

"No, buddy, I don't—"

"It's okay, Dex," I interrupt. "Sure, buddy. Come on up, just be careful of Preston's IV over there."

"Got it," he says happily before Dex lifts him onto the bed.

"I'm so excited to have another auntie. I'm going to have the best sleepovers with you and Uncle Preston."

I look to Dexter, alarmed. *Didn't they tell him what's happening?*

"We've talked to him, but GG put some other thoughts in his head, and we're having a hard time explaining reality," he tells me while glaring in GG's direction.

"Yeah, it's okay, Auntie Ems. Uncle Preston isn't going to die. He is just waiting for a knight's heart. See?" he asks, handing me a playing card with a king of hearts.

"Did you give Preston one of these at the wedding?" I ask, remembering I found one in his wallet when I was looking for his insurance card.

"Yup." The pure innocence of childhood is fucking killing me right now.

"I've got one for you, too. Here."

Turning it over in my hands, I see the new card is the queen of hearts. "Buddy, this is a king and queen."

"I know. The knight will give the queen a heart, and then the queen will fix the king. You'll see. Hi, Uncle Preston. Here, I brought another one just in case. I'm going to stick it on your heart. You just have to wait for Auntie to save you. You'll be okay, and then we will have an awesome sleepover! I can't wait. But just me, okay? Could I please have my own sleepover without my brothers and sisters? There's too many of them. Oh, and I love Auntie Ems. I want to be a doctor just like her someday so I can save people, too. She's going to save you. I know it. GG showed me. It's in the cards."

We all sit in awe as Tate talks to Preston for a full half an hour. We marvel at his innocence and weep at the knowledge we know will break his little heart.

I hold the cards in my hand for hours after Tate leaves. *I wish I could have saved you, Preston. I wish more than anything I could save you.*

"Mrs. Westbrook," someone barges into the room, yelling, "Dr. Terry needs you now. You have to hurry."

Sylvie stands immediately.

"Ah, no, the other Mrs. Westbrook. Dr. Camden, hurry, you have to come now." The woman sounds desperate.

I look between her and Preston. "No, I-I can't leave him."

"If you want to save him, you have to come right now, and we have to run."

I'm not sure I heard correctly, but Easton is lifting me out of bed and standing me on my feet while Colton drags me behind the nurse.

"But, Preston—"

"I'll be right here until you get back," Sylvie informs me as the nurse takes off running.

Colton drags me behind him.

Definitely a Westbrook trait, I decide.

CHAPTER 38

EMORY

*W*e run full speed up two flights of stairs, and it's only then that I realize I don't have shoes on. The nurse stops outside of a room and tells me to enter, but Colton has to wait outside.

What the fuck is going on?

My hesitation must annoy Colton because he shoves me into the room. As I'm stumbling to catch my balance, Dr. Terry comes into view. I can see someone in the bed behind him, but his upper half is blocked from sight.

No. Do not let this be Loki. Do not let this be Loki.

"Wh—"

"We have to move fast, Emory, if we are going to save Preston. You have left quite an impression on someone, but before we can proceed with the surgery, he requested that you read a letter. You must move fast, Emory. Time is not on our side."

My head is spinning.

Who did I make an impression on? Why does he keep saying save Preston?

He thrusts an envelope at me, then steps aside.

Mr. T?

Ripping open the envelope, I cry for a new reason.

Dearest Emory,

Thank you for making an old man's last wish come true ...

I'm running through the hospital again, sliding around corners in my stocking feet while Dr. Terry yells for me to come back. Down and down and down the stairs, I just cannot reach Preston's room fast enough.

Bursting through his door, I'm screaming. Dr. Terry, who is shockingly fast for his age, enters the room shortly after. Everyone is staring at me like I've lost my mind, and if they don't start following orders, I just might.

"Hook him up," I bark out on winded breathes. "Hook him up the CPAP now. Get him ready for surgery," I scream at Dr. Terry, who is the only one following my directives.

"Emory, what is—"

I turn in manic circles until my eyes land on the one person I'm looking for. Marching straight for him, I grab his ear and twist until he stands and begins to move out of the room with me.

"Jesus Christ, Emory. Let me go."

"We don't have time, please don't fight me. If you want Preston to live, you have to come now. We're running out of time."

That's all it takes. Everyone but Sylvie is running after me down the hall. It's like a crazed scene on a fake hospital drama, but this is real. This is my last chance to save Preston.

"What the hell is going on?" someone yells below me in the stairwell, but I'm so out of breath I can't reply, not that I really have the answers, anyway.

"Run," I yell as we hit the eighth floor again. Reaching the door, I once again slide into it, but this time get tripped up as my sock sticks to the door frame. I'm flying toward the bed just as Trevor wraps an arm around my waist to catch me.

"Dad? Emory, what the hell is going on?"

"Dad?" I ask, shocked, looking between Mr. T and Trevor.

"What the fuck is going on, Emory?" Trevor barks.

"I-I, here," I hand him the letter that's addressed to him. Trevor takes it but makes no move to open it.

"Open the fucking letter, Trevor. We don't have time. Please, please, read the letter so the lawyer will sign off on the organ donation. Please," I beg.

Slowly, he lifts the flap.

"Emory, what is going on?" Julia asks.

"This is Mr. T, the man I volunteer with at the infusion center. I knew he was sick, but not this sick. I just saw him last week. He left me a letter and said if I could get Trevor to read it, he would give Preston his heart. Somehow he already knew he was a match. I don't know how. I swear I never told him. I never even told him Preston's name, even though he pumped me for information every week," I shout.

"Ems, that," Julia says, pointing toward Mr.T, "is Trevor's dad, Romero Knight. He's known Preston since he was in diapers."

The room spins under me, and I lose my footing, but Trevor catches me.

"Did you read the letter?" I say when I catch my bearings.

"I-I just need a minute."

Ripping it from his hands, I yell, "We may not have that minute." I've lost all control of myself. I'm crazed, desperate, and completely willing to do whatever it takes to save Preston.

"Dear Trevor," I read aloud.

"Emory, don't," Julia begs.

"My biggest fear is that one day you will come to regret not speaking to me while I was alive. Please don't let that be the case, son. I do not deserve your forgiveness. I have done many things in this life beyond reproach, and I have to admit I did another to find out the fate of your friend, Preston. I hope that one, you'll forgive." I take a deep breath. I don't know the relationship between these two men, and I pray I am doing the right thing by forcing this issue, but Preston's life depends on it.

"I had stage 4 colon cancer, Trevor. It was fast, aggressive, and mean as hell. I need you to know this so you and little Charlie will take the necessary precautions. I know you don't believe it, but there are only three days I will take with me. Whether they go to heaven or hell has yet to be seen. The first is the day I married your mother. I pray I will see her again soon so I can spend eternity trying to make amends. The second was the day you were born. I wish I had been strong enough to change things when they went wrong. The third was the day I first laid eyes on Charlie and realized you would be the father I was never capable of being. While I had no part in it, I am proud of the man you have become, mio figlio.

"My heart is not all evil. When I first saw Emory enter the center with Preston, I knew I had to seek her out. If I can do one good deed in this life, I die a content man knowing I could do it, saving someone you love.

"Never regret the decisions you have made, Trevor. You are not the bad guy here. Every decision you have made has been in reaction to a bad one made by me. Be kind to yourself. Love your family fiercely. I hope someday you understand that I was not perfect, but I loved you with everything I had. Love, Papa."

Trevor takes a step forward and wraps me in a hug I was not expecting. "Thank you for being his person in the end. I know it couldn't be me, but I'm glad he had you," he whispers. "What do we have to do now?"

"I-I think the lawyer just has to sign the form," I say.

Trevor releases me and glances around the room. His eyes finally settle on an older gentleman in the corner. "Rex," he says in greeting.

The older man rises and hands me a piece of paper. "He's all set."

I look at Julia for help. "Go, Ems. Go do whatever heart surgeons do."

I don't wait another second. I take off for the fourth time in a full sprint.

Reaching the sixth floor again, I find Dr. Terry exiting Preston's room. "Scrub in, Emory."

"What? I can't. I don't have a license, I'm married to the patient, I—"

"We don't have another choice. There are only two other surgeons in this area that can perform this surgery. One is already in the OR, the other is on vacation in Tahiti." He hands me a badge. Looking down, I see Dr. Tao. "Put your mask on, and don't speak until we are in the OR."

"Dr. Terry, you could lose your own license for this."

"Are you going to tattle on me, Emory?"

"What? No, of course not."

"Then let me worry about my career. The most important thing is that we save Preston, and you are the only one capable of helping me. If my career is over for this, then so be it. I've had a nice, long one, but I've already lost one Westbrook. I'm not willing to lose another. There are not enough good men like them in this world. Now scrub in."

"Yes, sir." I chance a peek around the room. Every person there stares at me with hope in their eyes. I don't make eye contact with any of them again—the pressure threatening to suffocate me. Instead, I quickly cross the room and lay a gentle kiss on Preston's lips. "I love you."

CHAPTER 39

PRESTON

Fuck. Everything hurts. Where the hell am I?

I try to open my eyes, but they're glued shut. Air is being forced into my nose, and it's uncomfortable. The room is cold, and I can smell the underlying scent of rubbing alcohol under the oxygen being forced into my body.

Why is it so damn cold in here?

"I'll leave when he wakes up, not before."

"You can't eat in here, and you haven't eaten in days, maybe a week, Emory. You need to take care of yourself, or you'll be of no use to him when he gets home."

"Oh, he won't need me when he gets home. He has a large family that will take care of him."

"Ah, excuse me for asking, but aren't you his wife?"

"Sort of. It-It's complicated. Preston needed me—I'm not sure he will still need me when his heart heals."

What the fuck is she talking about? Sort of my wife? She is my goddamn wife.

The incessant beeping gets faster.

Wake up, asshole. Tell her! Tell her she's yours forever.

"If I had to guess, I'd say he didn't like your answer—"

Beep*Beep*Beep

That goddamn noise. Someone shut it up already.

"He's doing much better today, Sylvie. I know it's still hard seeing him like this, but I promise he's doing better."

"Dr. Terry told me you're the reason he's still alive, you know? When he thought he was going to lose him, you stepped in. You were literally the beat of his heart for a solid minute. You're amazing, Emory," my mother's strangled voice cries. "We all love you so much, Emory. We will always be here for you. Are you sure you have to return to Boston so soon?"

"I have to, Sylvie. I have to face Donny and make him pay for all he's done."

No! Not without me!

"I get that, sweet girl. I do, and you'll have our full support. I just hope Preston wakes up before you have to go."

"Me too. I'm not sure what changed. Ben said it's highly unusual for medical ethics reviews to be moved up with such short notice. I'd be nervous if Ashton weren't so thorough with his investigation."

That a boy, Ash! I knew he would come through. Why can't I say anything? God, this is fucking infuriating. I don't want Emory going alone to deal with that dickwad. I need to be with her.

"It can only be good news, Ems. I'm sure of it."

My mother is a saint.

"But we can't have you showing up looking so tired. Why don't you go home, get some rest? You haven't left his side since he got here."

"I'd like to stay, Sylvie. I'll sleep on the plane tomorrow. I don't want to risk him waking up when I'm not here if I can help it. But if it happens, I have a letter I'll leave him."

"More damn letters? Don't you think we've had enough

letter writing in this family?" my mother jokes, but there's an edge to her voice that's worrisome.

"I know, Sylvie. But like I told you, we've had a very unconventional relationship. I think it will be best if he has time to think about what he wants now. When we got married, his life had a very different outlook. I have to prepare myself that I may not be what he wants now."

"Tsk. That's bullshit, Emory."

You tell her, Mom!

"I still think he deserves his space to decide. I never even told him I loved him while he was awake. Would you marry someone who had not said they loved you?"

Yes. Yes, I did, and I would again because I felt it, Emory! I felt your love. Mother fucker, wake me the fuck up! I can't take this shit anymore.

Beep*Beep*Beep*

"I think Preston is trying to answer you himself. But yes, my answer is yes. I would have married Preston's father even if he hadn't said the words because I could feel his love. Words are nice, honey, but it's the actions the make the relationship."

*Beep*Beep*Beep*

～

"EMORY?" I barely recognize my own voice.

"Preston? Oh, Broken-heart. It's so nice to have you back. Let me grab my phone so I can touchin' the ladies to let poor Sylvie know you're awake. She just ran out for some coffee."

GG. She is never going to admit it is texting, not touchin'.

"Emory? Where is she?"

"She, well, she left this morning, son. But just hold yer horses, your mother's got somethin' for you. That girl saved your life, ya know? With her bare hands, she pumped your heart and got it to beat again. That's some kind of woman."

I nod, not sure I can deal with GG right now.

"Preston? Oh, thank God, honey. Thank God," my mother gushes.

"Mom. Water."

"Yes, yes. GG, go get the nurse, please."

"On it like hotcakes, Sylvie."

I can't help but roll my eyes at the crazy lady, then smile because I can roll my eyes at the crazy lady. My mom holds a straw to my lips, and I take a long sip. Nothing has ever tasted better. *Nothing except Emory.* Good to know that freaking voice hasn't gone anywhere.

"Emory? I need Emory."

My mother's expression darkens. "Preston, I know you have been awake for all of five minutes, but I need to ask you something. Then, you're going to have to think long and hard about your answer."

I swallow, a troubling feeling of understanding tickles the back of my consciousness, but I can't place it. "Okay."

"Why did you marry Emory?"

Images flash before me like a movie reel. In slow motion, I see a glimpse of our first meeting, our first kiss. I see the moment I realized I loved her and the conversations I've been hearing while asleep assault me like a bullet.

"Because I love her, where is she? She hasn't left yet, has she?" I'm trying to sit up, and a stabbing pain shoots through my chest. "Fuck—"

"Preston, I'm Dr. Montgomery. You have to stay still, don't try to sit up yet. You still have staples in, and you don't want to pull those out."

"Where, Mom? Where is she?"

Dr. Montgomery tries to fuss around me, and I stop him in his tracks with a murderous look.

"Would you like me to come back?" he asks.

"Yes," I say, as my mother says, "No."

"Preston, you will let this doctor look you over, and then

we can talk. While he is doing your exam, think long and hard about the truth of your answer."

"What the hell, Mom? Of course it's the truth. I love her."

She holds up an envelope.

"But if that happens, I have a letter I'll leave him." Emory's words hit me like a bolt of lightning.

"She doesn't believe I love her?"

Sylvie Westbrook, never one to back down from a challenge, smiles sadly at me. "I don't think so, Pres. So, what are we going to do to prove it to her?" Her smile goes from sad to devious in a split second, and I suddenly realize where all of my brothers and I get it from.

"Whatever it takes."

"Good answer, son. The boys are on their way to help, and the girls are already on their way to Boston. We'll get her back. Do you want to read her letter?"

"No. I think we've had enough letter writing in this family, don't you?" I smirk. "I want her to tell me in person."

CHAPTER 40

PRESTON

I wake to muffled voices and know my brothers are here. Not just the Westbrooks, but Trevor and Dex, too. If you've ever had eight boys together in a room, you know it's impossible to keep them quiet. When I open my eyes, I notice we're still down a man. There's only seven of us here.

"Where's Loki?"

"We aren't sure."

"Yet. We aren't sure yet," Ash amends.

"He hasn't been here?"

"No, Pres. We haven't heard from him."

I see every man in the room exchange a worried look.

"What? What aren't you telling me?" I demand.

It's my mom who steps forward. "Loki is listed as missing in action, according to Seth. They have multiple teams out looking for him."

"For how long? How long has he been missing?" My chest aches, and it has nothing to do with open-heart surgery.

"Two weeks," Ashton admits.

A silence falls over the room.

"Pres?" My youngest brother steps forward and takes a

seat beside me. "Seth and I are doing everything we can to locate him. We know his training far exceeds that of most operatives, so we have every right to believe he is lying low until it's safe to surface. Mom said we're here for another mission, though? I think ... I know Loki would want you focusing on this and let his team do their jobs."

Knowing I can't lose both Emory and Loki at the same time, I do as Ash suggests and focus on the one I can tackle today.

"Dexter, you might get your wish after all," I tell him.

"Yeah, what's that?"

"Prince Charming, I need you to make a MEP plan."

"Shut the fuck up." For a man Dexter's size, he jumps from his chair way too enthusiastically at the prospect of Prince Charming. "Wait, you're already married."

"Yeah, but she doesn't think it's real. We didn't exactly have the most normal courtship."

Dexter sits back in his chair with a hand on his scruffy chin. "So, what you're saying is, we need a grand gesture?"

"You are far too excited about this," Easton chimes in. While I tend to agree with him, I can't have him ruining the mojo.

"Shut it, East. This is important."

He holds his hands up in surrender and goes back to hugging the wall.

Two hours later, everyone leaves with their jobs in hand. I hate to admit it, but Dexter is a rock star at this fairytale shit.

(Dexter named the group MEP at 1:42pm)

MEP

Dexter: Plan's a go. Ladies, do your thing in Boston, then get her home by whatever means necessary.

Julia: Are the laws the same for abduction if you take them on a private plane?

Halton: Yes, Julia. Laws are the same. (eye rolling emoji)

Colton: Yes! I'm so psyched to be on the chain this time!

Preston: Don't fuck this up, Colt. I'm serious.

Easton: I've got the construction under control. Colt just has to follow orders, and we'll be fine.

Trevor: Julia, I swear to God, do not do anything illegal.

Julia: Whatever.

Preston: Julia!

Julia: Do you want the girl or not, Preston?

Preston: I'd also rather not have to bail your ass out of jail.

Julia: (Rolling eyes emoji)

Lexi: Lanes and I will make sure nothing goes off the rails.

Easton: That sounds promising.

Lexi: Fuck off, East.

Preston: Back on track here, guys. How long until you get to the hospital?

Lanie: Rolling up now! I've got a fanny pack of necessities. We'll get her home, Pres. Don't worry.

Lexi: She isn't even lying. A goddamn fanny pack!

Preston: Ladies, please take care of my girl. Gents, please move your asses and get this done before she gets back. I have one chance to make this right.

Halton: You know I hate every second of this, right? Why on God's fucking green Earth was I the one chosen to go dress shopping with Mom?

Easton: Because no one else can handle your grumpy ass.

Lexi: Halton is the grumpy one? I'm calling BS!

Easton: Don't push me, Lex.

Lexi: Or what? Seriously? What are you going to do?

Preston: GUYS! I don't know what the hell is going on

between the two of you, but can we focus here? This is about ME!

Julia: Lexi and Easton sitting in a tree. KISSING.

Lexi: Fuck you.

Easton: No, thanks.

Jesus, what the hell is going on here? Does Lexi just have this effect on every Westbrook brother?

~

PRESTON: WTH is going on? It's been hours.

Lexi: We aren't sure. They wouldn't let us in the room.

Preston: Fuck. I knew I should have been there.

Lanie: Pres, you can't fly. She knows we're here, and we'll take care of her, I promise.

Julia: Don't get your panties in a twist. I've got enough balls out here for the both of us. No one is going to mess with our girl.

~

PRESTON: You're killing me here. WTF?

Lexi: We just got in a cab. The trial went long, so they recessed until tomorrow morning. We'll be delayed until tomorrow night.

Preston: What the hell? Ash? I thought your intel was solid?

Lanie: It's not that. There are a lot of moving pieces that are being exposed within the hospital. We have to go. Emory's getting suspicious.

Preston: Is she okay?

Julia: She will be.

~

EASTON: The extra time is good news, Pres. We are rocking these buildings.

Dexter: It's a solid plan. We've got this.

Preston: I hope so.

Lexi: She loves you, Preston. I agree with Dex. I'm not usually one for the circus you've got going on, but in this case, I think she needs it.

Easton: Her? Or you?

Preston: What the fuck is going on with you two?

Lexi: Nothing.

Easton: Absolutely nothing.

～

PRESTON: Any word on her sisters?

Trevor: I've collected two. Waiting at the airport on the third. I'll bring them to Sylvie's house to get changed and fill them in on the plan.

Preston: Thanks.

Preston: How's Emory?

Lexi: In shock. It all happened really quickly. The FBI descended on the room before her judgment was even read. They took Donny the Dick Parade, the other doctor, and three board members into custody for fraud and a laundry list of shit none of us understood.

Preston: Take care of her. Please.

Lexi: Always. Lanie is playing Never Have I Ever with her over mimosas.

Preston: Are you kidding me? I need her sober, Lex! WTH? If she is drunk, none of this will matter.

Julia: Calm the hell down. Mimosas are necessary if you want us to get her on this plane without hog-tying her.

Dexter: Relax, Pres. Sometimes it's just best to let these Vermont girls do things their own way.

Easton: ...

Lexi: East, don't say it.

Easton: ...

Lexi: ...

Preston: As soon as I make Emory mine forever, the two of you are going to sit down and have a little chat with me.

Lexi: No can do, my friend. As soon as this is all set, I'm heading back to Vermont with GG.

Easton: ...

Colton: Does this have anything to do with what happened in Vegas?

Preston: What the hell happened in Vegas?

Lexi: Nothing.

Easton: Absolutely nothing.

Preston: WTF?

CHAPTER 41

EMORY

"*E*verything okay?" Lexi asks.

"Oh, yeah. It's just weird that none of my sisters are answering their phones. Someone always answers."

"They're probably just busy," Lanie says. "It's the middle of the day. Yeah, I'm sure they're just busy."

Did those mimosas go straight to her head? She is acting really strange.

"So, what do you say, Ems? You going to come home with us or what?" Julia asks without looking at me.

"What's up with the two of you?" I ask.

"Ugh, nothing. They're just lightweights who let the champagne get to them," Lexi answers through a clenched jaw.

"Hmm."

"But they aren't wrong," Lexi continues. "You should come back with us."

"I don't know, Lex. I think Preston needs the chance to figure out his life now that he knows he can and will live a long, healthy one. Facing death can make you do crazy things. I've seen it in patients before."

"He isn't your patient, Emory. He's your husband," Julia says.

Sighing, I know we are about to get into this for the tenth time today. "I know, Jules. But, he asked me to marry him when he had no other options. The world just opened up to him. It's okay for him to want different things."

"Don't you think you owe it to him to let him make that decision, though?" Lanie asks softly.

"That's what I'm trying to do," I tell them. "I want him to decide without any pressure from me."

"How can he do that if you're running from him?" Lexi points out.

I'm not running, am I?

"Listen, we won't badger you over this. But we do need you to come to the airport. We forgot a gift for you from Sylvie on the plane. She will kill us if we don't hand it to you personally."

"Julia!" Lexi and Lanie say in unison.

"What? We aren't going to get her on that plane unless we come clean and tell her we fucked up and have to give her something."

Note to self, watch the mimosa intake of these girls.

"Okay, that's fine. I can see you off, then take a taxi back to the hotel."

The rest of the car ride is silent except for the constant texting everyone else is doing. Peering down at my phone, my chest aches knowing Preston hasn't reached out once.

I climb the steps to Preston's private plane on the tarmac, probably for the last time. Glancing back at the girls, they all urge me to continue.

Maybe they're acting weird, knowing we won't have a reason to continue our friendships once Preston realizes I'm not his forever.

"Where—"

"In the cabin," they all shout.

"Are you guys alright?" *Maybe I should just clear the air now.*

"Listen, I know you're Preston's friends. I won't pressure you if things don't work out. I understand your loyalties lie with Preston."

"You freaking moron. We don't have loyalties. You're both our friends. That's why you have to forgive us for doing this," Julia says. Before I can blink, she and Lanie have shoved me into the small restroom attached to the private cabin.

"Go, we're all set. Take off, immediately," I hear Lexi yell.

"What the hell, guys? I said I'm not going with you. Let me out of here right now!"

"We can't do that. I'm so sorry, Ems. I promise this is for your own good."

I feel the plane start to taxi.

"Lanie, let me out of here right now! I can't go back to North Carolina. Not right now. Let me out."

"I'm so sorry, Emory. I will, we will let you out, just not until we're in the air."

"Are you freaking kidding me right now? Are you kidnapping me?"

"No, of course not. We're making an executive decision as your friends. Please, just trust us."

"Trust you? You just shoved me into a bathroom and told a flight attendant to take off so I couldn't get away. You want me to trust you?"

"Yes," all three girls say.

What the hell am I supposed to do now? I can't even call anyone because I tossed my purse on a seat as I walked toward the plane's rear.

Sometime after the plane has leveled off, the bathroom door opens, and all three girls stand in the doorway shame-facedly.

Julia hands me a shot, "Never have I ever been kidnapped?" She clinks glasses with me, and we both knock back a shot of tequila.

"You guys have some explaining to do." I say, pointing at each of them.

"We will, we promise. It will all make sense, but you just have to trust us for a few more hours. Please?" Lanie begs.

"Does anyone ever say no to you?" I ask, unable to stay mad at her stupid face.

"Not usually," she replies, grinning.

"So, you promise not to run and let us get our jobs done? If you want to leave after everything is said and done, we promise we'll take you to the airport ourselves," Lexi says seriously.

I'm so freaking tired from life, I don't have it in me to argue. Instead, I say, "Fine," as I land face-first on the bed. All three girls climb in next to me, and someone puts on a movie. We spend the next hour laughing and crying at the antics in one of my favorite movies, *10 Things I Hate About You.*

We have to be getting close. Glancing around at the girls, I realize only Julia and I are awake.

"Jules?" I whisper.

"Yeah," she smiles up at me sleepily. I think we've all hit our emotional limit.

"I'm really sorry about what happened with Trevor and his dad. I-I don't know what came over me, but I should have been more sensitive to the fact that his father had just died."

She rolls onto her stomach to face me. "What happened is, you were faced with the chance to save the man you love, and you did everything in your power to make sure it happened. Neither Trevor nor I fault you for that. Trevor had a really messed up relationship with his father, but I spent time with him not that long ago. He wasn't all bad. He made bad decisions and then didn't know how to get out of them. It cost his family a lot, but I don't think anyone can judge until you've walked in their shoes, you know?"

"I sat with him every week for a year. I don't think he was

all bad either, but I will always be sorry for forcing Trevor to deal with his death the way I did."

"Ems, if you hadn't, he may have lost his dad and his best friend the same day. You did what any of us would have done. I promise you, we all love you for saving Preston, even if he is a pain in my ass," she chuckles.

The plane touches down, and my stomach rolls like it just went over the cliff of a roller coaster.

"I'm nervous. I don't like surprises, and I'm not sure what you guys are walking me into. I don't want to force anything on Preston, especially not while he's in the hospital."

"Would it make you feel better if I told you we aren't going to the hospital?"

"Ah, maybe? Not really, no. That just gives me more questions," I admit.

Squeezing my arm, Julia says, "Never have I ever kidnapped someone who didn't end up better for it."

"Wait, you mean you've kidnapped someone else?"

The cheeky grin she gives me does not settle my nerves in the least. Lexi and Lanie laughing behind us worries me even more.

"You're a little scary, you know that, Jules?"

"Haha, Preston says the same thing. Come on, looks like the car is waiting."

Taking a generous breath, I follow the girls out of the cabin to the tarmac and the waiting car. Anxiety overtakes my body, and I don't know if it's the fear of having Preston or losing him forever that has my body trembling.

Almost an hour later, the car slows to a stop. Ducking down to see out the driver-side window, I see a ten-foot iron gate with an intricately placed W in its center is slowly opening.

"Wh-Where are we?"

"Not the hospital," Jules says as the car pulls to a stop in front of a palatial home. The front doors have the same ironwork W in their centers. While I'm staring at the doors, the girls all jump from the car and take off running.

Seriously?

Watching them run out of sight on my left, I'm startled by a knock on the window I'm sitting near. I feel like I'm stuck in molasses as I turn to see Ashton standing at my side. All the Westbrook boys have the same dark hair and eyes. They really are all carbon copies of each other, but Ashton stands there with his wire-rimmed glasses, reminding me of a handsome Harry Potter.

"Ash, what's going on? Did you know that the girls kidnapped me?"

He nods and smiles but says nothing. Instead, he opens the door fully and offers me a hand. Sighing, I take it, because really? What else am I supposed to do?

He leads me down a path that runs the side of the house. As soon as we reach the back, I'm hit with the sounds and scents of the ocean. I'm too busy gawking at the gardens, so I don't notice Ashton is standing before me with a blindfold.

"Are you kidding me?"

CHAPTER 42

EMORY

*A*shton smiles but shakes his head.

"Great."

Moving behind me, he places the silk over my eyes, tying it at the back. When he's finished, he gives my shoulders a squeeze. I swear I hear him walk away, and I start to panic until I hear Sylvie beside me.

"Don't be nervous, Ems. No one here would ever do anything but love you. I promise. I'm going to take your hand and lead you to our first destination. The boys have made sure it's a clear shot, but you should kick off your shoes just to be safe since we'll be walking in the sand for a bit."

"Sylvie?"

"I'm here, dear. Don't worry."

"How's Preston?" *When has my voice ever sounded so meek?*

"He's good now that you're back in the same zip code." I can hear the smile in her voice, and it soothes my frayed nerves. "Come on, it'll take a few minutes, so we should get moving."

We don't say much once we begin walking. I twist the ring I haven't taken off of my right hand since Preston put it on. It's become my go-to nervous habit in a short amount of time. Sylvie notices and gives my fingers a gentle squeeze, but otherwise, we walk in companionable silence. It feels like we're moving for hours, not minutes. It's crazy how the body compensates when one of your senses is taken away.

"Okay, hun. I'm going to leave you here for a bit. I'll be back to get you when you're ready. Count to ten, then take your blindfold off. You'll know what to do."

"Is this—"

I'm cut off by the sound of Sylvie. I swear to God, I think she is running away. *What am I supposed to do now? Maybe they're going to kill me off so I can't get Preston's money?* I can't even finish the thought without laughing, though. Figuring it has been at least ten seconds, I remove the blind from my eyes.

What the hell?

I turn to look behind me. *Nothing.* I don't see or hear anyone, anywhere. In front of me, sitting on the beach, is a Pepto Bismol pink house that I would bet anything isn't a permanent fixture. Examining it closer, it appears to be a façade, but the door creaks open, so I take a step back. When no one exits, I open it farther and poke my head in.

There are no floors, but there are four walls, and there's even furniture inside. When something catches my eye, I glance to my left and am shocked to see all three of my sisters charging me.

"Tilly? What are you guys doing here?" I ask as I wrap my arms around Sloane and Eli. Tilly forces her way in, and just like when we were kids, we stand in our little huddle hugging. "What's going on? How are you guys here? What is this?"

Eli looks to me with tears but says nothing.

"Please, please, don't tell me you're giving me the silent treatment, too?"

Sloane grins and mimes locking her lips and throwing away the key.

Freaking awesome.

"But—" Looking around, I notice everything is built-in miniature. It's like a playhouse little girls dream of. All the furniture is childlike yet functional.

"Once upon a time, there was a little family living in a little house," Preston's voice is fed through speakers in the open-air playhouse.

"Preston?" I ask, turning in circles, looking for him.

Tilly takes my hand and leads me to the corner of the room, where I see a rack of dresses in every color.

"I-I don't understand," I tell her.

She holds up one, while Eli holds another. All three of my sisters are trying to get me to choose one without speaking.

"I don't care about a dress. Someone, please just tell me what's going on."

"We choose the white one then," Sloane says and gets shushed by my other two sisters.

The three of them attack me with vigor. Eli and Tilly undress me while Sloane is forcing me into the dress they chose.

"You see," Preston starts again, "they were a little family with a little girl playing all the roles. The family loved each other fiercely, but just like Cinderella, one of the sisters never got to go to the ball."

"No, that's— Eli, I never regretted not going to the prom. I—"

"In this family, Goldie loved fiercely. She protected often, and she never once complained. She worked her ass off to provide for everyone she cared about. Then, one day, the evil troll tried to take it all away from her. Goldie's little family was forced to take a different path for a short time. That path led them to this little pink house on the beach where the sisters held a meeting."

I laugh as all three girls turn their backs on me and

pretend to converse in a small circle. *If this writing thing doesn't work out for Sloane, she should look into acting.*

"The little family was cozy and filled with love, but they decided it didn't fit. This family was just too small."

Tilly hands me a tissue, and I wipe at the tears that won't stop. Sloane attacks me with a powder brush, and Eli attempts to fix my mascara.

"I think that's as good as she is going to get," Sloane mumbles through pursed lips.

Eli scowls at her but holds up the blindfold to me.

"Come on! You cannot be serious?"

Her smiling face is the last I see before my eyes are covered again.

"I'm back, dear."

"Sylvie! What is going on?"

"You'll see soon enough. Come on, we have another destination waiting."

We walk for all of thirty seconds before she pats my arm. "Count to ten again, then you can open your eyes."

This time I do count. I need to calm my racing heart. When I reach thirty, I remove the silk from my face. Opening them, I laugh out loud. This house, much like the first, is a façade, but this one is bright blue. As soon as my eyes are open, I hear shouting coming from inside.

This time I don't hesitate. I open the door immediately and double over, laughing. All of Preston's brothers are in here. Dexter, Trevor, the girls, and all the kids, too. It's chaos everywhere I look.

"One day, Goldie found herself thrown into a new family by Prince Charming. This one was big and loud with people and drama at every turn. The loud family may not have had the same hardships as the little family, but they faced heartbreak just the same. Goldie was often overwhelmed by the new family's ridiculous ways, but she was determined to save them, too.

"The prince didn't make it easy on her, but it was in this loud family that he fell in love with his little Goldie. The problem is, Prince Charming didn't do a very good job of preparing Goldie for all the noise. He was so busy making his heart sing, he didn't realize that Goldie couldn't hear the song. Somewhere along the way, she thought she had just become part of the ensemble. In reality, she was his only melody."

Somehow, even the children are quiet, but there is no dry eye in this loud house.

"The prince called a meeting." I watch as all of Preston's family gathers into a circle, yelling and cheering. Making as much noise as they possibly can until Preston's voice drifts through the speaker again. "The prince decided that while Goldie loves the little family and the loud family, they just didn't fit."

Sylvie steps forward and hands me the blindfold. As soon as I place it over my head, I hear everyone scatter.

"One more stop. Are you ready?"

"I-I think so," I say nervously.

"Okay. You know the drill. Just count to ten."

I've never counted so fast in all my life. Ripping the tie over my head, I see the third house. This one is green, and I rush the door to find the little family and the loud family sitting in chairs looking back at me. This one is not actually a building at all. It is just the front facade that opens up to the ocean with everyone I love together—everyone but Preston. My heart sinks. *What did you expect? You know he's still in the hospital.* Then I hear his voice over the speaker, and I lower myself to the sand to listen.

"The prince knew long ago that Goldie fit just right. Like all fairy tales, they had their ups and downs. The prince may have gotten a new heart, but he knows it will only ever beat for his perfect fit—his perfect Goldie. Together, the little family and the loud family can make a happily ever after. Is that what you want, sweetheart?"

I'm sitting on my knees in the sand, sobbing like a baby. *How is he doing this?*

"Goldie?"

I jump when I hear Preston whisper and whirl around to see him on one knee behind me.

"You're going to get arrested for stealing my heart if you don't answer me soon," he grins.

How can he still have bad pick-up lines? My repertoire ran dry months ago.

"Jesus, Preston. What are you doing? You can't be down here like that," I scream, scrambling and flailing in the sand to get him off the ground, but Ashton beats me to it.

"It's okay, Ems. We have everything covered, but he will not get off his knee until you answer him. It's all part of his plan," Ash says with a wink.

"Answer? Answer wh—?"

"Emory Westbrook, will you marry me for real and forever?" In his hands is the ring I've only ever worn once.

I stumble back with my mouth hanging wide open. Glancing around, I see everyone is waiting on my answer. My hand flies to my mouth, and I flop forward in front of Preston.

"Are you sure this is what you want? That I'm what you want, Preston? I don't want you to feel like—"

"Emory, I have never once done anything I didn't want to. When I said you were mine, I meant it. I need you to understand that I still mean it. I want you forever. Please, Emory, give me your forever?"

"Yes, yes, Preston. I want to be your forever," I cry.

"Thank fuck. Come here," he orders, and I don't hesitate. When his lips touch mine, I know I'm home.

"Okay, break it up, you two. I promised Mom I wouldn't let him sit in the sand too long," Ashton chuckles.

"You look beautiful, Emory." Preston stares into my eyes for a long time. "I'm jealous of your heart, though."

"My heart? Why?" I'm staring at him in confusion when I see the devilish gleam in his eye.

"Because it's beating inside of you, and I'm not." He says it like a joke, but I can feel the heat behind his words.

"No way, Preston. I know you have not been cleared for that kind of activity."

"Fucking hell. This will be the second time you give yourself to me, and we don't consummate it," he sulks.

His words have an effect on me, though, and I feel my panties dampen.

Wrapping a hand around my waist as our family and friends clear a path to a makeshift dance floor, he leans in to whisper, "I bet I can make you come with only my words, though."

"Oh, God."

"That's what I can't wait to hear, sweetheart."

We start to sway to Ed Sheeran's "Perfect", and for the first time in my life, I feel at peace.

"How did you get those houses to the beach so fast? And what in the world are you going to do with them now?"

Preston chuckles. "Don't look at Easton's knuckles. He was out here all night with a crew to build them."

"What? Are you serious? All that work for an hour?"

"Not an hour, Emory. I needed to prove to you that I wasn't just looking for someone. I was looking for you. He will take them down tomorrow and rebuild them at some of the local Children's Homes for kids to play in. He'll have time to actually build walls and a roof for them, though."

"That's really amazing, Preston."

"So are you, Ems."

"We have so much to talk about still." *Does he know how much work we have to do to make this work? Don't ruin every-*

thing, Emory. I realize I'm holding my breath, waiting for him to answer.

"We will. We have a lifetime to work it out, but not tonight. I promised Dr. Terry we would be back in the hospital by six. For now, just dance with your husband."

"Preston?"

"Hmm?"

"I love you."

He pulls back to look me in the eyes. "I love you forever, Emory."

CHAPTER 43

LOKI

*A*rriving in Preston, Maryland, has taken a lot fucking longer than I expected. I can't remember an entire month, which means I don't know who my enemy is right now. It also means that everyone is the enemy. I've had to travel back roads and by nightfall. The infection in my leg is getting worse, and I could do nothing about it until I reached this safe house.

I've been watching this shack in the woods for six hours to make sure it hasn't been compromised. So far, so good. When dark falls, I cut through the clearing to the bomb shelter hidden in plain sight.

After I place my palm on the reader, a small door clicks open. Lowering my body so my eyes are level with the laser, I force them to stay open while it scans my retinas. After what feels like an eternity, the deadbolt opens with a pop. Glancing over my shoulder one last time, I slide into the darkened space.

I know the lights will flicker to life the farther I go, so I move on instinct down the narrow path leading underground. Slowly, the lights fight to activate, and my body finally attempts to relax. I will be safe here for a few days, at least.

As I round the corner, the narrow dirt path opens to a more sterile environment. I move quickly to open the flue to allow fresh air into the compact space. Pulling it back and forth a few times to ensure proper airflow, I put it back in neutral so it doesn't attract attention from ground level.

My vision is blurry from exhaustion, so I quickly grab a bottle of water and rubbing alcohol before falling onto the small cot set up in the corner. Removing my tattered clothing, I flush the wound with water, then pour alcohol directly on it. *Motherfucker, that burns,* is my last thought before darkness consumes me.

When I open my eyes, I don't know if I have been asleep for hours or days, but since I'm not sure what day I started this journey, it doesn't really matter. Stretching to work out the kinks, I'm relieved to notice my head isn't pounding quite as much, so I get to work.

Opening the cabinets that are all locked with biometric security, I set up shop. There's a generator that will allow up to four hours of power at a time. I hook up the laptop and start pulling out all the devices I'll need. Opening my network, I'm bombarded by messages, but the one that assaults me is the one I sent myself. "Four months. They know she's with you. Red." *What the fuck does that mean? Who is she?*

The four hours go by far too quickly, and I'm pissed to realize I found nothing in my research. I'm no closer to finding out who is after me or why. *Unless I didn't get everyone? Is it possible that I missed someone in their organization that would have the means to track me?* I pull at my hair in frustration, then yell, "I can't remember an entire month. How the fuck am I supposed to know who's after me?" My voice echoes in the small room, but then I hear a motor.

I jump from the desk and close the flue, then shut down

everything. Grabbing the guns from the closet, I sit facing the door. If someone is out there, they'll be waiting for me to exit the way I came. Lucky for me, I've always been a paranoid fucker.

When everything has been wiped, I press the button on my ring, and open the half-door. Lowering myself to my knees, I know crawling out of here with this leg will be a bitch. But, life or death doesn't give a shit about a little pain.

Once I reach the crawl space's safety marker, I pull the lanyard from my shirt and press the button. I hear the explosion and know I have seven minutes to make it underground to the edge of the forest. I'd thought about reaching out to Ashton, but now I know that would likely lead to his death. I'm on my own until I can get to them in person.

What the hell is happening in four months, and who the fuck is 'she'?

CHAPTER 44

PRESTON

"Sweetheart? Why don't you go home? You're exhausted, and I'm not going anywhere."

"I'd rather stay," Emory says through a yawn.

Since my surgery, she has been camping out in the recliner that I caught her using all her might to slide across the room one night.

"Emory?"

"What? Are you okay? Did I wake you?"

"No, Goldie. I've been awake watching you roll around in that chair for over an hour. What are you doing?"

Embarrassed, she lowers her gaze. "Ah, I haven't been able to sleep. I think I got used to your body heat, but there is no way I'm climbing in bed with you until you're healed."

A proud grin slides across my face as I watch her wrestle the chair into place beside my bed. Slipping my hand through the bars, she lays her head on my open palm and falls peacefully to sleep.

"You know, I have it on good authority I'll get to go home in a few days. It's probably okay for you to slip in next to me."

"I'd love that, but I'm working here now, and I don't want anyone thinking I get special privileges. It's important to me that I'm reinstated and work my way up the line just like everyone else."

"You're already working long hours, sweetheart. You need a good night's sleep."

"I will when we get home." I watch as her eyes blink slowly, then remain closed.

I'm going to have a lifetime with this stubborn woman. The thought brings me to tears. Just a couple of weeks ago, I thought our story was ending and now forever is possible. As I lay staring at her small frame slowly rising and falling with each breath, I vow to prove to her every day how much she means to me.

Confident she's asleep, I slip my phone off of the bedside table—time to call in reinforcements.

MEP

Preston: Phase two in Make Emory Preston's. Epic first dates. We did things a little backward, and I want to do this right.

Dexter: Have we created a monster?

Colton: Fuck, yes!

Easton: Jesus. Did they remove your balls during surgery, too?

Trevor: You just wait, East. Your turn is coming.

Easton: Fuck that. Never going to happen.

(Easton left the conversation at 9:34pm)

Ashton: What do you have in mind?

Preston: Dexter's the hopeless romantic. What have you got, Dex?

Dexter: How long do we have until you go home?

Dexter: When do you want the first date to happen?

Preston: I get out in five days. Date #1 in six days. Can we do it?

Dexter: You know we can.

Trevor: Dex lives for this shit.

Colton: Count me in!

291

Halton: I'm with East. Good luck, though.

Ashton: What the hell happened to the two of you? Grumpy mofos.

Preston: (eye rolling emoji) Great, Dex. What's the plan?

(Colton added Easton to the conversation at 9:47pm)

Easton: Jesus Christ.

$\approx$

WALKING into our home is an almost religious experience. I never expected to return, so everything looks different. Seeing it with new eyes, I realize there is nothing here that screams 'ours'.

"Ems? Do you like it here?"

Mid step, she turns to look at me. "What do you mean? Here, like, at your house?"

"That's what I mean. I don't want you to think of it as my house. Everything is ours. I want it to feel like ours."

Her face softens as she takes me in. "Preston, it's just new, that's all. I love it here."

I wrap her in a hug but don't fully believe her. Tomorrow, on our first official date night, I'll find out the truth.

$\approx$

THE DOORBELL RINGS RIGHT at six p.m. Colton may be a special version of Peter Pan, but he never lets me down.

"Ems?" I yell from the bathroom where I'm hiding. "Can you get that?"

"Got it," she says as I hear her walk down the hallway.

Poking my head out the door, I wait for her reaction.

"Colton? What the hell are you doing?" She laughs.

"You, Cinderella, have an engagement to get to," he says, rolling his hand as he bows.

Jesus, he went all out. He's wearing short pants with knee-high socks and everything. Coming up behind Emory, I stifle a laugh.

"Where did you get that outfit?" I finally cave and ask.

"Costumes For You," he says proudly. "Are you ready, madam?"

"Ready? Where are we going?"

"Step one in showing you I'm never letting you go. Come on, you don't need anything," I take her hand in mine and tug her toward the door.

"But, but you haven't been cleared to do much, Preston."

"It's a good thing we aren't doing much then, isn't it?"

We listen to her excuses for the entire elevator ride. As we step outside, words fail her. Hell, they fail me. There is a life-size version of Cinderella's pumpkin carriage, horses, and all in front of us.

How the hell did Dexter pull this off?

"What? How ... what?" she repeats.

"Come on, miss. Stroke of midnight and all," Colton says with a wink.

"But ... Why? Who?"

"Let's go, Goldie, you heard the man." I gently nudge her forward, and she climbs into the carriage.

Clapping Colton on the back, I whisper, "Thanks, brother."

"You've got a second chance, Pres. We all want to help make sure you live it to the fullest. She's good for you."

Swallowing the emotion, I finally choke out, "She is. Love you."

"Luvs."

Damn, Lanie is getting to everyone around here.

As soon as I climb aboard, the horses take off at a slow clip. Nuzzling in next to Emory, I wrap my arm around her.

"What did you do, Preston?"

Glancing down into her watery eyes, I kiss her forehead.

293

"We missed a lot of firsts, so this, my dear, is our first date of many."

After an hour, the horse and carriage drop us off at my favorite Italian restaurant, but I'm antsy for the next part of our date, and barely focus on what we're served. When we're finished, we step outside to find Colton talking to a bunch of co-eds. *Jesus, this kid.* Catching my eye, he slyly sends them on their way.

Taking Emory's arm, he helps her into the carriage. "Milady! Good to have you back. Are you ready for your next destination?"

Glancing over her shoulder, she says, "I don't know, I'm a little nervous."

Stepping in beside her, I promise, "Nothing to be nervous about, Ems. Now, or ever. I've always got you."

She nods once then takes her seat.

Turning to Colton, I whisper, "Everything all set?"

"Are you kidding? Dex has everyone on walkie talkies like he's a wedding planner. He will consider this a personal failure if it doesn't go perfectly."

Freaking Dexter.

"Thanks. Okay, we're ready then." Taking my seat beside Emory, I hold her hand as we watch the scenery go by.

The carriage slows to a stop in front of a vacant piece of property, and I see Emory glance around confused.

If all goes as planned, our future will all take place here.

Colton opens the door, and he leads Emory out with me right behind her. While we stand, looking out over an empty field, I feel questions radiating off her in waves. As she is about to speak, Dexter flips the switch, and it illuminates the area in fairy lights of various shades and sizes. In the center is a four-poster bed that appears to float in the space.

Wide-eyed, Emory gasps as she takes in everything around her. "Preston? Wh-What is this?"

"Speed dating," I say, pulling her forward.

"Speed— Preston. We're married."

"I know, sweetheart, and I'm going to make sure we stay that way forever. Come on."

I lead her through the path my brothers formed in the last few days. It takes us straight to the most massive bed I have ever seen. *Dexter must have had it custom made.* It's easily the size of two king beds.

"What the?" Emory whispers as I notice a screen rising twenty yards in front of the bed.

A spotlight clicks to life and draws our attention to another corner of the field. A neon light is hanging over a table that says Game Night. Hearing another noise, we turn in the opposite direction just as a light flickers to life, saying Sports Bar. That area is decorated like an Irish pub. In a whoosh, our attention is drawn to the large bonfire Ashton just lit.

"What is all this?" Emory says with a shaky voice.

"All our firsts. Dinner. The movie," I say, pointing to the projection that is frozen on *Ten Things I Hate About You.* "Game Night, Bar Crawl, Bonfire with S'mores, and Star Gazing," I say, indicating the bed.

"Holy— This isn't speed dating, Preston. Speed dating is asking rapid-fire questions."

"We're going to do that tonight, too, don't worry. By the time this night is over, I'm going to know all your hopes, dreams, and fears. Our life is just beginning, Emory. Because of you, my life is starting for the first time in ten years. I'm going to spend eternity showing you how much I need you with me, always."

"I-I don't know what to say," she says through tears. "I don't need these grand gestures, Preston. I—"

"You don't need them, but I do. I need to make up for lost time. For time I never thought I would have. Let's get a drink," I smirk.

She glances over my head in the direction of the ridiculous

bar the guys have set up, and laughs as Easton stands behind it in a vest and tie, scowling, but ready to take our order.

"Doesn't he look happy?" I chuckle. "What's your favorite cocktail, Emory? See? Speed dating." With a wink, I start walking toward East. Emory moves in tandem, and we reach him in just a few steps.

"Ah, I'm not much of a drinker, remember?"

"I do. That's why we had a special menu made," I say, handing it to her.

Emory's head falls back in laughter as she reads the drink names.

"The Broken Heart. The Fixem. The Never Have I Ever Again. The Goldie—"

She breaks off before she reads the last one.

"The Forever After," I fill in as music starts to play.

"What do you say, Ems. What can I make you tonight?" Easton grumbles. *The asshole.*

"I-I'll have The Forever After, please," she says quietly.

Leaning over, so my lips touch her ear, I whisper, "Good choice, Goldie."

Taking our drinks, we make our way over to the game table, and both laugh when we find a life-size cut out of GG propped up behind a row of tarot cards.

"She's absolutely nuts, but she wasn't wrong, was she?" Emory remarks.

"No, and that scares the shit out of me. Who knows what she's got up her sleeve next." Turning a card over, my stomach sinks noticing two babies are now face up. *I can't give Emory children.*

Sensing my sudden shift in mood, Emory places a hand over mine. "Pres? I think you made a smart decision having that vasectomy."

Shocked, I stare into her eyes. "You do? What about kids? Don't you want them?"

Something similar to sadness crosses her face. "Pres, I have been raising kids since I was seven. I'm not sure it's something I can do again. I'm not even sure it's something I've ever wanted, but I don't feel like I'm missing out on anything by not having them if that's what you're asking."

I nod, letting her words settle over me.

"Where do you see yourself in ten years?" she asks.

"I don't. I only see us. Here, happy, living, and loving life. What's your biggest fear, Ems?"

"Wow, jumping right into the hard ones, huh?" She laughs, buying time before answering. "I guess it's letting my family down. Letting you down," she adds so softly I almost don't hear it.

"Emory, look at me."

Slowly, she raises her gaze to meet mine.

"You can never let me down, okay?"

"You don't know that, Preston."

"I do because I have a faith in you that you haven't found yet. But you will, I promise."

With teary eyes, she asks, "Christmas dinner, ham or turkey?"

"Is that a real question?" I ask. "There is no debate. Turkey is for Thanksgiving. Christmas ham all the way."

"Agreed. Homemade or catered?"

"Emory, give me some credit here. Sylvie would kick my ass if holiday meals were ever catered."

"Okay, good. I've never been able to give my sisters a proper holiday dinner, but—"

"They'll never miss one of ours, I promise. Your family is my family, no matter what. We may need to invest in a bigger place, though," I say, happy we're finally on topic.

"Bigger? Preston, my dad's entire house can fit in your apartment."

"Our apartment, Emory. Ours." Now I know I've made

the right decision. "What's your dream home like?" I ask as I guide her to the bed when Lanie pops up out of nowhere.

"Hey, guys! We're going to get out of here. There is plenty of wood to keep the fire going. The remote is tucked into the headboard for the movie, and there are trays set up for your drinks. Have fun."

Before we can thank her, she's scurrying toward the road where I can make out shadows of my entire family. Family by blood and family by choice, it's all the same.

"How did you get everyone here for this?"

"I just asked, Emory. That's what family docs for each other. I wish you could have seen the shit we went through for Dex. But, back to the question." I hold her drink as she climbs up onto the bed that must be four feet off the ground, at least. "What's your dream home look like?"

After placing our drinks on the end table, I climb in next to her.

"Honestly? I don't know, Pres. I've never thought about it."

Tucking her into my arm, I pull the blankets up around our legs. "Let's dream it up together then. Mansion or cottage?"

"Ah, isn't there a middle ground here?"

Chuckling, I agree, "Okay, something in the middle. Country French-Style or Tudor?"

"Neither of those sound middle of the road. I guess if I had to choose, it would be Country French because I'd want it to be livable. I could never be comfortable in a show home."

"Me either, and I'm all for comfortable living. That's how I designed the penthouse. I wanted people to come in and feel at home."

"You did a great job."

"How do you feel about a sex swing in the bedroom?"

I catch her off guard, and she chokes on her Forever After.

"Geez, warn a girl," she admonishes when she's caught her breath.

"Sorry," I chuckle. "So, note to self, no sex swings. What's one thing your dream home would have?"

"Oh, that's easy," she answers immediately. "My dream home would have a library with floor-to-ceiling bookshelves and a rolling ladder, and lots of big, comfy couches to sink into while I read."

Done.

We spend the rest of the night building our dream home and asking every ridiculous question we can come up with. When we wake in the early morning light, the fire has gone out, and even under all the down, we're cold. I hold Emory for a few more seconds. Finally, I wake her, and we return to our temporary home.

CHAPTER 45

PRESTON

One month later

"Are you sure you want to set this up here?" Dexter asks. "Trevor and Julia have been spending a lot of time at his folk's house, cleaning it out. I'm sure they would stay there if you want to do this in my guest house."

"I want it here, and Emory understands. I don't have my stamina back yet. I want to oversee every part of this until we find him, and I can't do that if I have to drive back and forth."

"Loki's never gone missing this long before?" Emory's little sister asks.

"He's never gone over two weeks without checking in," Dex tells her.

I love my new sister-in-law, really I do, but she is this weird mix of Dexter, GG, and Lanie. She's a hopeless romantic like Dex, possibly even more gullible than Lanie, and asks the most inappropriate questions like GG. I don't know how to handle her.

"Ah, if we're using your extra bedrooms as war rooms, where is Sloane staying?"

Eli and Tilly went back to school before I was even

released from the hospital, but Sloane? She's like an extra appendage some days. With Emory spending more time acclimating to Charlotte Medical, entertaining her has fallen to me.

"I'm renting Loki's apartment downstairs. I can't believe how affordable it is. I couldn't rent a shoebox for that amount in Seattle," she says happily.

Dexter gives me a look that says, 'You're full of shit.'

"Yeah, crazy, right?" I give him a pleading glare. I need some alone time with my wife. Especially now that I've been cleared for more strenuous activity. *Fuck, I can't wait for her to get home.* Turning away, I adjust myself. *Get a grip, man. You cannot be cupping your dick while your in-laws are four feet away!*

Shaking her head, she smiles, and I'm still caught off guard by the similarities between her and Emory sometimes.

The front door bursts open with Trevor and Julia rushing through shortly after. "Seth got a ping?"

Dexter and I look at each other. Seth is on the other side of the apartment. We hadn't heard anything. A split second later, both our phones chime as Seth enters the hallway.

"There's news?" I ask with no pretense.

"Gather everyone in the family room," Seth instructs. "Let's go through this once, so we don't waste any more time."

I haven't figured Seth out, but I know he can be a real fucking prick sometimes.

"Stand down, Pres," Ashton whispers beside me. "I know what you're thinking. I think it, too. But, for all his faults, Seth is unwavering in his loyalty to Loki. I'm watching everything. I have ears everywhere, too, but we need Seth. He might be the only one that can lead us to Loki."

"Fine."

"Is everyone here?" Seth asks in his monotonous way.

"West," I yell.

"Brooks," Ashton finishes.

"Lanie is with the kids," Dex supplies as Colton, Easton, and Halt exit another room while my mother walks out of the kitchen.

"Emory is working at the hospital but should be here soon. I'll fill her in," I tell him.

"And I'm here," Sloane says. There's a perkiness about her I know will grate on Seth, and I love every minute of it.

Seth looks to Ash and me for confirmation of the new addition.

Shrugging my shoulders, I let a grin slip as I say, "She's family."

He grumbles something I don't catch, and I feel instantly lighter.

"Don't poke him, Pres," East chuckles.

"There were no adult remains found at the explosion site," Seth blurts uneasily.

"Oh, dear God," my mother says, clutching her heart.

"Civilians, Seth," Ashton says through gritted teeth. "Rein it in."

What the fuck does 'no adult remains' mean? Giving Ashton the side eye, I can tell he is thinking the same thing.

"Sorry. That means that Loki wasn't caught in it. Knowing him, he probably set the explosion himself to buy some time, but that's just speculation at this point. As you know, we have had nothing from him for six weeks. That's not his MO, so there is still reason for concern. Ashton has confirmed that Loki took out the entire operation. Anyone looking to take over will have no ties to any of you, so that's the good news."

"Then why hasn't he come home?" my mother asks, worry lacing her shaky voice.

"According to intel, the Russians have taken over that territory, and they won't go near Loki," Ash tells her. "But that doesn't explain why we haven't heard from him. There has to be a piece we're missing."

"Why would bad guys be scared of Loki?" Sloane asks.

"Are you taking notes?" *I think this freaking girl is taking notes like she's in class.*

She looks around guiltily. "Loki sounds like he would make a good hero."

Seth marches to her and rips the notebook out of her hands. "This isn't a fucking joke. Loki is the most highly trained special agent we have seen in decades. That doesn't mean he's invincible."

"Hey," I interject. "Tone it down, Seth. This is a lot for anyone to take. Sloane hasn't been here long enough to be desensitized like the rest of us."

"How is he different from other agents?"

Christ, where is Emory? Her sister does not know when to stop.

"Loki graduated the same year as Preston, Dex, and I, but he is two years younger. In book terms, he would be the hero, the nerd, the jock, the man from the wrong side of town, and the bad boy all rolled into one."

When Trevor finishes speaking, we all stare at him in shock.

"What? Have you read her books?" he whispers. "They are like fucking crack to Julia. I think she is going to break my dick if she keeps reading them. I swear, every goddamn chapter, she is climbing me like a tree. I've even thought about buying her a dildo just to give my junk a rest."

When I hear Dex exhale, I look at him and almost laugh.

"Thank fuck. I thought it was just Lanie's hormones all out of whack again. I actually hid in the closet last night when I saw she was reading another one. I'm chafed in places no man should ever chafe."

Are these two idiots kidding me right now?

"Please tell me you two numbnuts are not complaining about having too much sex," I say, running a hand over my forehead.

"You just wait. You don't understand what those books do to women," Trevor grumbles, cupping his sack.

Jesus Christ.

"Ah-hem. Are you ladies about done over there?" *Fucking Seth.* Giving him the finger, I motion for him to continue.

"The reason I'm giving you this intel is that the agency has called off the search. After he pinged a second time, they're considering him AWOL."

"What?"

"He wouldn't do that."

"Bull shit," I yell.

"I know," Seth sighs. "We know that's not the case, so I'm going to need your resources to bring him home. I can't do it on my own," he admits it as if the words wound him.

Ashton crosses the room first. "You have whatever you need at your fingertips. If you don't have it, ask, and I'll get it for you. Colt, grab the board. Let's map this out."

A second later, Colt is dragging a whiteboard into the room.

"We know he pinged a quarter-mile from ground zero three days after the explosion," Seth informs us, putting a pin on the map he just hung for us all to see and labeling it with the letter A. "His second ping was eight days later in Clinton, Pennsylvania."

"What's a ping?" Sloane whispers to Easton. I can recognize the instant he realizes he grabbed the wrong seat.

"A ping is a signal sent straight to HQ. It lets us know he is alive but not much else because the pings are retroactive. Meaning Loki is long gone by the time they go live."

"So, he's like a real-life super spy?"

"Jesus," East grumbles. "I guess."

Seth makes no effort to hide his annoyance. "Then nothing. For three weeks, we heard nothing. Five days ago, he pinged in Preston, Maryland. Loki would have known the agency wouldn't be following him anymore, so I have to assume he sent this one for us."

Ashton places another pin in Maryland, then ties a string labeling Pennsylvania B and Maryland, C.

"And just now, he pinged again in Hancock, Tennessee."

Ash ties another string with the letter D attached to it. "Loki's definitely sending a message," he says, stepping back from the map. "Clinton was our father's name. Then there's Preston, but what the hell is Hancock?"

"If you turn your head, it kind of looks like the letter U," Sloane says softly. Without warning, we all tilt our heads, too.

"Or the start of a W," Ashton counters.

"Five points West," Easton and I say together.

"Holy shit," Ashton murmurs.

"What? What the hell does this mean?" Seth yells.

"Our father always said there are five points in West. He would count the points of a W and said there was one for each of us. Take one away, and you only have U. He likened it to the 'no I in team' adage. He told us all if we were ever in trouble, to count on the five points. When Loki moved in with us, he used to joke that he would have to change our name to something with six points," I explain.

"I don't understand. So you're saying Loki's in trouble?"

"That's my best guess." *What kind of trouble are you in, Loki? Why haven't you called?*

"Let's assume he is giving us a signal. What does Hancock have to do with any of this?" he asks.

We all sit in silence until Halton stands suddenly. "Loki's nanny. The one who used to drive him everywhere. She moved to Hancock after he moved in with us."

"Are you sure?" *I don't remember anything about a nanny.*

"Yes, I'm sure. I remember because after we finished decorating his room at our house, he talked about her, and I couldn't stop laughing. For a ten-year-old boy, Hancock is a pretty fucking hilarious name."

"You know, I think he is right. What was her name?" my mother thinks out loud.

"Her name was Claire," Halton grumbles.

"How the fuck do you remember that?"

"Because there was a Claire in my class that year, and she drove me nuts," he says.

"Claire? Who lives in Hancock? That's all we have to go on?" Seth asks. His anger is bubbling just below the surface. "How many fucking people live in Hancock, Tennessee?"

"6,620," Sloane chirps from the couch.

"That's not too bad." *Is it?* "Ash, how many Claires?"

We all turn to Ashton, who is plugging away on a laptop. I see his shoulders tighten and cringe.

"None," he says, still staring at the screen.

"If this Loki is as smart as you say he is, wouldn't it make sense that he would have her using an unfamiliar name? I mean, if he ever thought he would need her as like a safe house or something?"

Sometimes the shit that comes out of Sloane's mouth is cringeworthy, but this doesn't sound too far off.

"I'm going to have to cross-reference by hand," Ash says, moving toward one of the tactical rooms. "Mom? What age bracket are we looking at here? How old do you think Claire would be?"

"Oh, Lord. I'm honestly not sure. Mid-sixties, maybe? Daddy had all Loki's legal files in that old filing cabinet when we became his guardians. I'll run home and look through that. Perhaps there's something useful."

"That would be great. Thanks, Mom," Ash yells over his shoulder as he kicks the door shut.

Walking my mother to the door, I hear Seth bark orders. By the time I kiss her good-bye, Trevor and Dexter are heading my way.

"Good luck with Seth," Dexter grumbles. "He's given us all jobs. We'll be by tomorrow for the party if you still want to do it?"

Emory and I have planned a Christmas do-over for everyone since the holidays were a bust for us all. We wanted to make up for ruining Dexter and Lanie's wedding, but they decided to put it off until spring.

Pinching the back of my neck, I roll it side to side. "Yeah, I think we should. Whatever is going on with Loki isn't going to solve itself overnight. Let's try to make the best of it." *Hopefully, this is the right decision.*

"Dexter?" Sloane calls from the other room.

"Fuck. Move, Preston, let us out," Trevor says, pushing past me.

"What? Why?"

"I know she's your family now, but she asks questions that would even make GG blush. She is using us for her stories," Dexter says in a panic.

"What kind of questions?" I laugh.

"Fuck you, wait until she comes after your story. She has a screw loose or something. She asked Dexter to explain, in detail, what it felt like when he came with Lanie for the first time."

I choke on a laugh when I realize he's serious.

"She asked me how many pumps it takes to come. Like I'm a goddamn lollipop. Now move before I run your ass over, open-heart surgery or not."

With a shocked expression, I watch two of my best friends run from my five-foot-two, overly inquisitive sister-in-law. *Shit, I'm going to have to talk to Emory about this.*

"Whoa, guys. Slow down, where's the fire?" I hear Emory ask just before she steps in the door.

Seeing her for the first time in hours, I growl. Actually fucking growl. She makes the clusterfuck happening behind me disappear.

"Hello, wifey." I wrap her in a hug and waste no time tasting her lips.

"Hello, husband. You really should let me wash the hospital off before you jump me like this, you know?"

"Oh, sweetheart. I am so going to jump you tonight. I even got the okay from my doctor."

CHAPTER 46

EMORY

I may be laughing, but one look into his eyes and I know he isn't joking. *What is he planning?* My body tingles at the prospects.

"Dexter?" I hear my sister call, and Preston cringes.

Eesh. What has she been doing now?

"Oh, hi, Ems! I was just looking for Dexter. I wanted to ask him another question," she says, peering behind us and realizing the guys have left. "Shoot, did I miss him?"

"Yes," Preston blurts, appearing uncomfortable.

"What, ah, what did you want to ask?" I'm terrified of her answer.

"Oh, just wondering what blue balls feel like. Lanie said he probably had them when he was in London."

I choke, and Preston pats me on the back gently. "Why on earth are you asking Dexter about blue balls, and why is Lanie telling you that?"

"I asked her," she says, shrugging her shoulders before turning back down the hall.

Oh no.

"Yeah. Apparently, she left Seattle before she finished her

last book, so she's collecting everyone's love story. In very vivid detail, Emory. Blue balls and coming kind of detail."

He sounds so freaked out, I almost laugh. Almost.

"Okay, I'll talk to her. What's been going on here?"

Preston fills me in on all the new details about Loki as I say hello and good-bye to everyone.

"Sloane? I'm just going to change, then we'll be out," I tell my sister, who is trying really hard to listen in on Seth's conversation.

"That's okay. I'm going to head downstairs now. I've got some writing to do," she says with a grin.

Ugh. Please do not let her be writing Lanie and Dexter's sexcapades.

I give her a quick kiss. "Okay. Love you. Did you have dinner?"

"I'm not a child, Ems. I can feed myself. Luvs," she says over her shoulder.

Good grief, she has been hanging out with Lanie.

I'm almost to our bedroom door when Seth appears in the hallway. "We have another ping. We think this one came from his childhood home."

"Shit," Preston hisses.

"It's okay. You go. I need to shower. I'll find you when I'm done."

"Our lives won't always be like this, you know? I promise you, we will have dull, married-couple days, too." Leaning in for a kiss, he whispers, "We'll also have hot, animalistic sex days. Very, very soon."

I glance down and see his words affect him just as much as they do me. I smile shamelessly. "I hope so."

"Fuck me."

I can't help but laugh at his pained expression. "Go, I'll be out soon."

"Okay. Emory?"

"Yeah?"

"I love you forever." I see it in his face. He means that with every fiber of his being.

"I love you, too, Preston. Always."

Stepping into the shower, I reflect on the last month. I worry that we've fallen too quickly into a pattern that takes most couples years to emulate. I won't ever tell Preston that, though. God only knows what kind of fairy tale magic he would pull out if he ever thought I had doubts.

"Don't ruin a good thing with your negativity, Emory. You are entitled to a happily ever after as much as the next person." Lexi's words run through my mind. They've become a mantra of sorts, but they do make me miss my friend. She left so suddenly, I feel like I missed something even though she assures me there's nothing wrong. Julia mentioned that something was wrong with the roof at the lodge that GG owns, so I guess it makes sense. It doesn't make me miss her any less, though.

Finished with my shower, I pad through the enormous space, happy that my husband is a smart man. Turning our home into Loki Locators HQ meant we had to shift some things around. Preston moved his office into the spare room across from ours. That allowed all the work to be done on the opposite side of the apartment. *"It's the only way we'll have any privacy,"* Preston had said.

Privacy is a hot commodity these days.

I sit quietly on the couch and listen to Seth talk.

"I have a team headed there now."

"Seth, I don't even know the last time Loki was in that house, but I can guarantee he has it locked down. I think my mother hired a caretaker after his parents passed, but I have no idea if she still looks after it. They will not allow strangers onto that property without a search warrant."

"Or you?" Seth counters.

Preston glances in my direction. I know he's desperate to get me alone again, but Loki is the priority.

"It's okay, you go with Seth. I'm exhausted anyway. I'll just get some sleep while you're gone."

Preston is on me in an instant. "Can I wake you up when I get home?"

"I hope you do," I say in a sultry voice I don't recognize.

He sighs loudly. "Let's go." A quick, hungry kiss later, he's walking out the door.

With them gone, I sit on the balcony. It's much cooler out now, but I find myself needing to clear my head more often than not. Everything in my life has happened so fast I'm struggling to accept it all as real.

"Goldie? Jesus Christ, you're frozen. You scared the shit out of me. I didn't know where you were," Preston's strained voice fills my ears just as I feel myself go airborne.

My eyes open in surprise to find myself plastered to Preston's side. *Shit! Did I fall asleep?*

"I ... wait, what time is it?" I ask, glancing around.

The house is dark as he carries me inside and straight to our room.

"Shh, it's late, and you are cold as ice."

I can't help myself. I nuzzle into his warmth. "I'm sure you can warm me up."

He growls into my neck, and my pulse quickens. I love that he responds to me this way. *No man has ever had this kind of reaction to anything I've done.* It makes me feel powerful, confident, and sexy as hell.

We come to a stop in the master bath, and he sets me on the counter as he turns on all three shower heads. I observe him as he holds a hand in the running water until it reaches the desired temperature. He is still the same Preston I met in Dr. Terry's office, but this man before me is different. The sad edge he held is gone. In its place is an open, honest man who continues to go out of his way to prove his love to me.

Will you ever be able to accept it? The phrase runs through my head like a curse. *Will I?*

"What's the frown for, sweetheart?"

I snap my attention to him, trying to shake the thoughts away.

"Nothing, just thinking. Any news on Loki?" I ask, changing the subject.

He stares at me, debating if he should take the bait. Finally, after searching my eyes, he caves. "We found a note, but it doesn't make any sense. We'll need a family meeting tomorrow before dinner to figure it out if Seth doesn't turn up anything tonight."

"Another full house," I say. I don't mean it to sound snotty, just an observation, but I can see it makes Preston feel guilty. "I-I didn't mean that. I—"

"It's okay, I think it, too. A lot. Especially now that I really, really need to have you all to myself." He motions toward his crotch, and I gasp.

Jesus, that thing is monstrous.

"Grrr, I do love that sound, Goldie. I want to hear it more often. Preferably when I'm inside of you." He grabs the hem of my shirt, and I raise my arms to help him remove it. His hands scrap the underside of my breast while his thumbs rub gentle circles through the lace of my bra. My nipples immediately love the attention.

"Your tits remind me of Mount Rushmore," he says, catching me off guard.

"Oh yeah?"

"Yes, and my face should be among them." He grins. His insanely handsome face searches mine just before he leans in to take one stiffened peak into his mouth.

I want to laugh, but it catches in my chest as he begins his ministrations.

"As your husband, it's my duty to see if I can make you come like this." He smirks.

"You can, you definitely can—"

I'm interrupted by a loud crash, and Preston immediately

goes rigid.

"Since I have the best alarm system available, and at least five special agents inside of the house, I'm going to assume that noise is your sister. Again," he sighs, resting his forehead against mine.

"She's never liked to sleep alone, but I had no idea it's gotten this bad since she's been away."

This is the fourth night in a row she has snuck back upstairs from her apartment. Most of the time, we just find her asleep on the couch.

"I'm sorry."

"Sweetheart, she's your baby sister. Now, she's my problem, too. I would never expect you to turn your back on her. But I'm telling you now, if I don't get you alone very soon, blue balls are going to be the least of our problems. Let's go see what she's up to this time."

Handing me my shirt, he turns off the shower then helps me hop off the counter. We spend the next two hours watching a movie on the couch with my sister. Preston sits in the corner, trying not to pout.

CHAPTER 47

PRESTON

*B*y the time we got to bed last night, Emory was fast asleep before her head hit the pillow. I hate that she is spending so many hours at the hospital, but I'm happy she will soon get the chance to do what she loves again.

Even my money and connections couldn't speed up the process. She has to go through all the proper channels like everyone else. I probably could have found a way, but she begged me not to, and she has worked way too hard for me to ruin it by playing the hero.

The house is blissfully quiet, and it gives my raging hard-on hope. Rolling over, I find Emory is already out of bed, though, and I groan. *Seriously, what else can possibly cock block me?* Jumping out of bed with more frustration than I care to admit, I take a cold shower, then go search for my wife.

As soon as I open my bedroom door, I'm hit with the scents and sounds of Christmas. Following the holiday cheer, I find all the guys, minus Loki, in the family room. They don't notice me, so I continue past them, toward the kitchen where I find Emory. Leaning into the doorway, I watch as she laughs with my mom. Crammed around my large island, Emory kneads dough with Julia, Lanie, Sloane, my mom, and Julia's mom.

When she notices me, she waves a flour-covered hand in my direction. She is covered in the white mess, but she has never looked more happy or relaxed. Not wanting to interrupt, I mouth, 'I love you forever,' and watch as her body softens. It happens every time I say it, and it encourages me to continue showing her how much I mean it. *I will never let her believe anything less ever again.*

Lanie's phone rings, and they all stop while she answers it.

"Hi, Lexi! Everyone, it's Lex." She presses a button on her phone and turns the screen around.

Easton is suddenly at my side. *Isn't that interesting?* Before I know it, we're all crowding around the kitchen saying hello.

"What do you mean? Hold on, I can't hear you. Everyone shush," Lanie yells.

"The roof is worse than we imagined, Lanes. I thought I could handle this, but it's going to take an entire crew, and since it's the middle of winter, everyone's busy on other mountains. There's snow pouring into half the rooms. I … I don't know what to do? I think GG is going to lose the entire lodge. I've had to cancel reservations left and right, there is no way for her to stay open, and we can't afford to shut the doors."

Lexi isn't someone to exaggerate. She also isn't someone to ask for help.

"Oh my gosh, Lexi. What can I do? What do you need? Should Dex and I come up?"

"No," Easton says forcefully at my side. "Fucking stubborn woman. I told her to let me help. I'll go, and if you don't like that, Lexi, too goddamn bad. I'll be there tonight." We all watch in shock as he storms off, yelling something about taking the plane.

"What the hell happened in Vegas?" I wonder aloud.

"All I know is Easton, Lexi, and I were the last one's standing. At some point, they put me in a cab and sent me home. East never made it to his bed that night. Judging by Lexi's appearance on the flight home the next day, she didn't get much sleep either," Colton explains, happy to supply the gossip.

"Oooh, is this another love story in the making?" Sloane asks, pulling a pen out of her hair like a ninety-year-old waitress.

"No," all the men yell in unison.

"Seriously, do you think something's going on with them?" Emory whispers.

"I have no idea. It's a scary thought, though. Those two would be voted most likely to kill each other for food in high school."

"There you are," Seth says gruffly. I swear this guy forgets whose house he is in half the time.

"Here I am. You need something?" I ask, wrapping an arm around Emory.

"I have Ashton carrying the board into the family room. Do you mind if we go over the new intel before you celebrate?"

I can't decide if it's sarcasm or anger in his voice, but since we're in the middle of a Christmas do-over, I go for charitable. "Sure. And, Seth? You know that you're invited to our Merry little fuckmas, too, right? Loki would want you here, and even though we don't say it enough, every person here appreciates everything you're doing to find him."

He stares are me, dumbfounded. "Ah … okay. Th-Thanks, Preston. I appreciate it."

Alright, I admit it. I've been a dick to this guy. I'll try to do better.

Clapping him on the shoulder, I say, "Anytime. Let's see what we have," then follow him into the family room.

Seth takes over immediately.

"I've been going over the intel nonstop all night. Unfortunately, I can't make anything of it. Ashton located the nanny's house yesterday morning, and my team converged in Maryland this morning. The house was empty. It appears she left in a hurry, and there's no trace of her. I think it is safe to assume Loki made it to her, but we have no idea if she left with him or was forced to leave later."

Out of the corner of my eye, I see my mom sitting silently.

"I think Sloane is correct in that he was leading us to all these places," Seth admits begrudgingly.

"The W? I knew it," Sloane cheers.

"Right. Anyway, we're checking out the other three points West but haven't found anything. The only other clue we have is from Loki's parents' house."

My mother gasps. The house Loki grew up in is next door to my childhood home. It shares a beach on Westbrook Bay. Halton makes his way across the room to hold her hand. The jerk isn't such a hardass when it comes to our mom.

"What did you find at the Kane house?" my mother asks.

Seth looks around, then pins a bloodied piece of paper to the board.

"Jesus, Seth. Are all the dramatics really necessary?" Ash scolds.

"Sorry, I-I just don't know what the hell any of it means."

Like everyone else in the room, I stand to get a closer look.

"That's Loki's handwriting," I confirm.

"I thought so, too," Seth agrees.

"Four points West—Sutton?" Emory reads aloud, but it's the next part I can't look away from.

Turning to find Julia, I know she sees it, too. "Is that your code?"

Julia nods her head. "It is."

"What does it say?" my mother asks. Loki is one of her boys. I can't imagine the pain this poor woman has lived through between the eight of us.

"They know she's with me," Julia says.

"What the fuck does that mean?" Seth barks.

"I … I don't know," she admits. "There isn't anything else? It looks like it's torn in half. There isn't another piece?"

"No, we searched everywhere," he says, running a hand through his unruly dark hair.

"Seth?" my mother asks gently, snapping him out of it.

"What can I do for you, Mrs. Westbrook?" At least he has manners when he chooses to use them.

"How many men do you have on this right now?"

"Ashton hired six. I couldn't get any from the agency because they have him—"

"We have a lot of men on it, Mom. Why do you ask?" Ashton cuts in.

"I'm wondering when the last time either of you slept? Or ate?"

They glance at each other, and know they are about to be mom'd hard.

"That's what I thought. Seth, you have ten minutes to give orders to the other men. Then we will all sit and celebrate this Christmas together. After that, we will all work around the clock to make sure you have everything you need to bring our Loki home."

"But time—"

"Time is of the essence. Yes, I know. I also know my Loki better than you think. Unless there is some reason the people you have hired are incapable of taking over for two hours, you will both join us." She doesn't wait for a response—she just turns and heads back into the kitchen.

"You heard her, Ash. I wouldn't fuck with her today. It's been a rough few months for her, too," I say quietly.

"Okay. Come on, Seth. When she says ten minutes, she means ten minutes."

Like two little boys, they scramble down the hall.

CHAPTER 48

EMORY

I take my seat next to Preston at the table. Sylvie sits to my left, and I can feel her worries weighing her down. That's why I'm so caught off guard when she clinks her wine glass with a small spoon.

"Can I have everyone's attention, please?" She clears her throat. Staring at the empty seats at the end of the table, she finally returns her attention to Preston. "I know that we are missing a few key members of our ever-growing family, but I feel strongly that we cannot let that keep us from celebrating the ones we have with us.

"Emory, my dear girl."

Shit. I feel the tears start, and I don't even know where this is going.

"You came to us in the most unconventional of ways, but now that you're here, we will never let you go. You held my son's heart in your hands, and you kept him alive. That alone will keep you in my heart forever, but it isn't the only thing. You not only held his heart, but you also captured it for eternity. We are all here tonight because of you.

"My late husband always said I was the glue that held our family together, but I know he would have felt the same had he been able to meet you. I always wanted a daughter, and God gave me you. Thank you for saving my son. For saving my family, and for helping Preston find his true self."

She reaches beneath the table and hands me a small box. Tears are flowing uncontrollably down my face, so Preston hands me a napkin. Even after wiping my eyes, everything is still blurry, but I finally get the box open with some help.

Inside is a delicate heart necklace encrusted with every dazzling jewel under the sun. I stare at it for a minute. It's the most beautiful thing I've ever seen, but I feel like I'm missing something. Tearing my eyes from it, I'm shocked to see everyone staring at me with their own tears forming.

"You see, I have a feeling you're still trying to figure out how your new life makes sense. We all had this made to show you. Each tiny jewel is the birthstone of someone in this crazy little loud family you have inherited. Everyone from handsome little Tate to GG in Vermont right back to me. The center stone was the diamond Preston's dad proposed to me with. You see, I spent a long time being the center of the family, but we would have been broken without you. I hope every time you wear this, you'll be reminded that you're the very center of this family you're still trying to figure out. We will always have your back, and we will always love you."

I'm so choked up, I don't notice that Preston has risen and is holding the necklace up in front of me. Holding my hair to the side, he fastens it, and I watch as it falls into place. It's beautiful, but it's the sentiment that has me breaking down.

"Th-Thank you, Sylvie. I-I don't know what to say."

"You don't have to say anything, dear. Welcome to the family, forever this time."

"Hey, that's my line," Preston yells, easing the heaviness that had settled over us. "Well, let's just get the tears out of the way now then, shall we?"

My eyes snap to his. "Preston?" I warn.

"Sorry, Goldie. I can't let my mom one-up me on our first Christmas together," he says with a wink.

Fuck. Glancing around, I see Julia and Lanie both digging in their purses. Julia comes out victorious first and throws a pack of tissues at me.

"Thanks," I mumble.

"Well, Goldie. We started out with a fake relationship that rapidly escalated because of the loud family you can now call yours. But it was somewhere along the fake that everything turned very, very real. I know I didn't do a good job of proving it to you initially, but I will spend the rest of my life loving you. You're it for me, Goldie."

Preston stands and grabs a large frame that I'm just noticing was leaning against the wall and hands it to me. It takes me a few minutes to figure out what I'm looking at, but I begin to shake when I do.

"It turns out, having a hacker for a brother comes in handy for all kinds of reasons. Who knew hospitals had cameras in some operating rooms for teaching purposes?"

"Preston, th-this is—"

"A photograph of you, Emory. Holding my heart in your hands and keeping me alive. I had an artist work on it, so it wasn't so macabre. But even with all the light changes and artful distortions, there is no mistaking you're my lifeline. You held my heart in your hands, and you carry it always. My heart will only ever belong to you, sweetheart. From now until forever, my heart is yours."

"I don't even know what to say," I sob. "I—"

"Well, I'm hoping you'll say we can hang it in our new home."

My head is spinning so fast I worry I'll get whiplash

"What are you talking about?"

Preston nods to Dex, who lowers the lights and turns on the projector. On the wall opposite us is a computer-generated version of our dream home, right down to the subway tiles in the kitchen we fought over. He presses a button, and the screen changes to the field where we had our first date. Another press of a button shows the groundbreaking of our new home.

"Where better to spend the rest of our lives than where we had our very first official date?"

I'm openly sobbing now and unable to form words, so he wraps his arms around me and pulls me onto his lap as he sits.

"If you ever have doubts about my love for you, Goldie, I hope you can look at these images and let them erase all your fears. I love you now and forever. You're my life, my love, my whole world. Dex and I incorporated all of our ideas into this version, but if you don't like anything, we have plenty of time to change it."

Just then, Dex pushes a button that reveals my library. The picture of me holding Preston's heart is the focal point.

"Oh my God, Preston!" I gasp just as someone barges into the room.

"Boss, alarm 7."

Seth visibly rolls his eyes before speaking. "That would be Loki's apartment again."

Sloane jumps up. "Ah, I thought I closed the door this time?"

"Ah-huh, come on. I'll take you down to check it out."

"Sorry, sis," Sloane gives me a quick kiss then follows Seth.

"That's okay. I'm not sure how many more tears I could take tonight," I chuckle.

Peering around at all the faces looking back at me, it finally sinks in. My family is no longer just my sisters and me. My family is this group of friends and brothers. My family is wherever Preston is. For the first time, family means everything it's supposed to. Love, life, and happiness. Forever.

CHAPTER 49

SLOANE

"*D*o you have to walk so fast? You realize you're nearly twice my size?"

Seth doesn't even slow his gait until we are just outside of my apartment door. I know everyone keeps calling it Loki's, but I signed a lease. I pay rent. For the first time in my life, I have my own space. *That you can't sleep in.* But that's beside the point. Who cares if I like to have people around all the time? *Everyone cares, Sloane. You have to get a grip.*

A strong rock of an arm barrels into my side, effectively blocking the hallway. Looking over, Seth stuck his arm in my way to keep me from moving forward. I'm about to protest when I follow his gaze and see the door is slightly ajar. But it's the blood on the handle that has him holding me back.

"You stay here, don't move. Stand against the wall and scream bloody murder if anyone comes down the hall. You understand?" he whispers menacingly.

I nod my head, yes, but in all honesty, I have no idea what I just agreed to. All I can think about is that my only means of making money is in my bedroom. My entire life lies in that Chromebook, and I can't lose it.

I stand stock-still while Seth presses a button on his

watch and then slides into the darkened apartment. I hold out for all of three seconds before I swear something touches my sleeve, and I bolt into the condo after him. Not sure which way he went, I head straight for my bedroom.

I'm about to enter the room when Seth stops me. "I told you to stay put. Goddamn it. Can't you follow one simple direction?" he hisses.

I'm so sick of everyone treating me like a moron, so I elbow him in the gut and slam my hand against the wall to turn the light on. He wouldn't be out here, hissing at me if he hadn't already cleared the apartment. *Right?*

I march into the room like I own it and stop dead in my tracks. Facedown on the bed is a large, bloodied body, and I scream. The body doesn't move, but Seth barrels into the room behind me. I'm already moving toward the bed. *Loki.*

"Stop, Sloane, stop," Seth yells, unable to see Loki's face from where he's standing.

I drop to the bed beside him. I may not be the doctor in the family, but I know how to check for a pulse.

"Go, Seth. Get my sister now. It's … It's Loki," I choke out. I've seen enough pictures I could tell his handsome face from a mile away. Even behind layers of dirt, blood, and God only knows what else, I can tell this is Preston's missing friend.

EPILOGUE

Preston

*P*reston: We will land in Italy at six p.m. Before that, we are off-limits. No one is to interrupt us. No one is to text us. No one, and I mean no one, is to call, email, or even set foot on the Greek Isles for the next seven days. I will lose my shit as you've never seen, and I swear to God, it won't be pretty.

Colton: So, what you're saying is, you want us to meet you in the Greek Isles?

Halton: That's what I read.

Easton: I don't know, maybe we need Dex to chime in.

(Easton added Dexter to the conversation at 3:06pm)

Dexter: What's going on now?

Ashton: Preston wants us to meet him in the Greek Isles.

Dexter: Really? I thought he was adamant about finally having alone time with Emory. Okay, hold on. Let me add Trevor. He is good at last-minute travel plans.

(Dexter added Trevor to the conversation at 3:15pm)

Dexter: Looks like we need last-minute bookings to the Greek Isles.

Trevor: Done. How many?

Preston: WHAT THE ACTUAL FUCK! NO! NONONO! Do not set foot on the Isles, or I will castrate you all. Meet us in Italy as planned, do not fuck with my honeymoon. We have had too much shit happen in the last year. Do not fuck with me. I'm a man on the edge. I swear to God.

Colton: I'm confused.

Halton: Me too. Alright, gotta run. See you there soon!

Easton: See you tomorrow.

Preston: I will kill every single one of you. I've wanted to be an only child my entire life. I will make it happen if you don't quit fucking with me.

Dexter: See you tomorrow, dude! Have a safe flight.

"I'm going to kill them. Honestly, I'm going to kill them."

Emory looks over my shoulder and laughs. "What did you expect?

Preston: I'm turning my phone off now. If I see any of your faces before I reach Italy, you had better guard your nuts.

"Do you all turn into five year olds, or is that special to your group?"

"Our group, Ems. They're as much yours as they are mine. Aren't you lucky?"

Her eyes soften. "I really am," she sighs.

"Can you believe it's already been a year? Where the hell has the time gone?"

She gives me an 'are you kidding?' look, and I chuckle.

"Life won't always be as complicated as it's been the last year. It can't, or none of us will survive."

"Your family does seem to like a lot of, hmm, what do you call it?"

"Theatrics? Drama? Chaos? Danger? Madness? Craziness? I mean, really, it all fits." I pull her into my lap.

"All of the above does seem to encompass the last year," she says, looking up at me through thick lashes.

"You're so freaking beautiful, Goldie. How did I get so lucky?"

"Well, for once, maybe you can finally thank your bad heart for something."

I'd never thought of it like that before, but she's right.

"You're right. Thanks to my bad fucking heart, I met the love of my life."

At my words, she sinks into my embrace. It's my favorite thing in the world—the moment she lets her guard down and is just mine.

"I heard you were looking for a *stud*," I say, rocking my dick up into her backside.

Her eyes widen, and she looks around for the flight attendant. Even after all this time, she still isn't used to flying private. The staff makes themselves scarce unless I press a button.

"Preston—" she begins to scold.

"I've got the STD, and all I need is U." The laughter falls from my voice as I say it.

She rears back, "Ugh, Preston. That's gross. Honestly, are you looking these up online or something? There's no way you can still come out with bad pickup lines on your own."

"You'd be surprised at how bad I can be when trying to pick you up, sweetheart. And I have all week, with no interruptions to do just that."

"Are you going to tell me where we're going yet?"

"Nope, it's a surprise."

"You don't think I'll guess it when we land?"

"You might."

"Then why not just tell me?"

"Because it's a surprise, Goldie."

She climbs off my lap to sit beside me. "Fine."

Chuckling, I imitate her, "Fine."

"Did you hear from Loki this week?"

"No," I admit. "Who knew he could change in the blink of an eye like that?"

"Well, in fairness, it wasn't really a blink of an eye. It was over four or five months, but I get your point. We also have no idea what they really went through, so we have to be careful not to judge."

"I know."

"Do you think he'll come to Italy?"

"I'm not sure. I've never seen Loki like this. I don't know what to expect from him anymore."

Taking my hand in hers, she kisses the back of it. "I'm sure it'll all work out for everyone," she says with a smile.

"Are you upset your dad won't make it?" Emory's father had been trying hard in rehab but suffered a stroke four months ago. We moved him to an assisted living facility where he will probably live out his remaining days.

"Yes, and no. I would like to think that Dad was working on his sobriety so he could be a part of our lives, but given our history, that's likely wishful thinking. I'm glad each of my sisters could have a conversation with him while he was sober, though. I'm not sure that has ever happened before."

"It really has been a dumpster fire of a year, huh?"

"It's not like any year I can ever remember, but I also wouldn't change it for anything. You've taught me how to accept love this year, Preston. All these years, I thought I knew what love was, but it wasn't until you that I learned what true love feels like."

"I love you forever," I tell her. Letting Goldie know how much I love her has become my life's mission.

"I love you, too, Pres. Always."

"Are you sure you're not going to want children, Ems?"

She turns in her seat to look at me. I know I just dropped a bomb in left field, so I hold my breath while I wait for her response.

"Preston, we've talked about this. I'm completely in agreement that your vasectomy was the best decision you could have made. We would never want to pass that gene on. I've never been sure when it came to kids. I started raising my sisters when I was just out of diapers myself. Honestly, I'm scared to do it again."

"But it would be different because we would do it together." I'm not even sure why I'm pushing this. I've never thought about having kids of my own.

"D-Do you want to have kids, Preston?"

"Honestly? I've never given it much thought until recently. Maybe it's seeing everyone with kids, or maybe it's because I have you beside me. I'm not sure. But I have been thinking about it more lately. Mostly, I just want to make sure you know that just because I can't have biological children doesn't mean I'm against it if you decide it's something you want."

"Well, it wouldn't just be me wanting something, Preston. That's a huge decision that would have to be made together."

Emory is silent for a while, and I decide not to push.

"You wouldn't mind raising a kid that wasn't yours?" she finally asks.

Turning her face to meet my mine, I tell her the truth. "Sweetheart, half of my family is made up of water, not blood. Family is whoever you choose it to be. Whether it's a part of you or someone else entirely, I would welcome any child into my heart because they would be ours."

Emory works to swallow before nodding her head. "Okay, good to know. Let's, let's just think about it, okay? Maybe we can talk again after our trip."

"Whatever you want, Goldie. All you ever have to do is ask. I love you forever."

"Forever and always."

Want to know what happened in Vegas that has Easton

and Lexi so fired up? Click the link below to find out, for free!
"What Happened in Vegas?"
Or visit my website: www.averymaxwellbooks.com

If you loved this book please consider leaving a review.
Reviews are how Indie Authors like myself succeed.
Thank you!
Please leave a review here!

Let's Be Friends!
Avery hangs out in her reader group, the LUV Club, daily.
Join her on FB to get teasers, updates, giveaways and release dates first!
Avery Maxwell's LUV Club

*Turn the page for a preview of Loki's story...

ROMANCING HIS HEART

Sloane

"Go, Seth. Get my sister now. It's … It's Loki," I choke out. I've seen enough pictures I could tell his handsome face from a mile away. Even behind layers of dirt, blood, and God only knows what else, I can tell this is Preston's missing friend.

"Fuck," I hear Seth curse as he sprints down the hall.

I run to the bathroom and grab a bunch of towels and wet washcloths with lukewarm water. Loki felt feverish, which probably isn't a good sign. Running back to his side, I drop it all on the bed.

With great effort, I'm able to roll him onto his back and climb onto the bed. Kneeling beside him, I use the wet clothes to wash his face. I'm looking for the source of blood as I go, but so far, find none.

Leaning over him to grab a clean towel, I'm thrown back when his hand closes forcefully around my neck. His eyes are wild as he asks, "Who sent you?"

He is crushing my airways, and I can't make any sound.

"Who. Sent. You?"

His middle finger twitches just enough I'm able to choke out, "Preston. I'm ... Preston sent me."

His fingers relax a fraction as I read the confusion on his face.

"Loki! Jesus Christ, let her go," I hear Preston's voice but can't see anyone as my vision blurs. I see the flash of my sister's hair as she plunges a syringe into Loki's side. I register shock before his eyes go glassy, and he falls back to the bed again.

"That is only a mild sedative. If he's violent, it won't last long," Emory commands.

"I'm not violent. She's trespassing," Loki murmurs before his eyes close once more.

"We need to get him to the hospital now," Emory barks again. Dr. Camden in control.

"No," Seth interrupts. "We cannot risk taking him to a hospital. We don't have enough information. Our intel says no one is chasing him, but I know Loki, he wouldn't have gone through all these hoops, missed Trevor's wedding, or Preston almost dying if he didn't at least believe someone was after him."

"I agree with Seth," Ashton says, entering the room. "Emory? Can you check him out here if we get you the equipment?"

"Ash ... I, he could have internal bleeding, broken bones. For all I know, he has a collapsed lung or something. He needs to be checked out properly in a hospital."

"If we get you basic equipment, can you rule out any life-threatening injuries?" Ashton repeats.

"Seth, do you think his life could be in danger if we bring him to the hospital?" Preston asks.

"I don't know," he says, appearing defeated. "I just know he wouldn't have gone to all this trouble if he didn't have just cause. If he believes someone is after him, and it turns out there is, then yes, his life would most definitely be in jeopardy admitting him to a hospital."

All heads turn to Emory. My poor sister, who just got her medical license back, is being asked to do something that goes against all the ethics she swore to uphold.

"I'll do my best, but if I suspect anything I can't handle from this bed, he goes to the hospital. That's my deal, take it or leave it."

I almost laugh. Emory has always tried to play hardball. If these guys knew her at all, they'd call her bluff, but the only one smiling is her husband, Preston. Good man that he is keeps his mouth shut. He knows she would tend to Loki even if they didn't meet her demands, but I'm glad when they do.

"Okay, done," Seth says.

"What do you need?" Ashton asks.

"We have an ECG and a portable UltraSound Machine in our closet upstairs. Let's start with those. Sloane, we need to get him undressed and cleaned up as best we can so I can do an exam."

Realizing she's telling me to help is a shock. Most people think I'm an idiot, but I should have known better. My sister raised me. She knows me better than anyone.

"Got it. I started with his face, which seemed to irritate him, so be warned," I tell her.

"The sedative will give us about twenty minutes. We'll have to see what Ashton can get for supplies. I can already tell Loki is severely dehydrated. That's why he's so disoriented, but we'll need to check for head injuries, too. Have we found where the blood is coming from?"

"My thigh," Loki croaks, causing both Emory and I to jump back, startled.

"Preston?" I yell. I don't mean to, but Loki's a little scary. "Come talk to Loki. Let him know we're with you, and we're just taking care of him."

"I can hear you, sugar," Loki groans as I lift his shoulder to get his shirt off.

"Yeah, well, you nearly strangled me to death the last time, so I'm going to let your buddy here do the talking for a bit."

His eyes widen in surprise at my words. His stare is intense and focused solely on me, and it sends a shiver down my spine. As if he can feel it, too, the left side of his lip curls up just before he nods off again.

"Hey, Loki. It's me, Preston. Where the hell have you been? I almost died and didn't get to give you a proper beat down for making us all worry. Now that you're home, we have to get you better so we can all take turns kicking the shit out of you."

I can hear the commotion in the hallway, and Emory turns just as the crowd from upstairs descends on us. Dexter and Sylvie are at the front of the line trying to enter, but Emory holds up her hand to stop them.

"I'm sorry. I can't have anyone else in this room. It's not a sterile environment, and I have no idea what I'm looking at in terms of his care. We'll keep you all updated, but I'm doing the best I can here. Please, everyone, go back upstairs."

Sylvie has tears in her eyes when she speaks. "My earthly Angel. You may have been sent to Preston, but in my heart of hearts, I know you're here to save another of my sons, too."

Jesus, talk about pressure! When has anyone other than my sister ever looked at me with such admiration, though? *Never, that's when.* I'm the family screw up, the black sheep. Black sheep don't get the looks of love that Emory so rightly deserves.

"Mom? Let Dex take you home, okay? I'll call you with updates, but you don't need to sit vigil."

"Don't you dare try to send me away, Preston Westbrook. I'll be waiting upstairs for an update. I'll go home when I am good and ready, you hear me?"

"Oooh, someones in truuuble," Loki slurs.

"I thought you said this would knock him out?" I whisper yell.

"It should have," Emory says, looking as confused as I've ever seen her.

"Excuse me, Mom. Ems, here you go," Ash says, entering the room. I see in Sylvie's face she's about to argue, but thankfully, Dexter guides her out of the room. "He has been trained for, well, let's just say he's been trained for everything. A horse tranquilizer wouldn't stop him."

"That's right, Ashy." Apparently, it doesn't knock him out, but he does get playful?

"I'm going to need more information than that to treat him, Ashton," Emory scolds.

He hands her a chart and a bag of supplies. She peers into the bag and looks up, ashen-faced.

"Where did you get these medications, Ashton?"

"The Agency supplies them." He doesn't elaborate, and I can tell he won't.

Opening the folder, Emory scans its data.

"Holy shit," she whispers.

When I try to get a peek, she snaps it shut, shaking her head and mumbling about HIPPA laws. I want to argue that we are in my bedroom but notice her concerned face and stop.

"What do you want me to do, sis?"

"Let's finish getting him cleaned up so I can run some scans," she says distractedly while Preston and Ash exchange a muted conversation.

"On it." Moving to the other side of the bed, I cut his shirt over his shoulder so I can slide it down his arm. His sleeve is folded tightly in the palm of his hand, so I try to pry it open. When his muscles finally relax, I realize he is holding onto something. Pulling it away, I unroll it and see it's the second half of the note.

"Ashton?" He turns his head and stops mid-sentence. Crossing the room, he takes the note from me. It's also written in some sort of code I don't understand.

"Is it Julia's?" Preston asks.

"Yeah."

"It's good codes," Loki mumbles, apparently still aware of his surroundings.

"What does it say?"

Ash isn't as fast as Julia, but he still solves it in record time.

"It, ah. It says, 'they're watching her. Four months Red. Get Sawyer out.'"

As if he were given a shot of adrenalin, Loki springs from the bed and turns in a circle. "They're coming for her."

Preston takes a tentative step forward. "Who, Loki? Who's coming, and who is she?"

He scans the room like a deer in headlights. "I-I don't know. I can't remember. I can't remember, but I know they're coming. They want her."

We all watch in horror as he collapses to the ground like a ton of bricks.

"Shit, help me," I scream, trying to break his fall.

Preston and Ashton are on him in an instant and help get him back in the bed.

"I'm going to have to sedate him. I can't do an exam with him wild like this, and if he can't remember, I need to prioritize a head injury check. Sloane, why don't you go upstairs with Seth. The fewer people we have in here, the better until I can assess properly."

"No," Loki bellows, lunging at me once again. Grabbing me around the middle, he pulls me to him. "They're watching her. She stays with me at all times."

I stare at Emory, wide-eyed, and more than a little scared. What the hell does he mean they're watching me? Did

Jackson find me already? How would Loki even know that? I begin to tremble as Loki sways.

"Shh, Red. Don't worry. I'll protect you." Loki pulls me to the bed where he falls back, taking me with him, and I'm trapped under his heavy arm.

I glance around the room in horror as everyone stares back at me. Finally, it's Emory who comes to her senses.

"Ash? You're sure this medication is labeled properly, and his medical charts are up to date?"

"Yes, ma'am," he says like a teenager about to get in trouble.

"Good. This will knock him out until we figure out what the fuck is going on." Emory takes a step forward and plunges another needle into Loki's arm.

Get it here: Romancing His Heart

ALSO BY AVERY MAXWELL

The Westbrooks: Broken Hearts Series:

Book 1- Cross My Heart

Book 2- The Beat of My Heart

Book 3- Saving His Heart

Book 4- Romancing His Heart

The Westbrooks: Family Ties Series:

Book .5- One Little Heartbreak- A Westbrook Novella

Book 1- One Little Mistake

Book 2- One Little Lie (Pre-Order)

Book 3- One Little Kiss (Coming Soon)

Book 4- On Little Secret (Coming Soon)

ACKNOWLEDGMENTS

There are so many people to thank for helping me with this book—first, my family. To my husband, my daughter, and three sons, thank you for your support. A lot has changed in the last year, and everyone is adjusting to having a working-stay-at-home Mommy, but we are figuring it out (with minimal complaining even!). Thank you for loving me and believing in me.

Renee, my critique partner for her many beta and alpha reads, late night texts and everything in between.

My BookBabble Girls, C.R., Mica, Mae and Claire. Without you, I don't know where I would be on this journey. Thank you for talking me down when I'm losing my mind. For picking me up when I'm down...I licked him first is a very real thing! And, of course, for your unending friendship. It means more to me than you could ever know. Thank you for being my very own She-Pack.

Beth, my dear friend, who reads my books even while working in healthcare during a pandemic! You keep me in line and I know I can always count on you to find my over-used words and to triple check my timeline! You truly are amazing, and I cannot thank you for all that you do. My books wouldn't be the same without you! XOXO

The Dragon Tamers- thank you for being my naughty-word connoisseur's, research assistants, and all-around helpers. Your texts always give me the push I need just when I need it.

My Beta-Readers, Kimberley, Christine, Mica and Melissa, thank you for helping make this book everything it could be. Your honest opinions, suggestions, and edits are more helpful than you could ever know. Thank you.

Last, but definitely not least, **YOU**, my readers. Thank you for taking a chance on an **indie author** and for loving my stories as much as I do. I can't do what I do without you, and I appreciate all the love and support you've given me. I hope to have lots more stories for you, so be on the lookout! **LUVS!**

Editor: Melissa Ringstead, https://thereforyouediting. wordpress.com/

Cover Design By Jodi Cobb at Dark City Designs www. darkcitydesigns.com

ABOUT THE AUTHOR

A New-England girl born and raised, Avery now lives in North Carolina with her husband, their four kids, and two dogs.

A romantic at heart, Avery writes sweet and sexy Contemporary Romance and Romantic Comedy. Her stories are of friendship and trust, heartbreak, and redemption. She brings her characters to life for you and will make you feel every emotion she writes.

Avery is a fan of the happily-ever-after and the stories that make them. Her heroines have sass, her heroes have steam, and together they bring the tales you won't want to put down.

Avery writes a soulmate for us all.

Avery's Website www.AveryMaxwellBooks.com

Made in the USA
Middletown, DE
21 December 2022

20117053R00210